W̶hat the critics are saying...

Gold Star Award! "…scenes are explosively passionate…plot is fast-moving…sex herein is outstanding…Ms. Springer has written a compelling and poignant novel that left me riveted to each page." ~ *Just Erotic Romance Reviews*

"…steamy… storyline is extremely well developed with a lot of intriguing and surprising details…wonderfully written with lots of sparks and also tenderness." ~ *Cupid's Library Reviews*

4.5 stars! "… Sara and Tom are fantastic as the hero and heroine. The chemistry between them is very hot, scorching actually, allowing Jan Springer to include some incredible love scenes…incredible suspense and tender, passionate love, this one will pull you right in." ~ *eCataRomance Review*

4.5 unicorns! "…This plus size novel sizzles with sexual tension and desire…love was heartwarming…a must read. ~ *Enchanted in Romance*

4 coffee cups! "Ms. Springer's story is a great blend of romance and adventure…a suspense thriller complete with ghost towns, murder and mysterious shadows lurking around a picturesque Peppermint Creek Inn…a keeper…~ *Coffee Time Romance*

4 Angels! "I have always enjoyed reading Jan Springer's novels. This one was no exception. She has a wonderful gift for bringing characters alive and making you feel for them and with them."~ *Fallen Angel Reviews*

4 Hearts! "The love is spicy and erotic while the suspense is deep and thrilling. Ms. Springer has proven herself, yet again, as a top-knotch storyteller!" ~ *The Romance Readers Connection*

Jan Springer

PEPPERMINT CREEK INN

ELLORA'S CAVE
ROMANTICA PUBLISHING

An Ellora's Cave Romantica Publication

www.ellorascave.com

Peppermint Creek Inn

ISBN 1419953370
ALL RIGHTS RESERVED.
Peppermint Creek Inn Copyright © 2005 Jan Springer
Edited by Mary Moran
Cover art by Syneca.

Electronic book Publication July 2005
Trade paperback Publication March 2006

Warning:

The following material contains graphic sexual content meant for mature readers. *Peppermint Creek Inn* has been rated E–rotic by a minimum of three independent reviewers.

Ellora's Cave Publishing offers three levels of Romantica™ reading entertainment: S (S-ensuous), E (E-rotic), and X (X-treme).

S-*ensuous* love scenes are explicit and leave nothing to the imagination.

E-*rotic* love scenes are explicit, leave nothing to the imagination, and are high in volume per the overall word count. In addition, some E-rated titles might contain fantasy material that some readers find objectionable, such as bondage, submission, same sex encounters, forced seductions, and so forth. E-rated titles are the most graphic titles we carry; it is common, for instance, for an author to use words such as "fucking", "cock", "pussy", and such within their work of literature.

X-*treme* titles differ from E-rated titles only in plot premise and storyline execution. Unlike E-rated titles, stories designated with the letter X tend to contain controversial subject matter not for the faint of heart.

About the Author

৪৩

Jan Springer is the pseudonym for an award winning best selling author who writes erotic romance and romantic suspense at a secluded cabin nestled in the Haliburton Highlands, Ontario, Canada.

She has enjoyed careers in hairstyling and accounting, but her first love is always writing. Hobbies include kayaking, gardening, hiking, traveling, reading and writing.

Jan welcomes mail from readers. You can write to her c/o Ellora's Cave Publishing at 1056 Home Avenue, Akron Ohio, 44310-3502.

Also by Author

৪৩

Author's Note

❧

The rustically romantic ghost town of Jackfish actually exists. Located in Northern Ontario, Canada, it was once a booming railroad town. Now abandoned, it gives a wonderful glimpse into our past.

As a matter of fact, Northern Ontario as well as other parts of Canada and the United States are drenched in abandoned villages or "ghost towns".

For the adventurous, many of these towns are physically accessible. All you need is to do a little bit of research in recent "ghost town" books, do an Internet search, grab a dependable map—topographical map of the area in question—and your imagination and go ghost town hunting.

For pictures and information on the ghost town of Jackfish, please visit:

http://thewritinghermit.crosswinds.net/jackfish.html

or http://www.janspringer.com

Happy Ghost Town Hunting! **Jan**

Peppermint Creek Inn

ଓ

Trademarks Acknowledgement

~

Prologue

ଛ

The hum of a car's motor drifted through the early morning mist sending a searing jolt through him. Instantly he was airborne, crashing shoulder-first into the deep muddy ditch, flattening himself like a chameleon against the ice-cold earth. Groaning at the blinding pain ripping through the wound in his back and the throbbing pain pounding his temples, he reached into the pocket of his tattered black leather jacket, his stiff, swollen fingers sliding past the icy handle of the gun to wrap securely around the note.

He knew he was taking a chance carrying the piece of paper around like this, but it was his only clue. If he got caught, he'd have to sink it deep into the cold muddy grave beneath him.

It was the only way to protect *her*.

The vibrations in the dirt grew. The smooth rumble of the motor swooped closer. He wanted to close his eyes. Wanted to pray he wouldn't be seen. But he could only stare up from the ditch. Stare up and face death head-on.

The police cruiser whipped by him at breakneck speed making him gag at the acrid smell of gas fumes. He held his breath as the officer's laser-sharp gaze sifted right over him, eagerly studying the nearby forest then the muddy road ahead. Within a blink of an eye the cruiser was swallowed up by the rustic kissing bridge he himself had crossed just moments ago.

Letting out a long, painful breath, he dropped facedown into the wet, cold dirt.

This time it had been too close. Next time he might not be so lucky.

Shards of pain racked against his splitting skull. The deafening roar of his heartbeat reassured him he was still alive.

But he needed some rest. Only one minute. Just one lousy minute and then he'd go looking for *her* again.

His eyes closed and he sifted into unconsciousness…

A twig snapped like gunfire through the still night air. His eyes popped wide open. His heart thundered in his ears as he scrambled out of the sleeping bag. His leather coat crinkled loudly and he cursed silently at the racket it made. He should have taken it off, but he hadn't been able to get warm after the swim.

He fought the bitterness of fear hunched at the back of his throat. Silence drifted around him like a cloak. Yet he could sense something – or someone – lurking around outside the abandoned cabin he'd been hiding in.

He dared a glance out the yawning, glassless window, and noticed the night grow darker as the moon slipped under a blanket of black rolling clouds. Lightning flittered excitedly in the sky.

That's when he saw it. A figure silently sneaking toward the building. Toward him.

Anxiety grabbed at the pit of his stomach, squeezing hard. Cold dread slithered up his spine and nestled onto the back of his neck like a coiled snake.

Suddenly a floorboard creaked right behind him.

Shit!

Out of nowhere, brilliant silver stars popped behind his eyes. The world tilted crazily and everything began to spin wildly.

He groaned in surprise as a pain so intense he never even knew something like it existed, shot through his head. His legs went rubbery and instinctively he reached out for support.

Wooden slivers sliced roughly into his hands. He winced at their intrusion and his brain tried to comprehend the overwhelming pain shooting through his skull.

"I got him! I got him!" An excited high-pitched man's voice screamed in his ears.

Dammit! How in the world had they found him? He'd been so careful. Made sure no one had followed him here.

Cold sweat blistered across his face. The urgency of his situation slammed into his gut. He had to get out of here. Now! Before it was too late.

Something slammed against the back of his thighs. His legs gave out and he crashed to his knees.

Nausea swept over him and he lost his dinner.

Trembling, he tried to stand.

Tried to move… To run!

Nothing happened. His legs didn't budge. The intensity of the pain grew intolerable.

He grabbed his fragmenting head in his shaking hands. A strangled curse broke from his dry throat.

The truth would die with him he suddenly realized with a shattering awareness.

The truth would die…

His eyelids fluttered open.

Bright sunlight streamed through the dense forest, blinding him. His mouth still tasted sour from the sickness. His head still hurt like a son of a bitch.

He tried to move, but the pain slicing through his back made him gasp, stopping him cold.

Oh, man! He was in big trouble.

Taking a moment to catch his breath, he then tried again. This time he managed to drag himself to his feet. Digging his injured fingers into the dirt, he climbed crab-style up the embankment and out of the ditch, stumbling like a drunkard onto the soggy dirt road.

He cursed silently at the fresh tire marks. The cop car hadn't been a nightmare as he'd secretly hoped — it had been reality.

He had to get moving. Had to stay ahead of them. Or else he was a dead man.

Forcing his legs to move, he headed in the direction the cop car had come from, keeping a firm grip on the note nestled safely in his pocket.

The small patches of sky shining through the towering pine trees turned from a brilliant blue into a gunmetal gray, ready to pump cold bullets of rain. The sky was falling and it was bringing with it an early Spring storm.

His teeth chattered uncontrollably as the wind wound tightly around him, forcing its way into his nostrils, down his sore throat and into his fire-racked lungs.

It was so damn cold.

Every which way he turned, the cold found him. He was so busy fighting to stay warm, he didn't see the fog-enshrouded meadow until he'd stomped ten feet into the opening.

It took him a few seconds of rapid blinking before he fully comprehended that, yes indeed, through the fading dusk, and behind the monstrous beech tree, he could see the silhouette of a giant two-story rustic log house. It stood proudly, smack-dab in the middle of the meadow.

It had to be *her* place.

Excitement pounded through him forcing much-needed adrenaline to surge through his veins.

He dragged himself forward.

The house was handcrafted with chinked square pine log siding, a rather steep new-looking sheet-metal roof, and several rugged-rock chimneys. Drawing closer, he stopped short when he spotted a snug-looking porch swing creaking on the wraparound veranda. His gaze lingered on the heavenly retreat, then flew with quiet desperation to the pretty lace-covered windows. Hopelessness flooded him and his heart fell into his stomach.

No lights greeted him from the house. And to make matters worse, one of the front windows had been smashed—leaving him with the distinct impression the place might be deserted. To verify his feelings, he spotted the charred remains of a massive log structure amidst a spattering of pine trees a few hundred feet away.

Despair descended over him with an icy shiver and he reached up to shove a frustrated hand threw his long dark hair, grimacing at the pain the gesture caused.

He was in a real heap of shit now. This place had been his last hope. Hell, his only hope. And it looked as though she wasn't home.

He'd better figure out what to do next or he'd be easy pickings for the nearest pack of wolves, black bears or—a hot edge of panic sliced into him—or he'd be easy prey for the cops.

Quickly he dug the note out of his pocket. It took a good minute before his wildly shaking hands were steady enough so he could read the scrawled words *Peppermint Creek Inn* and the one name hurriedly written beneath it. *Sara Clarke.*

Who was she? Had she given him the note? Or had it been someone else? When? Why?

No answers came to him. His memory remained a stubborn blank slate.

He'd looked at the words on the note dozens of times since he'd escaped from those two cops last night. He'd hoped for some sort of clue in the note. Nothing tipped him off. Not even the number "28" glowering in the bottom left-hand corner.

Within the blink of an eye, a monstrous raindrop obliterated the two numbers into a giant splotch of blue ink. Another drop quickly followed, splattering upon the paper. Without hesitation, he folded the note and jammed it back into the protective covering of his pocket.

He glanced pleadingly at the darkening sky but as luck would have it, a fierce, jagged lightning bolt slithered through the swollen gray clouds.

He needed cover. Fast!

He made it to the front porch a split second before the sky fell.

Chapter One

🔊

Sara Clarke wiped away the hot tears streaming down her cheeks and breathed a heavy sigh of relief as the yellow headlights sliced through the blinding torrents of midnight rain barely illuminating her two-story log house. When she got inside, she'd build the biggest, most cheerful fire in her bedroom hearth, curl under her snug comforters and sip on some refreshing peppermint tea to calm her frazzled nerves.

She'd force herself to stop thinking about the howling wind that threatened to send her screaming like a mad woman into the nearby isolated wilderness and she'd forget the scary racket the hard raindrops caused as they pummeled against the truck's windshield.

Most of all, she'd push away the memory of the gunshot slicing through another dark stormy night, a gunshot that had changed her life forever...

Blinking back her tears, she forced her attention upon swerving her vehicle around the giant potholes littering the deserted parking lot. A moment later, she pulled into her favorite spot beneath Peppermint Creek Inn's romance tree, the monstrous beech standing guard over her home. Leaving the truck lights on, she automatically searched through the silvery downpour to gaze upon the various sizes and shapes of hearts carved into the thick, smooth gray tree bark. When she spotted her heart, a rare smile curved her rosebud lips.

Jack Loves Sara, Forever.

Her husband had trapped the promise with a slightly off-center plump heart and a sizzling arrow with his Swiss jackknife the same day they'd purchased Peppermint Creek Inn.

Sara bit her bottom lip as the hot tears threatened to burst free. She didn't want to cry. Not again. If she did, she just might not be able to stop this time.

Taking a deep steadying breath she popped open the door to her truck. Damp, shrieking wind slapped cruelly against her as she stumbled from the pickup cab into the angry spring storm. Her trembling knees almost crumpled as they touched the ground. Cold, thick, gooey mud burst over her shoes and nestled uncomfortably inside her socks. Rain dropped like a cold bucket of water over her body, instantly drenching her.

In a flash, she grabbed her purse and slammed the door shut behind her. Using the truck's headlights as a beacon she darted up the slippery wooden wheelchair ramp and dashed across the wide veranda.

She wanted to believe it was merely the storm's fury that set her teeth to chattering uncontrollably and her body trembling like a leaf as she unlocked the front door. Or maybe it was the fact the tiny hairs on the back of her neck prickled with some eerie premonition as she imagined someone reaching out and grabbing her from behind.

She shook her head at the crazy thought.

The storm had spooked her. Once she got inside, she'd be fine.

A cool blast of air splashed a greeting as she opened the door. Pale yellow light from the truck's headlights sprayed a friendly glow through the doorway illuminating her cozy French-style kitchen and splashing spooky shadows over her furniture in the adjoining living room.

Walking a few steps inside, she dropped her purse and keys onto the countertop and smiled despite all her troubles.

She was home. Home sweet home. And that's all that counted.

Running her hand along the kitchen wall her fingers brushed against the light switch and flicked it on.

Nothing happened.

A feeling of unease swooped over her, and she stood still listening for any signs of trouble, but only the sounds of the howling wind rattling against the windows and the insistent tapping of raindrops splashing into the wood-planked veranda reached her ears.

It wasn't unusual for the electricity to go out when the wild Spring storms of Northern Ontario hit. Lines went down all the time, due to falling trees and lightning strikes in the transformers. So why were her instincts yelling at her to back out the doorway, climb into her pickup truck and get the hell out of here? And why wasn't she doing it?

Leaving the door wide open behind her, Sara defiantly squared her shoulders and stepped further into her kitchen. She sniffed the cold night air again, wrinkling her nose in disgust as a rancid breeze hit her nostrils.

Had something spoiled in the freezer?

She opened the refrigerator door. Inside, the air smelled cool and fresh. The electricity had gone out very recently, but where was the awful smell coming from?

Immediately she spotted the white lace curtains flailing in the wind and her broken windowpane.

And that's when she saw it. Lying on her kitchen counter.

Bloated and ugly. Black beady eyes stared unseeing at her.

Oh, gross!

The horrific smell came from a giant dead rat! She didn't have to ask who'd broken her window and thrown in the decaying rodent.

She knew.

It was the shadow! He'd been lurking around in the shadows vandalizing her property since her husband died.

Sara took a deep breath in a futile attempt to steady her pounding heart. It was the wrong thing to do. The disgusting smell made her stomach lurch.

She had to report this to the police. They'd probably laugh at her, pat her on the head and say, "There, there, dear, it's only the shadow again".

She'd heard the rumors about her. The lonely lady living deep in the wilderness, trashed her place every once in a while, just to get attention.

To hell with them! Someone had invaded her space. Again. And she wouldn't let them get away with it. As much as she hated to do it, she had to call the police. She lifted the receiver and tensed.

Dammit! The line was dead.

Suddenly she became as angry as the howling wind outside and slammed the telephone back into the cradle.

She was so mad she could wring someone's—

A dusky shadow splashed across the pine floor.

Sara froze.

Oh, shit!

Lifting her gaze, she spotted the tall, menacing figure silhouetted against the suddenly unwelcome glare of her truck's headlights in the open doorway.

The shadow!

It had to be!

She opened her mouth to scream, readied herself to run but he was faster. Within a split second, he flew to her side. A strong muscular arm slipped securely around her slender waist, pulling her against his rock-hard body. A large, hot hand clamped tightly over her mouth. It was a powerful hand. Strong enough to snap her neck like a chicken's wishbone.

She tried to fight against his grip but realized she'd only waste her strength. She stopped struggling and stiffened like a corpse in his arms.

"Don't scream." His voice sounded low and hoarse in her ears. Ragged, as if caught in the grips of a massive cold. "I'm not going to hurt you. Do you understand?"

Sara nodded weakly, wishing she could believe him.

He removed his hand from her mouth, leaving the other one to linger steadfast around her waist.

He held her close. Oh, so close. His body heat slammed into her like a furnace and his bristly cheek brushed erotically against the side of her face, making her feel as if they were chained together in an achingly seductive death dance.

Through the magical spell this man cast upon her, she felt the outline of something hard against the small of her back where he held her.

A gun? Yes! He was holding a gun!

Paralyzing panic burst into the forefront, gripping her insides with such mind-numbing terror, she almost bolted but his firm grasp on her waist anchored her.

She forced herself to breathe. To concentrate on what she should be doing to make him pay for everything he'd put her through. The bastard had finally come back. Returned to the scene of the crime.

And he knew she was alone!

She swallowed at the bile churning up her throat. The hot blood pounding in her head made her think of only one thing. Confronting this son of a bitch before he did her in. At least she'd die saying her peace.

She jumped in fright when his faceless voice suddenly asked, "Who are you?"

"Don't play games with me!" Sara spat. "You know perfectly well who I am. Just do it!"

"What?" he gasped in surprise, a dangerous tenseness swooped through him.

"Finish the job. Get it over with. Put me out of my misery," she cried.

"Listen, lady. I…I don't know what you're talking about. I told you I wouldn't hurt you."

"Oh? And I'm imagining the gun pressing against my back? Go ahead, damn you, shoot me!"

She wanted to beat her fists against his muscular chest and cast out the demons of hatred and anger she'd been holding inside for so long. But he continued to hold her captive.

Her senses swirled as his masculine scent swarmed all around her. God, he smelled so good. A delicate combination of leather, spicy soap and a hint of tangy wood smoke.

She almost laughed. The guy was about to murder her and she liked the way he smelled?

She was nuts!

"Where would you like to start first? A bullet in the back?" she spat. "Pull the trigger. I dare you." Hysteria sharpened her voice, but she couldn't stop. She'd waited so long for this confrontation. "Or maybe you'd rather do it point blank between the eyes. That's your specialty isn't it? Right between the eyes. So you can see the pain a split second before the back of the brain gets splattered all over the walls."

He didn't say a word. His warm breath raked her face. His hold loosened a little. A tiny seed of hope bubbled somewhere in the back of her mind. She drew in a deep breath in an attempt to steady her racing heart. Maybe the murderer had a conscience after all? Maybe she could talk him out of killing her? And turn himself in?

Suddenly the shadow let go of her and her pulses roared with fear as she saw nothing but the gun in his hand, its one black eye gleamed hideously at her. Her fledgling hopes plummeted.

He was going to shoot her!

Right between the eyes, but she wouldn't go down easily.

She prepared to nail him where the sun doesn't shine when the stranger lowered his weapon and moved into the harsh beam of light spilling through the doorway.

"Easy," he whispered softly. "I really won't hurt you."

For one brief, sweet moment, time stopped and Sara gazed directly into the most wonderful emerald green eyes she'd ever seen in her life. In that split second, she experienced the craziest idea she'd finally met her soul mate, the man of her dreams.

But something else haunted him. Something that made Sara jolt with recognition.

Confusion and pain shone in his eyes. Excruciating pain. Whether it was physical, emotional or spiritual, she couldn't be sure. But he definitely gave her the impression he was living in the same some sort of hell she'd been living in, and he was desperately trying to find his way out of there.

The thought that she had something in common with this madman sobered her and she abruptly sized up her opponent, gathering any information she could use to her advantage.

He was a big man. Strong. Well-built. Wide shoulders donned in a tattered black leather jacket covered in mud. Slim, sexy hips with tight, dirty blue jeans, which hugged his muscular legs like a cozy glove.

He appeared to be around her age. Most of his pale face was camouflaged by a good week's growth of scruffy, dark beard and a mustache. The rest lingered beneath a bounty of various sizes of scratches and bruises.

She found herself staring dumbly at the drying crust of crimson streaking from beneath the tangled hair draped over his right temple. The blood caked his slightly swollen eye, dribbled over his bruised cheek and disappeared into the thick mat of his mangy beard. The way he swayed slowly back and forth made her realize he was hurt.

Bad.

Like any wounded animal, he was extremely dangerous. And unpredictable.

"Do you know me?" The soothing sound in his voice had disappeared, replaced with a raw tension that frightened Sara.

Quickly she backed away from his menacing figure.

The kitchen countertop crashed painfully into the small of her back, stopping her dead in her tracks. With trembling hands she reached out behind her in a desperate effort to clutch the countertop for support as her paralyzed knees threatened to buckle.

"Sure I know you," she said and swallowed the bitter fear threatening to suck away her remaining strength.

His eyes took on a flickering of hope. "Who am I? What's my name?"

Was he kidding? Confused? Crazy?

Desperation tinged his voice and she sensed the fear overwhelming him. Compassion edged away her fright, but she quickly tempered it when she spotted the gun dangling in his trembling hand.

Plans quickly formulated in her mind. "I know who you are," she spat as her frantic fingers scoured the countertop behind her for the steak knives she kept in the knife holder. If only she could get to one of those knives. She'd use it to gouge out his eyes or stab him in the ear.

Something cold and velvety brushed against her fingertips. The rat! She could throw the rat at him! Surprise him. Give her a second to get away. That's all the time she needed.

She swallowed hard and willed herself to pick up the dead animal. But her hand just wouldn't cooperate. She continued groping madly behind her and prayed the darkness would conceal her search.

"I've told the police your description," she lied. "They'll be looking for you if something happens to me."

He recoiled in horror and truly looked shocked. "I told you I won't hurt you, I just—" He stopped suddenly, clutched his gun hand to his chest and bowled over, cutting loose with a series of raspy coughs. The sounds of which led Sara to again feel a momentary compassion for the man.

She pushed her sympathy aside and shot like a bullet past him and through the open doorway, bursting out onto the veranda into the fury of the storm. Pouring rain arrowed beneath the porch, poking her with icy fingers.

Suddenly a fiery bolt of lightning forked out of the heaving black sky stopping her cold in her tracks. It zeroed in on the romance tree as if it was a heat-seeking missile, hitting with an explosion like nothing she'd ever imagined could exist.

Brilliant white sparks sizzled wildly in every direction making her catch her breath. Above the shrieking wind and pelting rain, she barely heard the sharp cracking sound of the tree breaking.

A tingling sensation darted up her spine making the hairs on her neck stand in warning. Her head snapped upward. To her horror, the enormous tree swayed dangerously. Then it tipped precariously and began its descent. It hurtled toward her home.

And toward her!

She stood stock-still, mesmerized by the immenseness of the tree. Could this be the way it would end? Struck dead by Peppermint Creek Inn's romance tree?

God, she missed Jack. Missed the way he'd laughed, the way she'd felt so safe and loved in his arms. Maybe it would be better this way. Maybe—

Two strong hands curled over her shoulders and hurled her back through the open doorway as if she was a mere a rag doll, shoving her quickly onto the kitchen floor.

Then he flew on top of her, groaning as he landed. Squashing her beneath his heavy weight.

At that instant, a tremendous crash shook the house. She screamed as glass shattered and wood splintered. Automatically her eyes closed and her hands flew up to protect her head. It was all over in a split second.

Eerie silence followed.

She opened her eyes to complete utter blackness.

The truck's headlight beams were gone and most likely her truck, too. With a sinking heart, she realized her only means of a quick escape had vanished.

He rolled off her with a groan.

Lightning flickered through the windows and she saw him sitting close by. Fresh blood trickled down the right side of his face. His lips moved. He was talking to her. Through the noise of her crashing heart she barely made out his words.

"Are you okay?"

Was she dreaming? Had he cut her throat? And now she lay on the floor, her lifeblood draining from her and he was asking her if she was okay?

"Sweetness! Are you hurt?" his ragged voice seemed louder, more insistent as the noise in her ears subsided.

Mentally she searched her body for any pain and felt nothing. "I...I don't think so."

"Are you sure?"

"Y-yes." She fought back the tears of shock blistering sharply against the back of her eyes.

"You are one lucky lady. C'mon let me help you up." His white teeth flashed as he smiled in the lightning flickers and then he extended his hand toward her.

Sara hesitated only a moment before sliding her hand into his outstretched palm. He pulled her to her feet.

Without warning, the shakes hit. Full force.

Her legs wobbled.

Reaching out to him for support, her hand wrapped tightly around his upper arm. Muscles greeted her. Enormous muscles. Firm and unyielding.

Even through the thick, cool fabric of the leather jacket, she could feel them. God, but the man was built.

Something hot and wild stirred deep inside her womb. A sexual craving she hadn't felt for a long time. Something she thought she'd never feel again.

Explosive visions ripped through her mind, visions of this dangerous man wrapping his arms around her naked body, kissing her face and lips, fucking her senseless.

She shook her head of the unwanted thoughts. To allow these wonderful feelings to flood throughout her body was wrong. Very wrong.

"Hey. Take it easy. I said I wouldn't hurt you. Really. Everything is going to be all right."

The soft way he looked at her made her believe him...that is until she spotted the metallic glint strike off the item dangling from his wrist.

Squinting through the muddy darkness, she tensed. An awful shiver crept up the full length of her spine.

Oh, shit! The guy was wearing handcuffs! Hysteria edged into her mind again.

For God's sake! He was an escaped criminal!

"What do you want from me? Why are you here?"

"I need your help."

25

Was this guy seriously demented? "My help? Just like that. You stick a gun in my face, scare me to death and now you want my help? No way! I've had enough. I'm out of here."

She rushed past him and through the open doorway.

Shards of lightning blinked off and on through the sky illuminating the disarray compliments of the fallen tree.

Instantly she knew she couldn't get around the wreckage, not unless she went back into the kitchen, past him and out the door at the rear of the house. And right now she didn't want to go inside.

Back to him.

The lightning had parted the giant beech, as if God himself had swung an ax through the wild heavens slicing her tree perfectly in half. Half the tree had fallen into the parking lot, burying her truck beneath the debris. The other half had crushed the stairs, the entire wheelchair ramp, part of the wooden railing and a large runaway branch had ripped away the rest of the glass from the already broken windowpane.

All this in the exact spot where only moments earlier, she'd stood watching in horror as the tree had hurtled toward her.

The full impact of what had just happened sunk through the layers of her tattered emotions.

Shock. Anger. Finally, confusion. If he hadn't grabbed her and pulled her out of the way, she would have been dead.

The sobering thought struck a massive blow to her midsection. Her stomach convulsed violently. A cold sweat blistered across her forehead.

Inhaling a deep breath of cool Spring air, she welcomed the sweet aroma of freshly broken wood into her lungs and continued to stare at the remnants of Peppermint Creek's once beautiful romance tree. Its gnarled twisted fingers desperately reached out to her, screaming for her help.

She knew she wouldn't be the only one upset about the tree, for it held numerous initials and hearts from many people who came repeatedly to stay at the Peppermint Creek Inn.

She sniffled back a salty tear and felt her heart beating happily against her chest. A strange hushed tingle of excitement took hold of her cold, shaking body. A small giggle bubbled from her trembling lips as a more pleasant thought struck.

She was alive. She'd cheated death. Survived another tragedy. As abruptly as the laughter had erupted, it quickly died in her throat.

The stranger! Moments ago he'd threatened her life with the gun. And then he'd swiftly turned around and saved it. He wasn't the shadow after all. The shadow would have killed her, or so she imagined.

So, who was he? What kind of help did he want from her? Blinking back hot tears, she hugged her shivering body and waited for the shakes to subside. And she dug deep down inside herself, gathering some of the courage she knew she'd need to face this sexy stranger again.

Chapter Two

ഔ

Wincing at the blazing pain searing through his lower back and the massive headache battering his brain, he slumped heavily into the nearest chair.

Shit!

He shouldn't have scared her like that with the gun. Simply knocking on the door and walking in as nonchalant as possible would have been sufficient.

Earlier when he'd first spotted the house and the storm had first broken—he'd sought refuge on the swinging porch chaise. He'd fallen asleep, or more appropriately passed out. He'd slept hard, real hard, totally oblivious to the downpour hammering on the porch roof.

Eventually a noise had sunk through the soothing layers of sleep and he'd awoken and seen the two pinpricks of headlights bursting through the storm. Fearing the cops had found him, he'd quickly scrambled for cover to the side of the house. Then he'd seen the pretty woman sitting behind the wheel of the truck.

It seemed like an eternity that he watched her, mesmerized by her natural beauty. Instincts told him he'd seen her before. Somewhere.

But where? When?

He couldn't remember anything before last night.

Why he wasn't panicking about not remembering anything was anyone's guess, but for some reason, he felt as if he might be better off not knowing his past.

What he did remember was the woman stepping out of her truck and the fantastic way her long auburn hair had billowed around her heart-shaped face in the rising wind. In the blinking lightning she'd looked like a goddess coming out of the fiery heavens to fetch him and he'd almost stepped out to greet her, but a silent warning to be very careful had stopped him cold. Taking no chances, he'd pulled out the gun and followed her inside.

When he'd first seen her slamming down the phone, her cute face twisted in fury, he'd wanted to take her into his arms, to comfort her, to kiss away her anger but then she'd seen him standing there in the doorway and panic had raged in her eyes. He'd known she was about to scream, to run away from him and he'd grabbed her, instantly drowning in her wonderful, sweet, peppermint-scented body. He'd found himself transfixed by her sparkling eyes, yet it was the seductive curve of her rosebud lips that sent a scream of primal sexual hunger searing through his cock, making him want to dig his fingers into her tumbling mass of silky hair and kiss her 'til she begged for more. He'd almost done it, but thankfully self-control had prevailed, and he'd stupidly let her get away and almost allowed her to be killed by that damned tree.

When he'd seen the lightning strike, time had quite literally frozen stiff. Then the tree began toppling toward them and he'd been paralyzed by a hideous fear. Not for his safety, but for hers.

Thankfully, something had snapped inside him, and he'd felt himself inch toward her.

He'd wanted to scream. Yell at her to move. But the words had remained trapped in his paralyzed throat.

She'd just stood there, stiff against the railing. Mesmerized by the spiraling timber. As if she'd been waiting for death to strike.

Her earlier words hovered in the blackness of his mind like a heavy dark cloud. *Put me out of my misery*, she'd said. Had she in fact been waiting for the clutches of death to take her?

He'd grabbed her violently. Too damn violently. But he'd been so scared. He'd pulled her away from the ugly clutches of death. Hurling her toward safety. And best of all—back into his life.

"Thanks." Her soft feminine voice made him jump clear out of his chair. The unexpected movement sent excruciating pain sizzling throughout his back. He cursed under his breath. He hadn't heard her come back. Yet somehow he knew she would return.

She stood in the open doorway. Wild wind blew her auburn tresses every which way. Her short ski jacket provided hardly any protection against the bleak elements.

29

He cocked a teasing eyebrow.

"Thanks for what?"

"For saving my life!" she said suddenly angry, as if surprised he'd already forgotten what he'd done for her.

"My pleasure."

"Was it?" she snapped.

Her voice bristled like a porcupine but the memory of her soft body curving warmly beneath him on the kitchen floor was still fresh in his mind. The intense fire shooting throughout him as he'd covered her made his balls and cock stiffen painfully against the god-awful prison of his tightening jeans.

Through the lightning flashes, he watched her edge cautiously inside the door. She peered around, as if searching for something.

"The gun is over there." He nodded to the weapon swaddled by the dark shadows, where he'd dropped it when he'd run after her.

"Don't you need it any more?"

"No. Take it. It's all yours."

She darted a curious glance his way as if not really believing her immense luck. She reminded him of a child sneaking toward a cookie jar and he was the bad guy playing a horrible trick on her, changing his mind at any second and snatching the treasure from her hands. But she wasn't a child. Far from it. She was a woman. And in all the right places.

He tried to focus on her almost too-slim woolen-clad legs as she eased gracefully toward the gun. When she bent over to pick up the ugly weapon with her beautiful slender fingers, he was treated to a glimpse of her full, shapely hips and wonderfully rounded ass. God, he wouldn't mind driving his cock deep into her wet and warm pussy from behind. Plunging and thrusting into her, hearing her gasps of pleasure as he fucked her all night long.

Leaning wearily against the chair he was quite happy to see the satisfied smirk flash over her beautiful lips as if she was the cat and he, the helpless mouse. Then his stomach sunk a little as she raised the gun in her trembling hands and pointed it at his face.

The gun was empty. But she didn't know. The thought that she'd pull the trigger on him left him feeling quite disappointed. What else had he expected? That she'd embrace him for saving her life, even after everything he'd put her through?

He felt lightheaded, wiped out. All his remaining strength having been used saving her life. His eyelids felt as if heavy weights were pulling them down and he closed his eyes.

His head lolled back onto his shoulders.

He'd run out of time. And he didn't care anymore.

She was talking. He tried to concentrate on her words. Truly he did. But she sounded so far away.

Her sweet peppermint scent wrapped erotically around his fevered body, teasing him, coaxing him to move. To reach out and kiss her, but he was totally wiped.

Cool feminine fingers traveled across his hot forehead.

"C'mon, wake up. Open your eyes, damn you. Don't go doing something stupid like dying on me."

He lifted his heavy eyelids and her beautiful face hovered like a ghost amidst the black fog. A burrowed frown zipped onto her concerned face.

She was actually worried about him? A warm fuzzy kind of feeling he really liked floated around him.

"Where's your car? Is it nearby?"

"No car. Walked in," he managed to groan.

"What? How?"

"Legs."

She stood over him and studied him as if he were seriously deranged. He was beginning to think maybe he just might be. Why else would he have cops chasing him, an empty gun in his possession and a beautiful woman staring at him as if he was nuts?

"Okay. First thing we have to do is get you to bed."

"Only if you join me and keep me nice and warm."

He grimaced as a flame erupted before his eyes. For a split second, he thought he'd been mistaken about his gun being empty.

Thought she'd shot him in answer to his remark. Until the disgusting smell of sulfur hit his nostrils. She'd only lit a match.

"I'm sure your sense of humor will keep you toasty enough."

Ouch, he tried to say. But the word just didn't quite pass through his lips.

The yellow flame danced away from his eyes at a dizzying speed, joining another one farther away. A candle.

He closed his eyes as his stomach heaved. He'd just about drifted off when he felt her tugging at him.

"C'mon, wake up. Put your arms around my neck."

Wow. Any other time he'd be having a field day with that suggestion. But he was too darned tired. So he did as she asked.

* * * * *

Sara felt the curve of his hot fingers curl over her shoulders. His strong masculine scent grabbed her every breath and spread a slow burn throughout her again.

Leaning heavily on her, she realized how weak and wobbly he really was as they staggered down the cold hallway. There would be no way she could get him to an upstairs bedroom and the living room pull-out sofa was definitely out of question due to the cold air blowing through the nearby smashed kitchen window. Best bet was her bedroom at the back of the house with the cozy fireplace.

By the time they'd reached her room he was a mass of shivers and practically putty in her hands.

Steadying the stranger with one hand, she placed the short-stemmed candle on the nightstand beside the bed and hurriedly whipped away the soft feather comforters.

A moment later, she guided him onto the bed. His head immediately buried deep into the softness of her pillows and his eyes scrunched up tightly as if he was in pain.

Within minutes she had two oil lamps casting a warm buttery glow over the hand-carved pine bed harboring her fugitive and a rosy fire crackled happily in the bedroom fireplace.

"Mister, you are definitely not a stray tomcat. What in the world am I going to do with you?" she said as she stared down at the sleeping man.

Gently, she grasped his large hand into hers and grimaced at the unexpected mass of tiny wooden slivers protruding from the puffy holes in his callused fingers and palms.

He'd saved her life with these mangled hands? What had happened to him? Where had he gotten the slivers? The bruises on his face? And what was with the handcuffs?

Ugly, raw-red chafing marks bit deeply into his tender flesh around the handcuffed wrist. The other wrist looked just as bad. A twinge of alarm slithered sickeningly throughout her stomach. Under no circumstances would a prisoner be shackled in such a horrid way. Something else was going on here.

When she touched his neck, his skin felt cool and slightly clammy. Shock. She needed to get him warm and fast. Unzipping the leather jacket, she discovered damp clothes beneath. Quickly she grabbed the heavy down quilt and hung it over the chair near the fireplace to warm.

Running her hands along his now shivering broad shoulders, she felt his corded muscles with the skill she'd learned in numerous first aid classes. She slid her fingers slowly along his broad chest, across his ribs and underneath his body along his spine, all the while checking for broken bones or blood and loving the feel of his hard masculine flesh against her fingertips.

She didn't miss the large bulge between his legs as it pressed anxiously against his tight jeans.

Well! At least that part seemed in perfect working order.

Gosh, it sure was getting hot in here. Struggling out of her ski jacket, she whipped it away and continued the search to his lower back.

Suddenly he groaned and that's when she felt the warm stickiness.

Blood.

Oh, shit!

Struggling with the sleeves of his jacket, she managed to free it from his body and tossed it onto a nearby chair. Pulling up the damp black woolen sweater, the moist blue jean shirt and the once white T-shirt, she, as delicately as possible, rolled the unconscious man onto his side.

"Oh. My. God," she whispered trying hard to ignore the horrible chills racing up her spine as she stared at the puncture wound in his lower back.

There was no doubt in her mind what had caused it.

A bullet.

* * * * *

An hour later with the storm still hammering away outside her home, Sara dropped the blood-soaked bullet into the fancy Niagara Falls plate she'd bought on her honeymoon.

After she'd wrangled the clothes from his bruised and battered body, she'd boiled water and quickly collected the things she'd need to remove the bullet. The injury hadn't been too deep after all. Practically a flesh wound, the bullet having lodged itself in the fleshy part of his lower back. As far as she could tell, it had missed anything vital. However, he'd bled like a stuck pig and that accounted for his weakened condition.

Promptly she applied a poultice of her homemade peppermint antiseptic ointment to the bullet wound and bandaged it into place.

The dark-haired stranger stirred briefly as Sara tenderly touched the large bump on his temple. Someone had hit him. Hard. Too hard.

Sighing heavily, her weary gaze wandered to the knotty-pine bed in which the stranger lay. Her husband had built it and he'd done a pretty darn good job of it, if she said so herself.

Slowly, she reached out and lovingly ran her hot palm along the smoothness of the pine headboard. She'd enjoyed watching Jack's powerful sawdust-covered arms plane the sweet-smelling wood. His arms had sailed back and forth until the knotty pines would burst forth glistening happily like newly polished gems. A gentle sheen of sweat had covered his brow and his muscles had bulged proudly in his arms.

Dried glue oozed from the corners where the joints of wood had been pressed tightly together. Even the great amount of sanding hadn't dissolved the white substance shining through the stain in excess. All she had left of her husband was his handmade furniture and the memories. Memories of hard-working days dotted with a few carefree ones. Never thinking about tragedies that could befall them in the future. Never realizing just how little time they had had left together.

* * * * *

Through the entire night and the next day a fever raged through the unconscious stranger and Sara kept herself busy by dousing his shivering yet heated body with cool peppermint water and anxiously checking to see if the phone lines were working.

They weren't.

But one good thing had come out of this man entering her life. She was horny. So damn hot and horny she'd forgotten what it had felt like to be a woman. Every time she tugged the sheets off his gorgeous, wounded body and touched his burning skin, she wanted to climb onto him and allow his semi-erect swollen shaft to slide deep into her.

She hadn't felt this hot since…well, never. Not even with her husband. With him it had been a sweet kind of love, a caring partnership between two people who wanted kids and who wanted to grow old together.

Life with Jack had been…nice.

Just looking at this guy's hard, toned body complete with bulging muscles in his arms and the biggest cock she'd ever had the pleasure of seeing made her feel…wild, lusty, utterly carnal. Made her want to touch him…*down there*.

Inhaling a deep breath, she dipped her fingers into the cool peppermint salve she was using to treat the abrasions on the stranger's body. Most of the bruises and cuts were on his toned abdomen and chest, a magnificently wide chest doused with soft curly brown hair that she couldn't help but run her fingers through.

She felt his heartbeat beneath her hands as she massaged the salve into his hard muscles. Felt the male nipples dance against her palms. Felt the untamed way her breathing quickened as she touched him.

From the corner of her eye she noted movement between his legs.

She inhaled an excited breath as his gorgeously huge cock responded. Riddled with large veins, his shaft pulsed enthusiastically and the purple giant mushroom-shaped cockhead emerged from its sheath. Just as it had done all the other times she'd smeared peppermint salve onto his chest while he'd been unconscious.

Something hot and wildly beautiful uncurled deep inside her lower belly as she stared at his growing erection. She hadn't been with a man in so long. Hadn't even wanted to be with one since that horrible stormy night over two years ago.

Even the thin vibrator she'd purchased several months ago hadn't been able to break her out of her stagnant, non-existent sexual lifestyle. She'd used it a few times trying to bring back the gentle lust she'd felt with her husband. But she'd given up in frustration and had finally faced the fact she was sexually dysfunctional.

Well, obviously not anymore.

A heated flush zipped through her as she watched his balls swell, his cock grow hard, the dot of pre-come glimmer at the tiny slit.

Glancing at the stranger's face, she noted his full lips were slightly open beneath his scruffy beard as he slept. His eyes were closed and his breathing appeared slow and deep.

Smoothing the salve against the ripples of hard muscles covering his chest, her fingers itched to touch the hard-looking cock. Itched to wrap around his flesh and feel the thick veins bulge against her hands. To shove his hard shaft inside the lonely length of her weeping vagina and feel the pulsing jets of his hot sperm fill her empty womb.

That's what she missed the most about sex, the feel of a man's cock spewing his life source into her, the hopes of getting pregnant, of having a baby, a family to love.

She lifted her salve-covered fingers from his chest and reached for the thick base of his long cock. It jerked madly against her fingers.

For a heart-stopping moment, she thought he would awaken and find her doing something she really shouldn't be doing. But she just couldn't help it. She'd never seen a penis this large.

Thankfully, he didn't awaken.

Swallowing back her nervousness, she stroked her fingers against the satiny-hard chunk of his pulsing shaft. Touching him this intimately gave her a delirious rush of lusty pleasure and she found herself growing bolder.

Getting hornier.

Hot cream dripped onto her underwear as she stroked the swollen length. His shaft was much larger than Jack's, and he was the only man she'd ever had sex with.

His cock grew harder, thicker, and her belly tightened with ferocious need. The frustrated heat coursing through her vagina made her whimper. Made her want to have sex with him.

Have sex with him while he slept?

As if sensing the way her desperate thoughts were heading, he groaned erotically and she quickly let go of his cock. It stood at full attention and her face flamed as she peered at his face expecting him to see how hard she'd made him.

He wasn't watching her. He slept. Only this time there was the slightest smile on his now-closed lips. Her heart pounded in alarm and she wondered if maybe he'd somehow known she'd been playing with his cock.

Gosh, she hoped he wasn't feigning sleep. She didn't have a clue as to how she would explain why her fingers were wrapped around his big erection while he helplessly lay in her bed. Didn't know how he'd react to such an intimate invasion. For all she knew, he would grab her and throw her down on the bed, and fuck her ruthlessly just so he could relieve what she'd done to him.

Not that she wouldn't mind getting screwed at this point by her sexy stranger — anything to chase away the heated flush of arousal burning her.

Her gaze flew to the handcuff around his wrist and her arousal diminished somewhat. A guy wearing cuffs meant nothing but trouble. It meant he'd done something wrong and for all she knew, he could be a crazed rapist or murderer.

She needed to keep her hands off him. Needed to figure out what she was going to do with him if the phone lines didn't get working soon.

Most of all, though, she needed to have a long session with her vibrator.

* * * * *

One day later, Sara took her first worry-free break. She felt like one of the walking dead as she edged past the gnarled tree branches of the dead romance tree that had crashed onto her veranda and front yard. At the end of the porch, she leaned wearily against the wooden railing and inhaled the mild late-evening air.

The stranger had kept her away from her vibrator, as his fever had gotten worse. She'd been terribly busy taking turns dousing him with cool peppermint water, listening to his fevered mumblings of cops trying to kill him and using her husband's secret trick of unleashing his handcuffs. In the end his fever had come down, the handcuffs off, his wounds tended and try as she might to ignore them, Sara began believing the wild tales he muttered while he slept.

Whispers of drug deals, gunrunning rackets, and worst of all, bribing police officers. His feverish confessions raised many questions. Questions that wrapped themselves around her neck like a hangman's noose, threatening to rip her brain apart.

Biting her lip, she pressed a finger to her aching temple. From his delirious ramblings, she'd figured he was definitely a criminal neck-deep in illegal activities.

She dug into her housecoat pocket and withdrew the wrinkled note she'd found in his leather jacket. Her name and the name of her inn were scribbled on the paper. Who would send him here? And why?

Nearest she could figure out, the man needed a criminal defense lawyer. Her father-in-law was one, but he lived in New York City now.

She shook her head with frustration and gazed at the swirling black water of Peppermint Creek as it roared down the middle of the meadow. The normally quiet creek had swelled to three times its normal size during the Spring thaw, writhing like an out of control serpent, swallowing everything that stood in its path.

Chunks of gray ice floated by, sometimes catching on the low banks, then being knocked loose by another hunk of ice or other debris. The unlucky ones tossed freely out of the swollen water and left to die on the shoreline, slowly melting away.

When she'd come home the other night she'd barely been able to get the truck across the quickly flooding kissing bridge a mile down the road—her only way in and out—would by now be inundated with rushing icy water. It happened every Spring. Hopefully in a couple more days, it might be safe to cross, but with or without the truck, it would be virtually suicidal to cross before then. Unless she could find some way to mount its rough wood planked walls, climb over the steep roof and down the other side. After that another one mile hike over the gently rolling roadway would lead her out to the highway where she'd be able to flag down someone to drive her into town for help.

But even if the stranger was well enough to be left alone, she was too tired to make the attempt. She was totally drained from the tips of her toes right up through to the top of her rip-roaring headache.

The sweet, gentle tug of warm Spring allowed her to become lost in the soothing sounds of the oncoming dusk. The faraway cry of a lonely loon. The distant hoot of a gray owl and to her utmost delight, the occasional shrieks and croaks of frogs from the swamps of the nearby lake as they awoke from a long winter's nap.

In the dimming evening sky, an arrow of Canada geese whizzed past overhead, skimming the nearby treetops, busily chattering away as they headed north and tried to decide on an appropriate rest area to soothe their weary wings for the night.

The shadows grew deeper, casting a deserted misty glow over the charred remains of her ruined inn and the tiny cabins huddled in the nearby forest. Sara sighed and smiled wistfully as she remembered the first time she'd seen the desolate sprinkle of two dozen boarded-up wooden cottages among the towering pines. And the ghostly appearance of the huge deserted log house, as it sat proudly in the flower-rich meadow.

One look at Jack's sullen face, her in-laws' shocked expressions and finally at her sister Jo's doubtful look, had spurred Sara to square her shoulders, roll up her sleeves and tell them there was lots of work to do and they'd better not waste any time in getting to it.

It had been a challenge getting everything done by the target date of one year. They'd erected a two-story, sixty-room pine log inn that summer with the help of local craftspeople using the giant logs from their own property. They'd outfitted the log house with a new sheet-metal roof and sturdy windows, repaired the ramshackle cottages during Fall and furnished everything during winter. The next year the doors were opened wide for business.

Business had been brisk with a waiting list of at least one year. They'd been talking of expanding when…

Don't think about it, Sara. Don't go down that road again.

Sara shivered as the Spring breeze prickled against her bare arms and crawled through her housecoat and cotton pajamas. It was getting late. She had to get some sleep if only for a couple of hours or the stranger would be her nurse and not the other way around.

She shoved the note back into her pocket and at the same time heard the stranger's strangled cry from within the house. She sighed wearily. Another nightmare.

Quickly, she slipped inside the house.

* * * * *

In the nearby meadow, Sara didn't see the yellow flicker of a match being struck, or the burnt orange glow from a cigarette floating slowly out of the tree line a few hundred yards away. If she had, she'd probably think it an odd-looking lightning bug.

She didn't see the tall shadow stumble into the clearing of the meadow, to stand and watch the house for a full five minutes. And she didn't hear the shadow curse silently under his breath or see him whip the cigarette butt into the parking lot, then stomp angrily down the muddy, puddle-riddled road. If she had, she'd have known her problems could be starting all over again.

Chapter Three

ဆ

A biting sting on his cheek along with a sharp command to open his eyes snapped through the black fog claiming his senses. The intense feeling to run for his life shot through his veins, waking him with a start.

For a moment, he felt slightly nauseous as gray fragments of memory lurched through his cloudy mind. Fuzzy visions of gentle, caring hands bathing his fire-riddled body. Of warm feminine fingers stroking his hard cock.

"Easy now."

It was her voice. Soft and husky. Reaching out to him. Anchoring him.

His eyes popped open and he saw a dimly lit oil lamp on the nearby wall. It cast enough light to see her pretty heart-shaped face framed with tousled auburn hair, which cascaded in luscious silky curls down to the small of her back. Faint dark circles hung under her haunting brown eyes, yet they did nothing to dampen the somewhat shaky smile she cast his way.

His eyes narrowed curiously. She was smiling at him? Even after the way he'd forced his way into her house, threatened her life with a gun and—

A breath caught in his throat. He'd saved her life.

Had it been a dream? It couldn't be.

He still remembered every detail, every delicious curve of her soft, yielding body beneath him as he'd thrown himself on top of her and prayed the tree wouldn't crash through the house. Then a few minutes later she'd brought him in here, and then he'd promptly passed out.

He came fully awake with a jolt. The full implications of what he'd done to her hit him full force.

Pointing a gun at her was unacceptable behavior. He felt like a louse. An asshole.

"Welcome back. How are you feeling?" She sounded sunny, almost cheerful. Either she was a very forgiving woman or she was just being nice to him because he was on his deathbed. And from the way he felt, it was definitely the latter.

His tongue felt so heavy, he could barely form words.

"I feel like h—" His voice cracked and no other sound transpired.

"Like heaven sent you back to earth. Right?"

That wasn't exactly what he'd wanted to say, but it would do for now.

Her smile widened.

"Just to reassure you, your fever has broken and you haven't so much as coughed in a couple hours. I was afraid you might have had pneumonia, but I think I can safely say you've weathered the worst of the storm. How about something to drink? Think you can handle it?"

He moistened his dry lips and tried to nod again, but his hammering headache increased with the sudden movement. So he simply stared pleadingly at her.

"Be right back," she said.

Watching her tempting, shapely feminine hips sway deliciously against her pink housecoat, she strolled out of the room and his heart quickened its pace in his chest. Not to mention his cock grew painfully hard. At least his body's sexual urges were still intact.

His survival instincts were kicking in quite nicely, too. Without moving his head, he was able to sweep the rustic, homey room, and in no time flat had picked out the quickest escape route. A slightly open lace-covered, night-blackened window. Perfect.

And for a weapon? His gaze raked the giant pioneer-style stone fireplace where an old musket hung above the mantel. He cast it off as being too old-fashioned. Most likely needing a musket ball instead of bullets.

He let his gaze waver along the top of the gray stone mantel where a handful of interesting-looking, slightly dented antique tea kettles sat decked out in colorful cheery bouquets of dried flowers. He was pleasantly surprised when he realized he could even name a few of the blossoms.

Pink peonies, green ambrosia, pink clover, blue larkspur and marjoram. His favorite was a sandy-colored wicker basket loaded with crimson red mini roses delicately sprinkled with sphagnum moss.

The old teapots reminded him of cowboys, fresh-brewed coffee over an open prairie campfire and long dusty cattle drives. His past? Or some spaghetti western he'd seen on TV? He probed his mind, but it was still filled with mass confusion. Bits and pieces of memories and visions that didn't make any sense at all.

Clamping down on the blossoming panic that he still had amnesia, he continued the search for a weapon. And that's when he spotted it.

He grinned despite the pain in his bruised face. A woman alone could never be too careful he thought as his gaze pinned onto the shiny six-inch steak knife gleaming happily on the nearby night table. Obviously in her haste to get him that drink, she'd forgotten to take her protection with her.

With a knife close at hand, it was obvious she had not called the cops. And if she had, they'd both be cooling their heels on cold metal slabs at the local morgue. He didn't know how he knew this to be true, but he did.

Satisfied he was in safe hands, for at least the next split second, he settled snugly against the overwhelming softness of the pillow where he was greeted by her sweet scent. It was everywhere, on the pillows, on the comforter, on the sheets, even on him.

He stared at the pale apple green wood boards on the ceiling and then at the pretty moss green and sweetheart pink bachelor button floral printed wallpaper, anything to resist the delicious fragrance.

But it was useless denying the sweet scent, and so he let it cascade over him in cooling, soothing waves, allowing it to become a part of him.

Peppermint.

Sweet, wild peppermint tea.

Tender snatches of memory tugged delicately at his brain.

Peppermint. Sweetness.

Peppermint candy sticks.

Standing at full attention like green and white uniformed soldiers. Nestled snugly and safely inside the largest glass jar he'd ever seen.

Eyes wide with high expectations, and as delicate as a nine-year-old boy could be, he lifted the glass jar lid. Mouth watering with anticipation he withdrew one sticky, gooey peppermint stick. Before replacing the lid, he angled a pleading look at his mother who stood at the counter busily chatting with Mr. Lapp, the general store's owner. As if his mother sensed him watching her, she threw him a stern warning look and he gave up the idea of having two.

Sometimes when she was in an especially good mood, she allowed it. But today she wasn't happy. He could tell by the frown on her face. Tidbits of their conversation floated to his young ears.

"Thank you so much for extending us more credit, Mr. Lapp. We appreciate it."

Mr. Lapp, a kindly, elderly Amish gentleman who ran the store, smiled at his mother and patted her hand comfortingly. "All the farmers in de area have bin hit with de hail storm. You are not alone. Ya?"

He liked the way Mr. Lapp looked at his mother. Everyone looked at her in the same way. It was because she was so pretty. Her eyes twinkled and laughed and they were the same color as the golden wheat fields surrounding their farmhouse at harvest time.

She had the longest hair. Longer than all of his friends' mothers' hair. He was real proud when his friends commented on how her hair glistened an almost bright blue in the sunshine, and blacker than midnight coal on cloudy days. She even let him comb her silky hair sometimes. When she was in a good mood. But nope, today she definitely wasn't.

Replacing the lid on the glass jar, he quickly shoved one end of the warm stick into his mouth. Cool sweetness exploded against his taste buds, and once again, he'd found heaven.

The memory faded into the deep recesses of the black abyss. And his pounding headache returned with a vengeance. He tensed at its intrusion and took a deep breath.

Pain prickled through the right side of his back into his belly. Another memory rushed up from the black void like a gushing oil well.

It was dark. He was running through a meadow. Suddenly from somewhere behind him, the cop yelled, "Freeze! Or I'll shoot!" His voice sounded faraway. He would take the chance. He kept running.

A red-hot poker pierced his back, quickly followed by the harsh sound of a gunshot. He stumbled from the force of impact but he kept running. He charged into the nearby trees. Small twigs crackled beneath his feet. Large branches slapped painfully against his face. His lungs were on fire. The bullet wound in his back screamed for attention. Yet he kept running, headlong into the night.

Bullet wound!

His right hand moved beneath the covers and he allowed his fingertips to run along his warm flesh until he touched something taped to a throbbing area at the side of his lower back.

Yep, he'd definitely been shot.

His hand scuttled back to the front and brushed against his semi-erect cock.

His very naked cock!

A tinge of warmth scuttled across his cheeks.

What the hell?

Lifting up the covers, he peered curiously at himself. Except for some frilly, pale yellow linen-type bandages wrapped securely around his waist, his wrists and palms, he was unmistakably and totally naked as his pulsing cock poked up against the covers.

In the back of his mind lurked dreamy visions of the woman intimately touching his cock. His shaft pulsed harder, grew tighter. His balls swelled painfully. Other visions lurked through his mind. Memories of a bedpan and also of her long shimmering auburn hair trailing tickling lines across his chest as she'd bent over him, her face shadowed by determination as she'd worked on the handcuffs.

Dammit!

The handcuffs!

A considerable chunk of fear broke loose inside him, crashing like an iceberg against his chest as reality once again reared its ugly head. While he'd been lazily lounging in this comfortable bed, being tended to by a wonderfully attractive woman, the storm outside had died.

The hunt for him would start again.

Soon enough someone would come snooping. And when they found him —

He almost jumped out of his skin when the woman entered the room, a cluttered tray in her arms. She threw him a concerned look as she crossed the room toward him. As she placed the tray on a nearby twig table, he didn't miss her steal a quick glance over her shoulder to check on the status of the steak knife.

He didn't blame her for being careful. Any woman out in the middle of nowhere would be jittery. For all they both knew, he could be a dangerous lunatic fresh out of a mental institution for the criminally insane, or God forbid, the way his cock was growing and throbbing so painfully at the sight of her, he could be a sex-crazed serial rapist who preyed on helpless females.

But she appeared far from helpless. It needed a rare breed of pioneer stock to be able to withstand the loneliness of a secluded place like this one.

Unless she wasn't alone? His gaze swept quickly to her ring finger and a shiny gold band laughed up at him.

The knowledge she was married did nothing to remove the carnal heat raging through him as she hesitantly perched herself on the mattress beside him, slid her silky hand beneath his neck and gently eased his head forward until his dry lips lightly kissed the smooth edge of the ceramic mug.

She smelled real pretty, but the tea didn't.

Instantly he wrinkled his nose in disgust at the offending barbaric odor and turned his aching head away from the mug.

"Well, it's about time," she laughed with pure delight. The musical sound of her voice felt like salve over his tortured body. "I've been pouring this stuff down your throat without a single complaint from you." A tinge of seriousness entered her voice. "When I finally do get a complaint from a patient, I know he's going to make it."

Her meaning came across loud and clear. In the instance he never complained, it meant he'd kicked the bucket. So he'd better consider himself lucky to be alive.

He met her gaze with a knowing smile.

"Here." She reached over and grabbed another steaming mug from the tray. "Try some of this."

Again, she helped him lift his head to the mug. This time a cool minty mist sprayed a warm layer of dew against his cheeks and he eagerly sipped the steaming liquid. It scorched a blistering path of peppermint fire down his parched throat and he knew without a doubt this was the famous peppermint tea that tourists drove all the way up from the States to get to.

How did he know that? Another memory?

He continued to sip the delicious liquid and after it was completed, he tested his voice.

"Who are you?"

"I'm Mrs. Sara Clarke," she said as she lowered his head back onto the softness of the pillow.

The woman in the note. He'd found her. And she was married.

Why was he so dammed surprised and disappointed that she was married? On the subject of marriage, what about him?

He peered down at the bulky bandages holding his hands hostage but couldn't see a ring on his finger. The thought of not being attached to anyone or having no one care about him, made him feel — oddly enough — sad?

"My hands?"

"There were full of slivers. I've managed to get them all out."

He remembered reaching out, trying to grab at something, trying to keep from falling after someone had bashed him over the head.

"I remember being in a building. An old building. Abandoned."

She nodded her head thoughtfully. "There are a few abandoned buildings strewn around. We can talk about that later. First how about some more tea?"

"Please."

He watched her pour another cup, intense curiosity about this gorgeous woman finally taking hold. "How'd you get the cuffs off?"

"My husband used to be a police officer. He taught a lot of workshops. One of them was about handcuffs and how easy it was to get out of them with a makeshift key."

She reached for something on the table and to his surprise she held up a ballpoint pen.

"He put a small slit right here—" she pointed to the end of the pen "—and pried a piece of the metal away which gave him a small bit. Used alternately with a paper clip and lots of patience, it works wonders."

"Ingenious contraption," he replied with awe.

"Does the job," she laughed as she dropped the pen back onto the night table.

"You said he used to be a cop?"

He didn't miss her slight hesitation before answering. "He quit the force and we came out here to follow our dreams."

"And did your dreams come true?"

The flash of raw pain in her chocolate brown eyes just about made him sick. He'd struck a nerve and immediately recognized the "no trespassing" sign go up in her eyes. Quickly he changed the subject.

"That tea over there," he glanced slightly to the other mug containing the vile liquid and said with a chuckle, "What did you do, make it taste bad to pay me back for the way I introduced myself?"

The painful look on her face disintegrated into a cold frown that could have been made of brittle glass.

"Good guess," she replied icily.

She lifted his head again, not as gently as last time and pressed the mug firmly to his lips.

"Drink," she ordered.

He didn't sip. Instead, his mouth dropped open in surprise at her sudden chilly attitude.

"Hey. I meant it as a joke."

"I didn't."

Suddenly things began falling into place left, right and center about the Peppermint Creek Inn and her mistress.

Broken window. A dead rat. Burned-out remains of a recent fire.

"Aw, c'mon don't tell me you think I had something to do with wrecking your window? It was already broken when I got here. And I caught a glimpse of that rat on the counter. I swear I had nothing to do with it."

She didn't answer. Confusion brewed in her dark eyes.

"It looks like you've had some trouble around here. How long has it been happening?"

"Since you showed up a few days ago. Drink!" she ordered.

But he couldn't drink. He blinked in surprise at her, not quite grasping what she'd said.

"Did you say a few days? How many days?"

She must have seen a flash of warning in his eyes because she quickly withdrew the steaming mug from him and placed it on the tray before answering.

"Two days. You're heading into the third night."

"Oh, man, I have to go!" he tried to pull himself up but a sharp, searing pain drilled a hole straight through his back into his belly making him gasp aloud.

"You feel that?" Her brows knotted with concern. "That's a bullet hole. You won't be going anywhere for a while. So just sit back and relax will you? I don't want a repeat performance of the last few days."

Her large brown eyes suddenly took on a mischievous gleam and her features softened. She pointed to a nearby open doorway.

"And if you have to go, the bathroom is over there. I'm getting a little tired of empting the bedpan for you."

Her apparent stab at humor did nothing to remove the anxiety shooting through his system. She wasn't safe with him around.

"You don't understand. I have to leave. Now!"

Gritting his teeth against the searing pain slicing through his back and the battering ram inside his head, he made a second attempt at pushing aside the blankets.

"Oh, no, you don't," she cried and in one quick fluid motion her warm velvet hand dusted like sizzling steel against his chest sending one hell of a jolt shooting through his system. He stopped short, thoroughly enjoying the erotic feel of her restraining fingers loosely entangled in the curly hairs of his bare chest.

Gently but firmly she pushed him back against the pillows and hesitantly withdrew her hand. He didn't miss the windblown roses suddenly sweep across her cheeks before she turned her face away. With slim trembling fingers, she tried to smooth out a non-existing wrinkle on the comforter.

Was he imagining her shaky fingers? The wonderful blush? Did she also feel the attraction between the two of them?

It took him a moment to find his voice. When he did, he tried hard to keep it steady.

"Look. It's important that I keep moving."

Her head snapped up in sudden anger. "On the other hand if you bled to death, you wouldn't be moving at all, would you?"

"We all have to die someday," he quirked.

"Well, that counts you out, then. Only the good die young."

He felt the faintest smile crack his dry lips.

"So, are you just being shy or don't you have a name?" she asked softly.

"I—" His name was suddenly right there, on the tip of his tongue. And then it retreated with lightning speed, straight into the deep black abyss where his memories should have been stored.

He looked up and was surprised to see genuine worry lurking in those warm liquid fudge depths. Worry for him? Somehow, the thought seemed oddly endearing.

But all the wishful thinking in the world wouldn't change the facts. The facts were anyone who helped him would end up dead. He had no idea who he was, why he'd come here, and why he was being chased by the cops or why they wanted him dead. He just knew they did, especially after remembering the cop shooting him in the back.

"I'm going to be brutally honest with you, Mrs. Clarke."

"I wouldn't want it any other way."

"It's better if you don't know who I am. Better yet, for your own safety, pretend you never saw me."

Sara lifted her brows, an amused twinkle in her eye. "You mean, like you're a figment of my imagination?"

"Exactly."

The twinkle in her eye quickly disappeared and she frowned. "I'm sorry, but to be brutally honest as you so kindly put it, I don't lie."

"Not even for your own safety?"

"Nope."

He sighed in frustration. "Great. Just great."

"Why are you being so serious?"

"Because I don't know who—" He cut himself off, suddenly realizing he'd almost given himself away.

"You don't know who you are, do you? That's what you were going to say?"

How the hell did she know?

"It wasn't hard to guess. The way you acted the night we met. Demanding me to tell you your name. It was an odd request. While you were delirious, you kept asking me to help you find out who you are. Can you remember anything at all?"

"Everything's fuzzy. Bits and pieces. Images. Nothing I can put my finger on."

She frowned. "I've heard that memory loss is quite common after head injury and after a major trauma. In most cases people remember within a few days."

His stomach clenched into a tight knot. "Most cases?"

"Others take a little longer."

"How much longer?"

"I'm not a doctor." She hesitated before adding, "But what I've read it could be months. Maybe years. It's rare though."

Shit!

"I don't think I have that long. Someone's after me. And they want something. I can give it to them or not. Either way, I'm a dead man."

She visibly shivered beside him. "Do you have any idea who wants to kill you? And what do they want?"

He decided to tell her the truth. "I don't know what they want, but I know the cops want me dead."

Sara studied the stranger intently. His profile was defiant. He appeared to fully expect her to tell him the bump on his head had knocked more than a few screws loose, and there was no way in the world she would believe him. Funny thing was, she did believe him, because when she put everything together, it made sense.

He'd arrived beaten, a bullet in his back and handcuffs dangling on his wrist. While delirious, he'd said things. Things, which led her to believe the police didn't have a very high opinion of him.

Sara sighed deeply.

Her splitting headache still cried for her attention and she wished she could just climb into bed and throw the covers over her head. But that wouldn't solve anything.

"What else do you know?"

His forehead crinkled in disbelief. "You believe me?"

"Don't look so shocked. Tell me what you remember."

The briefest hint of a relieved smile passed over his lips.

"Listen. I don't want to burden you with my troubles. You're already in danger just by helping me out."

"You're going to have to trust someone. Right now all you've got is me."

He didn't say anything. Yet she noticed he still seemed tense. She needed to do something to cheer him up. Do something to get him to trust her.

"You know what," she said with a bit more enthusiasm than she felt. "You need a new handle."

"A handle?"

"A name. What's your favorite?"

He shrugged solemnly. "Don't know. You choose."

A name instantly popped into her mind. Yet she hesitated to use it. After all she'd already given it to someone else. Someone just as helpless and totally dependent on her as this stranger. And she'd failed him. Horribly.

Sara swallowed hard and pushed aside the disturbing thoughts. Pressed them into the corner of her soul, like one presses a precious flower for future remembrance between the covers of a weighty book. She buried them deep beneath the fragile pages that carried her fears, hurt and dashed hopes from the past two and a half years.

Blinking back the sudden sprig of hot tears, she took a deep breath, faced the stranger and tried to present a proper smile, but her lips just wouldn't cooperate. She noticed the odd expression creasing his rugged face.

"Is something wrong?" His gentle tone of voice almost unraveled her.

For a moment, she stared into his bright emerald green eyes and was overcome with the strangest urge of telling him her deepest fears and sharing her secrets. She'd never had such a strong urge to tell anyone this before. Now, without any reason she wanted to tell this man everything. To blurt out what had happened to her husband. To tell him about the shadow who'd been haunting her life.

Sara caught herself.

Was she nuts? What was the matter with her anyway? She should have her head examined. She didn't even know this guy.

Yet she wouldn't mind getting to know him better. Much better.

She wouldn't mind wrapping her hands around that thick cock of his. Maybe taking his delicious-looking organ into her mouth and swirling her tongue all around that mushroom-shaped cockhead.

Nip her teeth along the silky skin covering the rigid shaft.

Watch him squirm and buck as she took him deep into her throat.

"Mrs. Clarke?"

She blinked rapidly and quickly looked away so he couldn't see the reddish tinge of heat that must be crawling along her cheeks.

"Thomas. How's that?" She blurted out the name.

He said nothing and she cast a quick peek to see his reaction. She knew by the smile on his face that he liked the name.

"Thomas." The name rolled off his tongue with ease. "Tom. Mmm. Sounds good. It has a certain ring about it. Don't you think?" He cocked a curious eyebrow. "Why'd you pick it? An old boyfriend perhaps?"

The question almost toppled Sara. For a split second, she again wanted to spill her guts as she'd never done to anyone before. But the instant passed and she recovered quickly.

Impulsively she reached out to gently tug on his scruffy beard. His hair felt rough beneath her fingertips. Coarse. Sexy.

She noticed the soft gasp escape his lips and with lightning speed, Sara withdrew her hand.

"Because you remind me of a stray tomcat. Whiskers and all," she replied shakily.

He smiled a damned irresistible sexy smile that made her toes curl. Then he sunk his head a little deeper into the pillows.

"More like something the tomcat dragged in," he mumbled and his eyelids began to droop sleepily.

"You said it, I didn't," she laughed as she tucked in the sides of the blankets to keep him warm.

She wanted to ask him more questions, but they'd have to wait until he felt stronger.

"Mrs. Clarke?" he said sleepily and blinked to keep his eyes open.

"Yes?"

"Thanks for taking care of me."

"Thank you for not dying on me. I would have been a very unhappy camper after all the work I put into you."

"Why are you helping me?"

"You saved my life. And because you asked for my help."

"I'll have to figure out some way to repay you."

"You can repay me by getting some beauty rest, Tom."

She didn't miss the grimace etch along the wonderful lines around his mouth.

"I look that bad, huh?"

"Worse."

He sighed and he slid even deeper into the pillows.

"You'll get no arguments from me. At least for now."

His eyelids finally fluttered closed and from the steady rise and fall of his gorgeous, naked chest, she knew he slept.

Sara frowned.

Amnesia. The man has amnesia.

What she wouldn't do to forget her past, to forget that one stormy night. To forget all the pain she carried inside her heart.

At one point, she'd almost succeeded in losing her pain forever by taking the easy way out. But she was better now.

At least she thought she'd been better until that tree had come hurtling down toward her.

Would she be dead if Tom hadn't been here to grab her? Would she have simply stood there and accepted death?

She didn't know. What she did know was when the tree was coming toward her, for a split second, she wanted to forget her pain.

But he'd saved her.

She found herself studying his face as she'd been doing a hundred times over the past couple of days.

She marveled at how much she loved those crinkled lines edging like crows feet from the corners of his closed eyes. And she really loved the tender lines around his mouth.

While he slept, an almost youthful innocence splashed across his features making him very appealing. It was this innocence that allowed her to reach out and brush a stray curl of dark hair from his forehead.

As she touched him, electricity shot up her fingertips. In less than a heartbeat, she wanted to kiss him.

Slowly, without thinking, she bent down, her mussed hair falling across his face. His delicious peppermint tea-scented breath cascaded tenderly around her cheeks pulling her closer to him.

Gently, before she even realized it, she'd brushed her lips across his hot mouth. His beard and mustache tickled her face erotically. His full, sweet lips trembled beneath her feather-light kiss and suddenly he mumbled something.

Horror-stricken, Sara backed away from him, fully expecting his eyes to snap open at any second.

Thankfully, they didn't and he remained fast asleep.

As she watched him sleep, a whirlwind of emotions stampeded through her.

Fear perhaps being the most prevalent. Fear for the stranger lying in her bed. Of what would happen to him when he was better. And he was definitely getting better.

Already a bit of color had seeped into his face. And she'd noticed the intense way he looked at her. Noticed the sexual hunger in his bright, alert gaze.

She felt the hunger, too. An ache for her vagina to be filled by him. At that thought, exciting spirals of delight raced like a tornado through her and she tried to stop them by reminding herself that this man, this total stranger, was probably going to spend the rest of his life behind bars, or at the very least, die a very tragic death. Somehow, her mind wouldn't allow her to dwell extensively on that possibility.

Her heart wanted to believe he was a decent man, caught up in some bizarre misunderstanding.

Yet she couldn't help wondering what would happen when he regained his memory.

Would he revert to his criminal ways? Would he use his powerful arms against her, adding murder to his long list of self-described dream-ravaged criminal activities?

Sara eyed her sleeping Tom. He mumbled something again, and then fell silent. What would happen to him if his pursuers caught up to him? Would they beat him again? Shoot him again?

She bit her lip, battling the sudden icy wave of terror she felt for his safety.

He'd told her to pretend she'd never seen him. But how could she pretend? His simple touch had set her body on fire, opening a new world.

A world filled with exciting sexual cravings she wasn't sure she could ignore.

He was the first man she'd kissed since—

She shuddered involuntarily.

What had possessed her to do such a horrid thing? And with her husband's wedding ring still on her finger.

Yet Tom's kiss had felt so perfect.

Magical.

It made her forget her pain, if only for an instant. It reminded her there still was a life to live. And she didn't have to live it the way she'd been doing so.

Sudden guilt overrode the sensuous kiss.

The truly wonderful kiss that she pressed like a treasured fragile flower in between the tender pages of her book. Another keepsake to add to her collection of shed hopes and unfulfilled dreams.

Chapter Four

ℬℴ

Sara knew the direction her dream was heading yet she was helpless to stop it.

She'd been late for an exam in her still-life drawing class. Slept in because the storm had knocked out the power in her section of the city and screwed up the alarm on her clock radio.

Now as she quickly maneuvered her car through the downtown core of New York City, she spotted the flashing cruiser lights in her rearview mirror. At first, she figured they weren't for her. After all, many people broke the rules of the road without being caught.

But the pursuing vehicle drew closer with lightning speed. Within seconds, the cruiser climbed within a few feet of her rear bumper.

"Dammit!" She pounded the wheel in frustration. "Now I'll be really late."

Biting her lip nervously, she pulled over to the curb. The police car followed suit and parked behind her. She stared into the rearview mirror as a tall, stocky officer got out of the cruiser and slowly headed toward the driver's side where she quickly rolled down the window. Her pulse quickened when she stared up into his gorgeous cornflower blue eyes.

Easy, Sara. *She heard the low warning inside her head.* This could be the guy for you. *She would have laughed out loud if she wasn't sure the officer would write her a ticket for doing that too.*

"Good morning, ma'am," he drawled.

So polite. He probably had to be in his line of work. But he didn't have to be so cute.

"May I see your driver's license please?"

Sara swallowed hard and groped inside her purse with terribly shaky fingers, quickly finding her license. She tried to tell herself the shakiness was only excitement due to an imminent ticket, but deep down she knew it wasn't true. The man literally made her swoon.

"I'm sorry, officer. I'm late for my art class. Last night's storm knocked out the power and my alarm clock didn't go off and now I'm late for my final exam."

She handed him her driver's license.

His face screwed into puzzlement as he looked at the plastic-sheathed license.

"Sara Brady?"

Sara nodded. She recognized the look on his face. Many people reacted the same way when they discovered who they were talking to.

"The Sara Brady? The wildlife artist?"

Again Sara nodded, suddenly feeling really embarrassed. "One and only."

Now she would really be late.

"Wow! I've seen your paintings. The ones you donated for the Police Charity Ball this Saturday night. They're really lifelike. I enjoyed them. A lot."

"I'm glad you did, Officer?"

"Oh, I'm sorry. I'm forgetting my manners. Jack. Jack Clarke."

"Pleased to meet you, Jack Clarke."

"Pleased to meet you, too, Mrs. Brady."

Was he fishing? She decided to swallow the bait. Hook. Line. And sinker.

"Miss," she replied.

"Really?" A pleasantly satisfied smile crossed his lips and he handed her back her license. You know I shouldn't be doing this, Miss Brady."

"Doing what?"

"Escorting you to your class. Where is it?"

Sara told him then she asked, "You're not going to write me a ticket?"

"No way. Not after what you've done for the auction. Just stay close behind me, okay?"

Sara laughed, not believing her good luck. "Sure."

They sped quickly but efficiently through the traffic jams. Within minutes, he led Sara into the parking lot of the university campus with a few minutes to spare.

"This is unbelievable," Sara said excitedly as she lifted her briefcase out of the car and slammed the door shut. Turning to the officer, she was once again struck by his cornflower blue eyes and his wonderful smile.

"I really do appreciate your help, Officer Clarke. I'm in your debt."

"Please call me Jack. And it was nothing."

"Oh, believe me, it was something. They close the doors to the exam rooms promptly at eight. If I arrive late, I automatically get a failing grade."

"In that case I'm glad I could help you out, Miss Brady."

The hot way he stared at her made Sara blush.

"Thank you very much again for your help, Jack. It was really sweet of you. I guess I'd better get going now."

Hesitantly she turned, not wanting to leave him just yet but knowing she had to or she wouldn't get into the exam room.

"Miss Brady?"

"Yes," she whirled around so quickly she almost lost her balance.

"I shouldn't be doing this, but can I get your number?"

Her heart pounded crazily in her chest. Her knees suddenly felt weak.

"You already have my number."

A puzzled expression fell across his face and a moment later, he brightened.

"Oh, yeah, I forgot. On the paperwork accompanying the paintings." He waved. "Good luck on your exam. I'll call you."

And he did.

That very night.

Theirs was a whirlwind romance. Inside a year, they were married. Soon after, they decided to have a family. Jack quit the force and they moved out of New York City, heading north into Canada to purchase the Peppermint Creek land from a friend who knew a widow who'd offered it at a price they couldn't refuse.

And then they tried for a family.

Nothing happened.

They tried some more.

Still nothing.

Finally, they were both checked out by the doctor. Bad news had come in its worst form. Jack had an unusually low sperm count. The chances of getting pregnant the natural way were slim or next to nothing.

With the doctors encouragement they tried artificial insemination. After numerous unsuccessful tries, they finally gave up, resigning to waiting possibly many years to adopt. It wasn't too long after, Sara discovered she was pregnant and by the old-fashioned method.

She remembered his reaction when the doctor first told them on that sunny summer day they were pregnant.

"Twins? We're going to have twins?" Jack spluttered.

The doctor nodded slowly and smiled at both their shocked expressions.

"A baby. Oh, no, two babies! It totally blows my mind." He ran a trembling hand through his wheat blond hair.

"How do you think I feel? I thought I had the flu for the last month."

"Some flu. This is unbelievable." He twirled the hairs on his large mustache. An endearing gesture he used whenever stumped. Unexpectedly he let out a loud joyful whoop that quite visibly frightened the doctor and made her laugh. Suddenly he was taking her into his arms, swinging her around and around until she felt dizzy.

"Jack! Put me down," Sara pleaded.

He stopped and placed her feet delicately but firmly on the ground. His arms tightened around her waist as he gazed lovingly into her eyes. "I love you, Sara. I love you so much I could die."

A tremendous jolt shook them both and suddenly Jack tensed in her arms. Then he was falling. Blood pouring from a bullet hole between his eyes. Sara screamed. And screamed.

Sara awoke in a cold sweat and alarm rippling along her nerves. A frosty sense of foreboding settled over her, making her shiver in the gray light of dawn.

The horrible dream was back.

Please, she prayed, wiping away the tears streaming down her cheeks. *Don't let the dream start again. Don't let it start!*

* * * * *

Sara spent the entire day trying to forget the horrible nightmare as she busied herself with getting together some more orders of peppermint products for the general store in town. The locals may think she was crazy, but it didn't prevent them from buying her products.

Late in the morning, Tom woke to eat a hearty bowl of vegetable soup and a huge chunk of her homemade bread then drifted off into his nightmare-infested dreams once more. By late evening he looked halfway healthy.

His eyes burned bright with curiosity and his stomach was eager to chow down another bowl of vegetable soup, some mashed potatoes and Jell-O. Despite her protests and warnings that it may still be too heavy on his stomach, he managed to finagle a huge chunk of pound cake out of her.

She stood at the foot of his bed enjoying the way he wolfed down the last bite of his second helping. It was then she decided to ask the one nagging question she'd been dying to ask.

"Who gave you the note with my name on it?"

He stopped chewing and threw her a suspicious look.

"I wasn't snooping," Sara said, suddenly feeling guilty. "I was just looking for some identification. I found the note in your pocket."

He nodded. "I guess I'd do the same."

"Do you remember anything as to why someone would send you here?"

Disappointment coursed through her as he shook his head. "No. The note is the only clue I have. I don't even know if it has anything to do with me. I might have picked it up somewhere."

"I might have an idea."

At her comment, his head snapped up so quickly that he winced in pain, but his eyes shone with eager anticipation.

"But you aren't going to like it," she added.

He frowned. "Tell me anyway. Anything's better than having this horrible blank spot in my brain."

"While you were delirious you said things."

"Things?" he asked cautiously.

"You gave me the impression the police don't have a high opinion of you."

He frowned and her heart ached for him. "You may as well just say it. I'm a criminal."

"I see you've already come to that conclusion."

She came around to the side of the bed and sat down. "Any ideas you'd like to share?"

He nibbled thoughtfully on his lower lip as if trying to decide if he should tell her something.

"Mrs. Clarke—"

"Sara."

"Okay. Sara—" he tried a half-concerted smile "—I'm afraid I might be dangerous to you. I mean by the way I attacked you with the gun." He hesitated for a moment then continued. "And I've also had dreams. Dreams where I'm doing illegal things like paying off pimps and buying drugs and—"

"I know."

The look of surprise on his face made Sara laugh. "Like I said, you've been talking in your sleep. From what I can guess, I think you might have been sent here to get help from my father-in-law. He's a criminal defense lawyer and my sister is a private investigator. We can ask her to investigate what happened to you."

A frightened look shot across his face. Then all too quickly it vanished and he promptly tried to change the subject.

"Are your father-in-law and your husband away on business?"

"Actually he doesn't live here anymore."

"Your husband?"

"Garry. My father-in-law." She opted not to mention her husband. Maybe if he thought she had a husband he wouldn't get any funny ideas about jumping her bones the first chance he got.

And she could stop thinking about jumping his, too, especially after getting such a close and intimate exploration of his gorgeously, almost too long cock. After all, he was a stranger and a criminal. He'd confessed as much.

"Garry lives in New York City. His being a criminal lawyer and you being a—" She caught herself before saying the word "criminal". "You being in need of some help. It's the only thing I can think of as to why someone might send you here."

"Maybe they wanted me to try your delicious peppermint tea," he joked and suddenly his eyes fluttered sleepily.

"Maybe," she said softly and smiled as his eyes closed and a few minutes later, his chest rose and fell slowly.

Shoot. She'd lost him to sleep once again.

She didn't have anything more to go on now than she had before except he seemed comfortable with the idea of being a criminal, but not at all comfortable with the idea of seeing a criminal lawyer.

Perhaps she was being naive, but after the way he'd been treated by the police, wouldn't he welcome a helping hand from a lawyer? Unless—

Sara frowned at a new idea taking hold. Unless he was afraid of what a private investigator might find out and even a good lawyer wouldn't be able to save him.

* * * * *

The gray New York moonlight glistened brilliantly off the NY Chief of Police's white hair making it easy for Detective Pauline Brown to spot him. He was standing in the wide-open space near the towering oak tree at the north end of the park.

She wished they hadn't picked this particular park to meet. It was the closest to the cop station and there was a good chance someone would be lurking around watching them. Ever since that unfortunate incident last week when they'd been caught red-handed by that fool Matt, she'd been a nervous wreck. For one week, they'd waited on pins and needles, expecting all hell to break loose. But it hadn't.

Tonight she'd received the call they'd been waiting for. Unfortunately, it was bad news. Really bad news. She didn't want to be the one to tell the chief, but she had no other choice. He wasn't going to like this. Not one bit.

She frowned and walked briskly toward Chief Jeffries, her high heels clattering loudly against the cobblestone. A chilly gust of night air rumpled her long, straight blonde hair into a momentary static frenzy. The cold air made her clutch her Spring jacket closer to her chest as she approached the white-haired man.

Instantly she spotted the happy smirk plastered on his face. She hated his positive attitude. Overconfidence, especially at a time like this, was extremely dangerous. It allowed people to make mistakes. Real stupid mistakes.

"I trust you have some good news for me, Paulie."

"I got here as soon as I could." Pauline forced a smile as she planted a kiss on his cheek. "What did you find out about our man?"

"They had him."

"Where?"

"A ghost town called Jackfish, a few miles outside of the hick town Rainbow Falls. A couple hours outside of Thunder Bay. Sound familiar?"

"Like in Ontario, Canada? Where Justin lives?"

She nodded.

His face broke into an enormous smile and he rubbed his hands together with eager anticipation.

"So, he went up to Canada, did he? Did he honestly think he could escape me by hiding in the Canadian woods? Wait a minute. What do you mean they had him?"

"He escaped."

To her shock, the chief smiled. "Really? Well, I like a good game of cat and mouse."

Pauline blinked a few times. She hadn't expected this. There was a wanted man on the loose. A man who knew everything about what shady dealings they were involved in, and everything could explode around them any minute and the chief was in a happy mood? It was beyond her comprehension.

His eyes narrowed into tiny suspicious slits. "C'mon now, don't hold it back. What else?"

"They were holding him at the ghost town, waiting for Scout to get there and pump the information out of him when he escaped. A local cop went missing. He was last seen chasing after our man in the wilderness. Justin thinks our man killed him."

His smile widened. "Really? We'll just have to add that to our man's wanted list. I want you to head up that way and keep a lid on things with Justin. We need our man alive until we get what we want."

"There's more."

His white bushy eyebrows shot up in wonder. "Still more?"

Pauline nodded. "Justin says our man has amnesia."

"How interesting."

"Don't you find that a little too convenient, Chief?"

"He always was a smart fellow. But he wouldn't pull a stupid trick like that. Not unless it was true. You should know him better than anyone." He draped a comforting arm across her shoulder. "Don't worry though. You'll be his widow soon enough."

"What should we do next?" she asked, suddenly shivering in the chilly breeze. Or was it from his cold touch?

"Find him. Hold him for questioning. Then he, along with any potential witnesses, must be eliminated."

Pauline shivered violently as the seriousness of his words reached home. She wished it was over and not just beginning.

* * * * *

Dark, narrow alleyways, seedy smoky bars, traffic congested, smog-infested streets, hooker and drug dealing neon nights in which he felt numb, oddly not a part of.

And yet, here he stood talking and laughing with the professional ladies of the evening, buying their pimps drinks, lugging back a few himself just to be sociable. Paying off crooked cops with astronomical amounts of money in return for favors, dancing with some tall, sexy, blond bombshell he didn't even like.

Another dark night lured him deeper…

He was trapped in a suffocating, cold, black, damp room. Someone was leaning over him, checking to see if he was still alive after the violent beating they'd given him. Ash gray cigarette smoke twirled crazily on the night breeze, floating toward heaven, escaping through the tiny cracked openings in the rotting, sagging moss-covered ceiling.

How he wished he could escape the cold and these miserable handcuffs that burned raw fire deep into his wrists. He yearned to hop onto a smoke particle, using it as a magic carpet and quickly drift out of this hellhole.

The cigarette smoke hugged his clothes, seeped into his skin. The tart smell lingered in his nostrils, made his nose itch, burned a scratchy trail down his throat.

He could even taste it!

Tom's eyes snapped open.

Raw orange sunlight bore shards of pain deep into his eyes sockets. Yet he couldn't blink.

The shadow stood there. A black silhouette.

Right there! Outside the window. Watching him sleep.

For a split second, he figured he must still be in the trenches of his dream. But the unmistakable cigarette smoke curled like a billowing gray cloud through the open screen window, striking his face with offending odor. He swallowed back a cough. Cold perspiration shot across his forehead at lightning speed.

The shadow moved slightly, as if realizing it had been spotted.

Then it disappeared.

He wanted to laugh. Downplay what he'd just seen. Tally it up to some weird daydream, a side effect to the familiar pounding gripping his right temple. But the cigarette-scented air wouldn't allow him to let it go so easily.

Sara!

Was she in danger?

Bolting upright, he bit back a groan as pain sliced a sizzling arrow through his back and belly, yet he counted on it. Welcomed it. Used it to keep his mind focused on Sara, and not the paralyzing panic gripping his insides. He whipped aside the blankets and swung his weak legs out of the bed.

The room tilted precariously for a few seconds then everything righted itself. Gritting his teeth, he hoisted himself off the bed.

He hadn't gotten a good look at the person. But it hadn't been Sara. He didn't know how he knew she didn't smoke, he just did.

Adrenaline surged into his limbs urging him to run. To find her. To protect her from danger. Yet he couldn't bolt out of his room blindly, possibly rushing headlong into the enemy. He'd be useless if he got caught.

And Sara would be dead.

Despite the panic edging into his system, he knew he needed to stay calm. Assess the situation. Proceed with caution.

Thoroughly expecting trouble, the tiny hairs on his neck prickled to attention as he stumbled naked to the open window where the shadow had stood only moments earlier.

Leaning his bandaged hands on the inside sill, he pressed his face against the screened window and looked out. Nothing moved. Only the tall blades of green grass in the lush meadow swayed as the wind sailed against them.

If anyone had been here, they'd gone around the side of the house.

Grabbing the first thing he could, a pink towel draped over a nearby chair, he wrapped it securely around his hips. If he had to make a run for it, at least he'd be presentable to the surrounding forest.

With a trembling hand, he reached out and grabbed the steak knife on the twig table, then limped across the floor to inch the door open slowly. Seeing no one, he tiptoed into the quiet hallway.

The unmistakable aroma of fresh baked bread filtered into his nostrils. His stomach growled in hunger, but it was instantly pushed aside by the acrid taste of fear in his mouth as he moved quickly down the hallway and into a cozy living room. He barely registered the pull-out sofa with the neatly made up bed before he headed for the adjoining kitchen and stopped short as he spotted the giant sheet of plywood nailed over the broken window. Had

Sara done the repairs herself? Or had she asked someone to come out? Perhaps that's who'd been at his window. A handyman taking a drag.

But where was she?

Had she taken off? Had his confession of being a criminal frightened her and she'd decided to hoof it out to the highway and get the cops? Had she left him a sitting duck for the cops to finish the job?

Maybe she was on a personal basis with them. She'd said her husband had been a cop. What about the cop who'd been racing down the road? He was the same one who'd been holding him in that basement. What had he been doing on her road? Looking for her instead of him? Warning her about him?

Running a shaky hand through his scruffy beard, he shook his head in denial.

No!

No way. She hadn't even been here when the cop had come calling. Besides, she'd believed him when he told her they wanted him dead.

So where was she?

The familiar panic sifted through him again but he forced himself to hold it in check. Pushing against the screen door, he inched it open and winced as it sent out a violent creak.

Hesitantly he stepped onto the veranda and he sucked in a breath at the carnage that greeted him.

It looked like a bomb had exploded in the front yard. Parts of the beech tree lay scattered everywhere.

An owl hooted from a faraway pine tree startling Tom. And then he heard a strange sound. A metallic clatter. Like something falling over in the direction of the barn. Silence followed.

Swearing under his breath, he gritted his teeth and moved tenderly down the creaking wooden stairs.

The cold cement slabs of the walkway sent shivers shooting up his legs as he hurried barefoot along the path, heading in the general direction of the barn. A split second before he hit the clearing between the house and the barn, turbulent snatches of memory crashed into him, almost making him topple over.

Visions of a large, tilled plot of land surrounded by a pretty white picket fence. A brightly painted red hand pump stood proudly in the middle of the garden. He looked to his left and there it was. The tilled garden. The white picket fence. The red pump.

What the hell was going on? How did he know about all this and about the motorcycle he knew he'd find inside the barn? He hadn't felt these weird deja vu feelings of being here before. But maybe it was because the house and barn had been shrouded in almost total darkness when he'd arrived a few nights ago.

Or maybe he'd been just too darn tired. That night it had taken every last piece of energy he could muster just to climb up the front stairs and plop himself onto the cozy porch when the storm had hit.

The eerie deja vu feelings must mean he'd been here before. He must have met Sara. That's why she seemed so familiar. Why did she say she didn't know him?

But then again, she had admitted she'd given his description to the cops. Had said she knew him that night he'd arrived. Then she'd changed her story. Even given him a new name.

Why? What was she hiding?

Suddenly impatient, he ignored the angry protests of his sore muscles as he cautiously proceeded, quite intent on finding the shadow, Sara and answers to his arsenal of questions.

* * * * *

Muttering angrily under her breath, Sara picked up one of the two metal buckets she'd just sent sprawling onto the floor. Cripes! She was all thumbs today. First she'd spilled some red paint over the brightly colored Navajo rug covering the pine floor of her painting loft, and now she was knocking over her buckets. Ever since awakening from the dream, she'd been tense, on edge, as if waiting for something to happen. Surprisingly, along with the dream came that old familiar inkling of wanting to paint again. Something she hadn't done since *it* had happened.

But when she'd picked up the paintbrush and dipped it into the paint container, her hand had shaken so badly, she'd spilled the contents of the watercolor all over the desk and floor.

Sara sighed with frustration.

She'd been stupid to think she could start where she'd left off. It had been a dumb idea. Why she had even bothered to try again was beyond her.

The passion was lost. Finished. Gone forever.

Suddenly a bright yellow slant of light rushed across the stairwell leading up to the loft instantly capturing her attention.

A frosty warning of caution prickled across the rear of her scalp, scrambling down the back of her neck, settling like a cobra between her shoulder blades. Her heart did a triple beat as she quickly grabbed a palette knife off the nearby wooden bench.

The slant of light dissolved and she heard the door close quietly.

Silence followed.

Had to be the wind. She must not have closed the door properly.

God! She was jumping at every little sound. What a way to live. She had to relax.

Dropping the palette knife onto the nearby chair, she thrust the metal bucket under the nearby tap and half filled it with water before returning her attention to the carpet where she started vigorously scrubbing the red mess, all the while muttering irritably beneath her breath trying to convince herself that nobody was lurking around.

To distract herself, her thoughts traveled over the many things she needed to get done before the summer opening of her campground and the cabins. This morning she'd finally ventured away from the house. On her walk, she'd discovered a few trees had fallen over around the campground and one of the old cabins had a major leak in the roof.

It had taken hours to clean up the water damage and when the phone was working, she needed to make some calls to get the debris from the fire cleared away and then call in the log builders to see if they were still on schedule to come and rebuild the inn.

And then there was the poor romance tree. It needed to be cleared, chopped and stacked and—

The barn door creaked open again. Another buttery glow of sunshine spilled across the stairs leading up to her loft.

She kept scrubbing cursing herself for being so jittery.

It was just the wind again. Just the wind.

The bottom step creaked.

Oh, shit!

Not the wind.

Jumping to her feet, she grabbed the palette knife and clutched it tight in her hand.

Another step creaked.

Damn! No time for a proper weapon! She had to hide! But where?

She spied the bookshelf beside the staircase. Swiftly she tiptoed across the tiny room positioning her shoulder against the heavy maple bookcase containing all her paint supplies.

If she pushed hard enough it would topple onto the intruder as he came up the stairs sending him most likely to his death. Sara held her breath and waited.

The intruder was near the top now. She could hear his heavy breathing. Could hear the soft sounds of his feet upon the stairs.

A part of her mind wanted to shout a warning for him to leave or she would kill him, but surprise would be her best defensive. She would act first and ask questions later.

Before she could push against the bookshelf, a bare muscular arm reached around, grabbing her wrist. Another hand flew into sight, a gleaming knife smiling viciously at her.

She screamed as he pulled her easily from her hiding place.

Frantically she kicked out. Her foot cracked into soft flesh and she heard the knife clatter down the stairs.

Her assailant swore loudly.

Instantly she recognized the husky voice and stopped her second kick midway through the air.

"It's me!" he shouted at her.

His eyes were wide with surprise as he held her wrist tightly.

"You scared the daylights out of me!" she shouted back. "Can't you just enter a room like a normal person, without some sort of weapon. For crying out loud, I thought you were—" She stopped mid-sentence as she gazed at him.

The first thing she noticed was his very muscular, very naked chest. The second thing, the pale pink terry cloth towel slung low over his sexy lean hips. And the third, the dangerous daggers his furious green eyes were shooting directly at her.

"What's wrong?"

"You here alone?" he said as he let go of her wrist. His voice sounded low and controlled. Too controlled for her liking.

"Of course I'm alone. What's going on?"

He said nothing as he scanned the contents of her loft. His fierce gaze narrowed suspiciously, missing nothing as it swept past a sofa and the old beat-up oak desk she used to draw and paint on.

The broad muscles tensed in his abdomen and his eyes grew to mere slits as he surveyed the two wildlife paintings she'd strung along the white paneled walls.

First he concentrated on the watercolor of an enormous black bear flanked by her two frolicking cubs amidst a raspberry patch. Then he looked at another watercolor painting of a baby raccoon, his masked face peeking curiously through the tall blades of grass, watching a green frog sunning itself on a lily pad.

Then his gaze quickly riveted onto a nearby closet door where she stored her supplies.

"Tom, what are you looking for?"

He didn't answer.

Instead, his gaze flew back to her paintings, scrutinizing every detail.

"I'm getting some memories back," he replied icily without taking his eyes off the painting.

"Remembering?" Exactly what was he remembering? Was he reverting back to his criminal ways? Is that why he looked so furious?

Her heart began to thump wildly against her chest.

"Why haven't you told me the truth, Sara?"

"The truth? About what?"

"About who I am."

Oh for crying out loud. Was he sick again? Was that why he was behaving so strangely?

Automatically she reached up to feel his forehead.

In a wicked flash, his right hand sailed up with unbelievable lightning speed, capturing her wrist in a vise-like grip.

"What are you doing?" she gasped. She could hear the fear in her voice, realized he could hear it also. She straightened stiffly, not wanting to show him she was afraid of him.

She raised her eyes and met his smoldering gaze head on.

"Don't toy with me, Sara. I want you to tell me who I am."

"I've already told you. I don't know who you are."

"The other night you said you knew me. You said you'd given my description to the cops. Why? Who am I? What have I done? Why are you so afraid of me now?"

"Usually when someone sneaks up behind someone they have reason to be afraid. Besides, the door was opening and closing just before you came. I thought it was the wind. It spooked me. And I was terrified the other night. You had a gun. Naturally I assumed you were…" The words trailed off as she realized how mistaken she'd been. Or had she been mistaken? Her gaze fell to the tight grip around her wrist.

"Who? Who did you think I was?" he urged desperately.

"I…I don't know," she answered meekly. Now was not the time to bring the shadow into their conversation. Tom needed to spend all his energies on relaxing and getting better and not worrying about the fact someone was creeping around her place breaking her windows and throwing rats into her kitchen. It would just keep him on edge and unable to rest. He shook his head slightly, obviously not believing a word she was saying.

"Tell me this then. How do I know there's an antique motorcycle under the tarp in the far corner of the barn. And there's a lake and a huge campground not more than a few minutes walk up the hiking trail out back." He nodded to the adjoining door. "Or how I know you've got a bunch of finished wildlife paintings stored in the closet. How do I know all this if I've never been here before?"

Shock zipped through her. "How could you know about my paintings? That door is always locked."

"If you know who I am, why don't you just tell me? Do you know me? Have we met? Why do you look so damn familiar to me?" His grip tightened and Sara winced at the pain shooting up her wrist.

"I've never seen you before in my life. I told you all I know." She tried to pull away from him. "Please let go of me. You're hurting me."

His angry gaze dropped to his tight hold on her wrist and his eyes turned to a look of horror. He cursed heavily and immediately let her go.

"I'm sorry. I didn't mean to hurt you."

Quickly she backed away from him, her heart cracking like a jackhammer against her chest at his odd behavior. The back of her legs collided with an empty easel, knocking it over, the loud bang making her jump in fright.

She noticed Tom wince at the noise and his hand snapped up to massage the goose egg on his temple.

"I've been here recently, Sara. I know it."

"Listen, I've been away for a few days running errands. I just came home when you jumped me. Maybe you were here when I was away? I really don't know you."

Although I sure wish I did, a little voice whispered in her head.

She noticed a muscle jumped sporadically in his tense jaw. "Do you have a headache?"

"No," he muttered and avoided her gaze.

"You're lying. You just don't want to drink any more of my willow bark tea," she found herself teasing.

A flicker of a smile tugged at his lips. "Yes, on all counts."

"I've got something else for the pain back in the house." She touched his forehead allowing her fingers to rest there a wee bit longer than necessary.

The scorching way he watched her made her clear her suddenly dry throat.

"No fever. That's a good sign. So why did you ask if I was here alone?"

He shrugged his shoulders. "It was nothing. I just got spooked by a nightmare. Then when I woke up and…" He hesitated, his gaze flying to the window overlooking the yard.

A tinge of uneasiness swooped over her. Had he maybe seen the shadow?

"And what?"

"It's not important."

"Okay, let's just get you back to the house before you fall over."

* * * * *

A few minutes later, he stood watching Sara as she straightened up the sheets and the quilt on the bed. The way his loins tightened as her full hips swayed seductively while she plumped up the pillows proved he was definitely on the mend.

He found himself wanting to wrap his arms around her waist, to press his aching cock against her cute curvy ass and let her feel exactly how attracted he was to her.

Would she let him unravel the beautiful braid that ran down the length of her back? Allow him to sift his fingers through her shimmering auburn tresses?

He wanted to kiss her full, warm lips. Drown himself in her sweet peppermint scent and then—

"You need plenty of bed rest." Her determined words broke him from his fantasy just in time for him to see her pat the mattress and say, "Because I plan on putting you to work."

He almost laughed aloud when her cheeks turned a pretty shade of sweetheart pink as she suddenly realized what she'd just insinuated with her words and her gesture.

"I like that kind of work," he drawled teasingly as he climbed under the sheets she held up for him.

She smiled nervously. "I mean chopping wood. That is if you want something to do while we figure out why you're here."

"The thought of some good old-fashioned work makes me feel a bit stronger already."

He needed to get his strength back as quickly as possible. What other way to do it than to chop wood?

"I'll start first thing in the morning."

"I'll be the judge of when you start," she stated firmly. "Maybe in a couple of days. In the meantime, I'll get some medication for your headache. Do you feel like something to eat?"

"Maybe some of that peppermint tea? If it's not too much trouble?"

"No trouble." Sara turned to leave.

"Hold on! You forgot this!" Beneath the covers, he whipped off the pink towel, pulled it out and threw it toward her.

She caught it easily and he laughed as her face blushed an even deeper shade of pink when she realized it was the towel he'd wrapped around his waist.

"Like I've said before, you've got nothing I haven't already seen," she said and with the towel firmly in hand, turned stiffly and headed out the bedroom door.

Tom chuckled and snuggled into the fluffy peppermint-scented pillows. He felt halfway relaxed for the first time since arriving here. But he couldn't bask in this beautiful woman's company for long. He was placing her in grave danger just by being here.

There was something about this place that made him a bit too uneasy. In the loft, the wildlife paintings had instantly captured his attention. Why did her paintings seem so familiar? Why did their intense beauty give him such strange uncomfortable feelings?

And why did he think he'd been in her loft before? How had he known the adjoining closet in her loft contained more paintings? She'd said she always kept that room locked up. How had he gotten in?

More questions whirled. Had the barn door been opening and closing as a result of the wind, like Sara had said? Or had it been that person he'd seen in Sara's bedroom window? Or maybe that person had in fact been a dream? A flashback of a memory? If it hadn't been a dream, then why would the person simply be standing there casually smoking? Someone with bad intentions wouldn't be standing there? Would they?

He must have had some sort of illusion. The cigarette-scented air burning into his lungs could have been a flashback? Maybe his memory would come back in this way? Odd fragments of a puzzle. A puzzle he wasn't sure he wanted to solve. Whether it was a dream or reality, he couldn't leave Sara out here in the middle of nowhere, with a possible intruder lurking around. For now, he wouldn't tell her about the smoker. No use in getting her upset and frightened if it had just been a dream. When he felt a little stronger, he'd do some serious snooping around. Until then, he'd keep quiet.

Spent and totally exhausted, his mind fought against staying awake and he closed his eyes.

* * * * *

Sara stood at the living room window. Darkness protected her as she peered out into the inky night searching for any type of movement. Tom had been asleep when she'd gone back with the pain medication.

She was glad. It would give her time to think. To figure out why he'd come up into the loft, panic brewing in his eyes, brandishing a knife.

Had he had a nightmare and somehow gotten confused?

She didn't think so. He'd been searching for someone.

Had he seen the shadow? Had someone else other than herself actually seen it? The thought didn't bring an ounce of relief to her.

For more than two years, the hairs on the back of her neck had prickled a warning she was being watched. When it had first started, shortly after her husband's death, she'd thought maybe his restless spirit had been trapped between this world and the other. She'd feared his ghost had come back to haunt her because she'd been unable to save him.

Numerous times, she'd stayed up all night, waiting and watching for him. But she'd never seen anyone. Until one crisp night late last Fall, shortly after she'd closed the inn for the season, something had happened to make her believe she wasn't so crazy. She'd perched herself inside the loft, beside the picture window and watched.

The moon had been full force that night, beaming its white laser light across the front yard of her house and the meadow. It had been 3:15 a.m. when she'd seen the shadow saunter across the front yard, and up to her veranda. And she'd seen the orange glow of a cigarette.

She'd run out into the yard to confront the shadow but he'd disappeared.

Her fears of going crazy, of her husband's tormented spirit being caught in this world had instantly vanished. Her husband didn't smoke and a dead person didn't leave behind footsteps in the gravel of the parking lot. Since then, she'd been on guard.

Sara straightened and peered over at the telephone. She'd forgotten to check if the phones were working today. She reached for it, placed the receiver to her ear and smiled at the dial tone.

Punching in the numbers quickly, her mind raced as she formulated how to explain to Garry she was harboring a man who'd shown up at her house wounded, wearing handcuffs and that she needed him to help Tom.

The phone rang on the other end.

Once.

Twice.

Please answer, Garry.

Her hand tightened around the receiver as it kept ringing and ringing. Finally his answering machine clicked on.

She hesitated a moment then left a discreet message. There was no telling how long it would take before he picked up his messages.

For all she knew he could be in Florida with his brother on their annual fishing trip. She had no idea where they would be staying this time. But a good friend of his might know how to get in touch with him.

She looked up the appropriate number in her address book and didn't have long to wait before a nasal voice answered, "Det. Dan Rawlings. New York Police Department."

Sara hesitated a moment then took a deep breath and plunged ahead.

Chapter Five
New York, New York…

၈၁

"So you saw him pull the trigger?"

Garry Clarke suddenly shifted uneasily in his wheelchair as Sara's private eye sister Jocelyn Brady's question sliced through the quiet interrogation room.

They'd been ushered in there quickly, as if the chief of police—one of the witnesses to his twin brother Robin's fatal shooting—hadn't wanted anyone to know someone was asking questions about what had happened. And yet, as Garry's piercing gaze remained glued on the chief's pale granite blue eyes, he noticed the chief flinch at Jo's question.

It was just the barest of a twitch on an otherwise stone-serious poker face, but Garry recognized it as a sign. A sign that indicated Chief Jeffries hadn't told the entire truth about his brother's murder.

He'd met the chief on two previous occasions without Jocelyn. The meetings had been formal and cordial. Actually, the chief had been too cordial. To the point of bending over backward to show Garry the overwhelming evidence he had on the suspect. Yet something didn't sit right. He desperately wished he knew what it was.

In a last-ditch attempt to shake up the chief, he'd asked Jocelyn to tag along. Jocelyn, a striking woman, would arouse the chief's interest. The chief, being a man who always chased a skirt, wouldn't allow a beautiful woman to pass through his hands. Jo's distraction would let Garry survey the man from afar. Apparently his idea had worked.

"I've already told you, Miss Brady," the chief of police stated in response to Jo's question. "The murderer was standing as close as I am to you when he blew out Robbie's brains. I saw it and as you know, the suspect's very own wife saw it."

Garry suddenly felt sick to his stomach. Instead of being here talking about his dead brother, he should be down in Florida fishing with him, like they'd planned. But Robin's last minute cancellation had come as a shock to him. Up until almost the very end, Robin had been obsessively secretive about the type of work he did.

Finally, during the last phone conversation they'd had, Robin had revealed to him a few days before his death, if everything went according to plan, the debris would hit the fan when certain information about a certain New York police precinct got out.

Obviously, something had gone terribly wrong because his brother was now dead and buried. Allegedly killed by the hands of a crooked police officer.

The tiny nerve twitched again under the chief's right eye, drawing Garry's immediate attention. Their gazes locked. For a split second, Garry read the fear in those stone-cold eyes. Fear of what? What was he hiding?

In a quick sweep, the chief's eyes became shuttered once again. He pressed his hands onto his desk, stood and drew his attention back to Jo.

"If that'll be all, I've got a precinct to run," the chief said gently. He acted as if nothing out of the ordinary had just happened.

Jo took the hint, got out of her seat, leaned over the desk and shook hands with the chief. "I'm grateful to you, sir, for taking some time out of your busy schedule for us. You've been very helpful."

The chief managed a brilliant smile for Jocelyn. Most men did. And they should. Jo was a very attractive thirty-three-year-old woman with straight, chestnut-colored hair that dropped just below her shoulders.

Her sky blue-violet eyes always twinkled a welcome to anyone she met. But Jo never seemed interested in getting hitched. She always kept herself in a very cool business-like manner when she spoke to a man. And the moment they showed any interest in her, that famous icy exterior glazed over her, and the men just kind of slid away. One by one.

He sensed something had happened in her past to make her shy away from men and relationships. She'd never told him about it and he'd never pried. But she was very different with him. Always friendly and helpful.

Maybe because she figured he wasn't a threat. Being thirty-odd years older, a good friend and a father figure, he considered Jocelyn and her sister Sara, to be the daughters he'd always wanted but never had. The bullet that had shattered his spine and paralyzed him from his waist down had taken care of having any more kids, besides an only son.

Garry's thoughts drifted back to the chief and Jo who now stood.

"You come back anytime, Miss Brady."

Jo smiled. The cute little dimple popping out in her right cheek. "Oh, please call me Jo. All my friends do."

Garry's eyes widened at her words. She considered him a friend? A sinking feeling hit the pit of his gut and his hands tightened around the vinyl arms of the wheelchair. He should have filled her in on the chief. Told her the real reason he'd asked her to accompany him today.

"And I'd love to come back and visit," Jo said softly, teasingly. "Perhaps we could do brunch sometime?"

Brunch? God, he was going to be sick.

"That would be wonderful, Jo. I'm looking forward to it."

Garry threw the chief a stiff nod as a needle of anger sliced through him. He barely felt the smooth rocking motion as Jo turned his wheelchair and pushed him out into the corridor. When they were halfway down the hallway, Garry twisted awkwardly in his wheelchair and peered angrily up at Jo. A sweet, smug smile lifted her pretty lips.

Immediately his anger deflated into curiosity. Jo had taken her porcupine quills in for a reason. She was onto something.

"What gives, Jo?"

"What makes you think something's up?" she replied casually.

"You know why."

Jo slowed the wheelchair and leaned closer to Garry.

"Let me ask you something, Garry." She threw a cautious glance over her shoulder.

The corridor was clear.

"If one person shoots another person at close range, but not too close. For instance, like what the chief said, the killer being as close to the victim as I was to the chief today, right?"

Garry nodded.

"Well then, tell me this, Gar. Why would the autopsy report say Robin had powder burns on his face? Isn't that consistent with someone shooting him at point-blank range? Not a few feet away?"

Garry slowly shook his head. He'd thought she'd been onto something. He'd been wrong. "Don't read too much into it, Jo. He was using it just as an example."

Jo bit her lip thoughtfully. "Maybe."

"But? What?" Garry frowned. He didn't like the tiny sliver of uneasiness slithering across his shoulder blades. "C'mon, Jo, you have excellent instincts. What are you thinking?"

"Who would doubt the chief of police as a witness?"

"Yeah," Garry agreed softly as he finally understood her meaning.

Satisfied she'd made her point, Jo began pushing Garry's wheelchair down the deserted hallway.

* * * * *

The hot sun hung high overhead, radiating its welcome heat into the rich earth. A strong wind swept across the tall slender blades of the nearby meadow grass. Large puffy white clouds drifted from horizon to horizon allowing only moment's relief from the stifling yellow heat.

With her foot, Sara forced the shovel deep into the rich black earth, withdrew the burden of dirt, and then flipped it over as one might flip over a pancake. Then she wiped away the perspiration crawling from beneath her tattered straw hat.

"Darn it," she muttered angrily as she turned over yet another shovelful of dirt, allowing it to bake in the sun. She could have used the rototiller, but she needed to get a new spark plug. The old one hadn't been worth a hill of beans last year. Oh, who was she kidding. The rototiller would work well enough for now. Truth is, she just didn't want to wake Tom up.

She didn't need a half-naked man hanging around the house. Especially a man wearing nothing but a pink terry cloth towel, slung so low over his hips, she'd almost erupted from internal combustion. The sooner he got out of here, the better. He was too dangerous.

Too sexy.

Last night she'd dreamed that same dream again. About the day she'd met Jack, and the day they'd found out she was pregnant. This time a strange new twist had been added. Everything had occurred in the same sequence, up to the point when Jack had twirled her around and around until she'd felt dizzy.

At that point Jack's face disintegrated and Tom held her in his strong, yet tender arms.

And this time no gunshot ripped throughout the air. Only Tom who stood in front of her, gently unbuttoning her dress. Lifting it over her head. Gazing upon her nakedness with lusty eyes and a giant cock that stretched straight out as he eased her onto the bed and came down between her widespread legs.

She blew out an aroused breath at the sexy vision and wiped a bead of perspiration off her forehead, frowning as the tiny hairs on the back of her neck suddenly popped to attention.

Suddenly she had the distinct feeling someone was watching her.

Whirling around, she caught sight of a tall man standing at the picket gate of her garden, arms folded casually across his chest. He watched her carefully, saying nothing.

Alarm rippled along her nerves as she surveyed the clean-shaven newcomer. Was he looking for Tom?

Her grip on the wooden handle of the shovel tightened as did her protective instincts of keeping harm away from Tom. If this man tried anything, she'd be on him faster than a she-wolf on a rabbit.

Then she noticed the familiar smile edging up his full lips and aroused shock sifted through her system.

"Oh, my God! Tom?"

Drop-dead gorgeous. A young Mel Gibson look-alike.

"Wow," she heard herself saying, her insides suddenly trembling, her pussy creaming with heated arousal.

Tom's smile widened and she felt as if all her breath had stalled in her lungs.

Without saying anything, he popped open the picket gate and stepped into the garden, strolling confidently up the center path.

Sara leaned heavily on the shovel, her knees suddenly feeling weak as she watched him draw nearer. Heaven only knew she needed some sort of a crutch, because the crisp, clean smell of soap along with his erotic masculine scent slammed into her nostrils, making her quite aware of his maleness.

His hot gaze raked over her body making intense urges erupt deep inside her abdomen.

Oh, boy, she did not need this. She really didn't. But he looked so good. Handsome and clean-shaven. The dreaded paleness from being sick had vanished, replaced by a robust healthy color that made the yellowish-blue bruises barely visible. He'd tied his long, feathery dark brown hair neatly behind his neck. The rest of his hair was tucked beneath an old baseball cap that had once belonged to Jack.

"So? What do you think? Do I pass muster?" he asked huskily.

"You look...different." Heat flushed her face and it wasn't from the sun. She allowed her appreciative gaze to drop from his handsome face to the light gray muscle T-shirt stretched taught over his broad shoulders and muscular chest, then down to the gorgeous hip-hugging jeans she'd washed.

The shirt had belonged to her husband and Tom filled it out quite nicely indeed.

Yes, very nice.

Unconsciously Sara licked her dry lips.

Her face blushed warmer as she gazed back into Tom's prodding gaze. There was something shimmering in those green depths. Something hot, dangerous, sexy. Something erotic, aching to burst free.

It was something she wanted.

"I didn't recognize you."

"Good. It's my new master disguise. Amazing what a little bit of spit and polish won't do. I hope you don't mind about the hat?" He touched the beak of the hat. "But the sunshine's a bit hard on the eyes after being inside for so long."

"That's fine, but are you sure you should be up?"

Maybe in a couple days. But not now. She wasn't ready to fight off these wonderful erotic sensations coursing through her.

"Actually I feel pretty good today. I put some of your peppermint antiseptic onto the bullet wound. And I figured I'd air out my hands. If that's okay with the doctor." He held up his hands to show her he'd taken off the bandages. The tiny sliver wounds were healing very nicely leaving only red spots behind.

Sara found it hard not to sigh her relief that he was on the mend. "That's fine. As long as you keep them clean."

"Yes, ma'am." She noted the hint of humor in his voice as he saluted sharply and stood at attention.

"At ease, soldier," Sara quipped.

Tom relaxed then said, "You hungry?"

She nodded.

"Great stuff. I've got everything ready. I'm going to take you on a picnic."

A picnic? A sudden sprig of tears bit the back of her eyelids and she cleared her suddenly tight throat. She'd gone on many picnics when Jack had been alive. Could she go on one with a complete stranger?

He must have noticed her hesitation, because he shuffled his feet like a little kid as if he'd done something wrong and didn't know what. "I hope it's all right. I threw together a few things and found a basket in the pantry. I figured since it's such a nice day and you've been working so hard in the garden—"

"I'm not dressed properly," she blurted out using the first excuse she could come up with. She grimaced when she remembered how she'd dressed for gardening this morning. She wore an ancient pair of jean cutoff shorts, black Rolling Stones T-shirt and her hair hung haphazardly under the wide brimmed straw hat. She wished the ground would open up and she could disappear.

Besides, she couldn't go on a picnic with him. It was too—intimate.

Tom's eyes narrowed curiously. "What's wrong with what you're wearing?"

"I-I," she stuttered, looking for an answer. "I look like a scarecrow."

"A scarecrow, huh? Well you sure are the prettiest scarecrow around these parts."

Pretty? He thought she was pretty? Excitement coursed through her veins at his comment.

He pried the shovel from her suddenly nervous fingers, stuck the blade deep into the earth and slid his warm hand into hers.

Oh, dear.

Holding hands. Way too intimate.

Her flush got worse. Yet she didn't dare let go. It felt so good to be held. To feel a man's fingers twining with hers once again.

"C'mon, let's go. How about over there?" He pointed to the edge of the meadow where the dark shade of the black forest beckoned a cool invitation.

"Sure."

He led her out of the garden and through the gate, where he swooped over, grabbed the basket and the homemade family quilt she'd been unable to finish.

She bit her lower lip when she recognized the giant white lacy patch staring straight up at her. It was a piece of material from her wedding gown.

Doubt crept inside her head. How could she go on a picnic with a total stranger? Act as if nothing tragic had happened in her past. Yet that's exactly what she was doing.

They tramped through the tall meadow grass in silence, Sara's eyes never leaving the quilt. She'd hidden it in the pantry with the basket, after…well, after her world had fallen apart.

She recognized the patch of navy blue material from Jack's police uniform. Remembered the day he'd told her he'd quit the force. God, she'd been so happy.

She'd never liked him being a cop. Getting shot at. Never knowing if the next phone call would be the one telling her he was dead, gunned down by some crazed lunatic. But it had happened anyway, hadn't it?

Right out here in the middle of nowhere. A place they'd thought was safe. A place to raise their children. She angrily brushed away the stray tear dribbling down her cheek. Thankfully, Tom didn't notice.

Sara didn't realize they'd reached the edge of the meadow until the shade, cool and delicious, trailed over her heated body. The strong scent of baking pine needles and the wind flickering restfully through the sighing branches above them began calming her rattled nerves.

Tom threw her a concerned look. "You okay?"

Sara found herself grinning. "Just tired."

"You need food," he chuckled as he reluctantly let go of her hand.

Spreading the homemade quilt over the grass, he plopped the basket into the middle, slipped off his shoes and sat down cross-legged.

He smiled up at her, patted the ground beside him.

"C'mon, I won't bite."

Sara stood at the edge of the quilt, looking down at it, suddenly unwilling to step onto her past. She noticed the blue and white dotted gingham patch of her kitchen curtains from their first apartment in New York. She recognized the ragged patch from an old pair of Jack's trousers, the same one's he'd worn to the doctor's office on the day they'd been told the chances were slim she would ever get pregnant.

Life goes on. She told herself sternly. It has to.

Sara wiggled out of her shoes and stepped onto the quilt and onto her past.

She watched Tom as he gingerly removed the items from the basket. His grin was so innocent and intense. The last thing she wanted was to burst his bubble simply because she couldn't come to grips with her past.

Sara sat down trying to avoid looking at the patchwork coverlet.

"I hope you like this stuff. I prepared a feast fit for a king, queen and their entire empire. Cooked a heap of potatoes and made a salad and more stuff. Here see for yourself."

He handed her a foil-wrapped parcel. Gently she unwrapped it and gasped as a hefty sandwich emerged.

"You didn't have to go through all this trouble, Tom," she said without taking her eyes off the delicious-looking creation. Her mouth began to water. She hadn't realized she was so hungry and without further hesitation she took a big bite.

"Mmm. Very good," she mumbled between bites. "My compliments to the chef."

"You sound surprised."

"Actually, yes. Most men I know don't like to cook. Woman's work, they say."

"Well then, you must not have met up with the right man yet."

Right man? What was he insinuating?

He continued to heap a plate full of potato salad, bean salad, her homemade peppermint-pickled carrots and beets, acting as if he hadn't said anything out of the ordinary. He'd called her pretty, and now he said she hadn't met the right man yet? Maybe she was just reading too much into his words.

He wouldn't be interested in her. She was a widow living alone in the middle of nowhere, dressed like a scarecrow and not even wearing a touch of makeup. It was just her overactive hormones, she reasoned to herself or merely wishful thinking.

He offered her a heaping plate of preserves and salad.

Sara shook her head, gesturing her hand at him to take it away. "Oh, no. I couldn't eat that much."

But her taste buds were already into overdrive. She was practically drooling.

"Come on, take it. My beautiful scarecrow needs to put some meat on her bones. Besides whatever you don't eat, we'll feed to the ants."

His green eyes shone with encouragement and suddenly she began to feel better. Much better. She accepted the plate and chuckled. "We're going to have some mighty big ants running around here then."

He poured two glasses of ice-cold ginger ale and handed her one then held his glass up in the air. "To good food, good ale, excellent company and a fine ole day. Cheers!"

Sara couldn't help but laugh as the glasses clinked together.

"*Bon appétit!*" she mumbled between hearty mouthfuls.

They ate with occasional bursts of hearty chatter. Talking of nothing in particular until almost the entire assortment of food had been devoured.

Then she remembered her phone calls last night.

"I forgot to tell you that the phone was working for awhile last night so I tried to get a hold of Garry. He doesn't own a cell and I couldn't get him at his place so I called a good friend of his at the New York Police Department—"

Tom's mouth dropped open in surprise and he visibly paled. The easygoing innocent look flew from his green eyes and was replaced by a look of open distrust.

"You turned me in?"

"No! God, no!" Sara jolted with unease at the idea he'd think she'd betrayed him. "I never mentioned you. I only asked that Garry call me right away. And that it was urgent."

"Shit! You left a message with the New York police?"

"Really, you don't have to worry. His friend is very reliable. He used to be a lawyer, he worked with Garry and I didn't even mention you."

Tom shook his head and the tiniest bit of a smile flittered across his lips. "I'm sorry, I freaked. I really do trust you. Please, tell me what he said."

"I just told him I needed to talk to Garry about some family business and if he knew where in Florida Garry and his brother had gone fishing for their vacation. Every year the two of them take a couple of weeks off and do the fishing thing. Anyway, he said Garry was working on a very important personal case that had suddenly come up and he'd forward my message to him."

"How about your sister? Did you get a hold of her?"

"Well, actually the phone went dead again while I was dialing her number so I couldn't talk to her. It was still dead this morning when I checked. If it's the main line into here, it usually doesn't get fixed unless I tell the hydro people. If it's out on the main highway, then I'm sure they're working on it. I guess I really should invest in a cell phone."

"Might be a good idea."

"In the meantime, you can stay here at Peppermint Creek and enjoy all it's healing powers."

"And all this healing grub," he said, suddenly cheerful again.

She relaxed as Tom helped himself to some more of her homemade preserves. When his plate was once again full, he asked the question everyone asks of her when they come to Peppermint Creek Inn. "Tell me more about this place."

She loved it when people asked her to talk about Peppermint Creek Inn. It was her baby, now that everything else was gone. Draining the rest of her ginger ale, she shifted some plates aside, crossed her legs Indian style and began her story all the while her heart hammered against her chest at the intense way he was looking at her again.

"We bought the property from a widow. They were rich. He was involved in the gold and lumber industry just east of here, and he built the log house for her to use as a retreat. She'd always wanted to be a writer and used the house to write many novels in this solitude, but she never got up the nerve to send her work to a publisher."

Tom frowned. "Sounds kind of tragic."

Sara nodded in agreement. "When her husband retired, they both moved out here. Realizing they were lonely, they decided to open up a campground and had some rustic cabins built. Her husband died shortly after, and for a few years, she tried to keep the place going by herself, but it was too much work and the winters were horribly lonely so she decided to sell. But she only wanted to sell to someone who really loved nature. A friend of ours mentioned this place to us. Jack and I fell in love with the seclusion right away, but the others—" Sara shrugged her shoulders "—they took a wee bit longer."

"Others?"

"My partners. My father-in-law Garry and my sister Jo."

"Jo live here, too?"

"She did. For a while. But she moved back to Maine where she takes care of my parents' house when they are traveling. But they, as well as my brother and parents help out as often as they can. I usually have someone with me during the on season."

"And the winters? Aren't they too long for you and your husband all alone out here?"

Sara bit her lower lip and fingered her wedding band. Should she tell him? Could she trust this stranger not to harm her once he found out no one lived there with her? And could she tell him there wasn't a husband anymore?

Before she could figure out what to say, he answered his own question.

"Your husband doesn't live here, does he? You're just afraid to tell me because you don't quite trust me. Not yet anyway," he said confidently. "That's normal, Sara. Especially since I've revealed I'm a criminal."

"We don't know that for sure," she said quickly, suddenly surprised at saying those words. She was beginning to wonder why the police wanted this man dead. They didn't go around killing criminals, at least not on purpose.

He nodded thoughtfully. His eyes revealed nothing as he gazed toward the nearby diamond-studded lake, shimmering brilliantly beneath the sun's intense rays.

He changed the subject off himself and onto her again. It was becoming an annoying habit and she wished she could break him of it.

"So what do you do out here in the long, cold winters?"

"I manage to keep myself busy. I make my peppermint products from the peppermint I pick in the creek and when the winter blues set in, I go out and deliver them. That's where I've been the past few days."

"Products? You get the peppermint from your creek?" He sounded downright impressed and Sara found herself squirming with excitement.

Clasping her hands beneath her chin she said with longing, "Oh, you should see it here in the summer. The air is just drenched with the smell of the peppermint plants. In August, I hire a small crew of students who help harvest the peppermint and we dry them from the rafters in the barn. During the winter I make everything from peppermint-scented candles, bath and massage oils, soaps, antiseptics to candies, cookies, cakes and the list is endless."

Tom's brows rose with amused expectation and he licked his lips. "Peppermint cheesecake?"

Sara laughed. "That could be easily arranged."

"You really love this place. I can see it in your eyes," Tom said softly. The scorching way he looked at her made her a wee bit self-conscious.

Fingering a square of Amish blue material, she suddenly realized she couldn't remember what that piece represented. And at the moment she didn't really care.

"Well, sure. It's home. What's not to love?"

He shifted some more dishes off the quilt and stretched out full length beside her.

She tried hard not to look at him, but she couldn't resist glancing now and then at his long legs, his sexy hips or his thick sinewy arms as they bulged when he clasped his large hands over his flat stomach.

"Tell me more about this place," he asked as he looked up at the sky.

"What do you want to know?"

"Why it feels so relaxing here. Almost like something magic is in the air."

Sara laughed. "There'll be lots of stuff in the air in a couple of weeks. Black flies, mosquitoes, horseflies, deerflies—"

"Your laugh is very nice. You should do it more often."

Their gazes locked for a moment and her breath slammed into her lungs at the dark, lusty way he was looking at her. She could fall in love with this man. So easily. The thought shocked her senseless and Sara looked down, trying hard to concentrate on another square of material in her picnic quilt.

"The bugs don't keep the customers away?" he asked softly.

"They complain about it," she joked, avoiding eye contact. "But every year they come back in droves. I've had to cancel all the advance reservations because of the inn burning down but I'm still going ahead with the cabins and the campground on the other side of the lake. I'm going to have to get started on rehiring some of the people too for when I reopen. And I need a handyman to clear the fallen tree, repair some of the cabins."

"Maybe I could hire on temporarily?"

Sara swallowed tightly at his comment. Oh, dear. Having this hunk hanging around for a few more days was really going to be hard on her. Every time she looked at him, she wanted to jump his bones.

"I'm sure you're still too sore to do that sort of work."

"Actually it doesn't hurt too badly. I took a look at the wound in the mirror and it's not too deep. Just a graze."

He frowned as she shook her head. "It's more than a graze and I think it's still too soon."

"I can go slow. I really don't want to lay around another day, and I do feel a hell of a lot better. I wouldn't be offering if I didn't think I could handle it."

Who was she to tell him not to do something anyway? He was a grown man. He knew his limits.

"The phones are still out. What if something happens to you?" God forbid, she didn't want a repeat performance of him lying in bed totally at her mercy…touching him intimately while he slept.

To her shock, she felt her face warm up.

"I promise I won't overdo it."

Tom rolled over onto his belly and awaited her answer. Excitement flashed in his eyes as he gazed up at her with anticipation, his smoldering gaze once again locked with hers and she felt momentarily breathless. "I've had enough rest and relaxation the last few days to do me a lifetime. Besides, I'm stuck here, right?"

Stuck? Did that mean he didn't want to be here?

"Okay…sure. But don't overdo it. Okay?"

"You're the boss."

God! Was she insane? Hiring him to do stuff around her place when he was recuperating from a bullet wound? Keeping him here at Peppermint Creek Inn, in her bedroom with her sleeping on the couch right next door?

Oh, boy! Now that he was up and about, he was going to be even harder to avoid. Besides, how was she going to get at her vibrator with him around?

He nodded toward what had once been the main attraction of her establishment, the burned-out remains of her inn.

"I'm assuming that's what's left of Peppermint Creek Inn."

"I've got the contractors already lined up. I've given them the plans to the old inn so they shouldn't have too much trouble duplicating it."

"What happened to it?"

"Arson. This past winter."

"Arson? Why? Who? What was the motive?"

"They don't know. The police found empty jerry cans behind the barn."

Sara hauled her legs up against her belly and wrapped her arms around her knees. Sadness wrenched her gut as she looked at the black charred remains of the log inn they'd built from the trees on their property. It was a horrible shame someone had torched it.

"Someone's breaking your windows, throwing around dead carcasses, burning your buildings. You have any ideas who? Or why?"

A bite of tears touched her eyes as she remembered watching the orange flames roaring through the two-story building that awful night. "Let's not talk about it, okay? I just want to enjoy this beautiful day. It's been one wild and cold winter, and it just feels so good to have warm air on my face again."

Tom didn't reply. Instead, he plucked up a long, yellow blade of grass and plunged it between his teeth gnawing on it thoughtfully.

Closing her eyes, she relished the cheerful sounds of the chickadees singing in the nearby pine trees, the wind playing with her hat and his steady, deep breathing.

The picnic had gone quite well, Sara mused. She'd actually enjoyed herself and had forgotten how good it felt to simply relax, but Tom's next words ruined everything.

"This quilt is something special to you, isn't it? By the way you keep looking at it and touching it, it gives me the feeling that I shouldn't have brought it along."

Oh, shit!

She kept her eyes closed, trying hard not to frown, pretending as if the question didn't pierce her heart.

"I'm sorry, it's none of my business," he said quickly.

She bit her lower lip and tried to squash the tears that suddenly bubbled up in her eyes and trickled down her cheeks.

God, how embarrassing. How could she just lose it like this?

In a split second, he was beside her, cradling her in his strong muscular arms as if she was a sobbing, blubbering idiot.

She noted his gentle hand softly rubbing her back. Felt his other hand caress the full length of her hair.

"It's okay. Everything's okay," he soothed. "I'm sorry. So sorry."

Listening to the softness of his voice and the soothing touch of his hands, she found herself melting against his hard chest. His wonderful body heat seeped through her clothing and caressed her skin, and then she felt a finger touch the underneath part of her chin and her face being tilted upwards.

His velvety breath fell delicately against the tip of her lips unleashing spirals of desire deep into her vagina.

Her eyes popped open.

His face drew closer.

Oh, my God! He was going to kiss her.

His lips danced over her wet cheeks, feathery sensual brushes against her mouth that made her heated body jump for joy. Like a hummingbird drawing nectar from a tasty flower, her lips melted and parted into his firm, moist mouth. Eagerly she accepted the gentle probing of his tongue and a few seconds later the kiss deepened, turning from a gentle invasion into an intense exploration. From somewhere deep within her throat, a low moan stirred.

He responded with a sensual growl and his arms drifted to her waist. He hauled her closer, crushing her quickly swelling breasts against his muscular chest.

Her arms automatically flew around his warm neck, and she pulled his head deeper into the searing kiss. His hat fell off and the elastic he'd used to pull his hair back into a ponytail abruptly broke free as her fingers plunged through his silky hair.

She felt as if her entire body was melding with his. Becoming one. She'd never been kissed this intensely before. Never. She could lose herself in this man's arms forever and never return to reality.

Oh, God! She needed to lose herself in these sensations! Lose herself inside him.

"Please," she whispered against his mouth, not knowing what to say or how to say she wanted him to make love to her.

He sensed what she needed and his lips became more demanding, intoxicating. Fire raged through her and it stormed through him, too. She could feel how he tried to restrain it. Could feel his body tight with pent-up passion.

She found herself being pressed backward and whimpered as he lay her down onto the quilt.

Strong masculine fingers curled around the hem of her shirt lifting it up, baring her belly, raising it higher until her modest breasts were exposed to him.

She looked up at him. Saw the lust flushing his face.

A low erotic growl rumbled deep inside his chest as he looked at her nakedness.

"Your breasts are so gorgeous. Your nipples so velvety," he whispered as a finger lightly circled the areola of her left breast before twisting her nipple sharply, unleashing a coil of raw need deep inside her womb.

She shivered as both his palms smoothed over her mounds, cupping her breasts. His flesh felt hot, his fingers unbelievably gentle as he massaged her buds and twisted them until they were rock-hard.

The craving for him to make love to her roared higher as his head lowered and his luscious mouth sucked a nipple between his warm lips.

She shivered beneath the onslaught of lusty sensations.

Sweet mercy! This felt too heavenly to be true.

Reaching up, she smoothed her hands over his shoulders, her fingers exploring the hardness of his male muscles. Wonderful pleasure sifted through her and she found herself moaning, whimpering, needing to be loved.

She gasped as his mouth found her other nipple and he bit gently to this side of the sweetest pain she'd ever felt in her life.

"I want to lick your breasts," he growled as he broke the erotic bite and laved his tongue around the sensitized pain.

"I want to bite your nipples. Make love to them."

Again he bit into her flesh, harder this time but it was sweet just the same.

She wanted to tell him to do it, to make love to her breasts, to make love to her, but the words were somehow trapped inside her throat, paralyzed by the wild lust she saw in his eyes as he gazed down at her.

He un-cupped her breasts and his lips moved lower scorching a trail of fire as he kissed her pale belly until she quivered beneath him.

Long masculine fingers tugged open the clasp of her shorts and the sound of her zipper lowering on her shorts made her heart crash against her ribs. He tugged at her pants and she lifted her hips allowing him to move her pants and underwear lower. He slid them off expertly and his hot hands spread her thighs.

Her pussy convulsed wildly as he whistled lowly.

"You shave."

She nodded. She'd always shaved her pussy. Always kept it nude and baby-soft for Jack, in the hope he would take her whenever he wanted to, which hadn't been often enough for her.

After he was gone, she'd just kept doing it out of sheer habit.

"Do you do it for anyone in particular?" His words were tight, and she detected a tinge of jealousy in his eyes.

"No," she found herself whispering. "No one."

"For me then," he groaned.

She nodded.

"How long since you've been with a man?"

"More than two years."

He swore softly.

My God! She couldn't believe she was having this conversation. Couldn't believe she was allowing a perfect stranger to touch her like this. To look at her like this.

But it felt so right.

And it felt so beautiful.

He was climbing between her widespread thighs now and her mind screamed at him to stop.

But her body had a different agenda. Her body needed him. Needed him bad.

She could literally feel the hot cream of her anticipation slide down her channel toward him, moistening her, preparing her for him.

The instant his hot breath caressed the inside of her thighs, she couldn't stop herself from lifting her knees and spreading her thighs wider, tilting her abdomen higher, giving him a perfect view of her quickly moistening pussy.

She loved the way he looked at her, his eyes powerfully bright with feverish lust. His mouth moist as the tip of his pink tongue swiped over his lower lip.

"What do you want me to do, Sara?"

"Taste me," she found herself whispering, her belly clenching with excitement.

His eyes widened slightly and then his warm hands were intimately cupping her ass cheeks, tilting her hips even higher for him.

His head dipped between her legs.

She cried out as his delicious tongue swiped against her pulsing clitoris, hot and demanding. Mind-numbing strokes, sweet sucks and searing kisses had her bucking against his face in an instant.

Gosh! She felt so hot. So responsive.

So sexually wild!

Sweet mercy, the way his tongue lashed her clit felt fantastic! She groaned at the sensual quivers racing through her.

His hot mouth seared over her swollen pleasure nub and he sucked so hard she saw silver stars and felt her pussy cream soaking her inner thighs. He let go and his teeth nipped gently at her labia until she burned and moaned from carnal pleasure.

A finger slipped inside her tight, wet pussy and she jolted against his mouth. Erotic pleasures racked her mind, her body. A second finger slid into her. Then a third.

The pressure of his large, long fingers stretched her, had her lungs scrambling for breath.

She hissed as he began a tender rub against her swollen clit and his fingers began a slow thrust. In and out of her drenched vagina he plunged.

Slurpy sounds split the air and joined the intertwined sounds of their harsh breaths.

Her body tightened. Her tummy clenched. Her pussy throbbed.

The fiery heat of arousal slammed into her hard and fast, making her clench her teeth together at the powerful impact.

Oh, yes!

Beautiful!

Perfect!

Sexual tension exploded, making her jerk and writhe as the brutal waves crashed over her. She cried out at the heated satisfaction enveloping her. The pulsing orgasm carried her away. The intense pleasure quickly made her forget her past. But it made her remember how good it felt to be with a man.

It made her want more from him.

The pressure against her clit deepened, intensified. His fingers plunged harder. Faster.

Sweet mercy!

More erotic explosions ignited inside her. She gasped as another orgasm zipped through her, enveloped her, pummeled her.

She cried out his name. Grabbed his feathery hair, pushed his face into her hot and wet pussy.

Hips bucking, she pressed hard into him. Grinding her hips until the excruciating pleasure shimmered around her.

Tortured her. Relieved her.

When her orgasm subsided, she lay there on the quilt panting, sexually exhausted, the sticky cream of her arousal brushing against her inner thighs reminding her of what had just happened. Reminding her she'd just let a sexy stranger mouth-fuck her.

She heard him sigh deeply against her shivering pussy and she dropped her hands from his head. He moved away.

Opening her eyes, she found his face glistening with her arousal.

He smiled, but it didn't quite reach his eyes. Doubts peppered his face and she felt a hollow jolt deep inside her womb. Why was he regretting what he'd just done?

He stared at her long and hard before saying, "I'm sorry. I guess I shouldn't have done that." His eyes however lied. They were dark. Passionate. "I don't know what got into me."

She wanted to tell him it was okay. Wanted to tell him she'd asked him to eat her. But the words remained captive inside her chest while her heart pounded wildly in her ears as she reeled from her intense orgasms.

"I need to take a walk," he said as he grabbed his shoes and abruptly stood up. "I'll see you back at the house."

She watched his retreating figure. Watched the long masculine legs carry him away from her.

Warm wind whispered against her naked, wet pussy and her bared breasts. Her body ached for him to come back to her. Craved for him to make love to her.

When he disappeared into the trees, she found herself looking at the family quilt beneath her. Slowly she turned onto her side and ran a finger over the smooth silky white material of her wedding gown.

Memories.

Sweet old memories.

How could she keep them in the past, where they belonged? How could she forget her past and move on?

That was the million-dollar question. And if she had the answer, she'd be a very rich woman.

* * * * *

Tom cursed himself for the fifteenth time as he followed the narrow, winding path through the dense forest.

When Sara had broken down into tears, his only thought was to comfort her. But it had led to something else.

Something wild. Uncontrollable. Intense.

He hadn't been able to keep his hands off her. Had wanted to kiss her so badly. To touch her breasts, taste her pussy.

Automatically he licked his lips tasting the sweetness of her arousal still lingering on his lips. He'd never tasted anything so erotic in his life.

His cock hardened painfully against his jeans as he remembered how swollen and pink her clit had looked after he'd finished seducing her pussy.

The powerful need to plunge his cock deep into her vagina was scary. He'd never felt this way before about a woman.

At least not that he remembered.

Which led to the question—was he already married? Did he have a wife waiting for him somewhere? A girlfriend? He hadn't been wearing a ring. Could he maybe be single?

Oh, come on! Who was he kidding? Single or married there was no way he should pursue Sara in a romantic relationship. He was on the run. A fugitive with no freaking future to speak of.

He needed to put her and any romantic and sexual intentions out of his head. Needed to concentrate on figuring out why the cops were after him.

The path suddenly burst from the cool darkness of the woods into a large sunny clearing making him stop to admire the view. The entire meadow was covered in a lush dusting of tiny pale blue flowers.

Forget-me-not flowers. A symbol of true love.

His gaze lifted toward the far side of the clearing where he spotted a giant knoll surrounded by a white wooden picket fence. His stomach clenched tightly at the sight and he headed toward the knoll.

Hesitantly, he climbed up the rickety rock steps and opened the creaky gate.

His breath caught at what he saw.

A tiny cemetery, the dates on some of the gravestones going back to the late 1800's. In one corner, set aside from the rest of the markers, he noticed one large ragged pink rock.

Relatively new.

He tasted the bitterness of bile at the back of his throat as he read the names on that rock.

Understanding rammed through him and his stomach clenched. He hadn't even suspected.

He stared at the names etched forever into the giant, pale pink rock.

Davine Agnes Clarke. Beloved Mother of Jack. Beloved Grandmother.

Jack Richard Clarke. Beloved Husband and Father.

Tears sprang to his eyes as he continued.

Teresa May Clarke. Beloved Daughter and Granddaughter.

Tom Jack Clarke. Beloved Son and Grandson.

All had died on the same day.

Chapter Six

ഔ

When Sara returned to the inn, her pussy was aching to be filled by Tom's thick cock and the phone was ringing.

Raw excitement teetered with horrible dread as she lifted the receiver hoping this was the call she'd been waiting for.

"Peppermint Creek Inn. May I help you?"

"Sara? Sara? Is that you?"

The gravely masculine voice on the other end of the line struck such a spear of fear through her, she literally jumped and almost hung up.

"Hello, is anyone there?" the voice echoed.

She could barely hear the man's voice as her heart pounded wildly in her ears. Her hand tightened automatically around the receiver. She should hang up. Find Tom. Tell him to get out of here.

"It's me. It's Justin Jeffries."

Justin, the local cop.

She took a quick calming breath. She had to relax. Act as if nothing unusual was going on.

"Oh, hi, Justin," she said brightly, totally amazed to find her voice so steady even though she felt as if her whole world was crashing down around her ears.

"Where have you been?" his words rushed out in breathless excitement. "I've been trying to get through for the past few days. What's going on? Everything all right?"

"Everything's fine. Couldn't be better."

On the porch, she heard Tom's familiar footsteps. Unconsciously she licked her lips, his fiery hot kiss still fresh on her swollen mouth, her pussy clenched as she remembered the way he'd sucked on her clit.

"You make out okay with the storm the other night?"

"No problems," she lied.

Her heart picked up speed as she heard the rusty hinges of the kitchen's screen door creak open. Tom had returned from his walk.

"Glad to hear it," he replied cheerfully.

"How'd you know I was back, Justin?" She hadn't told anyone she was back home.

"I-I kind of figured you would be. After all the work you have to do. I can come over later this afternoon. Give you a hand?"

"No! Don't come over!" she practically screamed into the phone. She quickly rebounded. "I mean everything is under control. I don't need any help right now. Besides the road is flooded."

"I could take the hydro road in. I've got a four-wheeler. It wouldn't be much of a problem. I can bring you some supplies. A steak. Wine?"

Oh, God, he was hinting again.

"I've got plenty of food to keep me going. Please don't bother. I really don't need any help."

"You sure?"

"Yes, I'm sure," she stated firmly. Maybe a bit too firmly. Except for his steady breathing, there was a silence on the line. She wondered if he'd picked up on her nervousness.

"There's another reason I'm calling," he finally said. "Have you seen any strangers around lately?"

Sara's blood ran cold. She tensed and cast a quick glance over her shoulder.

Tom was leaning against the doorjamb, his muscular arms folded across his wide chest. He tried to appear casual, but Sara could read the uncertainty in his eyes and the tenseness coiling throughout his body. If he only knew who she was talking to, he'd flip.

"A stranger?" she said softly.

Tom's head snapped to attention and she waved a hand to him, signaling him to come and listen.

"My partner went missing over in the ghost town of Jackfish."

"Missing? Sam?"

She knew Sam. He was too pushy. A real lady's man. He hadn't wasted any time making the moves on her. Over the past two years, both Justin and Sam had become terrible nuisances, both stopping individually or together often and unexpectedly with any excuse to chat or have dinner.

Sara jumped when Tom brushed up against her and she held the phone out a little so they could both listen.

Justin continued. "Some hermit ambushed us while we were checking out the cottages near the ghost town."

Tom inhaled sharply and she hoped Justin hadn't heard it.

"The guy came out of nowhere. Caught me off guard, stole my gun and took off. Sam and I went after him. But we became separated in the woods. Haven't seen him or the other guy since."

"Are you all right?" Her voice sounded strangled, her confidence shattered.

"Aside from a bruised ego for letting him get away, I'll survive."

Her grip tightened anxiously on the receiver. "What does this stranger look like?"

Tom leaned closer obviously just as eager to know.

"It's a general description. Long brown hair. Brown beard and mustache. Real scruffy-looking character. Medium build. About six-one. Wearing a black leather jacket, blue jeans."

Black leather jacket. Scruffy. Blue jeans.

The words slammed into her stomach like torpedoes. And by the way Tom stiffened beside her, she knew he was experiencing the same reaction.

"If you see him around, he's armed and extremely dangerous. I don't want you to approach him. Just call me. Talk only to me. I'm in charge of this investigation. Are you sure everything is all right?"

"Fine."

Tom? Extremely dangerous? Was that why he'd shoved a gun in her face? Came into the loft with a knife?

She felt his reassuring hand slip around her waist and instantly relaxed.

No! Tom had been frightened on both occasions. He couldn't hurt anyone.

"Um… Do you know who he is?"

There was that slight hesitation again. "Who he is?"

"His name? Where he's from?"

Tom captured her gaze and held her. She read the fear in his eyes, felt the tension in his body.

"No. No name. We don't know who he is. Maybe I should come over. Check the place out. After all the trouble you've been having, it's not a bad idea."

"Really, Justin. Please don't. I'm fine. Besides there's no one around for miles, and why would a criminal come here of all places? He couldn't get through because of the road being flooded. If anything happens or I see someone, I can contact you."

"It's your call, Sara. Just be careful. Oh! And, Sara, I appreciate you keeping this information under your hat. Not too many people know about Sam being missing. It'll just cause unnecessary panic."

She frowned. "I'll do that. Thanks for calling. Bye for now."

She hung up.

"Get your things!" Tom hissed angrily as he pushed past Sara.

"What are you doing?" she followed him into the bedroom where he grabbed his leather jacket off the back of the twig chair where she'd placed it to dry days ago.

"I'm leaving and so are you. But we have to go separately," he said sternly and whirled around to face her. She inhaled a breath to steady her pounding heart at the look of fear shining brightly in his eyes. He was panicking.

"I'm not going anywhere."

It was as if she hadn't said anything. His narrowed gaze scanned the bedroom. "The gun. The handcuffs. Where are they?"

"They're safe."

"I need them. The law can't even suspect you've been harboring me. They'll kill you just as soon as look at you."

"They don't suspect a thing, Tom." Sara kept her voice as calm as possible. Hopefully her calmness would brush off on him.

He followed her back out into the kitchen where she reached into the cupboard to get the supplies she needed to prepare supper.

"Listen to me, dammit!" He was shouting now and she didn't appreciate being bullied around, but she understood his fear for her safety. She felt the same way about his. "I've overstayed my welcome. It's time for me to clear out. You need to find a safe place for yourself until this blows over. Go to your private eye sister's place and stay with her."

"What's the matter with you? I said I'm not going anywhere. This is my home. And no one knows you're here, why run?"

"My God, woman! Are you deaf? Didn't you hear that cop? He said I had something to do with his partner going missing. Aren't you afraid I might make you disappear, too?"

She turned around to see a muscle twitching crazily in his jaw and his eyes narrowed further.

Sara felt a sudden chill shoot up her back. He thought he would hurt her again. Grab her like he'd grabbed her yesterday in the loft. The thought struck her like pepper spray. Instinctively though, she knew there was no way he would hurt her, especially not after the way he'd tenderly seduced her pussy this afternoon after their picnic.

"Just relax, Tom. I trust you."

He threw her a look of disbelief. "How can you be so sure you can trust me? I practically assaulted you at our picnic. I couldn't keep my hands off of you."

"You only did what I asked you to do. Please don't read anything else into it."

A look of hurt flashed across his face and then it disappeared leaving Sara wondering if she'd even seen it.

"Besides, there's something wrong with Justin's story."

"What do you mean?"

"Justin said you stole his gun."

"Yes, I heard. It means I could have used it on his partner."

"That gun is not police issue."

"How do you know?"

"My husband was a cop. Justin and Sam are cops. Cops don't have those types of guns. Besides, it's old and too hacked up. Looks old."

"Then it's mine."

"Could be."

"And it was empty and that's why I took Jeffries' gun."

"Maybe," Sara said thoughtfully.

Tom frowned. "You know something."

"Why would you throw Justin's gun away?"

"I must have dropped it while I was running."

"Might have."

He shoved a furious hand through his hair. "Why can't you just admit I am a criminal? I took the cop's gun. Killed his partner. Then dropped it."

"Why drop a loaded weapon and keep the empty one?"

"Because I had it in my hand. I dropped it. There's nothing sinister going on here. I am a criminal."

"If you're a criminal then why do the police want to kill you?"

Tom inhaled deeply. "Okay, I see where you're going. Something else is going on here."

"I'm glad you're beginning to see it my way," she smiled at him, but his frown remained intact. "Besides this is the last place the police would think a criminal would be hiding."

"Why do I suddenly get the feeling I don't want to hear why this would be the last place a criminal would hide?"

"Because you don't want to hear that Peppermint Creek Inn is a private resort. It's geared toward—law-enforcement officers and their families."

She'd expected an explosion from him, but it didn't come. He merely blinked as if trying to analyze this new piece of information. Then he slowly nodded his head and gave a strangled laugh. He put on his jacket.

"Okay. If you don't want to leave, I'll leave before the cop shows up," he tossed over his shoulder as he headed for the door.

"Hold on!" She caught up to him and grabbed his arm in an attempt to stop him. Heated electricity jumped between the two of them and Sara quickly let go.

He must have felt it too because he looked at the area where she'd grabbed his arm then his gaze traveled up to her face. Every nerve in her body tensed and sparkled as he stared at her. His Adam's apple bobbed as he swallowed. He remained quiet for a moment then said slowly, "I didn't want to tell you, but I guess it's time. Yesterday, I saw someone lurking around right outside your bedroom window. I've been trying to make myself believe it was just a dream but it wasn't."

"What are you saying?"

"By the expression on your face I'd say you know what I'm talking about. Who is he?"

Her heart began a wild hammering against her chest. Her suspicions about Tom seeing someone had been right.

Was the shadow back?

"Don't be ridiculous. There's no one around for miles. You're right it was probably just a dream."

Wasn't that what she'd been seeing for the past couple of years? Shadows lurking around every corner.

"I smelled the smoke, too."

"Smoke?" she said dumbly. A wave of lightheadedness swept over her. Her knees threatened to buckle.

"Cigarette smoke. You don't smoke, do you?" Tom didn't wait for an answer. He withdrew something from his back pocket and held it in his outstretched hand.

"Found this, just a few minutes ago. Out in the parking lot. It's brand new."

Her mouth dropped open as she stared at the cigarette stub.

Tom frowned and looked at her in a strange way.

"What's the matter?"

She tried to shake the fear building in her head. Stupid to be afraid of a shadow. Stupid to be afraid of a cigarette butt. But why was she so scared? Terrified in fact.

"How is that possible?" she whispered.

"How's what possible?"

Tom had seen the shadow. Someone besides herself had actually physically seen the shadow.

This time the shadow had appeared in broad daylight. And Tom had smelled the cigarette smoke. Had found a butt. A fresh one.

"I can't help you, if you don't tell me what's going on, Sara." His voice was low. Soft. Gentle.

She bit her lower lip and remained silent. She wanted to tell him. Oh, God, how she ached to tell him everything, but she didn't know where to begin.

"Just a few minutes ago you said you trusted me."

Son of a bitch. He was right. She had said that.

She sighed her frustration and found herself whispering, "Sometimes when something really tragic happens in your life, it's so painful your heart just shuts down. You can't share the pain with anyone."

"Is that why you've stopped living?" His words weren't harsh. They were spoken softly. But they hurt nonetheless.

"Sara, when we close our hearts off to pain, they stay closed. We can't experience the other things life offers us. The joys, sadness, love." He nodded toward the quickly darkening sky. "The beauty in a sunset."

She followed his gaze to look out the bedroom window and saw the wisps of pink and pale lilac edging the giant blooming gray clouds.

In the past, she would have found the sunset a spectacular sight, something to look forward to every evening during the off-season. Now she couldn't feel anything. Only a deep clawing numbness.

He sighed his frustration, audibly giving into Sara's desire to stay then said, "I'm going to start clearing some of this brush off the veranda. Let me know if you want to talk."

She nodded and watched him walk out of the bedroom. Moments later she heard the kitchen screen door creak open and close gently.

Sara inhaled a deep breath and frowned.

Tom was right. She had stopped living. Given up on old friends, discouraged new relationships and completely lost her passion for painting. All she had left was the burnt down inn.

And her memories.

She had in effect become one of the walking dead.

* * * * *

Tom yanked brutally at the branches, wincing as pain sliced through his injured hands. But he didn't let the pain stop him. He continued to haul the branches off into the front yard. If he piled them the proper way and allowed air to pass through in an effort to dry the wood, they'd be seasoned enough for the summer guests.

The tree would bring great pleasure to the campers as they sat around the campfires at night, toasting marshmallows and hot dogs, singing songs and sharing ghost stories.

Hopefully the physical work would keep his horrifying thoughts at bay. Thoughts about what the cop had said over the phone to Sara. Thoughts about how the cop's partner had gone missing.

Did he have something to do with the police officer's disappearance?

The slightest ache began to throb in his right temple and his back was aching like a son of a bitch. Remembering his promise to Sara that he'd take it easy, he slowed his pace as he continued to snap the branches.

If he regained his memory, would he turn into a man with different priorities? A man with no scruples? A man who would kill another human being without any sign of remorse?

Is that why the cops had handcuffed him? Beaten him? Because he'd acted so wild and it had been the only way to bring him down?

He tried to remember, but nothing came to mind, only the thick, black emptiness. He shook his head in frustration. Why waste valuable energy on trying to remember? He needed to focus on the job at hand. To regain his strength. And to stay as far away from Sara as he could.

* * * * *

Hours later Sara stood in her kitchen, anxiously peering through the screen door into the brightly lit front yard. There was an eerie silence tonight. The frogs didn't chirp. No owls hooted. No faraway cries from the loons. Not even a breeze to keep her company.

Tom had kept himself busy breaking up the branches for kindling and then he'd chain sawed the tree into small sections, piling the logs so he could split them at another time. When it had gotten dark, she'd called him in for dinner, but he'd declined supper saying he wanted to get some more work done. So, she'd flicked the outside spotlights on to allow him to continue.

That had been over three hours ago.

And now, it was almost nine and Tom was nowhere in sight. The chain saw had been turned off over fifteen minutes ago and she'd waited for him to return. But he hadn't come back inside.

He was out there somewhere in the inky blackness. And she stood inside torturing herself with one horrid thought after another. Maybe he'd left without saying goodbye? Or maybe the shadow had taken him? Or maybe he'd fallen ill?

It was still too early for him to be doing all this heavy work. She should have stopped him. He should have better sense. Damn his stubborn hide. The old saying was definitely true, the bigger they came the more stubborn.

Slowly, she inched the screen door open and cringed as the hinges screamed like a wild animal into the cool night air. She'd forgotten to oil them again. Tomorrow, she'd do it.

A tiny flicker of lightning scraped across the western horizon and a freezing chill sliced up her spine.

A familiar feeling of panic shot through her system.

"Oh, God! Oh, God!" she whispered.

Not another storm. Not tonight.

Turning she readied herself to bolt back inside when Tom's gentle voice curled out of the darkness from the corner of her veranda.

"Talking might make you feel better, Sara."

"Tom! Damn you!" She spat angrily as she spotted him sitting quite snugly on the porch swing. He'd been here all this time, while she'd been mere feet away worried half-sick about him.

"You must be tired. You should be in bed."

"So should you," came his steamy reply. She didn't miss the sweet insinuation in his voice and it only made her more furious.

"I'm not the one who's been through a terrible ordeal," she hissed back at him. Wrenching the screen door open, she readied herself to retreat from the oncoming storm.

"Looks like you have. Why else would you be so scared of a harmless storm?"

"That is none of your business," she snapped angrily.

Stomping back inside she let the door slam shut behind her with such furious force the dishes clattered in the nearby hutch. Irritation burned bright inside her, and she slammed a pot down on the stove.

"Typical man!" Sara muttered under her breath, poured spring water into the pot and turned the gas on. "Always sticking his nose in where it doesn't belong."

A moment later, he came into the kitchen and sat down at the kitchen table. From the corner of her eyes she noticed him remove the work gloves he must have found in the barn. At least he'd had the sense of protecting himself. She watched silently as he rubbed his hands.

All her anger dissipated and concern for his well-being took over. The man looked totally beat. His feathery hair was tangled, dirt smeared his face, yet he still had the time to be concerned about her reaction to the storm.

"You want some ointment for your hands?" she asked after a minute.

"No, it's okay. I can get some later."

"You want some peppermint tea?"

"Sure."

They'd had their first couple of fights today and at the end of it all they could still sit down like two civil human beings and enjoy a hot cup of peppermint tea together before heading off to bed.

"I couldn't save your heart. I'm sorry. The tree shattered it beyond repair when it split."

He was talking about the heart Jack had carved into the tree. The pain of its loss cut deep, searing her insides and she had to bite her lower lip to keep from crying once again like a blubbering idiot.

Her heart was shattered beyond repair. Just like her heart. She merely nodded and kept her eye on the pot of water on the stove.

"I managed to save most of the others though. They're in the barn."

"It'll make their owners happy, I'm sure," she tried to keep her voice light and airy. It was a desperate tactic to hide the fact a silly wooden carving would have such a devastating effect on her.

He remained silent for another minute and then her world exploded.

"It's a nice view."

She jumped at his unexpected words. Instinctively she knew what he was talking about.

He'd found the cemetery. Found them.

The pot on the stove blurred. Angry, bitter tears spilled down her face and she quickly swiped them away with the back of her hand, only to have them replaced by another flood. She hated it when someone saw her crying. She'd done so much of it over the past couple of years. And she figured she should be over this mourning bit, but there was always something around that triggered another crying jag.

"I'm sorry," he whispered gently. His affectionate arms slid around her waist and his lean body pressed hot against her back. His warm breath sensuously caressed her neck.

"You can't run away from your pain forever. One day you'll have to stand and fight."

She found herself melting against him. Felt herself feeling safe and secure for the first time in a long time.

"All right. I'll tell you." Just saying those words already brought her immense relief.

A few minutes later, it was Tom who placed a mug of steaming peppermint tea in front of her. She fidgeted nervously with the cup's handle as he sat down opposite her at the kitchen table, a giant mug cradled in his large hands.

"I don't know where to begin," she said simply as she stared into the cup's steaming depths.

"Best place to start is at the beginning, sweetness."

Closing her eyes, she sighed deeply. When she opened them, his gaze was so green and tender and soothing she felt the dam burst inside her and the words just started tumbling out.

"It happened a little over two years ago. Indian summer. The night air blowing into the nursery was mild and pleasant. I was putting the finishing touches to the nursery. I'd decorated the walls with these really cute cartoon characters. I was talking to the kids. Y'know, things soon-to-be-moms do.

"The only thing left was to hang the handmade mobile. I'd made it myself out of scraps of fabric from the same material I'd used for the curtains. They were happy faces. All kinds of colors. Bright and cheerful. I'd walked over to one of the nursery windows to hang it when I looked outside..."

Sara gazed downward to the giant log structure of Peppermint Creek Inn barely visible in the glow of the bright white moon. All the shutters were clamped tightly over the windows to ward off the severe winter weather. The plumbing had been drained, and all the other things that needed doing for the winter close-up were finished.

She shifted her gaze to the cheerful buttery light spilling from the many windows of the tiny one room cabin office snuggled amidst the towering jack pine trees. The office looked like a sweet little gingerbread house, totally devoured by the immenseness of the nearby inn.

Inside the tiny building, she knew her husband worked furiously, getting the paperwork out of the way so he could get back to his favorite hobby of carpentry. He'd started a project during the summer. Carving out a new sign to hang up at the main road entrance. Many of the guests had complained the old sign was weather-worn and hard to see.

A low rumbling sound captured her attention and she lifted her gaze to the sky. "Uh-oh," she murmured to the twins. "Looks like Indian summer's over."

On the western horizon, just above the tree line, icy gray swollen clouds raced toward the moon with lightning speed. An earsplitting crack of thunder made her jump involuntarily and she laughed at her reaction. And giggled at the wonderful growl of thunder.

The thunder was an excuse. It was all she needed to tear Jack away from the paperwork. And this storm was it. Storms always made Jack horny. They brought out the best in their lovemaking. Starting out slow and torturous, then quickly reaching its peak with wildly ecstatic jolts and then they would lay in each other's arms, his sexual desires quenched for another little while and hers never quite fulfilled.

Now, suddenly in a hurry with delightful anticipation, Sara lifted the mobile over her head, ready to place it on the hook, when she heard it.

A strange sound. Something. A strangled cry?

Some horrible premonition of doom, an intense feeling of dread made her drop the handmade item. Made her heart begin to race wildly. Made the cold sweat smother her forehead and sent the intense feeling of fear rippling through her entire being.

She jumped as lightning flashed and thunder crackled a warning. Frosty air breathed against her through the open window, urging her to run through the nursery slamming all the windows shut. Running down the stairs, the overwhelming uneasiness stuck to her like glue. In the kitchen, she shook wildly as she stomped into her shiny black rubber boots and slipped on her yellow rain coat.

She'd never felt this uneasy before. Why was she so frightened? Why couldn't she stop shaking? Why did she have the feeling as if something horrible was happening?

Flicking on the porch light, she opened the front door and cried out as a cruel gasp of wind wrenched the door from her grasp, slamming it against the house wall with such force, Sara swore it sounded like a gunshot.

Swallowing the uneasy taste of fear clutching her throat she watched in surprise as a tuning fork of lightning stroked the stormy clouds not more than a quarter of a mile away. Thunder cracked another menacing warning. A prickle of shivers slithered down her neck as a wall of rain and wind hurtled through the pine trees toward her.

The tall meadow grass in the front yard fell under the groaning wind. Crinkled autumn leaves rolled around in tornadoes as if being chased by the devil himself. Shards of rain blew across the veranda in frightening sheets, slamming into her face. Sara blinked the cold rain from her eyes, braced herself and headed into the violent storm half expecting to see Jack racing across the parking lot toward her.

He didn't appear.

Instantly her boots plunged into mud as she took a shortcut across the yard, but with determined strides, she continued toward the glow cast by the office windows. The strong wind fought her every step of the way. In the end, she won the battle as she pushed the office door inward. The wicked wind blew her, along with a bushel full of colorful autumn leaves, into the room.

Breathless, she closed the door. She fully expected to see Jack sitting behind his giant desk, but when she turned around after closing the door, her husband wasn't there. Sara frowned as the eerie feeling of finding Jack intensified.

The room looked normal. The old weathered oak desk overflowed with papers and part of the wall behind the desk was taken up by a heavily loaded bookshelf. Aside from a few papers strewn across the floor, probably from when she'd entered, nothing else seemed out of the ordinary.

Except –

A distinct smell of cigarette smoke lingered in the air. Unexpected visitors? She hadn't seen a car outside.

A slow shiver began at the base of her neck giving her the feeling she was being watched. She glanced around the room. A flash of light glinted outside the window immediately drawing her attention.

"Jack!" she shouted at the fleeting shadow.

"Sara." A low, trembling whisper froze her dead in her tracks. It sounded so far away.

She stood still and listened. A tingling sensation prickled across her scalp as the howling wind frantically rattled the window frames. Leaves spit against the glass panes. Lightning flashed in the windows. Thunder roared. But she didn't hear another whisper.

Maybe she'd imagined the voice and the movement outside the window. Sara strolled toward the door. Jack was probably back at the house looking for her.

Her hand rested on the doorknob.

"God… Sara." The voice was a low harsh whisper filling her with horrific dread. This voice had not been her imagination.

Sara whirled around.

Her suddenly alert eyes raked across the room and she froze when she spied the bright red splotch staining a white sheet of paper on the floor.

Blood?

Had Jack cut himself and returned to the house? Had she passed him and they hadn't seen each other? Sure that's what had happened. Nothing unusual going on here. Just her overactive imagination, right?

Then, who was calling her?

The nagging feeling of unease crowded in around her. Her chest tightened painfully. Something was wrong. She could feel it.

Easing closer to the desk, Sara became even more uneasy as she spotted the trail of red drops until…

A scream found its way from her throat and her knuckles flew to her mouth as she spied someone slumped facedown on the floor behind the desk. A widening pool of blood spread dark crimson on the back of the man's white muscle T-shirt.

Please, God. No!

Jack didn't wear that shirt today, did he? He didn't, she said sternly. It's not Jack. Oh, God. Please. It's not Jack.

Closing her eyes, she blocked out the sight, reluctant to confront the possibility that this was actually happening. It is just a dream, a horrible nightmare. In a minute she'll wake up.

But his low moan of pain made Sara's eyes snap open propelling her to rush to the man's aid. Even before she cleared the side of the giant desk, *she knew it was Jack. She crouched down beside him, touching his cold flesh feeling for his pulse. The pulse was very weak, but it was there.*

"Jack? Jack, can you hear me?" He answered with a low moan. Immediately Sara grabbed for the phone on the desk.

The phone.

Her lifeline. Help. An ambulance.

A dial tone hummed loudly in her ears. Immediately she dialed 911.

It rang once. Twice.

White lightning flashed wickedly at the windows and she cringed as a horrible loud bolt of thunder ripped through the room.

They were plunged into instant darkness.

The phone rang a third time.

Suddenly the dial tone died.

"Hello! Hello?" she screamed into the receiver wishing she could climb into the telephone, and whiz along the lines to a place where she could find help.

Crying, she slammed the handset into the cradle.

Through the flickering lightning, she again thought she spotted movement at the window. Branches from a nearby tree? Or a person?

A weak groan erupted from Jack, demanding her immediate attention. She crashed to her knees and wiped the sweat from his cold forehead.

"I'm here. I'm here. My God! What happened?" Hysteria tinged her voice. She hoped she didn't frighten him.

"Sara — watch..." came Jack's gurgled moan.

He was trying to tell her something, but she couldn't make it out.

"Hush, Jack. Hush. The phones are down. I've got to get you over to the door. Then I'll get the truck and bring it up. We'll drive to the hospital and everything will be fine. You'll see, you'll see."

Hot tears slid down her face as she slid her hands under his armpits. She pulled at him. God, he was so heavy. But by sheer adrenaline, she managed to move him slowly from behind the desk.

She dragged her husband's limp form across the carpet, toward the door. From the corner of her eye, she tried not to look at the dark stream of blood following them across the floor. When she reached the door, she hurriedly lifted his blood-soaked shirt and swallowed at the sight of the red liquid bubbling from a hole in the middle of his upper back.

God! She had to stop the flow of blood. She should have done it earlier. Done it the moment she'd found him. Done it before anything else. And now his life's blood lay useless on the carpet.

Shit!

She was panicking. Not thinking straight.

Calm down!

Stupid! Stupid! Stupid! The words resounded in her ears as she examined the puncture wound in his back.

A knife?

A bullet?

Automatically her eyes lifted to scan the various windows. Nothing there. No movement and yet the wind still clawed frantically at the window frames, as if trying to get in at them. As if trying to finish the job.

Why would someone do this? Robbery? It was the only thing she could think of.

"Sara. Promise me." Jack's shaky voice interrupted her thoughts.

More tears sprang to her eyes. Everything blurred. She could barely see his moustache tremble as he tried to speak. Barely saw his gorgeous cornflower blue eyes as they stared unseeingly into space.

She was losing him.

She was losing it herself. She felt like screaming and screaming.

Hold on, Sara. Hold on. This is not the time to lose it. But the hot tears kept spilling.

"Shhh! Don't talk now. Save your strength."

She struggled out of her raincoat and thin white sweater. Bunching up the sweater, she pressed it securely against the wound, stemming the blood flow.

"Promise you'll find someone — else," he mumbled weakly.

Reaching out he placed his trembling hand on her slightly swollen stomach. "A father…f-for the babies. For yourself."

Oh, sweet God!

Horror stricken by his words, Sara quickly reassured him. "You're going to be fine. Hush now."

His hand fell down limply at his side.

Pulling hard at his heavy frame, she was able to angle him back first against the wall. She pressed the red wad of what used to be her white sweater in between her husband's shoulder blades and the wall and tenderly wiped off the perspiration beading his forehead.

"I'm going to get the truck. I'll be gone but a minute."

"Don't… Leave… Promise… First." His voice grew weaker.

"This is insane. We'll get out of this."

"Promise." His voice was fading.

She could see talking was taxing his remaining strength so she reluctantly agreed.

"All right. I promise. But I know I won't have to keep it."

She was glad to see the serene smile relax his tortured features, and then said quickly, "I'll be back."

Leaning over she kissed his cool, dry lips, feeling the urgency of getting help intensifying every split second.

Ripping open the door, she gasped as the cold wind bit deep into her skin. With one final look at Jack, she hesitantly closed the door behind her.

Was she doing the right thing? Should she stay with him?

No! She had to go for help!

Grey swirls of rain crashed down around her as she dashed through the storm. Terror grabbed at her legs. She couldn't run fast enough.

Lightning flashed illuminating her home.

She scrambled up the porch stairs and fell, her knees cracking against the hard wood. Gritting her teeth against the pain, she sobbed, got up and stopped abruptly at the screen door. Her breath came in painful gasps. Her gaze swung to the muddy footprints on her veranda.

Her heart sunk.

The footsteps led into her home.

The robber was inside!

Chewing on her lower lip, she whipped through her alternatives. She could surprise the culprit and smash a lamp over his head. But it would take time to locate him or them. The odds were stacked against her. And what would happen to Jack if the intruder got her first?

She needed to check the phone.

In the darkness, she opened the screen door slowly. Once inside she used her instincts to hone in on the phone. Grabbing it, she cried out at the dead dial tone.

Dammit!

The keys to the truck! She had to get the keys.

Tremors shook her as she waited for another flash of lightning. When it came, she quickly checked the rack where they kept all the keys to the buildings and to the truck. The key she was searching for was gone! It was always there!

Panic welled again.

She took a couple deep breaths willing herself to calm down. It helped because she suddenly remembered the emergency key.

Creeping further into the kitchen, she warily listened for any unusual sounds. Her footsteps echoed loudly as she tiptoed to the fridge. In the darkness, her hands frantically searched on top of the fridge and fell upon the welcome ceramic of an unused cookie jar where she kept the emergency key. She lifted the lid, and grabbed the key, slid open a nearby drawer and grabbed a steak knife.

Then she sprinted for the door.

Outside, it had started hailing. A volley of ice pellets attacked her, stinging her face, forcing her to lift her arms to fend them off as she blindly stumbled down the slippery steps.

Halfway across the yard, a sudden overwhelming gut-wrenching pain sliced through her abdomen. Crying into the frantic wind, Sara crashed to her knees. The knife flew out of her hands.

Dear Lord, they'd shot her!

After a split second, her worst fears came to light. The babies! Something was wrong with her babies.

The excruciating vise grip around her belly tightened. She bit down on her lower lip to prevent from screaming. She tasted blood. Blinding hot tears washed away the slicing cold numbness on her cheeks.

"I miscarried," Sara didn't even recognize her own voice. It sounded dead. Devoid of any emotion…

She shivered.

Tom's warm hands clamped reassuringly around hers.

"I don't know how long I laid on the freezing ground. But sometime later through the haze of pain, I heard a gunshot. I knew — I knew he was dead. Everything around that time and after is foggy. Jumbled. My mother-in-law — she died of a massive stroke that night when they told her the news. The murderer finished my husband by shooting him point-blank in the forehead. And to make matters worse that final bullet was never found."

Tom shuddered violently, but she continued. "If I hadn't left him...hadn't tried to move him..."

"Don't ever think that way. You had no other choice but to move him. You had to stop the bleeding and you had to leave him to get help. Don't you see that?"

Gently he tilted her chin, forcing her to look into his emerald green eyes. "Don't blame yourself. The killer is to blame. That's why we have to find him."

His voice suddenly took on a professional-like tone. "What do you mean by 'the bullet was missing'?"

"They couldn't find a bullet. It went clean..."

Shit!

She couldn't go on. She couldn't say out loud that the second bullet had gone clean through Jack's head, killing him instantly.

"It's okay. I think I get the picture," he said soothingly. "I know it's difficult. You don't have to answer any more questions."

"Please, I want to. I need to talk about it."

He inhaled deeply, slowly, and then nodded in agreement.

"Okay. You said the lights went out at the same time as the phone?"

"That's right."

"And you saw something at the window."

Sara shook her head. "I saw something move and a glint. I can't be sure it was even a person. It was too tall. Maybe it was a weird reflection of lightning against the glass."

"Which window?"

"The west side, it's the only one on that side of the building."

"How about the cigarette smoke? Did you tell the police about the cigarette smoke?"

"Yes, but they couldn't find any evidence of anyone smoking. No cigarette butt, no matches or anything to prove any intruders had even been there. That's when the rumors started flying. People said I made up the cigarette smoke and the glint in the window to throw suspicion off myself."

"People say crazy things when they're scared, Sara. But first thing in the morning, I'm going to take a look through that cabin and the ruins of Peppermint Creek Inn to see if I can't find something the cops missed. In the meantime, I want you to take your room tonight. I'll sleep on the couch."

"No, please, stay in my room. I've already got a nice toasty fire going in there for you and some clean sheets. Besides, I've still got some things that I need to do before turning in. I'd only keep you up and you look like you can barely keep your eyes open."

"It's still lightning out. Are you sure you'll be okay?"

"I'm fine. Thanks for caring."

It seemed as if he wanted to say something else, but he didn't.

"Good night, then." He smiled and headed down the hallway to her room.

"Good night," she whispered as she heard the door quietly click closed.

Chapter Seven

෨

Sometime around two in the morning, the storm finally hit. Thunder cracked intensely overhead rousing Tom from a deep sleep. The mattress shuddered under the brutal force of nature, and in a split second, he jumped out of bed. With her fear of storms, Sara would be frightened. He needed to check on her, reassure her everything was going to be okay.

Quickly he donned his underwear and made his way into the living room.

Silvery streaks of rain pounded against the glass panes and white lightning flickered constantly at the windows giving him a good view of the room.

To his surprise, she wasn't awake as he'd expected.

She was fast asleep.

And totally naked.

Tom blew out a ragged breath.

Was he having a sex dream? He almost pinched himself to make sure, but decided against it. This was one sex dream he wanted to keep going.

Allowing his hungry gaze to wander over every seductive curve of her gorgeous body, he found himself trembling with lust. Found himself wanting to smooth his hands over her silky plump breasts again, to caress her flat stomach, kiss her slightly rounded abdomen…

He swore softly.

The sheets and comforters were tangled in her feet, but her long legs were spread wide enough to give him an awesome view of her welcoming bare pussy. Fire zipped a scorching blaze through the thick length of his steel-hard cock and he shifted uncomfortably.

This wasn't right watching her while she was asleep.

For all he knew, he was married and this was wrong. But deep down in his gut he sensed Sara was the only woman he was interested in, the only woman he wanted.

Despite his feelings, he should leave.

His legs didn't budge.

He couldn't take his eyes off her as desire raged to new heights.

Oh, man, there were so many things he wanted to do to her lithe body, things that would have her screaming with joy, things that would chase away the sadness haunting her eyes.

And he wanted to lose himself in her warm beauty. Needed to forget his troubles. Forget everything except just the two of them.

He kept watching her, his breath escaping his lungs in harsh blasts. His balls were stretched tight and so full of his sperm he had to bite down on his bottom lip just to stop himself from climbing onto the bed, lowering himself between her legs and plunging his rigid cock deep into her succulent pussy.

He found himself wondering how she would react if she woke up to him fucking her? Would she scream and cry rape? Or would she smile and cry out her pleasures as she'd done while he mouth-fucked her during their picnic?

Slowly he moved forward, stalked toward her, watching her for any sign of movement. Waiting for her to awaken so she could see how stiff his cock was pressed against the prison restraint of his briefs.

Would she be scared at how aroused he was? Or would she eagerly accept his length deep inside her, clasping her long legs around her hips as he thrust madly into her?

Without thinking, he reached out and twirled her dark hair around his wounded fingers, sighing as the luscious silky strands soothed the rawness in his palms that had developed from breaking the branches of the romance tree with his bare hands. He'd been pissed off she hadn't wanted to open her heart to him about her troubles. Had ignored the pain in his back as he'd chain sawed like a madman then piled the logs in the parking lot near the truck. Thankfully, she'd confided in him later over a cup of hot peppermint tea.

The pain shining in her eyes as she'd talked about what had happened to her husband had just about killed him. He'd wanted to comfort her. To take her in his arms, make love to her. Make her forget her husband.

Show her how much sexual joy he could bring to her. Show her how much he needed her.

How he craved her in a way that made him wonder if it was normal to want to fuck a woman every time he looked at her. The desire for her had only increased when she'd so willingly allowed him to suckle her breasts this afternoon during the picnic and how eagerly she'd spread her legs allowing him to feast upon her delicious pussy.

She was hot. Hot and horny.

And so was he.

But he had no right taking advantage of her the way he'd done during the picnic. She'd been vulnerable. The quilt had been some sort of family heirloom. That much he'd figured out. He'd been a fool to drag it out of the closet where it had been hidden beneath the picnic basket. But he'd had no idea it would hurt her.

He seemed to be doing a lot of that. Hurting her. Pointing a gun at her—then a knife in the loft—and then enjoying her succulent body. He had no business sniffing around her. He had no future to offer her. He was a criminal. A man wanted by the cops who in turn wanted him dead.

Even as he thought those things, he knew he was lying to himself. Despite his troubles, instincts told him he needed her in his life. There was something about her. Something that told him she held the key to his identity. Even though she denied she knew him, there was a strange uneasiness floating at the back of his mind. He'd felt it when he'd seen her wildlife paintings in the loft. It was something he wasn't sure he wanted to explore.

Her sexy peppermint scent sifted deep into his lungs encouraging him to untwirl her hair and delicately caress her high cheekbone, trace a perfectly arched eyebrow and with the barest whisper of a touch, run a delicate finger over her long, thick eyelashes.

He came dangerously close to leaning over and kissing her slightly parted, pouting, ruby red lips when a thunderous crash shook the house.

Her eyes popped open. Fear flashed across her face when she spotted him.

"Easy. I just wanted to see how you were handling the storm," he explained, backing away and giving her space, although that was the last thing he wanted to do.

Obviously, he'd frightened her by coming so close.

The fear in her eyes only intensified.

"I better go," he said and twisted around to leave.

"Don't." Her silky whisper trailed through the darkness and stopped him cold.

Turning around he found her looking toward the windows. The fear was still there, accompanied by a worry wrinkle that burrowed across her forehead. His heart twisted for her. He knew she was thinking about the stormy night she'd found her husband in the cabin with a bullet hole in his back. The night she'd lost her babies.

"It's a bad one," she stated. He detected the shiver of fear in her voice—saw the trembling of her body.

"Bad enough to wake me up and I was sleeping like a dog." He couldn't stop his gaze from trailing over her nakedness again. Couldn't stop the ragged breaths from ripping out of his mouth or stop the blood from pounding into his heavily rigid cock.

At that moment, she looked away from the window and caught him ogling her. Her eyes widened as she realized her covers weren't on her and that familiar flush swept across her cheeks. Quickly she grabbed the closest comforter and pulled it over her.

Too late, sweetness. Your gorgeous nakedness has already been etched forever in my brain.

She smiled nervously, her gaze darting everywhere except on him.

"Thanks for coming in to check on me. I would have been scared if you weren't here."

"No problem," his voice cracked.

Another round of lightning flashed at the windows and he saw her shiver again.

"I'll set one of the oil lamps on for you and get the fire going again. It'll cheer you up."

"You mean help me forget…" she said softly.

He nodded.

"Thanks," she whispered shyly and seemed to sink deeper under the comforter as another roar of thunder shook the windowpanes.

He headed toward the fireplace where he spotted the items. Within a moment, a buttery glow shot from the oil lamp. He left it on the mantel and threw some pinecones he found in a bucket onto the glowing embers. A sharp crackling noise shot through the air and the cones quickly caught fire, fanning a burst of heat against his face. Then he followed up by tossing on some dry kindling and a couple of pieces of firewood.

"I guess it is kind of stupid of me to be so scared of storms, especially since I used to love them so much," she said a moment later when the fire crackled loudly in the hearth.

"When you're ready to enjoy the storms again, you will. It just takes a little time to work through things in life. They say time always heals wounds."

She shook her head and frowned. "But the scar always remains. It's always there to remind you of what happened."

Tom nodded. "True. The scar is always there. But the enjoyment you had before is also there, buried inside your heart. If you can find a way to dig it up…"

He let his words trail off as she smiled warmly.

"You sure you aren't a writer or a poet or something? You have a nice way with words."

Tom shrugged his shoulders. "Maybe in another life."

His breath caught at the way her heated gaze suddenly strayed to where his erection painfully strained against his underwear. He watched her eyes darken with carnal lust in the orange cast from the flickering flames. Darken with a scorching need. Noticed the way she licked her full lips.

Blades of lightning raced through his long shaft, pumping more pressure into his already swollen testicles. He groaned and found himself stalking toward her as if she was his sexual prey.

She didn't move as she watched him draw closer. Her hungry gaze riveted to his captive erection. He noticed she'd let the comforter loosen—it dropped just below her beaded nipples giving him an awesome view of her luscious globes.

He sucked in an aroused breath.

His balls tightened, became taut and sore. His erection demanded satisfaction, craved to sink into her mouth.

"Sara?" His voice sounded strangled and urgent as it tangled with the rain crashing against the windows.

She said nothing. Simply stared at his huge bulge as if she was mesmerized.

Man! The intense way she looked at him had his heart crashing madly against his chest. It seemed as if she wanted to devour him whole. It made the blood in his veins thicken and a roar of erotic sensations flooded his scrotum and cock.

"It's been so long since…" she whispered.

More than two years since she'd had a cock in her mouth? Is that what she meant?

Her eyes were so wide and eager and glittering with need that his knees weakened and he almost collapsed. And her mouth… Oh, man, her beautiful plump lips were parted and waiting for his thick flesh to slip inside.

He didn't know how she got there, but she was suddenly at the edge of her bed, on her hands and knees, her plump breasts dripping from her gorgeous body, her curvy ass in the air and her hot sensual breath splashing against his hard erection.

"I want to…taste you," she breathed.

Wow!

He couldn't believe it. Couldn't believe she would be so willing… Ah, hell, he was wasting time. His fingers quickly curled beneath the elastic of his underwear and he pulled it down over his hips.

The thin material slipped over his straining cock and she gasped as it sprang free from the material. Her mouth was opening, and then he was pushing his rigid flesh between those pretty lips, sighing as her heated cavern slid against the thick tip of his cock.

He watched in stunned awe as her mouth closed around his flesh and he felt a powerful sucking on his rod. The searing sensation almost blew his mind. Almost made him explode right then and there. But he held himself under rigid control. It was hard. Real hard not to come as she sensuously explored the tip of his mushroom-shaped cock with her hot little tongue.

He closed his eyes, only to see all too clearly a vision of him going down on her during their picnic.

His eyes popped open once again as her mouth moved away from his cockhead and she licked one of his bloated balls. He swallowed harshly as her sharp teeth nipped sensuously at the skin. Awesome sensations shattered his composure.

"No time for exploring, woman. I need you now," he hissed.

Grabbing both sides of her head, he guided her head back to his cock.

God! He couldn't hold himself back and when she opened her mouth, he thrust into her.

She was hungry for him. The frantic way her lips stretched over his rigid flesh, her cheeks drawing in and out as she sucked hard, proved it. She sucked so firmly, he growled at the erotic pleasures that constricted his belly.

The length of her tongue tenderly caressed the underneath area of his cock. Incredible pressure built along his entire shaft.

He began thrusting.

Her succulent mouth smoothed over him expertly. Her hands were fondling his balls now, and he gritted his teeth at the way she squeezed and kneaded.

God, she was good.

Her moist mouth continued to seduce his stiff rod.

His body tightened more. Tensed and coiled with need.

She sucked harder, drawing his erection deeper into her moist cavern with each plunge.

Oh, yes! He could feel the orgasm coming. Could feel his control slipping.

"I'm coming," he said in a strangled whisper.

Thunder crackled overhead. Stars flashed behind his eyes as he closed them and went with the oncoming lusty sensations.

And then his gut squeezed even harder, spasmed with an unbelievable carnal force and he just blew.

The climax ripped him apart.

Made him cry out. Made him thrust harder — deeper — faster as he strove for release.

She kept pace with his gyrations. Deep-throating him, giving him everything his tortured cock demanded.

She sucked harder. So hard, a deep groan of appreciation was ripped from his mouth.

"Sweetness!" he hissed.

His breath caught in his lungs and his hands held her head tighter, her silky curls flowed erotically over his wrists and brushed against his knees. His ragged cries shot through the bedroom as hot jets of sperm spewed down her throat.

Astonishing vibrations racked him.

Over and over.

Slamming through his balls, clenching his cock — her mouth squeezing all his creamy semen from him. And she drank every drop. Whimpering and moaning with every swallow as his jerking cock continued to unload.

By the time he was finished, her hot hands were curled intimately around each of his balls and she was holding on so tight to him he figured she was keeping herself from falling over.

He let go of her head and her hot bursts of breath caressed his scrotum and cock. She looked so beautiful with her face all flushed in the buttery light, her lips swollen and red from sucking him into mind-boggling oblivion.

Something warm and cozy, and intensely beautiful fluttered to life deep inside him. It blossomed and pushed through the black eternity of where his memories should be. Pressed through the layers of puzzling images of those hooker-infested nights he dreamed about, sliced through the visions of him slapping bills into the palms of cops with leering faces.

Instinctively, he realized he'd never felt this intensely about a woman in his life. And if he had, surely he'd remember such an overwhelming feeling of passion, this overwhelming need to be with a woman, wouldn't he?

He shook his head slowly, not quite believing he could feel this deeply about Sara Clarke. Although it wasn't too shocking, especially considering the fantastic way his heart had twisted the very first time he'd seen her coming up the walk that stormy night he'd fallen asleep on the veranda swing.

He frowned as she pulled away and slumped back onto the bed drawing the covers over herself.

No, he couldn't let this go any further.

She was a stranger to him. And he was a fugitive. A man without a past. A man without a future.

She didn't see anything in him except a lost man who needed a blowjob. It had been her female instinct that made her respond to him when she'd seen his cock straining for relief. That's all. Just a female instinct.

To his surprise, a playful little smile tilted up her lips. "I guess I shouldn't have done that."

She was echoing the words he'd said after he'd sucked her pussy following their picnic. Obviously she was feeling frisky, wanting him to join her in bed. Make love to her.

Shit! He'd screwed up again.

He pulled his briefs back up.

Another bolt of thunder shot through the room making her eyes grow wide with fear again.

"Please, stay."

He nodded.

She made no verbal invitation for him to climb into bed with her, yet he wanted to desperately. The flash of lust in her eyes said she wanted him to. But if he did, he'd mount her. Without a doubt, he would start fucking her. His cock was already growing hard

137

again. His mind already swirling with the carnal visions of what he wanted to do to her.

But he couldn't go to her. If he did, he wouldn't be able to leave her. He had to stop it here. Stop it before things got so out of hand she developed feelings for him. That's the last thing he wanted. She was still recovering from the tragedy of her husband getting murdered and miscarrying twins. He couldn't add to her pain just because he was horny.

He would stop it right here and now by sending her a message that would be unmistakable. It would hurt her, but a little hurt now was a whole lot better than a lot of hatred later.

"I'll stay…but on the chair."

The sound of her stunned inhalation stabbed at his heart, making him want to take her into his comforting arms again just as he'd done at the picnic. And look what had happened when he'd done that.

He gritted his teeth in frustration, and plopped his sorry ass into the nearby armchair and watched her. Watched how the playful smile slipped from her lips. Watched how a sad pouty frown marred her mouth.

"I can't let this go any further," he tried to explain.

She looked as if she was going to protest, but changed her mind. Instead, she burrowed deeper beneath the comforter and said nothing.

They both remained silent as the storm tossed around the house. Finally, her eyes fluttered sleepily and she fell asleep.

He stayed until the storm passed on and the sky began to lighten. Then he left her and took a very long and very cold shower. After getting dressed, he located the master keys on the giant key rack inside the kitchen door. Giving Sara one last look as she slept soundly on the sofa bed, he smiled at the warm way his heart twisted and then headed outside.

Everything was still dripping and wet from last night's storm when he stepped onto the wraparound veranda into the cool crisp gray dawn. The air felt damp and misty as it swirled against his bare arms, making him shiver violently. He should go back inside and grab the borrowed flannel shirt he'd draped over the kitchen chair last night, but decided against it. He'd warm up soon enough once he began to search through the contents of the office and the log structure. But first, he headed toward the truck.

Last night he'd cleared away the tree and branches. And now in the light he could see the damage inflicted on the cab of Sara's truck. The tree had crashed onto the vehicle—spider-webbed the entire rear window, cracked a side window and wrenched a deep dent into the roof of the cab.

But the dent could be hammered out and the windows replaced. It wouldn't look pretty, but the truck would still be drivable.

He climbed into the vehicle and jammed the key into the ignition. Nothing happened. He popped the hood, got out of the truck and lifted the lid. Some poking and prodding revealed a loose battery cable.

Retrieving an adjustable wrench from the toolbox he found in the extended cab, he quickly tightened the cable. Finding no more loose connections or visible leaks, he turned the ignition again and let out a tight sigh when the truck roared to life. Maybe, deep down, he had been hoping the truck wouldn't be repairable, enabling him to stay here in this peaceful place for just a little while longer.

The tiny one room office cabin where Sara's husband had been murdered was first on his agenda. Apparently, the building hadn't been used since the murder of her husband, because the desk and bookshelves were all bare and the place, after being scrubbed clean, had been left to accumulate cobwebs here and there.

He found the area where Sara had pulled her husband up against the wall to use it to stop the flow of her husband's blood. There was a slight nick in the pine wall, most likely where the missing bullet had lodged. He ripped out the plank with little difficulty and inspected it.

The bullet had never gone through. He searched through the fibers of insulation inside the wall just to be sure. It was quite obvious to him, someone, most likely the authorities, had already sifted through the fibers, because the insulation was loose and in disarray. Whoever had been searching here had done a very thorough job.

There was definitely nothing here now. Replacing the pine panel he ventured outside, to the west side of the tiny one-room office. Sara had said she'd seen something flash past the window on the fateful day of her husband's murder. Shortly after that, the phone and lights had gone out.

Tom nodded knowingly when along the west side of the building he located the incoming electrical wires leading into the cabin almost directly above the west window. A foot away he spotted the incoming telephone line.

After carefully examining the two lines, he trudged over to what was left of Peppermint Creek Inn's giant log building.

Damp air swirled around him as he stepped among the giant blackened timbers. He searched for anything suspicious, anything that didn't belong. He sifted through the charred logs, metal and skeletons of burned furniture with meticulous fashion. Examined every shred of burned carpet fibers, electrical wiring, anything that hadn't been burned beyond recognition.

Just when he was about to give up, he spotted something unusual. Something that made him wonder why the police hadn't located it, because if they had, the items would most certainly be in an evidence lockup, not littering a crime scene.

* * * * *

The cheerful chattering of a blue jay pulled at Sara. Slowly, ever so slowly, she found her way out of sleep and opened her eyes. The living room was sunny and warm. Pleasant. She yawned and stretched like a Cheshire cat all the while wondering how she'd been able to sleep so well. She hadn't slept this peacefully in years.

No dreams, no worries, absolutely nothing. Just oblivious peace. Peering over at the battery-operated clock on an end table, she gasped in surprise. Nine forty-five. How could this be possible? She was almost always up before six.

With a sudden burst of energy, Sara rolled out of the sofa bed. She felt great today. Absolutely fantastic. Just like floating on one of those giant puffy clouds she'd seen during yesterday's picnic when Tom had suckled her pussy.

Just thinking about Tom brought more happiness shimmering through her. She could understand his hesitation to make love to her last night. He was afraid he'd hurt her. Afraid their sexual attraction would lead to something else. A man with such restraint had to have a good soul.

This morning she planned on telling him she wanted him to make love to her. Wanted it with her every fiber. To hell with the consequences. She just wanted to be loved again.

The cheerfulness inside her continued to soar and the idea of feeling this happy frightened her a little, because it had been so long since she'd experienced it. Nonetheless, she liked this carefree feeling. She liked it a lot.

Bright sunlight spilled through the windows, coating the kitchen with a joyous warmth as she tied the sash on her robe and walked into the room. The fresh aroma of brewing coffee filled the air with a tangy aroma making Sara smile. She hadn't had a man make her coffee in so long and it felt good. Folding her arms across her breasts, she wondered where Tom was this morning. She'd checked his room, but it had been empty. His bed made.

She leaned over the kitchen counter, and peeked out the window and found him chopping wood. He looked up, waved, cast her a gorgeous, crooked grin that made her toes curl and returned to his chopping. He wore a white muscle shirt and Sara watched with awe as the muscles bunched up in his arms when he lifted the ax and swung a mighty chop, making the wood explode from his fantastic blow.

In one split second, from out of nowhere, she spied the dark, menacing shadow. It raced straight for Tom. He held a long, shiny steak knife in his hand.

Screaming, she crashed her palms against the window in a desperate attempt to alert him. The rattling was so intense she wondered why he couldn't hear it or her warning screams. He continued to chop wood, totally oblivious of the dark shadow who now stood right behind him.

She smashed her fists harder. Screamed as the gleaming knife lifted, ready to strike…

Sara awoke with a start.

An intense feeling of doom smothered her, making it hard for her to breathe. She was drenched in sweat, her limbs trembling uncontrollably. The living room was as quiet as a tomb and almost as dark. Wide-eyed with anxiety, she peered through the dimness at the clock. Seven twenty-five.

She let out a low sigh of relief. A nightmare. It had only been a nightmare. Or had it been a premonition?

Her heart suddenly picked up speed at the new thought. In a flash, she pushed aside the covers. On jittery legs, she threw on a robe and headed for the nearest window. Once there, she looked nervously into the front yard. The wood Tom had piled last night was still there, untouched. And thankfully he wasn't chopping wood.

Whipping open the window, she took a few deep breaths of the cool, damp air and tried hard to slow the jittery uneasiness still clutching her insides. She stiffened when she detected movement in the burnt-out ruins of the inn.

Instantly she relaxed. It was Tom.

He disappeared behind one of the charred walls of the Peppermint Creek Inn, but not before she saw the set look of determination in his face.

The thought that she had an ally made hot tears spring to her eyes. She'd been virtually alone in her fight to find out who'd killed her husband. Her sister Jocelyn and her father-in-law had done all they could, but they'd come up empty-handed.

Subconsciously her gaze scanned the surroundings looking for any other movement, any strange shadows. Thankfully, she saw nothing else.

Shaking her head at being so foolish as to allow a nightmare to dampen her spirits, she headed for the bathroom. She'd decorated the tiny room in floral-printed wallpaper, with a beige background and miniature sweetheart pink and red roses sprinkled throughout the pattern. The floral design gave the tiny bathroom an airy yet dramatic look.

She found a damp pink towel hanging off the shower rod and her heart picked up speed. Obviously he'd already taken a shower.

Grabbing the damp towel in her arms she inhaled the fresh fragrance of soap intermingling with Tom's masculine scent.

The aroma made her think of Tom standing naked in the shower. Sparkling drops of water sliding over the large, bunched muscles in his arms and across his wide chest as he rubbed the perfume-scented soap into his strong muscular belly. His large fingers curling around the rigid length of his thick cock as he pulled back his foreskin and cleaned his mushroom-shaped cockhead. She felt a delicious hot feeling spiral throughout her body as she remembered taking his cock into her mouth last night.

It had been a wild impulse to take him orally. The instant she'd found him leaning over her when she'd awoken from the thunder and seen the lusty glow in his eyes, she been turned on so hot she would have done anything to have him making love to her.

While he'd restarted her fire, she'd watched his cute, plump ass cheeks cradled behind his underwear, and had the overwhelming urge to rip the cloth from his backside and just run her hands over those masculine curves.

Then she'd gotten a good look at the gorgeous bulge pressing against his underwear and a fierce lust heat had consumed her. She'd wanted to see his cock so badly she'd almost reached out and pulled his cock out herself. When she'd seen his thick, pulsing flesh, the web of veins pulsing through his engorged erection, the hard swollen testicles, she'd wanted to taste him.

And he'd tasted so wonderful as his silk-encased rod slid between her eager lips.

She knew how to suck cock. Had done it to Jack, but Jack was small compared to Tom.

Tom's package was huge!

She blew out an aroused breath as she remembered how her lips had slid over his hot, pulsing shaft, how wonderful it had felt sliding into her throat. The taste of his semen had made her heady. The salty cream spurting into her mouth had turned her on as she'd envisioned Tom thrusting his cock deep into her quivering, drenched pussy.

His eyes had closed tightly as the pleasure had rocked him to his core. Pleasure she'd so freely given him.

She'd really expected him to come into the bed with her. Take her into his arms and kiss her, make love to her…

Sara banished the thoughts immediately. A terrible cloud of guilt crashed in around her. What had she been thinking? How could she even fantasize about this dangerous stranger, this fugitive with no memory, in such an intimate way and with her husband's wedding band still on her finger?

Just because she'd been without a man for over two years didn't mean she could jump into bed with the first one who sent shivers of passion shooting throughout her. Just because whenever she looked into his dark, charming emerald green eyes, she found herself flirting with all kinds of forbidden fantasies and desires.

She'd thought no other man could make her feel this desirable again. It would be too easy to fall into bed with Tom. Way too easy.

She'd seen the same desire, the same hunger in his eyes as what engulfed her.

But what about when he left? What if he stayed and she fell in love, and the police caught and killed him? She'd be devastated.

Tom had been right to stop what was happening between them last night.

She had to face reality. He was a stranger. A dangerously sexy man who she needed to stay away from.

Far, far away.

* * * * *

Tom was rummaging around in the barn looking for his gloves and a clean container to place the evidence in, when he decided to take a closer look at the antique motorcycle propped up in the far corner. It was dusty and red. A '55 Buch, if he guessed right. The chrome was in relatively good shape. Actually, the whole bike looked in pretty good shape. Maybe it still worked.

He unscrewed the gas cap and sniffed. The foul odor of gas made him grimace. Suddenly a surge of adrenaline shot through his veins. Bright flashes of light blinked in front of his eyes and before he knew it, he was sailing on a motorcycle…

Cold wind whipped past him, shrouding him in its chilly cloak. He shivered violently against the freezing onslaught. If only he'd been able to dress warmer. But there hadn't been any time.

The dark gray sky grew lighter as the sun threatened to peak over the horizon. Already the early morning traffic had thickened as he drove the straight ribbon of highway toward freedom. If his luck held, he'd cross the Canadian border into Quebec without a problem. The recently stolen bike plates would hopefully attest to that.

The vision disappeared as fast as it had appeared.

It left him grabbing onto the seat of the motorcycle for support. His face was drenched with sweat, his mind gnawed on the fear that had followed him out of the vision.

Stolen plates? Without a doubt, he'd been running from the law. Why else steal license plates?

Spearing a trembling hand through his hair, he closed his eyes and took a deep breath, trying to calm his growing fears.

Why else would he come here and stick a gun in Sara's face, and then almost attack her with a knife? He must be an escaped madman, that's why he was heading into Canada with stolen license plates.

The thought brought bitter bile rolling up into his throat. If he didn't leave now, Sara could be his next victim. In a blind panic, Tom headed for the open barn door.

* * * * *

Sara was singing her heart out when she heard the distinct sound of an approaching engine. A loud cry escaped her lips as she peeked out the screen door. Officer Justin Jeffries sat on top of a very muddy four-wheeler and he was cruising into the parking lot.

Oh, my God!

Tom!

Where was he? Had he heard the engine? Taken cover? Or had Justin Jeffries spotted Tom from afar and headed down to arrest him?

She felt herself sway slightly with panic, and immediately inhaled a few quick deep breaths to calm her suddenly racing heart. It took her a few more seconds before she was calm enough to move her legs.

With her insides trembling uncontrollably, she plastered a smile on her face and pushed open her creaking screen door just in time to see Justin's tall, thin body lean over his four-wheel, all-terrain vehicle and heft from a basket in the rear of the vehicle two dirt-spattered large paper grocery bags into his thin, spindly arms.

Yesterday, on the telephone, she'd told him she was all set with food and now here he was. She should have expected this intrusion. It was his pattern. He always showed up uninvited.

She should have warned Tom to keep a low profile. She could only hope and pray he had heard Justin coming. To have a policeman hanging around her place on his day off was the last thing they needed.

She tried to keep her cool as Justin strolled casually up the walk toward her. He wore very muddy midnight blue overalls and a baseball hat was pulled low over his forehead hiding his jet-black hair. The black mustache perched beneath his hawkish nose and those piercing deep blue eyes behind the too-thick glasses made Sara shiver a bit as she received the impression he was a turkey vulture and she his prey. It hadn't been the first time she'd sensed that feeling over the past few years.

"Morning, Sara!" he shouted cheerfully, all the while his narrow eyes scanned every inch of her place, leaving Sara with the distinct feeling her surroundings were being searched.

Mentally, she did a run-down to make sure she hadn't inadvertently left anything suspicious belonging to Tom out in the open that might lead Justin to believe she had a man around. She couldn't come up with anything.

"What brings you here so early in the morning?" Sara said as pleasantly as she could, trying like crazy to keep the tightness out of her voice. She could tell he'd picked up on her nervousness because he eyed her curiously and quickly nodded at the two bags in his arms.

"Compliments of the Widow McCloud. I mentioned you were flooded in and you had enough grub to keep you going, but the widow said she remembers all too well how it used to be in the Spring out this way. And how she'd wished she could get her hands on some fresh food while she was stranded. So she insisted I come and deliver these to you."

His cobalt blue eyes eagerly searched her face for approval.

"How thoughtful of her—and of you for bringing it over, Justin. And by the looks of you, you had a pretty tough time getting in through the hydro road."

"I must admit it was a wild ride and I did get stuck a couple of times. Took me two hours, but the fresh food had to get through."

He gazed over at the giant woodpile then at the splintered wheelchair ramp and the broken veranda railing. "Looks like you had some trouble. Your romance tree fell over, huh? Too bad. Lots of people liked that tree. Lot of initials in it. Lots of history."

Sara detected the disgust in his voice. She knew he hadn't liked her romance tree. Once she'd heard him say to one of her male clients it was silly to carve a heart and a couple's initials into a tree because the next thing you knew the sweetheart had herself another man. Sara wondered why he was so down on couples. She'd never seen him with a girlfriend or even heard him speak of one.

He wasn't such a bad-looking fellow—it was just his uppity attitude that had turned the women away.

He hoisted the large grocery bags uncomfortably in his arms, obviously waiting for an invitation inside.

It took every ounce of strength she could muster to say, "Come on in. I've got some peppermint tea brewing. It's about ready."

Her lungs deflated when he accepted the offer. She didn't know why she should be so shocked. He always accepted an invitation from her, and when she didn't offer, he'd invite himself in anyway. Besides, she had to act as if nothing was wrong. Act as if she wasn't harboring a fugitive from the law.

On the porch, he placed the groceries onto the swing and quickly got out of his muddy boots and coveralls before lifting the bags again. Sara held the screen door open to allow him to pass inside and before following him, she cast a quick glance around to see if she could spot Tom. She couldn't see him. Breathing a sigh of relief, she turned and went inside.

Justin Jeffries had already deposited the two grocery bags onto the countertop and had made himself at home by pouring himself a mug of steaming tea. She'd known him for years. He'd been a lifelong friend of Jack's. When they'd moved to Ontario, Canada, Justin had eventually followed by accepting a position at the local OPP detachment.

She'd never really liked him very much, and she didn't know why. He'd never given her any cause to dislike him. But she remembered her sister Jo's words. *Always follow your instincts, girl. They'll never steer you wrong.*

Since childhood Jack and Justin had been inseparable buddies, only God knew why. They were total opposites. Where Jack was laid-back and easygoing, Justin was over-friendly and as nervous as a field mouse crossing a busy highway.

She watched silently as Justin took a seat at the kitchen table. A large smile lifted his black mustache as he took a generous gulp of the peppermint tea. "Ahhh, it really hits the spot. Worth it to drive all those bumpy miles for your tea, Sara."

She nodded in polite approval, and sat down on the edge of her seat opposite Justin. Her insides screamed at him to hurry up and finish the tea and leave. For all she knew, Tom could walk inside without being the wiser that they had company — company of the worst kind.

"How'd you make out with last night's storm?" he asked as he took another sip, his eyes scanning her kitchen.

"Fine." Sara frowned as she remembered this morning's horrible dream of the shadow about to kill Tom. And now she realized her sick dream had been some weird, twisted premonition.

"It sure was a doozie," Justin laughed. "Lightning hit the church steeple. Killed the clock. It stopped ticking at 3:15 a.m. Electricity is out in some of the rural areas. Phones are still out all over the county. So, who'd you hire to cut and pile your romance tree? They come in through the hydro road, too?"

The question caught her unexpectedly, trailing a frosty shiver through her spine.

"Um—" She forced herself to keep eye contact with him. "What makes you think I've hired someone?"

"The flannel shirt on the back of your chair for one."

Oh, my gosh! She tried to keep her face blank as she silently cursed herself for forgetting about Tom's shirt.

"Actually the shirt belonged to Jack. I use it for my late evening strolls. And I did the wood by myself."

"You?" His eyes widened with surprise. "You use those gloves over there?"

She followed his gaze and spotted Tom's giant work gloves sitting on the countertop. Her gut twisted awfully.

"They are a bit big, I must admit. But I didn't want to get my hands all chafed."

His shifty gaze flew to her knotted hands on the table as he took another sip of tea.

"You sure did a good job lifting those heavy logs. I guess a lot of the manual work has fallen onto your shoulders without Jack around."

Sara stiffened at Justin's comment. "I manage."

Reaching out, he placed a cool hand over her clenched fists making her terribly uneasy at his touch.

"Sara, the case is still open on Jack. I know it's been a while and chances are slim but…" He shrugged his shoulders. "Someone might inadvertently say something or we could get a tip or maybe even find the missing bullet."

The last two words hung in the air like a guillotine over her head.

She didn't like where the conversation was heading. "I'm not giving up hope, Justin. The murderer will be caught. You can count on that!"

His gaze snapped to her face. "You sound pretty sure. You know something new?"

She wanted to tell Justin if anything was still around regarding Jack's murder, Tom would find it. Anything to take that utterly pitying look off his face, but she held back the sharp reply.

"No," she finally replied rather meekly. "Nothing new."

"Too bad. But if you do remember anything, even the slightest thing, let me know right away, okay?"

Sara nodded.

Seemingly satisfied, he removed his hand and drained the rest of the tea. She breathed a bit easier when he stood up and strolled toward the front door. Sara got up to follow him.

He quickly shrugged into his coveralls and boots and the moment he cleared the veranda he suddenly asked, "You mind if I take a look around?"

Sara felt her heart skip a beat. "Look around? Why?"

"See if everything is in working order." His reply seemed casual, but Sara could see he was far from casual as his suspicious gaze carefully scanned every single building.

"Oh, don't worry. I've got everything under control."

His voice lowered and his thin lips wavered into somewhat of a smile. "As I've said in the past, Sara, just call on me anytime to give you a hand. I've been known to work wonders with a hammer and saw."

"I'll definitely keep you in mind," she replied with fake brightness.

His gaze flew to scanning her buildings again.

She decided it was best to keep him occupied with conversation as she tactfully led him toward the all-terrain vehicle without his even realizing it.

"Have you found Sam yet?"

"Nope. I suspect he's fallen to foul play at the hands of that hermit. You sure you don't want me to look around?" he asked again when they reached his vehicle.

"I'm sure. I've been keeping my eyes open ever since you called yesterday. Haven't seen hide nor hair of anyone, except you, of course. Besides he's probably long gone by now. Most likely in the next biggest city trying to blend in so no one will recognize him. Isn't that what most criminals do?" she innocently added.

Justin nodded gravely as he climbed onto his four-wheeler.

"I better be going. Gotta get to work. Doing lots of overtime this week, organizing search parties for the suspect and looking for Sam."

"In that case, I'll definitely let you know if anyone suspicious comes this way."

"Thanks."

His eyes suddenly grew into mere slits as his gaze flew to the barn. "I could have sworn that barn door was open when I came in."

Sara's breath caught in her throat at his comment. "It catches in the wind," she said quickly. "I must not have closed it properly when I went out there to do some painting." He didn't need to know she'd gone out there yesterday, and it was entirely possible his wanted man was inside the barn right at this moment.

"Painting? You're painting again?"

She'd captured his entire attention.

Sara shrugged. "Just dabbling, nothing serious."

"Can I see what you're working on?"

She smiled sweetly. "Now you know better than that, Justin. No one sees my work until it's finished. I'm superstitious that way. Now, you'd best be on your way before you're late for work."

Taking her hint, he started up the engine. He let it idle for a moment as his suspicious gaze once again raked the closed barn door. Then his gaze fell upon her once again.

"How about I come over for dinner Friday night?" he yelled above the drone of the motor.

"I'll have to take a rain check. I'm using all my spare time painting," she lied. "I'd rather not have any visitors for a little while. I hope you understand."

Justin pursed his lips with a bit of a pout and gave her a quick nod. "Okay. Call me if you need me."

"I will," Sara yelled back.

He threw her a quick wave, revved up the engine a few times and pulled out of the yard like Evil Knievel himself. Sara breathed the biggest sigh of her life as she watched Justin Jeffries head across her meadow toward the towering hydro lines in the misty distance.

A few moments later, when Sara entered the barn, Tom raced down the loft stairs three at a time. By the look of concern on his face, Sara became alarmed. "What's wrong?"

"Go back outside." His voice was too low and too calm to her liking. Immediately alarm bells rang.

"Walk casually into your house. Lock all your doors and windows. Wait there for me."

Oh, God! He was scaring her!

"What's happening?"

"He hasn't left. He's out there watching the place." Tom moved into the shadows of the barn.

"How can you be so sure?"

"I saw something flash just beyond the knoll. Who is he anyway?"

"It's the police officer I spoke with on the phone yesterday."

Tom cursed beneath his breath. "I'm going out to keep an eye on him."

"No!" Sara grabbed his arm stopping him from leaving.

"Sara! Just do it! " Tom snapped at her and she trembled at the fear flashing in his eyes. "If something happens to me, you don't know anything. Hide all my stuff where no one will find it."

Before she could reply, he detached her death grip from his arm and disappeared like a ghost into the gloominess of the barn. A moment later, she spotted his silhouette climbing out one of the rear barn windows.

* * * * *

Adrenaline surged through Tom's body urging him to dash quickly ahead. He could hear his own ragged breathing as he sprinted from the side of the barn, and into the tree line. Dashing from tree to tree, all the while keeping low and cautious, he tried to ignore the painful ache digging deep into his back where the bullet wound lay.

He'd been heading toward the open barn door when he'd heard the engine of an approaching vehicle. Peeking through the doorway, he'd barely caught a glimpse of a tall man as he'd hoisted paper bags into his arms.

Even though the man's facial features were hidden behind the two large grocery bags, and the baseball hat slung low over his head, Tom had felt a strange pang of familiarity grip his stomach as he watched the man saunter up the walkway, a familiarity that clenched his gut into one hell of a tight knot.

He watched as Sara greeted the man. She seemed to know him and was unafraid of him. And she seemed friendly enough with him. He found himself wondering if maybe the newcomer was Garry, but dismissed the thought instantly. This man seemed young. Most likely his and Sara's age.

He'd cursed as Sara opened the door to allow the man inside. His eyes flew to the stairs and straight up to the loft. From up there he'd be able to look into the kitchen windows and keep an eye on the newcomer. Quickly, he brushed past the open barn door and headed up the stairs three at a time. When he was half way up the steps, he thought he heard the barn door creak shut.

In the loft, he'd snuggled up to the side of the giant picture window, keeping in the shadows just enough so he couldn't be spotted. He smiled at the excellent view of the east side of the house and sighed with immense relief as he spied Sara walk quickly past one of the side kitchen windows. Through another window, he spied the unwelcome guest at the kitchen table.

Unfortunately, the man's facial features were still hidden from his view as a result of the rising sun reflecting brilliantly against the glass panes. But the intense pang of familiarity still rode Tom.

He'd sat on pins and needles until a few minutes later when Sara and the newcomer finally walked into the parking lot. They chatted beside the all-terrain vehicle for a few minutes and when the man swung his gaze toward the barn, Tom ducked away from the window wondering if the newcomer had been so observant to notice the door to the barn door was now closed. Shit! Who was this guy? A minute later, he heard the roar of the all-terrain vehicle as it took off. Then he dared to peek out again.

Sara stood in the parking lot watching the man as he headed toward the power lines in the near distance. Except for bare feet, she was dressed in hip-hugging black jean shorts and a sweetheart pink short-sleeved knitted sweater. Her hair was tied into one long braid that cascaded down her back.

His first impulse was to run down the stairs, and out to the parking lot and gather her into his arms. To reach out and untangle her hair. Run his fingers through the shimmering auburn tresses. To slide his hand around her neck, and kiss her ever so gently on those rosy lips and tell her how relieved he was she'd gotten rid of that guy. But a minute later when he gazed up into the hills where the newcomer had disappeared, Tom spotted a flash at the top of a knoll, and he'd run back down into the barn to meet Sara.

Now Tom's entire back was drenched with sweat as he neared the area where he'd seen the flash of light over the knoll. He wasn't surprised when he spied the tall man entrenched into the side of the hill, binoculars raised as he watched Sara's place.

This time he was allowed a full view of the man's face. As soon as Tom's gaze fell onto the man, recognition speared a hole into his guts.

It was him!

The same cop he'd seen in the cruiser as it had whizzed past him the first day he'd stumbled along the road leading to Peppermint Creek Inn. Same jet black hair, thin black mustache.

The cheerful chattering of nearby chipmunks shifted into the background as a fierce pain shot through Tom's head. He grabbed onto the nearby tree for support as flashes of white light shot out of nowhere blinding him.

Images flickered…

The icy cold seemed to seep into his every muscle as he lay on the ground, breathing heavily. A sea of pain engulfed his every movement, his every thought. But he fought against it as he listened to the two men's raised voices on the other side of the wall. They were arguing about what to do with him. Hell, why not let him go? Problem solved.

There was such a weakness in him—he could barely clench his fist. But clench his fists he did, ignoring the painful bite of the handcuffs and ignoring the soreness in his muscles as he moved his legs up and down to keep them limber and warm.

He had to stay conscious this time. He had to escape, to stay alive because he was the only one left who knew the burning truth. The only one who could set things straight...

The vision abruptly vanished leaving Tom spent.

Too tired to retreat back to the inn and too tired to stand, he dropped to his side and allowed the tall, wet grass to conceal him from the cop. Wearily he massaged the painful knot in his temples, trying to make some sort of sense out of what he'd just remembered.

He was the only one who knew the burning truth. The only one who could set things straight.

Maybe he wasn't a criminal after all! Maybe someone wanted him dead because he knew too much. The two cops had been arguing over what to do with him.

If he was a criminal, why not arrest him? Take him in? Not hide him in some weird dungeon and try to figure out what to do with him.

Hope soared inside him and he fiercely clung to his new theory. Maybe he wasn't a bad guy after all?

He stayed hidden in the tall, sweet-smelling grass and continued to watch the cop as the cop watched Sara's house. After awhile, looking seemingly satisfied, the cop left.

But Tom remained rooted to the same spot until his growling stomach urged him to return to Peppermint Creek Inn.

* * * * *

Bright sunshine streamed through the kitchen windows as the sun shot over the pine trees, cascading Tom in its late morning glow. Since he'd returned, his demeanor had changed.

His cheeks were rosy, his complexion healthier than she'd ever seen it and his appetite—

Sara smiled as he shoved his fourth fresh-baked, giant, luscious Widow McCloud biscuit drenched in golden butter and blueberry jelly into his mouth. He was on his third cup of pure black coffee. And he'd devoured a heaping plate of blueberry pancakes. He reminded her of a bear fattening himself up for winter hibernation.

"And all he did was watch the house?" she asked.

He nodded, his delicious-looking mouth working away at the biscuit.

God, he looked so good today. So handsome. So masculine. So sexy. A man she could so easily fall in love with.

The heavenly taste of coffee scalded her throat as she took an unexpectedly large gulp and almost choked, but managed to keep a straight face when Tom threw her a curious glance.

Love?

No way. Couldn't be.

Lust, maybe, but not love.

"You're staring."

Sara blinked. "What?"

His lips curled into a gorgeous smile. "I said, you're staring."

"At what?" she said dumbly. God, what was wrong with her all of a sudden. She couldn't even keep her eyes off him. Her face grew toasty. Just the sun streaming through the windows. That's all. Just the sun.

"At me!" Tom laughed heartily. "What's wrong with you this morning, Sara? You've been unusually quiet. You don't have to worry about Jeffries coming back. You said yourself he told you he was busy setting up search parties for the week. Why are you so— preoccupied?"

"Preoccupied?"

A quick concerned frown trashed his smile. "You're not sick are you?"

"No. No. Would I be hungry if I was sick?" Hungry in more ways than one. She should have made him leave. He'd be gone now, and she'd be snuggled away with all her work. No sexy man hanging around the house. No sexual cravings for him to make love to her. No problems.

But since he was still here, she might as well ask him the big, burning question she'd been dying to ask ever since she'd seen him sifting through the ruins. "You didn't find anything in the building that I should know about did you?"

His mouth halted in the middle of a chew.

"Could we hold off on that question until I've had another biscuit?"

"I can tell by your face, it's not good news. So let's have it now, Tom."

He shoved the last piece into his mouth and stood. "Okay, I'll be right back."

She waited for a few anxious minutes until he strolled back in with a lunch-size brown paper bag.

"You went grocery shopping?" she teased half-heartedly as she set her coffee mug down on the table with a slightly shaky hand. By the watery smile on his face, he wasn't too pleased at what he'd put into the bag.

"I went shopping, but not for groceries. Do you have some plastic wrap?"

"Sure."

A moment later Tom was ripping some clear wrap from the box Sara had given him. He placed a strip of wrap across an area of the table, free of any dishes. Then he wrapped some plastic around his hand and delved into the brown paper bag.

"You're not going to like what I've come up with." The serious tone of his voice had her heart thumping madly. She watched anxiously as he withdrew some green shards of glass and laid them one by one on the plastic wrap. Next, he pulled out what appeared to be a full green wine bottle with a yellow shoestring hanging out of the spout.

"What in the world is it?" Curiosity raked through her and she reached out to grab the bottle.

"Don't touch it," he warned. "It may still have fingerprints. It's highly unlikely, but you can't take any chances."

"What is it?"

"A homemade bomb."

Chapter Eight

ﺏ

Sara couldn't believe what she was hearing. "Did you say a bomb?"

He nodded and she leaned forward to stare more closely at the green wine bottle.

So innocent.

So deceiving.

It was filled with a liquid. A gray putty was stuffed into the mouth of the bottle. From the putty, sprouted a yellow plastic-looking string about six inches long, with a blackened end.

"There were more out there. This is the only one that wasn't broken. I checked four of the burned-out rooms. There were green glass fragments in all but one of them. And the one that didn't contain glass, I found this bottle. Right outside the building, under some debris, opposite to where a window would have been. My guess is whoever started the fire, broke the windows, placed the bottles just inside on the ledge, close to the curtains, lit the fuses and boom. Instant fire." He nodded to the wine bottle. "From the looks of it, the person lit this one and it went out before it could explode or somehow rolled along the window ledge, dropped outside the building and fizzled out. When was the fire? Three? Four months ago?"

"New Year's Eve," she whispered.

"About five months ago. It probably rolled into a snowdrift and disappeared. That's why the fire marshal missed it."

"We don't have a fire marshal. The fire department is on a volunteer basis around these parts."

Tom scowled. "Who was in charge of the investigation?"

"Justin and Sam."

Tom's eyes narrowed suspiciously. "Why am I not surprised. They're the ones who said it was arson?"

Sara nodded. "They found the empty jerry cans. They'd been removed from the barn."

"The gas from the jerry cans is most likely what the suspects used to fill the bottles. Don't you normally keep your barn door locked with all those supplies in there?"

"Yes, usually."

"Who else has access to the keys to the barn?"

"Practically everyone. All my summer crew. Family members. Whoever needs the keys to the barn and truck easily. The keys to the cottages and the inn are securely locked up in one of the upstairs rooms. But during open season, they're kept under close watch behind the lobby desk at the inn."

"So pretty much anyone coming in through the front door could have picked up the key during the open season, made a copy then put the key back before anyone was the wiser then came back in the winter, removed the jerry cans, used them." Tom's brow knotted thoughtfully for a moment then he asked, "Or a better scenario would be someone could have taken the key shortly before the fire. Did you by any chance have company that day? Or maybe earlier in the week?"

"Jo stayed for a few days around then. I can't think of anyone else."

"Are you sure? It was around New Year's. You must have had some holiday visitors dropping in around that time."

Sara shook her head slowly. "I don't— Oh, my God! Cran Simcoe dropped by. He's the town drunk. But it couldn't be him."

"Why not?"

"We never let him inside. He showed up drunk and Jo told him to take a hike."

Tom sighed. "Okay, so he's out of the picture. What about Jeffries and this Sam character?"

"Yes, they did drop in."

"And both were in the house? Unescorted?"

"Yes, of course. They're police officers. I trust them."

Tom shook his head in disbelief. "Why is it people automatically trust cops? They're human like the rest of us, Sara. They make mistakes, and some are corrupt, too." The statement was made without anger or hatred, but as if he were stating a plain fact.

His voice grew lower, gentler. "The nearest town is how far away?"

"Thirty minutes drive if you go the speed limit," Sara joked.

But Tom didn't smile. The look of seriousness gave Sara an uneasy feeling.

"You didn't notice anything odd that night? Strangers in the area? Footprints in the snow? Odd smells? Noises?"

"We called the fire crew the minute we saw—" Sara stopped mid-sentence as she suddenly realized something. "You know what? I heard something odd that night now that I think about it. I heard popping sounds. A couple of them. I was half-asleep and well—you know how it is when you're half-asleep, things just don't register."

"Jo never mentioned hearing anything?"

"No. She sleeps like a log, especially when she's here. She says it's the fresh northern air. She didn't come downstairs until I started yelling. That popping sound had woken me up. I wandered into the living room and that's when I saw a strange light flickering against the curtains. When I looked out, I saw the inn on fire. We called and the fire department and the crew were here pretty fast."

"How fast?"

"I'd guess maybe ten to fifteen minutes. I don't think they were following the speed limit though if that's where you're going."

Tom managed a thin smile. "What I'm getting at is how did these volunteer firemen get suited up so quickly and get to the station house and then here in ten to fifteen minutes from when you called if the town is thirty minutes away."

"Actually, I wasn't the first one who called the fire crew that night. Justin was cruising down the highway when he saw a suspicious-looking vehicle racing out of the road onto the highway.

When he came into the road, he saw the orange glow in the sky and called the fire department."

"How convenient," Tom whispered snidely under his breath. "Can I ask you a question about your husband's murder?"

Sara bit her lip and nodded.

"How did you get help for yourself that day?"

"Thankfully Sam and Justin were on their usual rounds and found me."

"Did they find you before or after you heard the gunshot?"

Sara's mouth dropped open in shock at the horrible question.

Tom frowned and placed a calming hand on hers.

His delicate, caring touch didn't feel one bit like Justin's cold, clammy hand. His hand felt warm and soothing, and Sara suddenly felt safe.

"I'm not sure. Things are jumbled like I mentioned."

"I'm sorry." He attempted a weak smile. "I shouldn't be so callous. It's just that someone murdered your husband and bombed your inn, and both times the cops were here in the nick of time to help you out. I just find everything a little too convenient."

"I can see why you may want to suspect them. They probably know how to make bombs. But why would policemen want to bomb my place and kill my husband?"

"It might not even be them. Practically anyone can make a bomb. The ingredients are in our households, in our stores, on the Internet. Everywhere. A bottle, a fuse, gas, a little putty. It's so simple a three-year-old can make one given the instructions." He threw her such a serious business-like look—it suddenly made her think he was some sort of professional himself.

"As to why they would want you out of here, I don't know. It's not like you have any competition out here. There has to be another reason. We just have to find it."

Sara shook her head slowly. "You're way off on this Tom. Way off."

"You said Jeffries got suspicious and called the fire department. How did he know to call them? Your place is situated in a valley surrounded by high hills and so far off the beaten track. How could he see the smoke? Or flames? Or a glow when there are so many trees along the road hiding everything from view? It just isn't possible."

As Tom spoke, Sara began to realize he was right. Everything did seem too convenient. "Okay then, if Justin set the fire why would he call the fire department to put it out?"

Tom shrugged. The question had apparently caught him off guard. "Good question."

"And why would they not kill me after killing my husband if they wanted this place so bad?"

Tom chuckled. "Another good question. Maybe you're right. Maybe I am way off base. Oh, and before I forget, I checked out the office."

Sara swallowed at the chunk clogging up her throat. "Did you—find anything?"

"I have a theory. When you saw the flash and movement at the window, the lights and phone went dead soon after, right?"

"That's right."

"The window sill is pretty wide. It could easily be used to hoist someone up allowing them to climb onto the sill to disconnect the line to the phone. The line to the lights is just a reach away."

Sara shuddered.

"Did the cops mention anything about the wiring?"

"No."

"Then if my theory is right, whoever disconnected the wires, reconnected them either before or during an investigation."

Sara's head spun. "You mean the murderer might have hung around. He could have been watching me as I was miscarrying. God, that's sick."

"Whoever shot your husband is sick, and you're in danger out here all alone if he's not caught. And Sara...the flash in the window could have been the refection off someone's belt buckle or someone's glasses. Maybe even Jeffries' glasses."

Sara couldn't say a word as she let the information absorb into her mind. Tom leaned forward in his chair and said softly, "I'm sorry but like I said it's only a theory. It might not be him. Could have been anything flashing. A knife. A button. It's just that this morning when I saw the flash on the hill alerting me to his presence, I just kind of thought of what you'd said about seeing a flash in the window."

Sara nodded, trying hard to still the chills ripping through her. The last person she would ever think would harm Jack was Justin. They were best friends. "I understand, but I still can't believe Justin could do something so sinister." She focused her attention back to the green glass fragments and the wine bottle.

"What do we do with all this stuff now?"

Tom removed his hand from hers, grabbed his mug of coffee and took a thoughtful sip before answering. "We'll give this evidence to Jo and Garry."

"What do we do until then?"

"We wait and see if anymore shadows turn up."

* * * * *

Three days later Tom yawned as he flopped wearily onto a comfortable living room armchair. It had been a tough day and his muscles screamed for relief. Thankfully, the days had passed without any more unexpected visitors and he'd spent most of his time working alone while Sara filled more orders for her peppermint business.

He'd constantly looked over his shoulder as he tackled the various odd jobs of reshingling leaking roofs on a couple of old cabins, doing some plumbing, repairing the porch, rebracing the front wheelchair ramp and replacing the glass in the kitchen window.

He'd been surprised to find everything he needed in the workshop inside the barn. Sara's husband Jack had been a planner. He'd stocked his workshop with everything imaginable.

From kegs of roofing nails, shingles, glass panes, right down to the exact size of washers fitting a bathroom tap. And when he'd bought something, he'd bought it in bulk, taking advantage of quantity discounts.

Tom had been here more than a week and because the phones were still out, there'd been no word from the two people Sara said might be able to help him. He was beginning to wonder if they'd ever be able to return Sara's calls. Not that he was in a hurry to find out about his true identity.

Far from it.

The intense physical labor during the day seemed to be exactly what he needed to keep his sexual urges about Sara in check. By the time he ate supper he was too pooped to pursue her the way he wanted.

Nights, however, were another story.

There were dreams. Lots of them. Some of ripped him awake and he'd lie in bed drenched in a chasm of fear and cold sweat, torturing himself, racking his brains, trying to remember what the dreams involved. Then there were dreams he remembered, erotic dreams of Sara that left his body heated with carnal desires, his groin hard and aching and demanding satisfaction from her.

God, did she know what effect she had on him? Did she know every time she looked at him with those luscious chocolate eyes, his cock remembered how perfectly her mouth had slid over his shaft? Or how his mouth watered at the thought of wanting to suck the warm pleasure cream from her body again?

She'd cast a spell over him the moment he'd first seen her, and he didn't have the foggiest clue as to how to remove it.

Quite frankly, he didn't want to remove it.

If only he didn't have this awful black cloud hanging over his head. He wouldn't hesitate to be near her. To kiss her. Make love to her. But until everything was cleared up and he was a free man, all he could do was think about any excuse to stay away from her.

"The tea'll be ready in a minute. Do you want some cake with it?" Sara called from the kitchen.

"Sure," he answered back.

His weary gaze wandered around the rustic living room. He never got enough of looking around the place, rugged yet romantic, cozy and comfortable. A place where a man could kick off his shoes and relax after a hard day working outside.

Most of the wood furnishings were made of knotty pine by Sara's late husband Jack. The pine blended warmly with the cinnamon brown paneled walls. Bright colorful Navajo blankets with rich looking paisley were draped casually over the stair railing and the sofas, adding cheer throughout the room.

Twig birdhouses, wicker fishing baskets overflowing with a variety of wild flowers and more of those tin kettles were strewn casually here and there. Snowshoes, canoe paddles and fishing rods hung on the walls. A very cozy outfit, indeed.

Tom yawned again.

Boy, was he ever tired tonight. He'd spent the entire day, chain saw in hand, walking the various hiking trails, clearing debris and fallen timber off the pathways.

He groaned, and leaned over to throw another log on the dying fire, the ache in his back signaling a warning to take it easy when from the corner of his eye, he spotted a thick book, a photo album actually. It was stuffed under a pile of magazines on a twig table. He pried it out and flipped it open to a picture.

Sara had been slightly plump. A tomboy. Short surf cut. Auburn curls tangled warmly about her heart-shaped face. And so goddamn cute.

Her husband Jack had been a tall man with wheat blond hair and a droopy, bushy mustache. A towering good-looking man who'd dwarfed over Sara.

And the way they looked at each other… So much love in their eyes. Tom found himself wishing Sara would look at him in much the same way.

He continued to leaf through the pages at a leisurely pace, thoroughly enjoying the photographs of Sara and her husband doing various chores around the inn. Pictures of a vacation in Niagara Falls. And a few of Sara paintings. She always looked so cheerful.

So happy. So in love.

He flipped to another page. A family portrait. Of five people. Three women and two men. Standing in front of the log house. There was Sara and her husband Jack. An attractive woman who looked a lot like Sara. Must be Jo, Sara's sister, the private investigator. Beside Jo stood a striking elderly woman, who Tom guessed as Sara's mother-in-law and also an elderly man sitting in a wheelchair. Garry? The father-in-law. That accounted for the wheelchair ramp out front.

"Why you look like the hounds of hell are at your heels?" The gruff voice came out of nowhere crashing into Tom like a torpedo. Before he could orient himself as to where the voice was coming from, violent bursts of flashing lights blinded him.

"You're losing your touch, little buddy!" It was the same man's voice and Tom tried fiercely to see who was yelling at him. But there were only the white lights, pain in his temples and the man's gruff voice.

The flashes of light stopped as abruptly as they started, leaving him shaken to the core. He let the photo album slide to the floor. The room tilted awkwardly. A sick feeling knotted his stomach, twisting hard.

Oh, shit!

More visions were coming!

Burying his suddenly fragmenting head in his hands, he gasped as another volley of bright searing lights slammed into him.

He sat inside one of the numerous circus tents, sitting opposite the toothless old gypsy woman. He tried to read her leathered-up face as she lay out the tarot cards, but it remained expressionless. A few months ago, he would have laughed at anyone who suggested he come here and see a physic or card reader, but here he sat. Eager. Desperate. Hopeful.

The old lady turned over the last card.

A deep frown burrowed across her face. She shook her head.

He shuddered. His heart sank.

A skeleton card lay on the table.

Death called.

The vision dissipated and before he was able to catch his breath, another volley of white flashing lights crashed into him almost knocking him sideways.

More pain.

More voices.

Dammit! It was happening again!

* * * * *

"Here's your tea and cake," Sara called as she entered the living room carrying a tray, stopping abruptly when she discovered the room was empty.

A slight trace of fear slipped around her.

"Tom?"

No answer.

Maybe he'd gone off to bed. He'd looked beat when he'd come in for supper. But he wouldn't go off without saying goodnight, would he?

"Tom?" she called a little louder. Fright edged sharply into her soul.

"Out here."

As soon as she stepped onto the side veranda, she knew something was wrong. He stood at the railing, his body tense as a coiled spring—his fingers kneading his right temple. A bottle of aspirin sat on the porch swing. A half-full glass of water shook crazily in his hand.

"Are you—?"

"I'm okay," he said shakily as he turned slightly toward her.

There was something in the dismal look of his eyes that frightened her. They were filled with pain. Tremendous pain. He'd lost someone very near and dear to his heart.

"You've remembered something."

"It's nothing," he muttered irritably and returned his attention to the darkening sky.

Lightning flickered crazily over the trees.

Sara jolted. Her heart began to pound wildly.

"Let's go inside."

"I'll tell you what I've remembered, if you'll stay out here for a couple of minutes. You can leave any time after that."

She cast a nervous glance at the almost black sky. The uneasiness crept up a notch. A fist of fear threatened to cut off her air supply.

"The only way you'll get over your fear of storms is by confronting it and going through it." His voice sounded so warm, so confident.

Sara shook her head and retreated a step. "I just want to go inside."

"Come closer," he encouraged gently.

The look of tenderness in his emerald eyes drew her to him like a bear to honey. He reached out and pried the tray from her grasp, placing it on the nearby porch swing. Her hands automatically clenched into tight fists at her sides. A lonesome cry from a loon out on the lake startled her. Her insides churned violently with the bubbling fear.

When Tom reached out, she didn't hesitate a second before flying into the safety of his arms. His hand slid around to the small of her back, caressing her there. It felt so wonderful.

Instinctively, she pressed her head against his strong muscular chest and listened to his heart beating. The sound was a delicious, steady, soothing rhythm and for the first time in a long time, she felt truly safe.

"It's okay," he whispered gently. "I'm with you."

Another bolt of lightning zipped across the velvety black night. This time, Sara didn't jump in fright. His face was mere inches from hers and the intense look in his eyes fascinated her.

There was need. Hunger. Caring.

He stood so close. It would be too easy to wrap her arms around his neck, pull his face downward to hers, to kiss those enchanting lips. He smelled so intoxicating, so masculine. It took all the strength she could muster to break the spell.

"What do you remember?"

He took a deep breath and stiffened against her.

"Mom." The word came out in a low rush, a quietly whispered anxious sigh. "I remember my mother. How the cancer was eating away at her. She was suffering so much. After a while the doctors told us they couldn't do anything more. She wanted to go home to die, and so we took her home."

"Oh, God," Sara closed her eyes for a moment, absorbing the pain of Tom's words.

When she opened them again, he was staring straight into her eyes. Searching for something. Understanding? A fellow comrade? Someone to share his grief?

"Our house smelled of death. Little by little, day by day she got worse. Begging us to put her out of her misery. We went nuts trying to find help for her. We tried everything. I even went to see some old gypsy card reader to get some help. She came up with the death card."

He was shaking so bad.

Sara reached out and touched his face. "I'm so sorry. It's so hard to lose someone you love."

The first growl of the oncoming storm cascaded over the surrounding hills. Sara barely heard it.

"'Time heals the wound of loss' my mom used to say," Tom whispered in a strangled voice. She felt his warm breath caress her cheek. "You never forget. You grieve. It's a part of the healing process. But you never forget."

"How'd you get through it?"

He took a deep wobbly breath and let it out slowly. His jaw clenched tightly for a moment before answering.

"It was tough. For all of us. But I focused on my belief that there is a higher power out there, a great designer. Someone who knows what they are doing and why. Mom went that way for a reason. I haven't figured it out yet. Maybe I'm being naive for even trying. I kept repeating to myself over and over again that I'm going to get through this. I'm going to make it. Then one day I realized I had."

"I almost didn't make it," Sara whispered.

"I kind of got that feeling." He reached up, his gentle callused fingers brushing away the fresh tears slipping from her eyes. "There's a haunted sadness in your eyes. Can you tell me about it?"

Sara hesitated a moment, feeling uncertain and afraid. She'd never told anyone. Not even her closest confidant, her sister Jo. Not a single soul. She'd felt—well, embarrassed for trying to take the easy way out.

"It happened a few weeks after they died. Just after Christmas," Sara began. "It was the first time I'd been left alone. Mom and Dad had gone back home. Garry needed to get away. His heart was breaking. He'd lost his wife, his only son, only grandchildren and he was losing me, too. His brother managed to talk him into visiting him for awhile in New York City.

"Jessie, my brother, bless his heart, wanted to sell his apple farm business to stay and take care of me. But I put up a good front. I told everyone I was fine. But Jo, she seemed to feel I wasn't doing so well. I couldn't get rid of her. No matter how hard I tried. Kicking, screaming, crying. She was always there, hovering around me. It was almost as if she sensed what I wanted to do…"

Sara checked if the door was unlocked then stole into Jocelyn's bedroom. She'd always felt safe and secure in Jo's room. Maybe because of all the chats they had together when she came for visits.

Or maybe it was the room itself and the way Jo had decorated it. Frilly white laces. Soothing tones of forest green and buttery warm yellow. So comforting. So safe.

But today she didn't feel safe or secure. She felt nothing but the deep hollow emptiness. A black hole stretching endlessly.

Her therapist told her she was depressed. If this was depression, they could have it. She had nothing to live for anymore. Her family was gone. Wiped out. All she wanted was to be with them.

Sara edged to the closet where Jo kept it. After a couple of minutes of frantic searching, she found it hidden way in the back. Her sister had moved it.

Jo suspected. They all suspected.

Her fingers fell on the smooth wooden box on the top shelf. With suddenly trembling hands, she slowly removed the item from the closet and sat down on the bed. She stared at the box for a long time, then what seemed an eternity later she opened it and delicately withdrew the gun. It was cold and heavier than she remembered.

Years ago, Jo had shown her how to load it, how to clean it and how to fire it. But Sara hadn't been interested in shooting the thing, much to the dismay of her little sister who believed every woman should learn to defend herself any way they could. Just in case.

Sara felt oddly removed from everything in her life now. The past weeks had been a horrible ordeal. Burying her husband, her babies and her mother-in-law.

On top of that, all the curious stares, hand pointing and hurried whispers from the people in town. For the past two weeks, she'd been preparing herself for this day. Jo rarely left her alone. It was as if she sensed Sara would snap at any minute.

But every Monday morning, Jo left for town to pick up the cinnamon-covered donuts that Widow McCloud at the general store made for Monday Special. Jo loved her donuts. How many times had Sara been envious of her little sister? She ate so many donuts and yet never gained a pound. But when Sara ate more than one in a sitting, her stomach seemed to grow its own donut.

But Sara didn't worry about her own weight anymore. No family. No appetite. No problems.

She wondered how Jo would react when she discovered her body. She knew Jo would feel guilty for some time. After all, Jo had her own demons to deal with. But she'd come through and gone on with her life.

Sara wished she'd been able to do the same. But it just hurt too much.

She thought about her father-in-law Garry and how he'd react. Or her parents. Oh, God, she couldn't deal with it. Not now. Not when she was so close.

In the end, everyone would be relieved of her. She'd been a burden to them all. Altered their lives to baby-sit her just because she hadn't been able to handle it.

Yes, she liked Jo's room. So soothing. So safe.

It was the perfect place to do it.

Hesitantly, Sara's trembling fingers picked up the bullet she needed for the job. She loaded the gun. She thought of Jack. The twins. Of how it should have been.

She wanted her final thoughts to be of them.

She cocked the gun.

The sound pierced through the quiet morning like a gunshot and she jumped at the harsh noise. Just a matter of seconds and it would all be over.

She would join them soon. They'd be the big happy family just like they'd always planned.

She wondered if she would have the guts to do it. She sat there looking out the window. Everything was covered in sparkling white snow. The trees, the buildings, the parking lot. It looked as if someone had dumped icing sugar on everything. She knew it should look pretty but it didn't. Nothing did.

She imagined Jack, rolling a giant snowball through the drifts. Their two-year-old twins following him. Both bundled up in winter gear to ward off the winter weather, their faces red from the cold, eagerly watching what their dad was up to. And when Jack put the smaller snowball on top of the two other giant snowballs and placed his own hat and scarf around the makeshift snowman, the children laughed. The sweet sound like crystal chimes.

She could hear her children's laughter so clearly.

She wanted to join them. To be happy with them. Jack's laughter boomed with her children's.

I'm coming, my darlings. I'm coming.

She lifted the gun, oh so slowly.

Jack's laughter boomed outside. The children giggled excitedly.

Her family was waiting for her. She pressed the cold smooth barrel of the gun until it kissed her left temple.

Her finger tightened on the trigger.

Suddenly Jack's voice interrupted her thoughts. "You promised me, Sara. You promised."

"Jack?"

Sara swung around, her eyes wide fully expecting to see her husband standing in the open bedroom doorway.

No one was there.

For a moment, she thought she'd pulled the trigger and had been reunited with her family.

But she was alone. Desperately alone.

And then she realized it wasn't true. She wasn't alone. Jack had been here for her. She'd heard his voice. He'd been here all the time. She should have felt relieved at the realization, but she wasn't. He'd made her feel guilty, guilty for not honoring her promise to him.

Then she knew. It wasn't time to go to them. Something waited for her. It could be around the next corner. The next day. Or further down the line. Something was out there.

A burning curiosity began to take hold. She wondered what Jack had in store for her. Why else had he come into her life at such a bleak period, but to offer hope?

"The promise you made to him to find someone else." Tom's hushed voice cut through her memory.

Sara closed her eyes and bit her lower lip to prevent herself from crying. His arms tightened around her, comforting her.

"And from then on you were on the run. Trying to escape the promise you'd made to him. Keeping the pain of his loss from grabbing hold of you. Trying not to remember how your family died. And when you finally allowed them into your heart, you saw them, experienced your children's laughter, heard Jack's voice. Is it any wonder Jack, the man who loved you so dearly, who probably loved you more than his own life would want nothing more than for you to live? Would want your happiness?"

His words found their way into her heart and Sara felt her spirits lifting. She cocked an inquiring eyebrow at him.

"Are you sure you're not a psychiatrist?"

Tom laughed. "I still may not know who or what I am, but I'm definitely not a shrink." His voice suddenly grew serious. "I guess it's what I learned from my mom. She tried to teach us. To prepare us a little on how to deal with death and life. Take it as it comes, the good with the bad."

"Us?"

"No names. But I know I have two younger brothers. A dad. I can't see their faces, but I know they're out there. It's just feelings I have. Just like things I remember Mom teaching us. About healing rituals. Something that might be able to help you."

Sara frowned. "Rituals?"

"Remember the old saying something old, something new. Something borrowed, something blue."

Sara nodded. "A wedding ritual, a symbol of transition. When a woman gets married, she wears something old, to remind her of her past, of what she's leaving behind. And she also wears something new, a symbol for her future. So you're saying I should find something to symbolize my past, my losses. Create a reminder of what I've lost."

Tom nodded. "Then you have a healing ritual. When you enact a ritual of your loss—bury it, destroy it, give it away or show some way it is no longer a part of your life."

"You make it sound so easy."

He frowned and squeezed her tighter against him. "Believe me. It isn't."

Suddenly she felt better. Better than she'd felt in a long time. Realization and understanding wrapped around her like a newfound, long-lost friend. "And that's why people attend memorial services and visit gravesites of their loved ones. To obtain some sort of closure."

A hint of a smile entered his voice. "And why societies build memorials in an effort to heal from social traumas—whether it's for thousands of people lost in a war or for one person who meant so much. Remember though," he cautioned. "You can't fix everything in a split second. It's sort of an experience in the larger process of recovery. You have to examine and process your trauma, mourn your losses, deal with the symptoms, then rebuild your damaged self and finally rejoin society."

"Are you sure you're not a shrink?"

Tom chuckled. "I don't think so. But you know what?"

"What?"

"Looks like the headache is gone. What do you say we go in, sit by the fire and have our tea and cake?"

"You're on."

Before Sara could make a move, Tom's entire body coiled with tension, his hand tightened painfully around her waist and suddenly Sara became aware of everything around her.

The cool breeze bristling against her face. The sweet smell of the oncoming rain. The unmistakable feeling they were being watched.

Before she could voice her suspicion, he grabbed her shoulders and shoved her. Hard. She crashed stomach first onto the wooden planked floor, her breath escaping in a wild rush, his weight crushing her against the veranda as he flew on top of her. Much the same way as the first night they'd met.

A split second later she screamed as a gunshot disintegrated the overhead porch light, showering glass over both of them.

Chapter Nine

ᏸᎧ

"Sweetness?" Tom hissed anxiously.

"I'm fine. Who do you think it is?" Sara shook violently as she peered through the veranda slats.

"Stay down!" Came his harsh reply as he rolled off her. "Get inside. Lock all the doors."

Before she could stop him from blindly taking off and stumbling recklessly into extreme danger, he'd slipped into the heavy cloak of darkness.

* * * * *

Though Tom's eyes were still unaccustomed to the sudden darkness, he dashed headlong through the night. Crouching low, legs and arms pumping viciously, he bolted in the general direction of where he figured the shot had come from. The road.

Someone had shot out the porch light. On purpose? Or had someone been aiming too high and missed. The gunshot had triggered the unwelcome headache and more visions. He'd lain on the veranda for a few precious seconds. Totally useless. Not knowing where he was. Engulfed by memories.

He'd snapped out of it long enough to make sure Sara was safe. And now he ran through the night like a madman. Visions sucker punching him all the way.

One by one, the blows fell.

Crimson.

Blood seeping.

Shouting.

Glass breaking.

A gunshot.

It sure as hell made concentrating on being careful pretty difficult.

Up ahead he could hear someone running along the road. Tom's legs pumped harder. Adrenaline rushed like wildfire through his veins. Around the next bend lightning flashed and he spotted the intruder attempting to climb into a pickup truck.

Instantly Tom was airborne. He crashed into the tall, chubby figure. A surprised gasp escaped the assailant's lips as they both slammed against the open truck door with violent force. Tom grabbed the man's shoulders and spun him around, the overpowering smell of whiskey made him wince.

Raising his arm, he was quite ready to smash his fist into the man's face when he halted midair. He'd been expecting Justin Jeffries. This was a man he'd never seen before. A somewhat rumpled looking fellow about Tom's own age who scrunched up his face like a prune, waiting for Tom's fist to hit.

Instead, Tom grabbed the man by his shirt collar with both hands. "Why are you shooting at us? Who hired you?"

"Hired me?" There was genuine surprise in his slurred voice. "Are you kidding? C'mon. Quit rough housing me, you're gonna ruin my threads."

Tom's grip tightened and he shook the man hard. "I'm going to ruin more than your threads if you don't answer me!"

"I thought you were Jeffries!" he blurted fearfully.

Tom was suddenly taken aback at the man's confession. "Jeffries?"

"The cop. I was trying to scare him off."

"Why?"

"Keep him away from you and—Sara."

Tom didn't know why, but he believed this drunkard. There were two types of people who always told the truth. Kids and drunks. And by golly this man was sauced.

Tom let him go and the drunk immediately reached out to grab the truck door in an effort to keep standing. He figured it was more from the booze than from Tom's surprise attack on him.

"Who are you anyway?" the drunk asked curiously.

"Never mind who I am. Who are you?"

"Cran Simcoe. You gonna turn me in?"

"Only if you don't answer my questions."

The man visibly shrunk. "What do you want to know?"

"For one, why do you want to shoot at Jeffries?"

"Because—" The drunkard hesitated. "You sure you won't turn me in?"

"Just answer my questions," Tom replied firmly.

"Sara's had enough trouble lately, she don't need his kind around her."

"What kind is that?"

"Trouble is all. Heaps of it."

"Why do you think he's trouble?"

The drunk shrugged. "He just is."

"C'mon. You must have a reason. You didn't shoot at me thinking it was him without a reason. So spill your guts."

The man remained silent as he studied Tom, probably wondering if he could trust him. He decided to try another approach to get an answer out of him.

"Do you smoke?"

"I don't have any cigs if you're trying to bum one off me."

"Answer me." Tom growled. He made a threatening step toward Cran Simcoe.

"Sure I smoke. Cigarettes. Cigars. Pipe. Anything I can bum off someone."

"You've been here before. You were the one smoking." It was a statement not a question. The man had the same short dumpy profile as the one he'd seen in the window the other day when he'd woken up.

The man didn't answer, but Tom could tell by the way his face grimaced he realized Tom knew the truth.

"You saw me in Sara's bedroom that one day. So why'd you think I was Jeffries tonight? Wouldn't it be logical I'd be with her on the porch?"

"Heard talk," Cran said simply.

Tom sighed quietly. Now he was finally getting somewhere.

"Talk?"

"I was in jail a few days ago on a disturbance charge. Heard Jeffries talking on the phone. Said he was keeping an eye on Sara's place for this person on the phone as best he could. But the guy this person was looking for hadn't showed up yet. I'm figuring you're the guy Jeffries is talking about."

"Why didn't you tell Jeffries about me?"

The man got edgy, angry. "Why the hell should I? Like I said —"

Tom chuckled and gave the man a settling pat on the shoulder.

"I know you don't like him." He was getting the feeling he had an ally in this drunk. Somehow, it felt rather comforting.

"Are you the one who's been lurking around here the past couple of years vandalizing Sara's place?"

Lightning flashed at that moment and Tom saw the look of horror on the man's face.

"I've been keeping an eye on the place not wrecking it." The man was truly insulted.

"So you've taken it upon yourself to be her protector."

"Her husband was a good buddy of mine. Got the booze out from under me." His voice grew hard. "Then his old partner shows up and Jack didn't help me out anymore. He kind of got sidetracked with his old buddy."

Tom's eyes narrowed suspiciously. "What old partner?"

"Jeffries of course. Don't you know anything?"

Apparently not. It was something Sara had neglected to tell him.

The drunk's voice grew angrier and louder as it sliced through the damp night air. "Then some low-life scum of the earth murdered Jack. I figured I owed him for helping me out. Figured I could repay him by looking out for his widow. Drop in once in a while, since the cops aren't doing their job, letting the hooligans getting away with bothering Sara all the time."

"You ever see who's doing all the damage?"

Cran shook his head. "Na. Whoever's doing it is good."

"What makes you think that?"

"They always do it when she's not around. But me? I'm not privy to when she's not around. Me and her don't get along much. She doesn't like it when I've been drinking."

"I find it hard to believe Sara can't get along with anyone."

The man merely shrugged in answer. "The way I figure, someone's got the inside scoop as to where she's going to be and then comes in, does the job and gets out."

"So Jeffries and Sara's husband had been partners in the NYPD?" Tom mulled over this new bit of information. Partners depended on each other. Shared a deep bond. Trusted each other. Saved each other's lives. Killed for each other. Maybe even killed each other.

The man weaved dangerously. "That's what I just said isn't it?"

A crack of thunder ripped through the air and thick drops of rain began to fall, forcing Tom to think about getting to shelter soon.

"You're welcome to spend the night, Simcoe. Wait out the storm. Maybe dry out. After all you owe it to Jack and yourself to stay on the wagon."

He didn't want this guy driving around in his condition. Besides, it would be better if the man stayed close by and he could keep an eye on him. After all, he was the only other person who knew Tom was staying here at the inn. He hadn't said anything to Jeffries yet, but if the man got some more whiskey in him it may loosen his tongue enough to sign Tom's and Sara's death warrants.

"Naw," The man swayed again and lifted his arm in a parting wave. "Wouldn't want to cramp your style."

Cran let his arm drop and began to clamber into his truck. Tom was about to protest when the drunk suddenly swayed dangerously and began to fall backward.

Catching him quickly, the guy had passed out cold. He shivered at a sudden thought. Luckily the man had passed out now and not behind the wheel of his truck out on the highway, possibly killing himself or worse, someone else.

He grabbed Simcoe's keys where he'd dropped them on the seat and pocketed them. Lifting the man, he threw the drunk across the bench seat, and locked him in. He'd tack the keys to the front door of Sara's house tonight so when Cran Simcoe awoke with a hangover and came looking for them, he'd find them easy enough.

Cold rain ran down Tom's back in rivulets and his teeth chattered uncontrollably when he climbed up the wheelchair ramp and stepped onto the porch out of the cold downpour. Everything was dark, except for the occasional streaks of lightning.

"Sara," he called as his hand reached out to open the screen door. "It's me. I'm back."

No answer.

A tingle of fear slithered through him.

Shit! Where was she? He cursed out loud as anger roared through him for being stupid and leaving Sara all alone here after the gunshot.

He jumped when a few feet away the porch swing creaked in the darkness as if someone's weight shifted. In one terrifying instant he thought another intruder was in the midst, his arms came up ready to defend himself when her icy voice curled out of the darkness.

"Did you have a nice time?"

Her anger barely put a dent in the overwhelming relief of finding her okay.

"I thought I told you to get inside!"

He clammed up when lightning blistered across the stormy sky. Sara didn't wince at the sight as she stared at him coldly. She looked really ticked off.

He threw her a sheepish look. "I'm sorry for taking off like that. I didn't think—"

"No!" she snapped. "You didn't think. You didn't think at all."

He winced at her angry tone.

"This is twice you took off on me, heading straight into danger. Don't you know you could have been killed? Have you so little regard for your own life?"

"My life?" He thought she'd be upset with him because he'd left her alone and in danger.

"Yes, your life. Since you don't care a rat's ass about you, why should I?" She abruptly stood. "I'm going to bed. Finish your tea."

She was inside the house, the door slamming shut behind her before he could get a chance to explain about Cran Simcoe being her shadow.

"Great," Tom muttered to himself as he picked up the cold cup of peppermint tea sitting on the tray. "Just great."

Taking a huge gulp of the liquid, he shivered involuntarily as the icy chills sliced through him.

Suddenly blinding flashes of light slammed into him. He fought the urge to scream.

He couldn't scare Sara. Couldn't let her see him like this.

Blindly he collapsed on the porch swing, buried his head deep into the soft cushions desperately fighting the pain ripping through his brains as the visions came forth.

Crimson.

Shouts.

Shattering glass.

A gunshot.

Blood gushing and gushing and gushing.

* * * * *

New York City...

Jocelyn Brady couldn't wait to get the news she'd just gotten to Garry. She knocked quickly and waited for his reply before entering the adjoining hotel room. She found him staring through the rain-soaked window into the dark abyss beyond, a severe frown working away at his wrinkled face.

Her heart went out to him. Garry had been eagerly waiting for his brother to get some sort of business out of the way so they could go on their annual fishing trip down in Florida, but instead tragedy had struck.

Garry's brother was now dead and Garry was hell-bent on avenging his brother's death.

"Your sister's been trying to get a hold of me," he said as she entered.

"Sara? Is she all right?" She didn't like the concerned look he tossed her way. He was always worrying about Sara living alone in Northern Canada, especially since what had happened to his son Jack and then Peppermint Creek Inn burning down this past winter.

"I don't know. A buddy of mine called from NYPD, said she left a message with him a few days ago. He didn't tell her about Robin. Thought it might be better coming from me. He had to leave town in a hurry and had forgotten to pass along the message, so I just got it today when he returned. He said she wanted me to call her. She also left a message on my home answering machine. Said it was important. She sounded…stressed. I tried calling her, but apparently the phone lines are down."

Jo couldn't help but feel a tinge of anxiety rip through her. "What do you mean she sounded stressed?"

"I don't know. Something in her voice…she just didn't sound right."

Shit! She was definitely buying her sister a cell phone for her birthday. If only to prevent herself from worrying silly every time she couldn't get a hold of her because of those damned phone lines going down all the time.

"Okay, I'll phone my parents later on and see if they've heard anything and then I'll call her myself, too. But in the meantime I've got something for you, Gar." Jo quickly withdrew a notepad paper from her pocket.

"I asked a friend of mine who works with the FBI to run a computer check on all the pertinent information in the suspect's file. Y'know social security number, medical insurance number, stuff like that. She pulled in some favors and one of her contacts gave her a phone number to call and to use the name I've written on the paper."

"You try the number yet?" Garry asked.

"Not yet. I figured you'd like to do the honors."

"You know me so well, Jo. Let's give it a try shall we?" Garry wheeled over to the phone and Jo handed him the slip of paper with the information.

Garry cocked an eyebrow as he scanned the number. "A Washington DC number?"

"Thought it would pique your interest." Jo slipped off her violet raincoat and sat down on his bed, legs crossed Indian style.

Garry's weathered face broke into a smile as he picked up the phone and punched in the phone number. He nodded his head to indicate someone had picked up the line on the other end.

He gave his name and frowned. Instantly Jo knew something was wrong. Maybe her friend had goofed and given her the wrong information.

"Isn't this the uh—" He scanned the sheet for the name her FBI confidant had given her "—the Turdus residence?" Garry's hand tightened around the receiver and he hissed desperately. "Hello? Hello? Are you there?"

He threw Jo a questioning glance and she leaned forward anxiously watching the tiny beads of sweat pop across his forehead. Obviously she'd gotten Garry's hopes up to a frightfully high level. She hadn't meant to though, she'd only wanted him to feel better.

Jo jumped as Garry slammed down the phone.

"What happened?"

"A woman answered really casual-like. The minute I mentioned my name, the tone in her voice changed. She got all flustered, recovered quickly then told me I had the wrong number and hung up." His eyes narrowed suspiciously. "She's hiding something, Jo. I got the feeling she knew who I was."

He made a grab for the phone. "I'm going to get a trace and call back that number."

"Hold on, Gar." She placed her hand over his weathered one to stop him. "A trace will take too long. Let me try first."

Reluctantly Garry gave up the phone to Jo. "All right, maybe you'll have better luck."

Jo dialed.

She cleared her throat then pointed a finger in the air to indicate someone had picked up.

"Hello, My name is Jo Brady. I'm a private investigator looking into the murder of Detective Robin Smith. The FBI gave me your number along with the contact name Turdus."

The woman on the other line paused a moment before answering in the same casual tone she'd said "hello" in. "I'm sorry but you have the wrong number, Miss Brady." Before the woman could hang up Jo replied in an angry tone. "If you don't help me out here, I'm heading straight to the *New York Times* and telling them everything I know and believe me it's plenty. They'll be breathing down your neck faster than you can say —"

"Take it easy, lady, please."

"Don't tell me to take it easy!" Jo shot back. "A friend of mine has been murdered and you've got answers. Do we exchange or do I go to the press?"

Jo could hear the woman's anxious breathing. She sensed she had her confused and scared. She needed to attack before the woman had a chance to think straight.

"Don't keep me waiting, lady." Jo barked, fully enjoying the brilliant smile tipping Garry's mustache into the air. "I demand to speak to your superior. Now!"

There was a muffled sound as if the woman held her hand over the receiver and was saying something to someone. Then the woman came back on the line, her voice sweet and professional. "One moment please. I'll put you through."

"She's putting me through," Jo whispered to Garry who now was anxiously wringing his hands in his lap. She sat straight up as another woman's voice spoke. "Good afternoon, Miss Brady. How may I help you today?" Instinctively Jo knew she'd hit the right person. This woman's voice held authority and confidence.

"You can start by talking to me face-to-face and not hiding behind a phone." She saw Garry grimace and she held her breath.

Maybe she shouldn't have demanded a face–to-face meeting. Maybe she'd blown it. Maybe—

"All right," the woman sighed in obvious surrender.

Jo blinked not quite believing the answer. The woman had agreed. Just like that. Why?

"Miss Brady? Are you still on the line?"

"Y-yes. Tonight. A public place."

"I'm sorry that cannot be possible. I'm too far away from your location. I'll have to fly in to a secure area and the secure area is a bit too far from where you are to get to at a safe hour."

Jo's mouth dropped open. How did the woman know where Jo was staying? "Tomorrow morning would be more convenient to meet. You may bring Mr. Smith along as an escort, but I will not be able to reveal my identity to either of you. Any information I supply will be entirely anonymously. Is that understood?"

Jo shook her head in disbelief. The woman knew she was with Garry. Did they have the lines tapped? Call display? Or were they watching her?

Her gaze flew to look out the window. She could see nothing but a black curtain of rain. She returned her attention to the woman. "Um…yes that would be acceptable."

Jo made a mad grab for a pen and paper.

"This is a secure line, Miss Brady. The address I'm about to give you is highly confidential. Please don't leave a paper trail."

Jo's hand stopped in midair. Her eyes grew wide with surprise. Once again her gaze flew to the window and the yawning darkness beyond.

"And if you do decide to write this address down, our procedure to follow is to quickly memorize it, then destroy it, preferably flushing it down the toilet."

"Like *Mission Impossible*." Jo joked.

The woman chuckled slightly. "I'm glad you get the idea, Miss Brady. From your reputation I'm sure I can trust you."

"You know me?"

"Let me say your reputation precedes you."

Jo noticed Garry strain his neck in an effort to see the address as she wrote it down. Jo turned slightly, blocking his view. If he got a hold of the address, he might slip out earlier without taking her. She sensed he was already wishing he hadn't brought her in on this, especially now when things did not seem as they looked.

When the woman finished the address, Jo crinkled the paper into the palm of her hand.

"Thank you," she told the woman.

"You're welcome, Miss Brady. Until tomorrow then."

The woman hung up.

Jo gently placed the receiver into its cradle, and slowly shook her head in wonder.

"We're set to meet tomorrow at eight a.m. It's over in Queens. I know the area. And get this. She seems to know where we are staying. And she knows me."

Garry's white bushy eyebrows furrowed into a frown.

"And she knows we're together," Jo continued. "And she told me to memorize the address and destroy it by flushing it down the toilet."

"Are you serious?"

"Deadly."

"Hold on, Jo. It may be some sort of a trap. Whoever killed my brother might be waiting there. I think you've already done enough. I'd rather you back out of this."

Obviously her instincts about Garry wanting her out of the picture had been right. "No way, Gar. I'm in. Let's hit the sack early tonight so we'll be bright-eyed and bushy-tailed for the meeting. I'm gonna go down to the hotel restaurant and grab some donuts before I call my parents and try to get a hold of Sara. You want to come along?"

"Sure. I'll come along." Garry rolled his wheelchair toward the door.

"Hold on a sec, Gar. I want to try something."

Jo picked up the phone and hit the redial button. On the second ring, she received a pre-recorded message saying the number was no longer in service. She tried the number two more times with the same result.

How'd the number get changed so quickly? Even the government couldn't move this fast. It was as if the woman had been waiting for Jo's call. But that was ridiculous. Wasn't it?

Before heading out, Jo quickly memorized the address, ripped up the paper and flushed it down the toilet.

* * * * *

Early the next morning the rain fell in torrents and Sara drove a newly disguised Tom to the outskirts of town. She'd been given a terrific shock when she'd found him sipping peppermint tea at the kitchen table when she'd gotten up. He'd cut his hair very short, almost military style, and dyed it blond by using an old carton of unused blonde hair color that had once belonged to Jo when she'd been a blonde.

He still looked as sexy as sin with his new look and she wanted to keep him tucked away safely at Peppermint Creek Inn, but now that the road was passable, he'd insisted on coming along with her to drop off her peppermint products and pick up supplies. She'd begged him to stay back at the inn, but he'd told her he had cabin fever. His other argument being perhaps he'd been in the town before and would see something that would jar another memory loose.

She gave him some spending money and they made arrangements to meet back at the side of the road in two hours. Zipping her husband's raincoat up and pulling the hood over his blond head she watched with a heavy heart as Tom slipped out of the truck, threw her a wave and disappeared into a gray swirl of rain.

* * * * *

Rainbow Falls was an old mill town, topped full of rustic clapboard houses and stores. A few men hung about under the canopy in front of the hardware store when Sara pulled into a free parking space. The parking lot in front of the dull gray-planked hardware store was already almost full of pickup trucks at this early hour, most of the trucks in similar condition to hers. Old, battered and beat-up over the years.

Times were tough in this small town. The pulp and paper mill, the major employer within miles, had been working at less than half-capacity over the last few years. With the assistance of a concerned citizen's environmental group headed by her late husband, the government had implemented new pollution constraints, whereas the mill had opted to downsize its output production, instead of upgrading their pollution controls.

Word had it the mill was on the chopping block. Living on borrowed time. It was only a matter of months before the rest of the workers would be thrown out on the street.

As she passed the crowd of men, she felt the suspicious glances penetrate her back. She knew every one of them, but none hailed a greeting as she headed toward the dull gray clapboard structure housing the building supplies.

The sweet smell of hay and seed hung heavy in the air and the rickety floors creaked beneath her feet as she entered. Inside the front door lay a long wooden counter that separated the customers from the cashier. About five people stood in the line up. All conversation died and heads turned to watch as she passed by.

Sara moved slowly, meeting everyone's gaze quite openly. Luckily, no one said a word today. It was if they all sensed she was in a mood to fight.

After passing the customers, she grabbed a cart and headed down the aisles, picking the items from the list Tom had supplied. Her gaze took in the wooden shelves upon shelves stacked full of sacks, bottles, cans and kegs of items.

Toward the back of the store she could see the monstrous heaps of hundred-pound sacks of feed and seed the locals would be needing soon.

"Got yourself a new man, Sara?"

Sara froze as she recognized the whiskey-wrecked voice of Cran Simcoe. Once a good friend of hers and her husband, he had turned into one of her worst tormentors. After Tom's revelation early this morning about Cran being her shadow, she'd been shocked to say the least. Sure, his intentions had been honorable or so he'd told Tom last night, but he'd given her so many sleepless nights and made her question her sanity.

Her instincts told her to curse him up and down until he left but she had to think about protecting Tom. Trying to ignore him she reached for an item she needed on the shelf then turned her back against him fully intent on getting out of here as fast as she could.

"I'm talking to you, girl," Cran slurred. "What's the matter, cat got your tongue?"

Damn him!

Go away!

"I'm hoping your new man is a hell of lot better than that backstabbing husband of yours was."

His comment lit her fuse.

Son of a bitch! She wouldn't let him talk about Jack that way.

Taking a deep frustrated breath, she counted to three then slowly turned to find thirty-five-year-old Cran staring intently at her at the end of the aisle.

He swayed slightly. Barely eight o'clock in the morning and the man was already drunk.

"You have something to say about my husband, Cran Simcoe, you'd better say it to my face." His high forehead wrinkled in surprise as she quickly headed toward him. Obviously he wasn't used to seeing her being so bold. When she reached him, she recoiled from the sour smell of whiskey on his breath. Behind him, she noticed about a half dozen older men milling in the nearby corner. All turned to watch.

From what Tom had told her last night, this man thought he owed her husband a debt for helping getting him off the booze. He'd stayed off for awhile, but when Cran had been one of the men laid off at the mill, he'd hit the bottle once again. Sara finally understood why Cran had been tormenting her all this time.

Obviously he was the type of man who had to join in with his peers, instead of standing on his own two feet and fighting for what he believed in, which was obviously protecting her. Suddenly she came to the realization that the hatred she saw in Cran's eyes wasn't being directed toward her but toward himself for using her to impress his drinking buddies.

"What happened to you losing your job was your own fault, Cran. Had nothing to do with Jack."

"Your husband helped to downsize the mill, Sara," an old crony from the group yelled back.

"A mill that was polluting the area, Mel Roberts," Sara replied calmly to the man who'd spoken. "You know very well the mill was warned in advance of the upcoming regulations. They chose to downsize rather than upgrade. Had nothing to do with my husband. All Jack did was guide the government people to the sources of pollution and give them a fair hand at the hearings."

"He's the one who put us out on the street," Mel grumbled angrily.

"Better you out on the street, than the fish and wildlife dead, Mel. Oh, but I forgot you're a hunter yourself aren't you, Mel? So maybe you wouldn't care much about the wildlife." She knew it was a cheap shot. The hunters around these parts hunted within the government limits.

But it irked her when someone shot at animals. Sometimes when the animal was wounded, the hunters didn't bother to track them down and put them out of their misery.

She turned her attention back on Cran. "As for you, Cran, Jack was a thousand times better a man than you'll ever be in your entire life. If you picked up anything from my husband when he helped you off the booze you'd better start remembering it and put it to good use by getting some professional help. Jack's probably looking down and shaking his head in disappointment at seeing you this way." A loud snicker cut loose from the old cronies.

Cran's eyes narrowed into dangerous slits and his voice lowered so only the two of them heard. "You better watch your step out there in that wilderness, missy. You never know what can happen when you're all alone." She bit down the urge to tell everyone Cran was her shadow but decided against it. He would only deny it and no one would believe her anyway.

"You better go and dry out, Cran, or you just might find yourself facing charges of hunting out of season along with

191

attempted murder. I have the bullet from your gun in my porch wall to prove it."

Her message sunk in loud and clear and he slowly nodded his head. To her surprise a bit of a smile tipped his wide lips. Abruptly, he turned and walked out of the hardware store all amidst more chuckles from the elderly group.

Chapter Ten

ॐ

Sara was still ticked off at her confrontation with Cran when a few minutes later, she entered the general store/post office, her arms laden with a huge plastic-wrapped cardboard box crammed full of the peppermint products Widow McCloud had ordered for this month.

"Howdy there, Sara."

She jumped as Widow McCloud appeared from behind the nearby post office counter. At first glance, people thought Mrs. McCloud a man because of her short feathery cut and long witchlike nose, but her affectionate demeanor made up for her odd looks.

"Haven't seen you in a long while, dear."

All her anger evaporated at Widow McCloud's friendly voice. The old woman was one of the very few people who had remained friendly with her despite Jack's involvement with the environment group and the rumors about her possibly being involved in his murder.

She found herself laughing as the woman's eyes widened with delight and she clasped her hands to her chest as Sara placed the carton box onto the countertop. "You brought the goodies! I'm just about out of every line. The customers are getting hostile." Widow McCloud squealed happily and took a quick breath before continuing. "I hope you enjoyed the groceries I sent over with Justin."

"Thanks, Hilda. The flood lasted a bit longer than usual this year and it was a blessing to have fresh food for us."

The old woman's eyebrows rose in wonder. "Us?"

Shit!

An icy shot of adrenaline squirted through Sara's veins when she realized her mistake. She recovered quickly.

"I made Justin some breakfast to thank him," she lied. "Have you got any mail for me?"

The older woman didn't so much as acknowledge Sara's question. Instead, she asked, "Did you hear about Sam going missing?"

"I heard about it," Sara said flatly. Mrs. McCloud had awful matchmaking skills.

She'd been trying to get her together with Justin and then with Sam for a long time now and obviously didn't expect Sara's non-passionate response. But Sara had never had any romantic feelings about Sam or Justin and had made it abundantly clear to the elderly Mrs. McCloud on several occasions, but the woman still kept trying.

She just hadn't been interested romantically in any man, at least not until recently when Tom had shown up in her doorway.

The older woman frowned with puzzlement then bent over and disappeared behind the counter. A second later she reappeared with a shoe-sized box filled with mail and slid it onto the countertop beside the giant box Sara had brought in.

"I'll be a minute to search for your mail, dear. Why don't you look around," she said as she began sifting through the mail.

Sara meandered through the store finally ending up at the pain-relief section where she picked up a bottle of painkillers in case Tom had anymore headaches. As she turned around, she froze.

In front of her, directly at eye level, piled in neat stacks were condoms.

Oh, my God!

Should she?

She snuck a peek down the aisle. Mrs. McCloud was still busily searching through her mailbox. Her eyes flew back to the shelf.

Which one should she pick? She'd never bought any before. Jack had always taken care of that kind of stuff.

She bit her lip as an intense excitement zipped along her veins. In a split second, she reached out, snatched a pretty-looking box she hoped appropriate and quickly tucked it under her arm.

Turning to look up the aisle back toward Mrs. McCloud she exhaled as she was still busily picking through the makeshift mailbox.

Sara could already hear the rumors flying! Sara Clarke bought a box of condoms today.

Maybe she should put the box back. She didn't really need condoms. She didn't really know Tom. Only that he was gentle, and caring and gorgeous and sexy and God did he know how to make her orgasm with his mouth.

Dejectedly, she took the box out from under her arm where she'd stuffed it and was about to lift it up to put it back on the shelf when she noticed Mrs. McCloud watching her. The knowing look on her face told Sara she'd been found out.

Oops. Better keep the box.

Reluctantly, she headed back to the counter where she hesitantly plopped the headache remedy and box of condoms onto the counter beside the small pile of her mail Widow McCloud had compiled for her.

She could feel her face grow hotter as the other woman's curious gaze raked across the condoms.

"I'm so glad you're getting back into the swing of things," she chuckled as she tipped the prices of the two items.

"It's for a friend," Sara replied quickly. It wasn't as if she was lying. The condoms were for a friend. And hopefully if everything worked out, Tom would be more than a friend.

The tiniest bit of a knowing smile tickled Mrs. McCloud's thin lips and she knew the woman didn't believe her. Her face grew even hotter.

She felt as if she might die of embarrassment when Mrs. McCloud suddenly gasped, "Oh! I almost forgot. Another package came for Garry. I'll be but a minute."

The old woman bustled off and Sara almost leaped out of her skin when the bell jangled behind her signaling a customer. Her eyes flew to the box of condoms sitting naked and in full view of prying eyes. At that moment, Mrs. McCloud erupted from the back room with a tiny brown wrapped package that fit snugly in her hand.

Sara rolled her eyes when she saw the package. Another one of Garry's junk mail collections. The man was forever ordering cassettes and books from various clubs. Obviously, he'd forgotten to give this particular company his new address.

"This came via personal courier late last week. Sue said the man was a catch, a bit rough around the edges but that could be fixed. You remember Sue, don't you?"

Sara nodded. How could she forget Sue? The woman had it made with a gorgeous husband and lovely two-year-old triplets. Why Sue would leave her beautiful children for a few hours every Friday night and work at the store was beyond Sara.

"Sue said if she wasn't already taken, she'd have scooped up the fellow along with his Harley motorcycle into her husband's fishing net and taken him home without a second thought." Mrs. McCloud laughed as she produced a brown paper bag and thankfully placed the items inside.

"Said the man made an odd request, though. He asked if she'd make a copy of a videotape for him. Even gave her fifty dollars U.S. for her trouble."

Grateful that the evidence, so to speak, was in the bag, Sara quickly grabbed it. But by the look on Mrs. McCloud's face, she wasn't finished with her yet. Her next words confirmed her suspicion.

"Any ideas when Garry is dropping in for a visit? I haven't seen him in a while."

Widow McCloud had her sights set on poor Garry. He did everything in his power to discourage Mrs. McCloud up to a point. It wasn't his style to be downright rude to her and Sara figured it would be the only way for Garry to get rid of the older woman.

"He might be dropping by soon. Speaking about him, can I use your phone to make a collect call?" Maybe she could get a hold of Jo.

"Sorry, hon, but the phones are still out all over town. According to Justin, the storms caused a lot of damage. I'd loan you my cell phone but I gave it to Sue. Her hubby is away on business and she's all alone with the babies. I do believe Justin has a cell though. I'm sure he'd be glad to loan it to you."

Widow McCloud smiled sweetly and Sara couldn't help but tense at the thought of seeing Justin again.

"Thanks. I'll see if I can track him down," she lied.

"So, when do you think Garry might be dropping by? Any specific day?"

"Sorry, I'm really not sure." The sooner, the better. "But the next time I speak to him, I'll definitely let him know you were asking about him. I really have to go now. Next time I'll buy you a cup of tea and we'll catch up on things."

Mrs. McCloud brightened immensely. "That'll be a real treat, dear. But can't you wait a moment for a check for your products?"

"I'll catch you next time. Bye," Sara waved and practically ran over the elderly couple who had entered the store moments earlier.

* * * * *

Tom stuffed the tiny present he'd bought for Sara into the pocket of his raincoat and whipped the raincoat hood snugly over his head before stepping out of the hobby shop into the chilly downpour.

He'd been up all night, pacing back and forth through the house, trying like the devil himself to figure out what those visions of blood and flashing lights meant and also trying to conjure up a way out of this mess without Sara getting hurt, when he'd found the carton of blonde hair color in the upstairs bathroom and promptly cut his hair and given himself a dye job.

He had to admit, he now looked totally different as a clean-shaven blond. Far different than the scruffy character with whiskers when he'd first shown up at Sara's home.

Nonetheless, it was best he kept a low profile, grabbing the things he needed before hoofing it back to their agreed meeting place just outside of town as soon as possible.

He smiled as he spotted Sara's truck still parked outside the hardware store. She was grabbing the items from the list he'd given her of the things he'd used in order to keep supplies on hand back at the inn for emergencies this season. As he walked, he kept his gaze glued to the hardware store's front door in hopes of catching a glimpse of Sara coming out. Doing so, he almost bumped into a tall dark-haired man standing right outside the hobby shop door.

"Excuse me," Tom said politely as he tried to sidestep him.

"Haven't seen you in these parts before."

The familiar voice froze him solid. Through the downpour he made out the dark framed glasses, the moustache.

Shit!

"Name is Jeffries. Officer Justin Jeffries."

I know who you are, he wanted to spit in the cop's face. But that wouldn't solve his problem. Obviously, the cop wasn't going to let him go. He'd just introduced himself and Tom realized he had two options. Be stupid and polite and face him head-on. Or else be smart and run.

Tom opted for the first. After all, he had the hood covering his newly dyed and cut hair, and he was one beard and one mustache less now.

He turned around slowly, preparing to defend himself, but to his cautious surprise, the cop extended his hand.

Blinking the rain out of his eyes, he shook hands with the cop.

"Howdy." Tom said casually, hoping the shakiness traveling like lightning speed through him wouldn't show up in his voice. "Name's Smith. Tom Smith."

The man openly stared at Tom. "You related to Garry Smith?"

He shifted uncomfortably under Jeffries' curious gaze.

"Nope."

"Just visiting?" The cop's cold voice dropped a chilly shiver upon Tom's spine.

"Passing through," he replied.

Jeffries' eyes squinted narrowly behind his rain-spattered glasses and Tom suddenly realized Jeffries might not be able to see him clearly or have an idea who he was talking to. On the other hand, he might. Tom didn't miss the cop's right hand snake smoothly to his holstered gun.

"You look a bit familiar to me. Have we met somewhere?"

Those words froze Tom's smile. "Don't think so. Never been in these parts before."

The answer seemed to satisfy Jeffries and he nodded and his hand flew away from his holster, he saluted and turned on his heel.

Tom watched warily as the cop strolled casually down the sidewalk. He'd been lucky Jeffries hadn't recognized him. The rain had been his savior today. But how long before Jeffries figured out why he looked so familiar? One hour? One day? How long before Cran Simcoe decided to spill his guts and tell a friend that Sara had a stranger living out there with her?

He cursed softly beneath his breath.

He'd been crazy to even flirt with the idea of leaving Sara. He would have to try again to persuade her to seek safety somewhere else. And if her stubborn pride got in his way and she refused to leave, then he'd have to stay and protect her himself, because there was no way in hell he was leaving her alone.

* * * * *

"How does a person get amnesia?"

Dr. Smokey McKay's dark gray eyes narrowed with curiosity as she leaned forward in her creaky old overstuffed leather chair and shoved the pen she'd been using to scribble notes on a patient's chart, behind her ear.

"Why are you so interested in amnesia all of a sudden, Sara? Has this something to do with your memory confusions when Jack was murdered? Or is it something else?"

Sara swallowed hard and squirmed uncomfortably under Smokey's intense gaze. The woman knew Sara so well. She could almost feel herself blurting out about Tom and decided against it. She knew without a doubt she could trust the shrink, but it was best not to get her involved.

"Actually, um, I'm thinking of writing an article about my experience. That's all."

"That's all, huh," Smokey said doubtfully. "I know you too well, Sara. Something's going on isn't it?"

Sara laughed nervously. "My God, I've only asked you one question. How can you be so interested in one lousy question?"

"Because, Sara, you are positively glowing. Something happen to you over the winter? Have you met someone?"

Sara shifted uneasily. The question had caught her off guard.

"I'm just doing some research for Garry that's all. Nothing suspicious about that."

"Writing? Or research? Which is it? Besides I didn't say there was anything suspicious about your question," Smokey replied gently. "Why are you being so defensive?"

Sara grabbed her purse off the desk. "Maybe this isn't such a good idea, Smoke. Just forget I asked."

"Wait!" Smokey urged. "I'm your doctor. If you have questions, I'm obligated to answer. You don't have to tell me why you want to know. I'm sorry for being so pushy. It's just you've changed so much, Sara. You look so alive. Healthy. I'm just surprised. Please have a seat. I won't ask any more questions."

Sara sighed and plopped back down on the chair. If she'd known Smokey would get so suspicious, she'd never have come to her for help. She knew she should tell her. Tell her everything about Tom. His amnesia. How attracted she was to him. How she wished he'd make love to her. Sara shook the racy thoughts from her head as Smokey spoke.

"I know dealing with memory is very tricky," she said. "And every case of amnesia is unique. What exactly do you want to know?"

Sara's grip tightened on her purse. "How does someone get amnesia?"

"We still don't know everything about it, but people can get amnesia in a variety of ways. A serious illness, a blow to the head or as you well know some sort of mental trauma can make a person block out certain aspects of their life. What specific questions do you need answered?"

"This is a strictly hypothetical question, of course."

"Of course." Smokey smiled and urged Sara to continue.

"If someone say—killed someone and didn't remember it or anything else for that matter, what are the chances of his ever regaining his entire memory back?"

"It depends. If the person is deliberately blocking out something because it's too painful to remember, for example killing someone, it's called psychological or defensive amnesia, whereas the memory is being suppressed unconsciously not deliberately.

"He may say he wants to remember, but in fact really doesn't because his life is so pleasant at the moment he fears the memory return may complicate matters. Whereas if the amnesia is caused by head trauma, the memories may return with time or may never return, depending on the severity of the case.

"Either way the longer the person has amnesia, the worse the chances are of regaining their memory."

"And what happens when they regain their memory? Will he remember what happened to him during the period he was lost?"

"When a person has amnesia they are in what we in fact call the 'fugue state'. The person has no recollection of who they are or where they come from. Certain aspects of their lives are retained such as foods they like, traffic laws, how to walk, how to talk, things like that.

"The person who has amnesia will go on living, making new memories and sometimes the fugue state dissolves allowing the person to remember who he is and where he came from. They can return to their normal lives again.

"But will they remember what happened during a fugue state? It depends on the individual, and again it depends on how long the amnesia lasted. The longer it goes on, the poorer the chances of even remembering what happened in a fugue state."

She had the answer she was looking for. There was a chance Tom wouldn't remember who she was when he regained his memory. The horrible thought made her feel like crying. But she didn't. Instead, Sara squared her shoulders defiantly. She wouldn't think about it. She couldn't.

Smokey leaned forward in her chair, her eyes narrowing. "There's a case I had when I was living down in Florida. You could use it for your article or research, if you're interested."

"Sure. Tell me."

"A woman and her family went down to Mexico for a trip. One day her husband took the kids shopping and she decided to settle under a palm tree to read a book. She was reading when suddenly a coconut fell on her head. She couldn't remember who she was or where she came from. She wandered away from the hotel and was reported missing.

"Eight years later, she reappeared at the same hotel, her previous memories totally intact. She believed she had just returned from sitting under the coconut tree. Much to the woman's surprise, her family wasn't there.

"She went home to discover her two children were almost teenagers and her husband had declared her dead and remarried. Making matters worse, he married her very own best friend." Smokey shook her head. Her reddish brown curls bounced with wonder. "Needless to say, their lives were totally turned upside down. Eventually the husband did go back to his first wife. And then after a few months, a man showed up on the woman's front door claiming to be her husband. Apparently she'd married during her fugue state and had two more children."

"You mean she didn't remember remarrying or having any more children when she regained her memory?"

"She remembered nothing. As I said, she thought she'd only returned from her vacation. Tests were made to determine if the children were hers and all results pointed she was indeed the mother. But she was unable to be their mother because all maternal instinct had been wiped out."

Sara bit her lower lip trying hard not to show any emotion as Smokey watched her curiously.

If Tom regained his full memory, there was a chance he wouldn't even know who she was. And he might also have another family out there waiting for him to come home. A family who loved him.

And if there was a family out there? Could she let Tom go?

Could she pretend he never existed and move on with her life? Or would she return to those horribly depressing months she'd fought so hard to overcome after her own family's destruction?

* * * * *

Queens, New York...

Garry and Jo stared through the ten-foot-high chain-link fence at the abandoned-looking red brick building housed smack-dab in the industrial section of Queens, New York.

"This is definitely the address," Jo said. "My memory might not be the greatest but I'm one hundred percent sure this is the place."

She winked at Garry as she held up her palm to show him where she'd rewritten the address.

Garry's forehead wrinkled in surprise. "I thought you flushed it down the toilet."

"I did. But not before writing it down somewhere else." She shrugged her shoulders. "Hey, you never know. You might wake up one day with amnesia or something."

Garry smiled as he continued to eye the building. "Looks deserted. Kind of spooky. Not a place to be hanging around, even in broad daylight." He wheeled his wheelchair closer to the fence. "Do you think we've been scammed?"

Jo shook her head. "For a place that looks abandoned they sure have a fancy security system." She pointed to the overhang over the front door. "And a high-tech surveillance camera."

Garry cocked a curious eyebrow as he spied the shiny camera scanning them.

"Why don't you sit tight, Garry, while I check this out." With a sudden burst of speed, Jo leaped up the fence, her fingers grasping the chain links.

"What are you doing, Jo?" Garry shouted from behind her.

"Trying to see if anyone is home," she yelled back as she scrambled monkey-style up the fence and down the other side.

Within a minute she stood at the front door gazing at the number pad encased in cement in the wall.

"Now why would someone have such fancy gadgets in this neck of the woods," she mumbled beneath her breath. Jo reached into her back pocket and withdrew her wallet.

"Careful, Jo," Garry shouted. "I know what you're thinking of doing."

Jo winked at Garry as she withdrew her credit card. "This should get us some action," she said. In one quick fluid motion, she swiped the card through the swiper and punched in a few random numbers.

Sirens and bells screamed throughout the air.

Bingo!

Garry cursed loudly outside the chain-link fence.

The front door burst open and three men dressed in black, with drawn guns surrounded her.

"You must be the welcoming committee," she said cocking an inquiring eyebrow at them. From the corner of her eye she spotted another "welcoming committee" surrounding Garry.

"Take it easy guys, I'm a P.I. My ID is in my wallet." She held the wallet out at arm's length so the goons could see it. "I'm also armed. The gun is in my right shoulder holster. Just so you know."

A tall, very pretty woman with shoulder-length auburn hair dressed in a smart navy blue blazer and short skirt erupted from the building. She was followed by two more armed men dressed entirely in black.

"I know who you are," the woman said sharply. "You've just broken into a high-security government building. If you don't answer some questions mighty quick, you and your accomplice are going to jail."

"You better show us a federal arrest warrant mighty quick or we're walking," Garry yelled from the other side of the fence.

Jo picked up Garry's hint and turned to leave.

"No. Wait!" the woman shouted at Jo.

Jo stopped and turned to the woman. "You've got questions. We've got answers," Jo lied. "How about you tell us what you know and we'll reciprocate. Have we got a deal?"

"Deal," the woman mumbled. "Come inside."

* * * * *

"Listen, I'm sorry I snapped at you last night. When you took off like that I was worried for your safety," Sara said as they headed back home in the truck with the rain drumming against the roof of her cab like a thousand impatient fingers. Ever since she'd picked up Tom at their designated meeting spot, he'd been quiet. Brooding. Actually, he'd been quiet since early this morning, barely touching his breakfast and saying few words to her except for when he'd argued he would be going to town with her.

When he'd finally spoken to her, he'd said only enough to tell her Cran Simcoe was her shadow, and in his opinion a harmless one at that.

Tom didn't acknowledge her apology. As a matter of fact, he totally ignored her as he stared blankly out the passenger window.

"Tom? Did you hear me? Or are you simply not going to answer me?"

"I just don't feel much like talking is all." A muscle twitched in his jaw.

It didn't take a brain surgeon to figure out he had another headache.

"I'll make you another cup of willow bark tea when we get back."

"Sure."

Sara frowned. He really must have a doozie of a headache if he wasn't protesting the awful tea.

"There's some extra-strength painkiller in the paper bag right there." She pointed to the bag on the bench seat between them then suddenly realized her mistake.

Oh, shoot!

The condoms! They were in the bag!

Sara made a grab for the bag but realized she was too late.

He'd already opened it and was looking inside.

She watched in shock as his face suddenly turned pale as a ghost. Her foot had already hit the brakes when he shouted his warning. Tom barely made it out of the truck in time.

* * * * *

Tom grimaced as Sara placed the second cup of the bitter tea in front of him and sat down beside him.

"So what gives?" Sara asked.

"The headache. A little."

"Quit goofing off. I'm serious. Why'd you react like that in the truck? Was it — " Sara hesitated.

She wanted to know if he'd seen the condoms buried underneath the mail. She didn't think he had, but still, she would appreciate knowing if the thought of making love to her repulsed him so much he'd become violently ill and almost passed out.

Instead she went with her instincts and asked, "Did you have another memory flash?"

He frowned in response and picked up the cruel smelling brew, took a deep breath and gulped down a giant mouthful. Another grimace quickly followed, this time obviously from the horrid taste.

"Yes. I had a memory flash. I've been having more of them over the past few days."

"Well, I'm glad you could confide in me." Sara angrily crossed her arms.

Tom nodded, the fine lines around his mouth deepening as his frown increased. "I'm sorry I didn't tell you. I should have."

Her anger quickly faded to compassion when she realized he indeed was truly sorry for not telling her.

"Are they about your family? Do you remember their names?"

"Nothing about my family." His words were drenched with dread and Sara shivered under the onslaught of the troubled look in his eyes.

"What…what do you remember?"

Anxiety curled around her. She remembered what her shrink Smokey had said, that if he remembered his past he might forget her.

"I couldn't see his face. But he was an older man. He was lying on the floor. There was—" Tom shut his eyes tightly as if to squeeze the memory away "—lots of blood."

Sara swallowed hard at the scorching look of pain twisting his face and she tried to dispel the fear creeping across her shoulder blades. There were questions to ask. Questions she didn't want to rise, but she had to. "Did this man have red hair? A pencil-thin mustache?"

"No, he had white hair."

"Thank God." Sara let out a breath of relief.

"It's not the missing officer?"

"No, it's not. Did you see yourself killing this man?"

He shook his head. A frustrated frown crossed his face.

"Good. That's good."

Another hurdle crossed.

"But I didn't see myself not killing him," he said tightly.

"Let's keep this positive. Remember innocent until proven guilty."

"Okay, okay," he whispered and nodded his head. "Positive. I can do that."

"Is there any more you're not telling me?"

"No, it's always the same. I've tried to see who he is, but I can't make out a face. Just white hair and lots of blood."

"It'll come with time," Sara said gently.

"I don't know if I want it to come." His jaws tightened and released and he stood. His strong muscular legs took him over to his raincoat hanging on the peg by the door where she heard paper rustling as he searched for something in the pocket.

When he returned to the kitchen table, he sat down and plopped a small paper bag on top of the table in front of her. For a horrible instant, Sara thought it was the bag containing the condoms.

Then she relaxed when she saw the writing on the bag indicated it was from the hobby shop.

"Open it. It's for you. I bought it with some of the spending money you gave me," Tom said, his expression was soft and tender.

Her heart clutched warmly and curiosity burned inside her as she peered into the bag. The minute she saw its contents, her stomach did a somersault. Shaking her head, she pushed the bag away as if it were contaminated.

"I can't."

"You can," Tom replied gently.

He withdrew the white box of charcoal sticks along with a strip containing four photos. He held up the photo strip for Sara to see and tried to smile the same way he'd smiled when he'd sat in the photo booth in the drug store he'd gone to as the camera snapped shots of him. Sara found herself smiling at his antics.

"I figured I'm an impartial object for you to draw," he chuckled. "And don't say you don't do drawings of people because I've seen the paintings hung up in those cottages. And I especially like the one of the twins making a snowman. Is that how you imagined them to look?"

Sara nodded. He'd hit the nail right on the head. They had been her twins, or who she'd imagined them to be at their various ages.

She stared at the box of charcoals as if it was the devil itself. "I can't draw you. I can't draw anything anymore. It's gone."

"A talent like yours never goes away. You've got to dig deep down. Bring it back to the surface. I'm a safe enough subject don't you think? I come with a blank slate so to speak. Will you give it a try? Please? For me?" he coaxed, his eyes blazed with a fierce heated confidence, urging her on.

Sara gave in and took the strip of pictures in hand, examining them carefully. It would be kind of nice drawing his handsome features. Those long, delicious black lashes, the endearing lines around his mouth, the wonderful slant to his green eyes.

"Sure, I can try."

That gorgeous crooked smile fluttered across his features catching her off guard again, making her pulses pound, making her pussy cream with anticipation.

"Good that's all I'm asking, Sara. Keep your twins alive in your paintings. Keep me alive."

Sara jolted. "Why are you talking this way? You sound as if…" She shook her head slowly. "I don't know, almost as if you were going to disappear on me. Are you?"

His Adam's apple bobbed as he swallowed hard, obviously not wanting to tell her but knowing he had to.

"I ran into Jeffries."

"You what?" Her mind whirled as terror rammed into her. Justin Jeffries had seen Tom. She needed to get him out of here. Needed to get him to somewhere safe until she heard from Jo and Garry.

"I spoke with him."

"Did he recognize you?" She gulped down her fear. "Of course he didn't. That was a stupid question. If he had, you'd be in jail or — No, he doesn't know who you are."

"His glasses were pretty soaked and he had trouble seeing me, but he said something that got me thinking it might be just a matter of time before he puts two and two together. He asked me if we'd met somewhere before. I think we should leave today."

"Okay."

Tom blinked at her with apparent disbelief. Obviously, he hadn't expected her to agree.

"On one condition though," Sara quickly added.

"Name it."

"We start looking for answers ourselves."

Sara noticed the sparkle of interest light up his eyes as he leaned forward in his chair.

"How's that?"

"You up for a visit to a ghost town?"

Chapter Eleven

ଚ୨

A late afternoon mist gently hovered over Jackfish Bay. The rain had cleared out early afternoon and the sky had turned a brilliant warm blue.

They'd driven down the narrow winding road to the ghost town and parked the truck in a clearing near the train tracks. Now as Tom stood on the tracks, scanning the gray rippling waters of Lake Superior his gaze immediately pinned onto the large rocky island about a quarter mile out in the bay. The eerie feeling of déjà vu slammed into his stomach like a fist and he suddenly found it difficult to breathe.

That island. Why did it draw him so intensely?

Closing his eyes, he focused on breathing in the cool, breezy lake and tried to conjure up a memory. Within seconds one appeared.

For a flash of time, Tom stood on the rocky island's shoreline. The gentle lapping sounds of water did not soothe him as he stared at the ghost town littering the main coast. A seagull flapped overhead. The sunshine beat against his naked body. But still he shivered.

He felt so damn cold. Even his teeth betrayed him. They wouldn't stop chattering.

He looked at the chilly black waters. Could he make it off the island? Did he even want to try?

The vision disintegrated leaving Tom with nothing but more questions.

He'd gone into that water? At this time of the year? But why? Why had he gone out to the island? Any sane person could see it was too cold for a swim.

Maybe he'd been here last year? But as his gaze raked over the rocky island, he felt relatively comfortable with the idea he'd been here not too long ago.

The peacefulness of the area shattered as Sara called excitedly from somewhere ahead. Shifting the heavy knapsack on his back, he cast one last wary look at the island before quickly leaving the railway tracks. He followed the worn path leading up an incline. On the other side of the grassy knoll, he spotted her anxiously waving to him.

"Over here," she called.

He trudged through the tall grass to meet her.

"Here it is." Sara made a sweeping motion with her arm. "Good old town of Jackfish."

Tom gazed at the sight.

Many of the debilitated wooden structures had caved in through the seasons. Some stood at awkward and tilted angles. Others stood proudly, their empty black windows yawning at them.

"You've been here before, haven't you?"

He nodded, meeting Sara's anxious gaze.

"Nothing I can put my finger on. But yes I get the feeling I've been here before. And what I'm wondering is why? Why would I come to a place so isolated?"

"You must have had a good reason. And if what you are feeling is true, this confirms what Justin said about you being here with him and Sam. They are the ones who handcuffed you and beat you to a pulp."

"I could have put up a good fight when they tried to arrest me."

"Sorry, but I won't buy that angle. Justin didn't have a mark on his face and he didn't look like he was hurting. Beating a prisoner is illegal, Tom. Shooting him in the back isn't proper procedure either. Now more than ever, we have to prove your innocence. The only way for us to do it is to keep looking around and see if you can remember."

Before he could say anything, she was heading down the pathway. Her arms and legs moved with a determined confident stride, urging him to follow her.

A cold feeling of dread began a slow creep along his spine as she led him along the path running adjacent to the railway tracks. She pointed out various abandoned buildings and what they'd been.

Eventually they stumbled across a lone cottage perched on a cliff. Beside the cottage sat a two-story shell of a leaning building. The name "Jackfish" was haphazardly scrawled on a wooden shingle nailed to the derelict, a public announcement to anyone who dared enter the ghost town's confines.

"It was 1884 when the railway blasted its way through here, leaving a railway construction town in its wake. This was the hotel for the workers." Sara pointed to the building. "They had a town dock. It's gone now and at one point three dynamite factories were erected to make dynamite to blast the bedrock for the rail bed throughout Northern Ontario."

Tom tried to imagine himself working for the railroad. With Sara as his wife. A passel of kids. A house with a white picket fence. Leaving her for weeks on end to work on the railroad would have been hell, but coming home to his lovely Sara would have been heaven.

He peered over at her as she gazed at the deserted shell of a building. The pained and haunted look she'd carried since he'd met her had disappeared, replaced by eyes bright with fevered excitement.

She looked so alive, so damned beautiful that it took every ounce of his strength to keep himself from pulling her into his arms and kissing those full, luscious lips, from cupping her heavy, silky breasts in his hands and tweaking her plump nipples.

His cock suddenly strained against his jeans with razor-sharp awareness and he almost groaned, almost gave himself away.

"Tom? Did you hear me?"

"Sorry?"

"I said we've got about two hours of daylight left here. Is there any particular area we should scout first? Anything that draws your attention?"

"Everything draws my attention." *Especially you*, he added silently. "You pick."

Sara smiled prettily and he could feel the lust traveling through his system, could feel his belly tighten with awareness, his cock grow thicker, harder, longer.

"All right, this way."

He followed her up the overgrown walkway, her cute hips swaying seductively in front of him as they trudged toward an ancient-looking relic of a building with a horribly sagging roof. Climbing up some moss-covered stairs they stepped onto the creaking veranda.

"Ooooohhh, kind of spooky in here." Tom chuckled as he bent over slightly to enter the low doorway of the semi-dark cabin interior. Cool, damp air blasted against him. "Casper, where are you, ole buddy?"

"Quiet, you'll wake him up," Sara whispered as she gazed wide-eyed at the debris of dented tin pots and other tin items littering the strangely tilted floor.

Tom's eyes narrowed curiously as he followed her gaze.

"What are you looking for?"

"Antiques."

He couldn't stop the laugh from escaping him. "Antiques? This junk?"

Sara ignored his remark and with a shout of glee that momentarily startled him, she twisted her way through the debris, and bent over. From a nest of yellowing papers, she pulled out a slightly dented old-fashioned rusty and white enameled coffeepot.

"It's perfect. Absolutely beautiful," she said as she held it up and stared at the derelict-looking object with sparkling eyes.

"Beautiful?" The thing looked beyond repair. He cocked a cynical eyebrow trying to find what she saw in the rusty piece.

"One man's garbage is another man's treasure. Turn around," she instructed.

He did as he was told.

"What are you going to do with that rusty old thing anyway?" he asked as he felt the flap of the knapsack lift up.

"For your information, many of my dried flower bouquets, which I set in your so-called rusty things have won first, second and third prizes at the Fall fairs."

"Prizes?" he mumbled doubtfully.

Then he remembered the slightly dented teapots filled to overflowing with all kinds of beautiful dried flowers on the stone mantel in Sara's bedroom. And again strewn about her living room. The same teapots that made him think of campfires and spaghetti westerns.

"That's right. Lots of prizes," she said with utmost confidence that made a smile lift his lips.

He sucked in a harsh breath as he felt her luscious body heat slam into his ass as she dumped her treasure inside the knapsack. His body tightened with awareness. His mouth suddenly went dry as he imagined how wet her pussy would be as his tongue slid deep into her tight channel. How hard her velvety vaginal muscles would clamp around his thick rod as he filled her right to his hard, aching balls.

"The next one goes in my pack." Her giggle broke him from his sensual thoughts and he watched as she set upon searching for more of her prize materials. Bending over, she picked up an enamel water pitcher, and Tom cursed silently at the seductive curves of her luscious ass pressing against the tight pants she wore and wondered if she'd allow him to take her anally.

He held his breath at that thought.

He'd make her get on her hands and knees. Make her push her face into the pillows and lift her bare ass way high in the air. He'd run his hands over her velvety cheeks until she moaned for more. Then he'd slide a butt plug into her, a big plug that would prepare her for him.

Her face would be flushed—her erotic moans would drift through the air as the plastic sank into her tight depths. He'd make her wear it. Make her wait. Make them both wait. The ache of anticipation of him taking her anally would drive them both crazy with lust. When she was finally ready, he'd remove it and thrust hard into her. She'd love the pressure of his cock sliding up her ass. She'd bite back at the pleasure-pain, her breaths coming in harsh gasps as he fucked her over and over until she cried out for mercy.

She must have noticed the look of lust on his face because she was suddenly staring at him with a heated need that made his heart do a double take.

He barely heard her next words as his mind reeled from the beauty of that sexy bedroom expression on her flushed face.

"You'll change your mind about my treasures once you see the finished product," she whispered softly as she held up yet another junky-looking tin pot. "A lot of sandpapering," she added softly. "A splash of aluminum paint, followed with perhaps a dusty rose color or maybe pioneer yellow or an Amish blue—"

"All right." He cut her off, his voice sounding strangled, aroused. "I get the picture. That one's yours. Turn around."

Sara handed him the disgusting spider-webbed antique and he lifted the flap dumping it inside.

"Just watch out for those sandwiches I have in there. I don't want pancakes for supper tonight."

"Too late," Tom teased.

He dropped the flap and she twirled around to face him. Her eyes flared with heat and he noticed the way her plump nipples were poking hard against the thin T-shirt she wore. He knew she wanted him just as badly as he wanted her.

Perspiration broke out on his forehead as he restrained himself. He could take her right here, right now. Push her against the crumbling wall, slide her pants and panties down and plunge his heavy, thick cock into her warm, wet cunt. Her face would scrunch up with the pleasure and he'd catch her cries with his eager kisses.

Without warning, she stood on her tiptoes and planted a playfully light kiss on his nose. Before he could grab her, she turned around and danced like a water nymph out the door, leaving him alone with a magnificent hard-on that just about made him scream out in frustration.

It was at that point he wondered if she had planned on coming here to this rustically romantic ghost town so they wouldn't have to worry about the cops coming down the road to the inn and them being discovered at any moment.

Here they could relax.

They could enjoy themselves.

Enjoy the carnal pleasures that were pent up and begging to break free in both of them.

"C'mon, let's go see what other treasures we can find," she called from outside.

"You're the only treasure I'll ever need, sweetness," he whispered softly beneath his breath and followed her outside.

* * * * *

Two hours later, twilight shadowed a warning to Tom that it was time to execute the plan he'd been formulating as they'd scavenged through the ghost town of Jackfish. Leaving Sara alone while she examined a three-legged stool with her flashlight in yet another deserted house, he sauntered out into the cool evening air.

Down by the moonlit Jackfish Bay he saw the cozy little boathouse they would spend the night in. Smiling, he grabbed both their knapsacks and headed into the romantic nightfall.

* * * * *

Aside from the gentle breeze rustling the leaves outside the glassless window of the debilitated cabin and the lapping water of the nearby bay, Sara found it quiet. Way too quiet.

But the silence wasn't new to her. With the help of her shrink Smokey, she'd finally been able to come to grips with the idea she was now alone and Jack and the twins were gone. After that realization, she'd more or less settled into a relatively quiet existence at Peppermint Creek Inn, keeping the inn running with the help of some hired students and bored housewives, and going into her peppermint product business. Since Tom had entered her life with his sexy heated looks, which made her burn and yearn to be fucked, she realized she couldn't go back to living alone.

Thoughtfully, she bit her lower lip. Today when she'd suggested they leave Peppermint Creek Inn, come here and stay at the ghost town where he had last been seen, she'd secretly planned a seduction, something he would hopefully remember if the memory of his other life came back. She was being selfish also, because she wanted memories, too. In case he remembered his past and on the off chance he forgot her like the woman who'd gotten hit in the head with a coconut in Smokey's amnesia example, she'd at least have had Tom for one night of passion.

She craved to find out what kind of lover he would be. Would he be gentle and tender, or aggressive and fierce? Maybe he would be a sweet combination of both? From the sexual satisfaction she'd experienced from his suctioning mouth on her swollen breasts and his expert tongue inside her pussy during the picnic, he wasn't shy about taking what he wanted. And her experience with him that night when she'd taken his thick cock deep into her throat proved he wasn't shy about his own sexuality either.

By the heated looks he'd thrown her way today as she'd tried to pretend she hadn't noticed, had made her hornier than she'd ever been in her life. At one point when they'd first arrived, she'd even sensed he would simply grab her and slam her against the nearest wall, rip her clothes off and start fucking her.

God, she'd wanted him to.

But he hadn't.

The sexual need in his eyes though had been unmistakable.

Sara closed her eyes and inhaled a deep, stirring breath. She could smell the oncoming rain drifting in the air. It was cool and damp with the distinct scent of ozone. It reminded her again of that horrific day. The day Jack had been murdered and of her miscarriage. Storms would probably always remind her of what had happened.

Just on cue, thunder rolled quietly in the distance.

Sara's eyes popped open and she looked up just in time to catch the lightning flicker briefly in the glassless window. A brief surge of adrenaline shot through her quickly followed by something new.

A surge of power. A new hope. An inner sense of strength. Some kind of instinct that allowed her to believe she would eventually get over her fears.

The fear of a relationship. The panic she felt with storms.

And now was as good time as any to start chasing away those doubts.

Digging deep down inside herself for the courage and with her hand wound tight around the flashlight, she slowly headed outside into the blinking lightning in search of Tom.

She didn't have long to look for him. Down at the edge of the sandy Jackfish Bay she quickly spotted buttery candlelight spilling from an open windowsill of a lone boathouse. Swallowing back the flare of excitement, she headed through the gnarled grass until she reached the rotting boardwalk that surrounded the slightly tilting boathouse. Stepping onto the walkway her heart picked up a fast pace when the boathouse door suddenly opened.

He stood there.

In the growing darkness she made out the tense muscles rippling in the hard contours of his naked chest, the fine fluff of chest hair that arrowed down and disappeared beneath his low-slung jeans and led toward that enormous bulge between his legs.

She swallowed at the erotic sight.

He cleared his throat and her head snapped up to find his blazing green eyes locked onto her. Heated hunger brewed there and Sara felt her body responding with incredible speed.

Felt her breasts swelling, her nipples hardening. Her clit pulsed wickedly and her vagina grew wet with her arousal.

"You finished with your tin pot hunting?" he asked, his voice a hot sensual purr.

She found herself nodding, suddenly unable to speak.

"I've prepared our nest for the night. Care to inspect?"

Reluctantly she broke the magical pull of his scorching gaze, followed him inside and realized he'd beat her to the seduction. At the far end of the walkway, dark, rippling waters seeped into the ancient boathouse and splashed a soft welcome to her. A lone candle flickered in the mild breeze on one of the windowsills and streaked a creamy glow over their sleeping bags, which he'd laid wide open, one on top of the other, on the narrow wooden floor of the empty boathouse.

Her heart pounded violently in her chest at the sight. A tinge of both arousal and fear ripped through her as she noted the frayed ropes on the rusty mooring rings in the nearby wall.

Had he put those ropes on the moorings? Or had they been here already? Did he want to tie her up? Was that the kind of dark lover he would be?

"Does it pass inspection?"

She found herself trembling as he came up behind her. Her mouth went dry as he pressed himself against her backside. Her cunt creamed as she literally felt the thick length of his cock scorch against the thin material covering her ass.

What should she say? Should she ask him if he planned on tying her down and fucking her? Did she even want him to? She barely knew him. She'd never done something like that with Jack, but she'd fantasized about it a lot. Fantasized about a stranger tying her down and making love to her. Fucking her over and over again, until she was a screaming bundle of passion.

She found herself leaning into him, encouraging him, wanting him to start taking off her clothes.

"So? What do you think?" His voice sounded dark, sensual.

"I think we should maybe get out of our clothes," she whispered.

Her pulses raced at the sharp inhalation of his breath.

She whimpered as his warm lips moved against the back of her neck. He kissed her there, his hot breath sending shivers down her spine. Long fingers clasped with hers and he led her to stand over their sleeping bags. That's when she noticed the gorgeous rusty tin teapot with a striking bundle of yellow daffodils set in it nearby on the floor.

She couldn't help but grin at the pretty sight.

Once again he drew up behind her, pressing his huge erection against her ass. His warm arms snaked around her waist and his chin rested on her shoulder.

"I know it's a bit of a primitive setting, but the flowers and candlelight are for you. To set the mood," he whispered.

"I've been in the mood ever since I met you."

"I didn't know if you wanted me to—" he tenderly kissed the curve of her neck "—fuck you, after the way I behaved the other night."

He was talking about what had happened after she'd taken his gorgeous, heavy cock deep into her throat.

"I understand. You aren't sure of anything. Neither am I. There doesn't have to be any strings. I know we don't know each other very well. But you're the first man…" She heated up at what she was about to confess. "You're the first man I've been sexually attracted to since Jack died… The first one I've wanted to make love to. I need to…"

I need to feel you deep inside me. Need to feel alive again.

"You want to feel like a woman." His tongue licked sensuously at the side of her chin sending a shimmer of erotic sensations into her mouth.

She nodded.

Leaning harder against her, he began a sensual slow dance rubbing of his erection against the curves of her ass cheeks. Her ass moved eagerly against her body, her insides grew hotter with every seductive gyration.

"And I want to bring you pleasure, Sara."

Her breath caught as his hand settled on her belly, the heat of his fingers sinking beneath her belt line, scorching against her abdomen.

Oh, God! Hurry. Make love to me. I am so ready to be fucked.

His finger slipped over her bare pussy, slid apart her already drenched folds and gently he stroked her swollen clit. Her teeth clamped together and she stifled a cry as her belly clenched with the insanely erotic sensations rocking her.

Another finger poked into her creamy vagina and she trembled with desire.

"What I do know is I've been wanting you. Needing to fuck you in your pussy and up your ass every night while I lay in bed.

Why do you think I've been working so hard every day? Staying away from you."

In the ass? She'd tried that a couple of times with Jack and hadn't really cared for it. But she found herself wondering how it would be with Tom.

His fingers left her pussy and his large hands slid sensuously over the curves of her hips quickly maneuvering her around to face him.

His eyes were heavy-lidded, his nostrils flared with arousal and the look of pure lust on his face took her breath away.

"I want to be inside you, Sara."

She watched as he unbuttoned the stud on his jeans. Her heart pounded at the sound of his zipper lowering. She noticed he wasn't wearing any underwear as she was given a view of his taut abdomen and dark curly pubic hair. Suddenly his thick savage-looking cock sprang free and strained toward her as he worked his jeans down his legs and stepped out of them.

"Undress for me, Sara. Undress for me while I watch."

His eyes were darkening. His voice barely a strangled whisper as he stood proudly in front of her.

Oh, God, he looked absolutely stunning.

Fire flushed through her and she stared at his big chest as it heaved with his every breath. Muscles rippled beautifully in his biceps as his arms came in front of him. One hand grabbed the base of his hard cock—the long fingers of his other hand kneaded his swollen testicles.

He nodded and she took it as her cue to begin stripping.

The walls of her cunt spasmed at the erotic sight of Tom touching himself and she could literally feel the thick, hot moisture pooling inside her panties.

Her fingers were ultra-shaky as she lifted the hem of her shirt and pulled it over her head. Her breasts felt heavy, enormously full as she unclasped her bra and let it drop.

He swore quietly as her breasts dropped free. He let out a ragged breath.

Her heart beat frantically as she stepped out of her pants and then drew her underwear off.

When she came up, Tom stood right in front of her, his fierce gaze raking down her body. A low growl of approval rumbled somewhere deep in his chest. It was a wild sound, an erotic noise that sent her nipples to tightening and her pussy clenching around air.

"You are so damn sexy I cannot get enough of looking at you."

His hands came up and his trembling fingers touched each side of her mouth. There was an odd sadness shining in his bright eyes along with raw sexual need.

"Ever since I saw you that first night, I've had the feeling I've seen you before. That feeling has only gotten wilder with every passing day." He brushed his fingers along her chin and down her neck, tracing them over the swell of her breasts to her dark nipples where he stroked them lightly, brushing the tips until they ached, the tingling sensations ripping shards of arousal into her vagina.

"I've had the feeling I fell in love with you even before we met. You think its reincarnation or something?"

She settled her hands upon his lean hips not quite believing what he was saying. How could a man fall in love with her even before meeting her?

"We've never met before. Believe me, I would have remembered if we had, and personally I do believe in reincarnation, so it could be that."

He nodded and continued to play with her nipples. His body heat skipped against her and all she wanted to do was get closer to him.

Pinpricks of erotic sensations were fanning outwards from her nipples, spreading quickly. When he squeezed the fullness of her breasts, passion sizzled like lightning arrowing a line of fire straight into her pussy and saturating the area between her legs with her sticky dew.

His feverish hands cupped her breasts tightly and his lips opened, his warm mouth quickly taking a quivering nipple captive. His white teeth bit down hotly against her flesh making her cry softly. The moist tip of his tongue dabbed gently at the sweet hurt and she pressed her breast against his mouth impatiently.

The tender dabbing of his tongue vanished turning into a hard suck, which made her squirm against this sudden change.

Tender, one moment, fierce the next. A very nice combination.

Her eyelids grew heavier as he sucked her other nipple into his mouth, sending sharp bursts of pleasure spiraling around her.

She could feel the hard, long outline of his thick cock press against her upper thigh. Could taste the desperate need to have his heavy flesh kiss her wet pussy lips. To slip inside.

His mouth finally left her breasts and came up to plunder her mouth. His lips were hot and moist from suckling her, his breath puffed harsh and excited.

She moaned at the pleasure rippling to life in her belly.

A hand slipped between her widespread legs and he was touching her pussy, tenderly rubbing her engorged clitoris sending hot spasms pulsing up both her channels.

Her pussy wept as her vaginal muscles clenched on empty air.

"Tom, fuck me," she cried, breaking the intoxicating kiss.

She heard his breath catch, felt the fingers exploring her pussy slip away from her cunt.

"Hold on," he whispered. Dropping down he dug in the pocket of his pants on the floor bringing out a handful of condoms. Dropping all but one, he stood and caught her shaking her head at him.

"I wasn't snooping or anything. I was looking for some more shaving lotion and found them where you put them in the bathroom mirror shelf," he explained as he quickly slipped a rubber onto his engorged shaft.

"The name I gave you fits perfectly," she giggled. "You're just like a curious tomcat. You find everything."

When he was outfitted with the condom, she curled her arms around his warm neck and her fingers enjoyed the smooth feel of male muscles in his back. Drawing him against her, she looked straight into his eyes.

"Make love to me, Tom."

He smiled and her heart twisted erotically in her chest.

"I aim to make love to you all night long, sweetness. I just wish it was under better circumstances. Wine, music, romantic candlelight."

"Your mouth is my wine, love. The frogs croaking outside, the music and you've supplied the candle already."

"You deserve so much more."

"Shh." She brushed her lips against his hot mouth. "This is absolutely ideal. We have our own beautiful little boathouse and I've got you. It couldn't be any more perfect than that."

His heated gaze dropped to look down between them and she inhaled as she felt the hard, round crown of his cock head press hotly against her vaginal opening.

Then he poised his thick flesh right there making her squirm impatiently. He seemed not to notice her distress.

"You know, you are awesome. Most women would probably have turned me in the first chance they got. You've been so caring, saved my life and you've given me a place to stay."

He pressed his engorged head into her vagina.

Oh, God! He was so big! So blessedly huge. Eagerly she awaited more of his hot flesh to enter.

He didn't move.

Instead, he started chatting again. "And now you're even allowing me to fuck you."

Sexual frustration began to build.

"Allowing me to love you."

"Can we discuss this some other time?"

"Why? You don't like to listen to me talk?"

It was then she noticed the humor lacing his voice, the perspiration dotting his forehead.

"Bastard, you're teasing me," she whimpered, realizing that not only was he going to be a lover with tender and fierce tendencies, he was going to tease her into a sex-frustrated death.

At her words, his hot mouth descended upon hers with such consuming tenderness it shocked her. Her pulses faltered. Hot spirals of pleasure coursed through her mouth.

His strong masculine scent seeped into her nostrils making her dizzy with desire. The smell of him made her crazy. Her knees weakened as his cock tunneled deeper into her moist vagina, stretching her as she'd never been stretched before.

Shit! That felt so good.

His erection sizzled, pulsing as his hard heat powered into her slowly.

Oh, so wonderfully slow.

He was being careful. Careful not to hurt her and she was thankful.

Soon his engorged shaft was buried inside her.

He held her hips tightly. Hotly. Firmly.

"You okay?"

"Yes."

"Feels good?"

"Oh, yes."

"You're so beautiful."

"Stop teasing me. Start fucking me."

"I'm serious." His warm breath whispered across her lips.

"So am I."

"You know I don't think I've ever fucked a woman standing up."

Somewhere along the way, she'd closed her eyes. She opened them, a spear of dread rippling through her arousal.

"You're remembering something?"

"No. But don't think for a moment I haven't forgotten how to make love to a woman."

Liquid pleasure showered her at his words.

"Thank God."

"You really are so damn beautiful, Sara. So beautifully tight."

He slowly withdrew his cock, and then came into her again. The well-lubricated walls of her pussy allowed him a tight yet painless access, and this time he penetrated her quicker, harder.

Sensations gathered, erotic vibrations that danced to the tune of his increasingly deeper, fiercer thrusts.

Inside her, his shaft pulsed with every long stroke.

With eagerness, she met his every plunge. Her vaginal muscles began to tremble. The pressure of his penetration seared through her, the lusty pleasures grew and grew.

"Oh, yes!" she sobbed.

Never before had her pussy been stretched so wide. She could actually feel every engorged vein of his cock pressing against her pussy walls. Could feel her muscles frantically clamp around the heated length of his gorgeous rod.

His throbbing flesh moved in and out of her parted pussy lips. Erotic groans broke free from his chest, the sounds only adding to the building pleasure.

Panting against his neck, she bucked her hips harder and harder against him, nearing quickly toward the killing joy.

Every muscle inside her grew tight as he pummeled her cunt without mercy. The sensations spiraled, snowballed, exploded.

Sara screamed as the seductive haze gripped her.

She crashed harder against him. Dug her fingers into his arms fiercely. Bucked until she let go and felt nothing but pleasure.

Pure pleasure.

Heavenly sensations that splintered her apart.

Oh, God! So beautiful!

The orgasm splintered, pummeling her a few delirious moments, ebbing away the next.

He continued to thrust.

Entering her, over and over again, until she was crying out from the wickedly delicious sensations.

Until her legs could barely hold her.

Until he came.

* * * * *

Cool air curled in through the open window of the boathouse and brushed along her naked backside where Tom had instructed her to lay on the sleeping bags with her bared ass up in the air and her face down.

They'd rested after their lovemaking.

But it hadn't been long before Tom had reached for her again.

She could hear his harsh, excited breathing as his warm palms slid seductively over the curves of her ass as he explored every inch of her hungry flesh.

"You've got the cutest ass I've ever seen, sweetness," Tom's velvety whisper pierced her erotic excitement.

"Yours isn't too shabby either," she replied, wiggling her ass, eager for him to slide his luscious cock deep into her pussy from behind. Her hard nipples twitched and tingled as she rubbed her swollen, aching breasts against the coarse material of the sleeping bag beneath her.

"I've got something here in the knapsack I want you to wear for me. I found it in your bathroom drawer." Oh, my gosh! Had he found her vibrator? Oh! How embarrassing. She'd totally forgotten to hide it. Holding her breath, she watched as he dug around in the knapsack and withdrew a butt plug.

Oh, shit! He'd found the plug. Jack had made her wear it when they'd tried to spice up their sex life.

"I want to you start wearing this to prepare yourself for me." Her face flushed at his words and he cocked his head, curiosity flashing in his eyes.

"Did you enjoy anal when your husband did it to you?"

She shrugged her shoulders. "It was something he wanted me to try once."

"Just once?"

"Actually twice," she said and her heart picked up a mad pace as he placed the plug onto the sleeping bag and began to caress the curves of her ass cheeks again.

God! His touch was so gentle, so caring, so arousing. A dark spear of pleasure seared through her as a hot finger slid between her plump pussy lips to stroke her swollen clitoris. The intimate massaging increased until it was almost a pleasure burn. Until she sucked in a breath and wished he would just penetrate her vagina in one swift thrust.

"Was it something you wanted?"

She hesitated. What if she told him the truth? What if she told him she hadn't really cared for it? That she'd only wanted to please her husband. Would Tom not do it, if she told him she didn't care for it? But she wanted to please him, too. She didn't want him to think she was a stick in the mud for at least not trying with him.

And she really did want to try this with him.

"The truth, Sara."

"I only did it because he wanted it. I didn't particularly care for it."

"Did he stroke your clit? Like this? Before he took your cute ass?"

Her thighs tensed as his finger eased off the pressure and smoothed firmly over her pulsing nubbin.

Oh, yes, that feels so good.

She couldn't stop her hips from gyrating, from wanting him to speed up the erotic caresses.

"No, he didn't," she bit out suddenly realizing Jack hadn't really taken the time to pleasure her when it came to sex. Maybe that's why she'd always been so eager to have sex when a storm came. It was about the only time he got excited.

"His fetish was making love to me during storms," she confessed.

"That's one I haven't heard before." His finger stilled momentarily on her aching clit, then he began rubbing her again. She could literally feel the hot cream of her arousal seeping along her vaginal channel and dripping from between her thighs.

"And now you hate storms."

"And you're playing shrink again," she said softly, pushing her pussy harder against his rubbing finger, trying to increase the erotic sensations his touch was creating.

"I am, aren't I?" Humor edged through his voice. "You're getting nice and wet down here. Unfortunately it's the wrong hole I'm lubing."

She cried out her dismay when his hot finger left her clitoris all alone and howling for his touch. Twisting her head around, she found him once again sifting through his knapsack. His hard, long, swollen cock stabbed out from between his legs as he dug out a container of her peppermint salve.

She trembled at the sight.

He was aroused again. His cock turning an angry purplish color, his cockhead fully out of his sheath and ready to penetrate her.

"This will do the trick," he said and came up behind her naked ass again.

Heat flared through her as he spread her tender ass cheeks apart.

She cried out as a liberally lubed finger poked into her tight ass, the sensitive muscles clenching around the intrusion while he explored her depths.

He dipped inside her puckered hole several more times, spreading the cooling peppermint salve, relaxing her anal muscles even further and going deeper with every entry. "I'll change your mind about ass-fucking, Sara. And one day I'll take your cute ass from behind. There's nothing like seeing your own cock sinking into a woman to." His finger popped out of her hole and her eyes widened as she felt the generously lubed, smooth, arrowed end of the butt plug press against her anus.

"When a man knows how to do it right, a woman will beg for it, over and over again."

His voice sounded dark, erotic. His finger continued to massage her tense, aching clit.

Oh, sweet heavens! Surprised excitement at the thought of being anally penetrated by the plug had her brushing her nipples harder against the sleeping bag.

She cried out as it pressed past her sphincter muscle and he slid it in. The pressure was enormous, stretching, burning.

He moved it into her slowly but confidently.

As the plug sank into her, a finger massaged her swollen clit, rubbing sensuously until she could literally feel her sticky cream of arousal seeping along her inner thighs.

"Oh, yeah, sweetness, take it all in," he bit out. "God! It looks so erotic, having a plug disappearing into your hole."

Agonizing pleasure-pain slid up her ass as it slid into her. It was a good burn. Something she'd really never experienced before. Not even when she'd inserted it those few times at Jack's insistence. Suddenly the plug stopped and her ass throbbed thickly.

"It's in," he whispered, his finger increasing the friction on her soaked clit.

Pleasure sensations were mounting. Twisting through her quickly.

The invasion of the plug tormented her in a beautiful kind of way and she found she loved the feel of it searing into her, impaling her ass.

The finger at her clit quickened its movements, poising her at the edge of unimaginable bliss.

And then his thick cock slowly sunk into her drenched and ultra-tight vagina, pushing into her, until she was trembling at the lusty sensations.

"Feel good?"

"Very," she hissed through gritted teeth. "Damn good."

He chuckled and began pulling his steel-hot cock out again. She cried out as he came into her again, all the while his finger teased her ultra-sensitive clit.

Her ass flamed beautifully—her clit throbbed.

Both actions complemented each other perfectly.

She found herself moving her hips backwards, meeting his now steady, even, deep thrusts into her.

Soon she was on fire.

Her pussy felt so hot as he stroked her clit sensually, and impaled her vagina, thrusting into her in ecstasy-inducing strokes, encouraging a tremendous climax to explode around her in a kaleidoscope of sensations that threatened to shake her apart.

"Sweetness, yes, that's it," he cried out as she bucked herself against his thrusts, impaling herself on him.

She could feel his cock thickening, pulsing, burning inside her with every violent plunge.

Oh, yes! He knew what he was doing.

Lusty flares raced through her. Tore her apart. Made her scream.

He let go of her clit and her pussy spasmed violently, her muscles eagerly clasping his penis. Her ass clenching wildly around the plug.

He continued to piston his steely cock into her.

Fast and furious.

Filling her wonderfully.

Heat. Pressure. So much pressure.

She loved the way he filled her. Loved the way he groaned as her vaginal muscles tightened around him.

Brilliant sparks of pleasure enveloped her. She rode the waves. Peak after electrifying peak — the killing joy crashing all around her.

She convulsed all around him. Violent tremors of lust blinding her.

He groaned, a lusty sound that tore at her heart.

And then he was coming. Thick hot jets of his sperm spraying into her, out of her, down her thighs, mingling with her own juices.

Afterwards, they made more love through the night, their sensual cries mixing with the waves slapping against the boathouse.

When the early streaks of buttery sunshine slipped through the windows, they were exhausted.

Tom collapsed onto the sleeping bag and she drew the other one over both of them, watching the way his long lashes curled over his closed eyes. Watching a loose wisp of hair feathering over his damp forehead. Pink blush stained his cheeks.

Gosh, he was a handsome man.

A fierce lover.

Her cunt felt sore from the fucking. It was a nice soreness though.

A tenderness she wanted to experience again and again, just as he'd said.

She curled an arm around his warm shoulder and snuggled against him, pressing her belly against the warm curve of his ass cheeks.

She smiled and closed her eyes instinctively knowing there would never be another man in her life.

Only Tom.

* * * * *

The sun was just disappearing behind the island out in the bay when Tom strolled along the outskirts of a tangled clearing in front of an abandoned house they hadn't yet investigated.

Stumbling through the snarly grass toward the building, his thoughts turned to last night and to today. To the intense all-day sex they'd shared between them.

He remembered the heated way Sara always looked at his cock just before he'd thrust into her quivering tight pussy. Remembered the awesome sensual cries that split through the air when she came.

Man! She was so gorgeous. So hot. So sexy.

Without warning, a loud crack erupted from beneath his feet and in a split second, he was floating through the air.

* * * * *

In the boathouse, Sara went still as the odd noise ripped through the evening air. It almost sounded like wood snapping.

It was followed by silence. Dead silence.

A shiver of unease rippled along her nerves and she padded barefoot to the open doorway just in time to see the flickering lightning on the other side of the bay. She shivered at the sight and tried hard to contain her anxiety of another storm approaching. Clasping her arms over her naked breasts, she quickly surveyed the nearby hillside for any sign of Tom. She saw nothing but the shadowed silhouettes of abandoned houses nestled in the hills.

He'd said he'd wanted to take another look around before they turned in for the night. They'd decided they would head back to her place first thing tomorrow morning for some more supplies and to check if the phone was working yet. She wished she'd invested in a cell phone. It would have been easier to contact her family and check for messages. Because they hadn't found anything helpful here for Tom, she realized her sister and father-in-law were their last hope. Surely those two would be able to help him.

Smiling into the twilight, she hugged her arms tighter over her swollen breasts and felt the aching tips of her raw nipples brush against her flesh. The magnificent things he'd done to her body last night had just about driven her insane with lust. For a man who couldn't remember most of his past, he sure knew how to bring out the sexual needs in a woman.

And now they had another full night of lovemaking ahead of them in their cute little boathouse.

Gosh, right now she felt like she was the luckiest woman in the whole world. The intense feeling of happiness almost frightened her. Almost made her feel that same awful uneasiness she'd felt during that dream she'd had a few mornings ago. The dream where she'd seen Tom chopping wood and the shadow coming up behind him with the gleaming knife.

Sara shivered as a swift blast of cool air breathed over her nakedness and suddenly she got the feeling something was wrong.

Very wrong.

* * * * *

Tom felt the cold, wet grass and slippery weeds brush against his fingertips and let out a deep sigh.

Thank God! He'd made it to the top!

In a couple of minutes he'd be out of the well he'd fallen into and Sara wouldn't have to know what he'd found down there. He winced as a sharp blade of light shone in his face and he felt a smooth velvety-warm hand slid into his grasp.

A wonderful minty scent wafted around him.

Shit! He didn't have to guess who'd found him.

Sara said nothing as she dropped the flashlight and pulled hard on his hands, allowing him the extra strength he needed to get onto safe ground. For such a willowy woman, she possessed a physical strength he'd never expected. By God, she'd need the strength if he decided to tell her what he'd discovered down the well.

Within moments he stood beside her, and began brushing the dirt and dust off his jeans. It took a conscious effort to keep his gaze averted from her. If she looked into his eyes, she'd see the truth.

"You really should watch where you're walking," she teased, her hands slid over his chest and arms as she checked him for injuries. But she wouldn't find any significant new ones. At least not physical wounds. The ones he carried were held deep inside him, and instinctively he knew they were ready to ambush him at any time.

But time was the enemy.

He tensed when Sara eyed the dark hole that had coughed him back to the surface. She wouldn't see anything. It was too dark. But if she picked up the flashlight where she'd dropped it on the ground by her feet, and shone it down there…

His stomach heaved. He bit back the sour bile coming up his throat.

Thankfully the cool breeze off the nearby bay slapped wonderfully against his hot face. He breathed deeply, swallowing the cool air, allowing it to calm his shrieking nerves. It did nothing to dissipate the violent trembling taking hold of his body. He frowned and looked away from the abyss.

"You okay?" Her voice was a concerned tender whisper.

He didn't answer her. Instead, he swooped the flashlight out of the weeds.

"C'mon. Let's settle in. There's another storm coming tonight." He grabbed her hand and pulled her away from the danger lurking in the dark depths of the well.

* * * * *

It was late and the storm would blow too far to the north to threaten any rain. The full moon glistened like a spotlight through the glassless windows of the boathouse.

It and a headache blasting at his temples kept Tom awake.

He'd wanted to make love to Sara tonight, knew she'd wanted it, too, but one look at his face, and she'd made him take a couple of painkillers and told him there would be no sex until he felt better.

Besides sex was the last thing on his mind at the moment.

Frustration gnawed at him and he pulled at the knapsack cradling his head trying to get comfortable. The rough wood-planked floor beneath the sleeping bag felt so darned hard. But that wasn't what bothered him. He felt restless. Itching to get moving. But to where?

Ever since he'd fallen into the well he'd felt different. A little more confident now that he knew his memories were slowly returning. A lot more scared of what his memories would reveal.

He closed his eyes and breathed the cool night air. The air smelled of rotten wood, fish and Sara. Her wonderful minty scent felt like an aphrodisiac. It seeped into his every pore. Clung to his skin like pure velvet. It claimed him. It was one with him.

He tried to ignore the warmth and softness drilling into his side from the woman who lay curled up against him. But her sweet body heat reminded him of the fierce lovemaking they'd shared last night and today.

After experiencing her passionate side, he wanted even more from her.

He wanted a relationship with her.

A lifetime of love.

A future that just might not be there for them. It might only be a matter of time before he was killed or incarcerated. Then he'd never see her again.

A horrible chill gripped him at that thought and his eyes popped open again. He turned and looked at her. In sleep, she looked like a sweet angel. Her full lips curled upward in a pretty, irresistible smile. What was she thinking to put such a wonderful smile on her peaceful face?

Her breathing was steady and rhythmic, slowly but surely lulling him to sleep. He closed his eyes and listened to her lullaby. In the distance, he heard the rustling sounds of the night creatures as they slowly crawled through the tall grass, heard the occasional splash of a fish jumping in the water outside the boat.

His mind grew heavy with sleep. *He mustn't drift off*, he chastised himself.

He should stay awake. If he slept, he'd remember.

He tried to lift his heavy eyelids. But they didn't budge. Too late! Too damn late! He didn't want to remember what he'd found in the well…

He was floating through the air, his stomach sinking as if he was on a runaway elevator. Darkness wrapped around him. Cold, damp air welcomed his descent. He could feel the rough, tightly packed rounded stones scrape past his fingers as he instinctively reached out to grab something, anything to break the fall.

The right side of his head cracked bluntly against the rock wall and for a moment he saw stars. He cursed his rotten luck and continued to grab madly around him. Something hard slammed into his leg. He reached out and his hands clamped around a cold, round, wooden object.

A momentary searing pain ripped through his shoulders and for a second he felt they would pop out of their sockets. However, the fall was broken. He swayed from his arms for a moment on what he figured to be a log stuck horizontally across from wall to wall of the pit he'd fallen into.

He allowed himself a minute to catch his breath, and then he pulled himself upward, his arms shaking with the effort. A moment later, he sat upon the beam.

Reaching out, he dug his fingers into the nearby wall and pried a trickle of dirt and a round palm-sized rock loose. He let the rock drop. A loud splash echoed throughout the cavern. If he were to venture a guess he'd have to say he'd found the local watering hole.

He cast a glance upward. He didn't have to wait long. *Lightning flickered. It illuminated the entire opening.*

Eight feet. He'd fallen at least eight lousy feet. It had seemed an eternity.

He took a deep breath of the cool, putrid air and exhaled slowly. Damp air ambled through his clothes. It nestled onto his skin, and sunk deep down into his bones. He shivered violently. Another flicker of lightning spilled down toward him.

"Damn," he hissed under his breath when he spotted something at the bottom of the well.

* * * * *

In the morning, Sara awoke to find herself curled up against Tom like a cat snuggling her master for warmth. His strong supportive arm lay protectively under her head acting as a pillow.

She sucked in her breath and lay quiet, relishing the exotic feel of his warm body heat as it seeped into her skin. She wanted him to wake up, to take her into his arms. Wanted to feel his hard, hot mouth press against her eager lips. Ached to feel his firm body on top of her. To become one with him. His long, thick cock sliding into her warm pussy.

Thrusting. Plunging deep inside her.

Explosions of desire raced up her spine as he suddenly snuggled closer. As if sensing her thoughts, he nuzzled his face into the side of her neck. His other arm slowly reached around her waist and pulled her closer to him. But his eyes remained closed, his breathing slow.

She remained wrapped in the silky cocoon of his strong arms and reveled in the ticklish feel of his day-old beard pressed pleasantly against her cheek. She watched him sleep for a long time in the chilly breeze of the early gray dawn.

After awhile when he didn't awaken, Sara reluctantly wiggled away from his warm embrace. Reaching for the nearby knapsack, she searched for an apple to nibble on when her hands fell upon her sketchpad.

"What in the world?" she found herself whispering as with further searching she discovered Tom had also stuffed the slender box of charcoals into the pack along with the strip of photos he'd purchased for her.

He really wanted her to get back into her art.

She found herself grinning as she looked at the pics and then at him sleeping soundly.

Why use his picture when she had a live model right here?

Maybe she should surprise him with a drawing? Show him how cute he looked when he slept. The instant her fingers slipped around a thin velvety piece of black charcoal, she began to feel the familiar excitement pound through her veins. In a flash, she became lost in the angles and various shadings of Tom's sleeping face.

She sat cross-legged, drawing from her heart. The smallest details of his face emerged onto the sketch paper. Wonderful tiny lines stretched around his sensuous mouth. Cheerful laugh lines crawled away like crow's feet from his sleeping eyes. And those gorgeous, long dark lashes. Oh, God, how she loved those luscious lashes.

In the past, she'd sketched like this. Sitting all day in front of her subjects. Drawing wildlife animals one day, a scenic meadow another day, and toward the end of her painting career, her imaginary children had intermingled with the wildlife world of the north.

Her husband would seek her out in the late evenings where he'd find her in her studio or out in the forest working to near exhaustion, trying to beat the drowning light just to finish a sketch or a painting she wanted just right before calling it a night.

At the thought of her dead husband, Sara lifted her gaze from the completed sketch, a wistful smile on her lips. She found herself looking at her surroundings. Really looking and for the first time in a long time she saw the beauty of nature.

She realized why Jack's spirit had come to her on the day she'd almost pulled the trigger. He'd wanted her to experience these feelings of love and beauty once again.

She stretched lazily and stood.

In a moment she was dressed in a pair of shorts and a powder blue pullover that would keep the early morning chill off her.

Grabbing the sketchpad, the charcoal and her flashlight, she gave Tom a long, loving look and then tiptoed out of the boathouse.

Bright sunshine and abandoned houses greeted her as she walked through the old town, which smelled mildly of fish. The smell didn't make her wrinkle her nose in disgust. She understood it belonged here.

Just as she belonged here — amidst the healing nature of the wilderness.

For some strange reason, the abandoned houses looked picturesque today. And so romantic. Each conveyed its own aging character.

Their scarred and weather-beaten wooden foundations, once homes for quite a large town, stood defiant. Their lonely, vacant windows watched her as she walked past them. Soft pastel shades of early morning sunlight splashed gently against their peeling paint and green tinged moss-covered roofs. The soil beneath her feet seemed thin and barren, and she wondered how the townsfolk were able to tend to their vegetable gardens in this rocky paradise.

In a sizable clearing, warm sunshine swirled around her, chasing away the chill of the shadows and the gray mist nipping at her heels. She stopped to bask in its warmth and sketched a couple of close-by buildings.

She realized she'd come back here again one day with her paints and pastels and capture on canvas the romantic colors and history of this ghost town called Jackfish.

As she finished the sketching, Sara tucked the book under her arm and continued her peaceful walk through the derelict town. She stepped over rotten boards, careful to avoid the protruding rusting nails and she lost herself for a moment in the cheerful chatter of a couple of chipmunks as they chased each other up one tree and down another.

Then she continued walking.

As she fought her way through the wild tangled clump of raspberry bushes, she quite unexpectedly stumbled upon the yawing chasm of the local well.

The same well Tom had climbed out of last night.

Sara stopped in front of it.

It would be dangerous to leave it like this. Someone else could fall in and be seriously hurt. She would search for sturdy boards in a bit, but first she needed to take a peek.

Flipping on the flashlight, she shone the yellow beam into the hole.

The well was deep. Horribly deep. And so dark.

How in the world had Tom been able to climb out of there? No wonder he'd been so quiet and distant last night. He'd come so close to death. Understandably, the experience had left him shaken.

What if he'd been seriously injured? Or killed? Sara shuddered at the horrible thought. What would she do without Tom in her life?

She stilled the flashlight. A pang of uneasiness slithered up her spine. Something was down there.

She lowered herself onto her belly, all the while dipping the flashlight deeper down the hole with her right hand. Cold, damp, dusky air swelled from the bowels of darkness. It swarmed against Sara's skin, instantly making her shiver in revulsion.

A piece of silvery metal flashed in the lamp's beam.

A belt buckle? A belt. Dark blue pants.

Surely she was seeing things. Surely she was having some sort of horrible nightmare and she'd wake up snug and secure beside Tom.

Her grip loosened and the flashlight dropped into the hole. The bright light gave Sara a momentary clear view before it flickered off as it drowned in the murky water.

"Oh — My — God!"

Her hand flew to stifle the scream threatening to erupt from inside her throat. Cold shivers draped over her body. Her pulse raced wildly. In a split second, she leaped to her feet.

"Oh, God. Oh, God. Oh, God," The words strummed through her like a death chant. She had to get away from here. Far away!

Blindly she stumbled backward away from the unseeing eyes that peered back at her and cried out as a sharp plain sliced deep into her heel. She jumped as safe, warm arms wrapped around her waist to steady her.

"You okay?" Tom's whispered voice was soft and full of concern.

"Sam Blake is down there! He's the missing officer. We have to tell someone."

Tom's entire body tensed against her. "Why? What good would it do? He's dead."

Sara broke from his embrace. Anger tore at her every fiber as she surveyed the casual way he glanced at the well opening.

"You knew already last night. You could have at least told me. Why didn't you? Why are you keeping me in the dark?"

"Believe me, you'd rather be in the dark. I just wanted to protect you."

Sara responded by twirling away from him and she stumbled as the pain sliced through her heel.

He grabbed her by the elbow preventing her from falling.

"What's wrong?" His concerned gaze raked over her.

"My foot. I stepped on a nail."

His grip on her elbow tightened with alarm and he ushered her quickly to a nearby fallen log. Slipping off her running shoe, he quickly peeled the blood-soaked sock from her foot.

Tom frowned. "When did this happen?"

"Just now."

Her heel throbbed like a bitch. Shit! That hurt!

"We have to get you to a doctor. You need a tetanus shot. You could get lockjaw."

Before she could protest, Tom swooped her off her feet and into his arms.

"No arguments," he stated firmly.

Her anger with him vanished when his hot body warmth seared through her clothes as he carried her along the overgrown path his handsome face mere inches from hers.

"Tom, please put me down," she whispered feeling quite breathless at being so near to him. "I've already had a shot."

He looked at her, doubt flaring in his eyes.

"It's true. Right after the fire, as I cleared some debris I cut my wrist on a piece of metal. See? I immediately went to my doctor."

Sara raised her arm and showed Tom the thin two-inch scar streaking diagonally across the underneath part of her wrist.

His eyes darkened and he let out a deep breath of relief. "Then let's go down to the lake and wash it out."

With her still cuddled in his arms, he headed toward the shimmering dark blue bay.

Every nerve ending in her entire body seemed to be on fire as she valiantly fought her desire for him. His strong muscular arms cradled her securely as he swept her onto a warm piece of driftwood near the water's edge. Delicately, he dipped her foot into the cold clear water all the while his body heat kept slamming into her, making Sara pant for air.

He worked diligently, splashing the cold water against her sore heel, thoroughly intent on cleaning the small wound.

"I meant to tell you about the dead man," Tom said as he worked. "But like I said, I wanted to protect you."

"I don't need your protection, Tom. I need your trust," Sara replied softly.

His head snapped up and he nodded.

"Okay, you've got it."

"No more secrets?"

"No more. I promise. How's your foot feel?"

"Just a little sore. I'll live."

She noticed his gaze stray to the one lone abandoned house set into a nearby hillside, far off the train tracks. A house they hadn't explored yet.

His eyes narrowed.

"What is it?"

"Something about that house."

"Should we go and explore it before we leave?"

He hesitated before answering. "I think that's the house they held me captive in."

* * * * *

Ever since he'd fallen in the well last night, frequent flashes of memory had bombarded him. Amidst the turbulent snatches, he still couldn't grab onto his name or where he lived. Instinctively he knew the whirling vision of a dead man lying in his blood with someone yelling in the background was a recent event. The vision of him being held captive in a dark, damp cell was also recent. And in the abandoned house straight ahead of him lay the answers. He was so sure of it, he could taste the sour bile in his mouth.

Trudging across the railroad tracks, he led Sara along the overgrown path to the desolate white-planked house. The black tar-papered roof sagged a little but the rest of it remained in relatively good shape. As they neared the cabin, impressions shelled him. Images of darkness. Ice cold seeping deep into his bones. Angry voices of two men having a violent argument.

This was the place where he'd been held.

Perspiration popped out on every square inch of his body. He felt clammy. Cold. Terrified. The urge to run felt so strong he turned to leave.

"What's wrong?" Sara's soft voice stopped him cold, and he looked back at the innocent-looking cabin.

"Nothing."

He was too close to run away now. His memories lay somewhere in there.

"C'mon let's go inside," he whispered. His hand tightened around hers and excitement intermingled with fear as they trudged onto the rotting porch. Pushing the gray wooden-planked door open, he entered the house first with Sara right behind him.

A musty odor of rotting damp wood greeted them along with crumbling shelves filled with cobwebs. Giant spiders watched his every move as he passed them. An old refrigerator lay half sunk into the rotting floorboards.

"Nice kitchen," Sara whispered from behind him. "Looks like someone was looking for something, too."

Tom noted that the floor planks had been ripped from the foundations and gaping holes eyed him from the walls. Somebody had obviously done a good job searching the premises.

Instinctively he knew they were way off the mark. He'd outsmarted them. His heart slammed powerfully against his chest as he followed his instincts and walked further into the house.

Chapter Twelve

ɞ

Tiptoeing across the rotting floorboards, Sara eyed the long strips of white paint that hung haphazardly from a dangerously sagging ceiling and buzzing hornets made their homes in the corners of the main room.

"Look, over there."

She followed to where Tom was pointing and noted a splintered hole in the top of the window jamb.

"A bullet hole?"

"If I don't miss my guess."

Tom bent down and picked up an old rusty kitchen knife and in a few steps he was at the window digging at the hole.

A moment later, the bullet popped out of the rotten wood. Turning it over in his hand, he examined the slug.

"It seems to be the same size as the one I dug out of your back."

"Could be from the same gun."

Excitement roared through her. Here was possible evidence Tom had been in this house and someone had been shooting at him while he was escaping. This piece of evidence might come in very handy.

Quickly he shoved the bullet snugly into his back pocket and took her hand again.

"Watch your step, sweetness. I don't want any more nails digging into those pretty feet of yours. I have better plans for them."

"Such as?"

"Sucking on your toes for one."

"I've never had a man suck on my toes before," she giggled.

"Better get used to it."

"Is that a promise?"

He halted and her breath stopped deep in her lungs at the intensity of his gaze.

"I'm going to try like hell to clear my name and make a future for us. But I can't do it by trusting the cops. If Garry and Jo can't help me, then I may have to run, but I promise I'll come back to you."

"If you run, I'm coming with you."

She saw the flicker of hesitation in his eyes and a shiver of uneasiness curled through her.

"I know I said no strings but you do want me to come with you, don't you?"

"I want you safe, sweetness. You can't be safe with me."

She wanted to argue with him, but they were at the staircase now.

"I was held down there," he said tightly and let go of her hand.

A moment later, he began to descend into the dark basement.

Brushing past the hanging cobwebs, she quickly followed him down the narrow staircase.

The air flowed cold and damp down here, instantly reminding her of the well and its contents.

Abruptly she stepped off the last step. And stopped behind Tom.

Except for a tiny streak of sunshine streaming through a small pane-less window toward the far corner, pitch-blackness greeted her.

"We should go back to the boathouse and get a flashlight," she said as a shiver of unease rippled up her spine. The spooky darkness of this place gave her the creeps. At that instant, she heard a sizzling sound and the bright yellow flare of a match.

"You come prepared."

"Boy Scouts," he whispered and pointed to a lone wooden door in the wall.

"That's where they kept me."

* * * * *

Tom shivered as he struck another match and watched the shadows flicker along the wooden door.

Against the back of his neck, he could feel Sara's warm breath bristle invitingly and he was really glad she was here with him. She gave him the courage to step forward. To find out what had happened behind that door.

Yet at the same time, he didn't want to open it either.

As if she knew what he was thinking, Sara whispered gently, "We'll never find out if you don't go forward."

She was right. It was about time he confronted those memories.

Taking a deep breath, he gave the door a rough shove. It creaked inward. Ice-cold air slammed into Tom hurling him back in time…

He'd awoken, almost frozen, lying on the cold, wet ground, his hands cuffed to a drooping chain adhered to an iron loop protruding from the stone wall. His head was literally splitting apart. Nausea almost overwhelmed his senses. He pulled himself upward, his sore hands burning with the effort.

Finally he managed to pull himself into a seated position and hugged the wall for any warmth he could find. He winced as the excruciating headache edged up a notch.

Gazing down at his hands he found the source of pain and was surprised to see the tiny, puffy puncture wounds in his palms. He had no idea what had happened or where he was, but he wasn't going to hang around to find out.

It was dark in here, but not so dark he could not make out the silhouette of someone huddled in the nearby corner. Almost immediately, he noticed the tiny candle flickering on the ground near the person.

He almost called out. But his heart sank when he saw the clothes the man wore. A cop's uniform. The man's eyes were closed. His chest rose and fell in steady rhythm. Sleeping on the job? *Tom's breath hitched at the thought.*

Y'know the old saying, when the cat's away the mice will play. He gazed around the room, quickly checking for an escape route. The room was tiny. About six feet by three feet. And maybe six feet high. How appropriate, he thought wryly.

For all intents and purposes he may as well be six feet under, because aside from these challenging restraints, the only way out would be the wood-planked door. Suddenly the heavy door burst open crashing against the rock wall like a sharp rifle crack. Tom jumped in surprise. The cop in the corner remained in his crouched position. Not moving. His eyes stayed closed.

He got the feeling the cop was feigning sleep. And waiting. He watched the newcomer crouch slightly as he stepped into the cellar. His heart sunk even lower. Another cop.

He noted the reddish moustache and the red hair.

Sam Blake. The man lying dead in the well. The shock of his remembrance almost broke Tom from his memory but he fought against the surprise, pulling himself back into his train of thought. He wanted to remember this. He needed to remember.

The cop glared angrily at the other officer crouched in the corner, but he said nothing.

Then he turned and stared down at Tom.

Tom stared back, defiant.

Sam Blake looked to be about six-foot-three. Maybe taller. The skinniest-looking guy he'd ever seen. His hair, what floated out from beneath his cop's hat, was a dirty rusty red, the same color as the pencil-thin mustache hanging beneath the man's bulbous-like nose.

His gaze narrowed on the cop. "Who are you? What the hell am I doing here?"

The cop's anger dissipated. His lips upturned into one awful cruel smile.

"So! You're finally awake!" the cop drawled and slowly crouched down in front of him. "Thought I'd beat you a little too hard during the last round. Had me worried."

"What do you want?"

"We're not going to play that game again, are we?" he said sweetly.

When he gave the cop no answer, a cruel smile crept across his lips and his voice lowered to a deadly tone that sent a shiver of dread slicing through Tom's bones. *"I'll cut to the chase this time. You got it. We want it. Tell us where it is and we'll let you go. It's as simple as that."*

He blinked not knowing how to comprehend what the cop said.

You got it? We want it? Got what? Shock waves of nausea spilled through his gut.

"I don't know what you're talking about."

Blake's mustache twitched. The cruel smile evaporated and his black beady eyes narrowed into tiny slits.

"Don't toy with me, rat. I want the goods. I want it now," he demanded between clenched teeth.

Rat? Why was he calling him rat? What the hell kind of name was that? And what was the cop talking about?

"Listen, there must be some kind of mistake. Just tell me what it is I'm supposed to have."

Blake's hand slithered downward. Toward his boot.

He gulped nervously as the cop's black leather gloved hand slid into the boot and produced a .32. His blood ran cold as Blake lifted the gun slowly. Deliberately.

In seconds the barrel was pointed straight at him. Directly between his eyes. Not more than three inches from his face.

His stomach twisted into a sickening knot.

"You don't have to do this, man," Tom whispered. He didn't recognize his own voice. It sounded flat. Totally devoid of any emotion.

"Just tell me where it is."

He flinched when he heard the clicking sound shatter the silent room. He watched in horrified fascination as the cylinder revolved to position a shiny new .32 bullet into the chamber.

It was at this point he became fully aware of the saying "your life passes before your eyes". However, nothing was happening. At least not in his case. Heck. Nothing passed before his eyes. Just a .32 and a grinning madman.

A trickle of sweat dribbled down his forehead as his mind fought desperately against the exploding panic gripping him.

He didn't have the faintest clue as to what this man was talking about. Maybe the guy would listen to reason?

"Listen, man. I'm serious here. I don't know what you're talking about."

"Wrong answer," came his sharp reply.

He braced himself. The gun pointed directly at his brain. The bullet would most likely knock him out before he could even feel a thing. Attempting to keep that one thought plugged squarely in his head, he felt some of his fear vanish.

Panic dulled. Anger at being held against his will subsided. A warm feeling of peace greeted him and he found himself alone. With peace and with God.

Then as if in a dream, he watched his own shackled hand slowly lift and float toward the gun, pushing it gently aside.

"You can't kill me," he said casually. "I have something you want."

Blake's eyes grew into giant marbles as his face twisted into an evil mask.

"You are a dead man, rat."

The gun swung on him. A gunshot rang out.

Tom jerked at the searing sound. He squeezed his eyes shut and his heart lunged into his mouth. He held his breath and waited for the life to pour out of him.

Endless silence rang throughout the room.

After a few moments, he realized cold air still entered his trembling lungs. Amazing. Somehow, the bullet had missed. He was still very much alive. And very much terrified. Or very much dead. But dead men didn't have splitting headaches did they? Or the God-awful shivers.

Reluctantly Tom opened his eyes to find Blake lying facedown on the hard rocky floor in front of him. A spreading blossom of red pooled across the man's back.

Horrified at the sudden turn of events, he'd turned his aching head to find the other cop, the one who'd been feigning sleep, standing in the corner. A small gray wisp of smoke curled from the gun in his hand. A satisfied smile lifted his lips.

Tom cursed beneath his breath as he remembered the cop's face.

Jeffries. Justin Jeffries had saved his life.

* * * * *

A fresh, warm, fish-scented breeze wafted off the bay, gently rustling Tom's blond hair. He stood stiff as a board. His jaws clenched tight as if he was fighting off some demons. His scowling emerald gaze scanned the nearby rugged cliffs.

He seemed extremely upset, yet he hadn't said a word to her as they'd trotted up the stairs from the bowels of the debilitated house. He'd headed straight for the shoreline and begun to scan the surrounding hillside. She wanted to ask him what he was searching for, but she opted to remain quiet. Past experience had taught her he'd tell her in his own good time.

Suddenly his eyes narrowed. She followed his gaze. She didn't see anything out of the ordinary, and yet—

Sara peered closer. A casual observer wouldn't have seen a thing.

It took a moment but she definitely saw a tiny metallic glint twinkle in the sunshine about halfway up a nearby rocky cliff.

"How's your foot?"

"Fine."

"You up for a little hike?"

Sara nodded, puzzled by his suddenly excited behavior.

"C'mon," he grabbed her hand, leading her along the sandy shoreline, across the train tracks and toward the hillside.

* * * * *

Fifteen minutes later, they were both out of breath from the taxing climb as they stood on a narrow ledge of the steep cliff staring wide-eyed at a shiny, expensive, brand new-looking, flashy green motorcycle laid carefully on its side. And it wasn't just any motorcycle. Gold lettering, written proudly across the gas tank revealed the words "Harley-Davidson".

Two shiny black helmets were strapped to the black leather seats.

"Who in the world would leave such a beautiful bike out here in the middle of nowhere?" Sara asked softly.

"It's mine," Tom replied excitedly as he surged forward.

"Yours?" She watched in surprise as his rippling muscular arms lifted the bike into a standing position and kicked out the kickstand.

A set of old, weathered black leather saddlebags hung from both sides of the bike. They contrasted sharply with the newness of the machine. Tom set upon searching through them.

Sara pushed a wisp of hair out of her eyes and surveyed Tom closer. He didn't strike her as the biker type. But on the other hand— The night he'd first arrived. Of course! He'd been wearing a heavy black leather jacket. Biker wear.

Tom's curse drew her attention. She felt her eyes widen as from one of the saddlebags he removed a fat billfold and with precise expertise began to count.

Bank robber. The obscene thought popped into her mind. There must be thousands of dollars in his hands. Where would he get that kind of money?

Drug money?

She shook the crazy thoughts away. She wouldn't go down the second guessing route. There must be a good reason why he had so much money on him.

"Man, there must be ten grand in here. Tens, twenties and fifties."

He tucked the bills back into the wallet and handed it to Sara.

Immediately she searched the contents for some ID. There was none.

"These bills are all U.S." Her eyebrows raised in wonder.

"And they're clean."

"Pardon me?"

"Not counterfeit," he elaborated. "And in no particular order. That means its not dirty money. No one can trace it when it's spent."

As if he suddenly realized what he was saying, he stopped talking and lifted his troubled gaze to peer at Sara questioningly.

"How do I know this stuff? And why would I be tooling around with all this cash?"

"Maybe you're a banker?" She threw him a smile and ran her hand gently over the gleaming bike marveling at its beauty. She noted the two shining black helmets strapped to the leather seat.

Two. One helmet was old and scruffed — the other one was shiny and new. Had someone been riding with him? Did the extra helmet belong to his girlfriend? His wife?

From the saddlebag, Tom withdrew a small leather pouch, which clinked with repair tools, a couple of tins of food, a can opener and a map of Ontario. Unfolding the map, they noticed the ghost town of Jackfish had been circled in black.

Cocking his head with curiosity he tapped the map with his fingertips. "I remember asking someone, a young lady I think, about any place that was really cheap to stay at. She mentioned a couple of hotels in town. And suggested I might be interested at taking a look at the ghost town of Jackfish while I was in the area."

"Where did you talk to her? How did she look like? Maybe we can find her and ask her questions about your conversation you had with her. You may have said something to her to indicate who you are."

He frowned and shook his head. "I don't know. I can't conjure up a face or a place. But —" His gaze flew over the nearby ground.

"What are you looking for?"

He took a few steps, bent over and overturned a fist-sized rock.

"This!" Tom lifted a set of keys.

"Obviously you're regaining your memory." She didn't know if she should be happy for him or sad for herself.

"Some of it. I'll give you the details once we get out of here."

"Wait a minute!" Sara grabbed at the keys. "Your key chain. That long key. It looks like the key to my barn and this one." Sara pulled at a short stubby key. "Is the key to my house." She pulled at another one. "And this is to the loft." She lifted her questioning gaze and met his confused green eyes. "Where did you get them?"

He shook his head slowly. "I haven't a clue."

"This explains how you had access to my barn. How you knew about the pictures in the loft. And that old bike in the barn. You were there."

Sara continued to examine the keys carefully. "These keys are from the first set we made when we'd first bought the inn. We only gave them to family. You know what this means?"

She raised her gaze to meet Tom's and jolted at his tortured look.

"I could have stolen them from someone you know." His voice was low and tight.

Sara shook her head. "It means someone I know trusted you enough to give the keys to you."

"Or I could have taken them off someone's key chain that indicated where they belong."

"You could have." Sara decided to agree. She wasn't surprised to see the look of shock cross his face.

A somewhat watery smile settled on his lips as he suddenly realized the game she was playing with him.

"Sorry. I should be positive. I was just—"

"Being negative." Sara laughed, and then grew serious. "Someone knew I was out of town and gave you the keys so you could stay at my place."

Tom finally nodded his head in agreement. "Okay. I can look at it from your perspective. Someone gave me the keys knowing you were out of town. That means someone close to you. But why haven't they called to check if I'm here? Or left a message on your answering machine?"

"I'd forgotten to turn the machine on when I left on my trip. And then the phones have been out most of the time you've been here, that's why there aren't any messages. See? Easy explanation."

"You're right." Instantly Tom's demeanor changed and he hopped onto the bike, laughing like a little kid meeting his best friend after a long separation due to summer break.

Sara's breath caught as she realized she'd never seen him so happy. Cute crinkles zipped from the edges of his eyes and his laughter was joyous and free. It was contagious. She enjoyed this new man emerging right before her eyes.

Jamming the key into the socket, he turned it and the bike instantly roared to life.

"Your chariot awaits, my dear," he chuckled and jumped off the bike, bowed and extended his hand in a sweeping motion toward the motorcycle.

"I can't get on that," Sara gasped as the full meaning of his gesture hit home.

Placing his hands on her waist, he pulled her towards him. Her heart accelerated with excitement as he pressed his large cock against her pussy.

"Why not? Don't you trust me?" She detected the mischievous glint light up his eyes.

"It's not that," Sara lowered her lashes so she wouldn't have to look into his face. So he wouldn't see her embarrassment." It's just…well, I've never been on one before," she shyly admitted.

He grinned tenderly. "Is that all? You can be my good-luck charm then." Seeing her concerned look he added, "You'll like it. Believe me."

He unstrapped the newer helmet and handed it to her. "Have to put this on. For safety."

Obviously he wasn't going to take no for an answer so she plopped the light helmet over her head. It fit perfectly and made her wonder who had worn it last. The girlfriend? Or the wife?

An odd feeling she didn't much like ripped through her. Anger? Jealousy? No way was she jealous. She'd never been jealous in her life before and she wasn't about to start now. With a stubborn tilt to her jaw, she reached up and fumbled awkwardly with the strap.

"Here let me," Tom offered.

For an unbelievably long time he stared into her eyes, his wonderful masculine scent invading her nostrils. With feather-light fingers he adjusted the strap, the touch of his flesh making her pulse quicken and her breasts tighten.

"All ready?"

Sara gave him a slight nod.

Reluctantly he let her go. "A few tips about motorcycles. Keep your legs away from those exhaust pipes. They get hot and I don't want you to get burned. Use the pegs. You can use the handle here to hang onto or you can wrap your arms around me. And you'll have to move with me, too, when I turn. Okay, that's about everything. Hop on!"

Sara swung one leg over the smooth warm leather seat and sat down. The vibrations startled her for a moment as they traveled up her legs, thighs, along the butt plug he'd re-inserted after breakfast and rocked against her pussy.

She sucked in a sharp breath and straddled the seat, enjoying the way her pussy spasmed and creamed with arousal.

"Ready?"

"Uh-huh," she said trying hard not to be nervous about this first time.

She jumped when he sat down in front of her and revved the engine. Her hands automatically flew off the awkward handle and she wrapped her arms securely around Tom's firm belly, pressing her swollen breasts against his hot back. Pure pleasure coursed through her at this erotic position and she moaned softly.

He threw her a concerned look over his shoulder. "You okay?"

"No problem back here," she lied. *Except for what your cock sliding into me wouldn't cure.*

"Hold on tight, sweetness," he shouted above the roar of his bike.

Sara clamped her thighs tighter around Tom's hips enjoying the vibrations from the bike and the wonderful sensations assaulting her body. He wasn't kidding when he told her she was going to like this.

"Let's go get our stuff at the boathouse!" he hollered. "Then we'll haul the stuff back to the truck and I'll drive the bike back home behind you."

Hearty warmth splashed through her as he called Peppermint Creek Inn home. She didn't have too long to relish the newfound feeling for he suddenly popped the clutch and the bike lurched forward slamming more sensations deep into her pussy. She tightened her grip around his lean waist as the bike began to descend, pushing her pussy harder into his luscious ass. Arousal mixed with fear as they plunged down the sharp angle of the slope. Closing her eyes, she buried her face into his broad shoulders as the bike hit a rock and jolted them, knocking her up off the seat momentarily.

Oh, shit! We're going to crash! Her mind screamed. But they didn't. Her ass hit the seat again and she melted harder against Tom's strong frame.

Within seconds, she began to relax. Well maybe not relax, but she certainly began to enjoy the hot sunshine caressing her face and bare arms. She found herself smiling at how expertly he maneuvered the powerful cycle down the steep embankment and she was grateful to the cool wind for banking the fires that began to rage once again inside her, now that she knew she would be safe on this bike.

Being so close to Tom was a heaven she never knew existed. Every movement in his body sizzled against her and she found herself wishing this carefree, erotic ride would last into eternity.

Chapter Thirteen

సా

They were fully prepared not to stay at Peppermint Creek Inn but after checking the answering machine, Sara discovered Jo had called while they'd been away at Jackfish.

Her sister left a message stating she and Garry were together working on a very serious case. They'd received her urgent messages and Jo would call back either tonight or tomorrow. Much to Sara's frustration, Jo didn't answer her cell phone or her pager when Sara quickly returned her call, thus forcing Tom and her to remain at her home to wait.

While Tom kept an eye out for unwanted guests, Sara prepared them both a quick hearty lunch. Afterwards they ventured to the seclusion of the back porch taking up residence on the top steps, sitting beside each other sipping some cool peppermint tea. It was at this point Tom began explaining everything he could remember when being held prisoner in the basement of that cabin in Jackfish.

Sara's hopes soared. Justin had killed Sam in order to save Tom's life. But then just as quickly her hopes deflated when she saw Tom's grim face.

"There's more isn't there?"

He stared into his mug for a moment then confirmed her question. "A lot of it is jumbled from before Blake entered the cellar room. But I do remember when Jeffries shot Blake I passed out." He grinned sheepishly. "Too much excitement I guess. When I came to, Jeffries was leaning over me, unlocking the cuffs from the iron ring. The minute he unhooked me and tried to snap the cuffs back around my wrist, I pushed him so hard he went crashing straight into one of the stone walls." He winced at the reminder. "Must have hurt because he just lay there stunned. To this day, I don't know how I managed the strength to do it or how I found the staircase in the darkness. But I did. When I reached the top I fell over Blake's body."

The blood in Sara's veins turned to ice.

"There was a gun on the floor beside him. I heard Jeffries running up the stairs behind me. I grabbed the gun and tried to shoot a warning shot but it was empty."

"Is that when he shot you?"

"No. I flew out one of the windows when he started firing." He presented the bullet they'd found in the wall and handed it to her. "This bullet should match the ballistics of the one you dug out of my back. I was halfway across a clearing when he got me a few seconds later."

"I just don't understand why he saved you from Blake and then tried to kill you when you were escaping."

"I think he realized what he'd done then planned on setting me up to take the fall for Blake's murder. All he had to do was stick to his story about my stealing his gun. That's how he would explain the bullet in his back. I mean who are the authorities going to believe? Me? Or a cop? And then there's the empty gun I picked up…"

Tom stopped in mid-sentence and grimaced. A tortured look scarred his features. And then Sara knew.

"You said when Blake pointed the gun at you it had one bullet in the chamber. But when you fell over Blake's body and picked up the same gun, it was empty. Either you're lying, which I really don't believe or you're omitting something you don't want me to know."

"It isn't pretty."

"For crying out loud from what I saw down in the well nothing you say is going to shock me."

But she was wrong—Sara realized it the moment Tom continued. "When Sam Blake aimed the gun at my head that night in the cabin, like I said there was only one bullet in the chamber. I'll bet you'll find that bullet between Sam Blake's eyes." The impact of his statement made Sara go weak. If she hadn't been sitting down, then she might have been in big trouble.

"You're saying Justin killed my husband because Blake was killed the same way?" The sudden realization she'd been entertaining her husband's murderer a few days ago brought a river of hot rage spiraling to the surface, making her hands knot into hard fists. The next time she saw Justin Jeffries she would kill him with her bare hands.

"Jeffries did it to Blake, it's highly likely he did the same to Jack. Fits the profile anyway. On top of that, he has a bad habit of showing up in places right after bad things happen."

Yes, Justin did have a habit of showing up when he was needed. The bastard!

The top step creaked as Tom shifted his weight, his concerned eyes raked her face. "You okay?"

"It's a shock," she admitted.

"You didn't want to believe it was Jeffries because of his past partnership with your husband."

"They depended on each other on the force. They seemed so close. They were best friends since they were kids. How did you find out about them being partners?"

"Cran Simcoe."

"And he doesn't like Justin either." She shook her head in puzzlement. "It's funny, come to think of it."

"What?"

"No one likes Justin. Jack and I seemed to be the only ones he got along with." She spotted sudden understanding flash brightly in his green eyes. "You've figured something out haven't you?"

He nodded. "The first day I arrived here I saw Jeffries driving out of your place in a cop cruiser."

"I asked him to look after my home while I was away."

"And you did that often? Asked him to keep an eye on your place."

"Yes. Like I said, I've seen shadows lurking around here. Not to mention someone torching my inn. How did I know if my house wasn't next?"

"If he was checking out your place, he couldn't have missed the broken kitchen window that first time he drove in. Unless—"

"Unless he broke it himself," Sara finished for him. "And why the rat?"

"Send me a message. Blake called me a rat just before he was about to blow my brains out. Maybe I double-crossed him. Maybe the money we found belongs to him or to Jeffries. Either way, somehow Jeffries knew I was coming here and he left the rat to scare me off. Keep me away from you. Keep you out of this."

"Maybe he found the note in your pocket, that's how he knew."

"He might have, but I don't think so. I was just plain lucky I found the slip of paper scrunched up at the bottom of an inside pocket myself. If he found it, he wouldn't have put it back into my pocket. If I was found dead with the note, then you'd be under intense interrogation. Jeffries doesn't want you hurt. And I think I've figured out why he's gone out of his way to protect you."

"Well don't keep me in suspense."

"He's in love with you."

"Oh, come on. Don't be silly." Sara laughed, unable to grasp the idea Justin Jeffries would be in love with her.

"You said you're the only one he gets along with. And why would he follow you two to Canada from New York? And what kind of a man would drive two hours through mud on an all-terrain vehicle to deliver you groceries when he already knew you were okay and he was supposed to be out looking for a man who's wanted for the disappearance of his partner?

"And all the other times he's showed up unexpectedly. When your husband was murdered. When the inn was on fire. I'm sure he's dropped in other times, too."

Sara's mind whirled as the truth of Tom's words sunk in. Justin Jeffries had been a pest since her husband had died. Always underfoot. Dropping in uninvited for dinner. Sometimes even bringing dinner.

"You think he killed Jack because of me?" she asked tightly. If that was the case, she would never be able to live with something so horrible.

Tom shrugged and said softly, "People have killed for love before, and if this is the case, then, dammit, don't you dare think it is your fault. He's the one who is sick."

She's the one who felt sick. "I don't want to hear any more." Abruptly, she stood.

In her haste, she accidentally brushed against her empty mug she'd set onto the edge of the stairs. The mug tipped over and rolled. Before she could catch it, the mug crashed onto the stone patio, shattering into splinters.

"Oh, darn it," Sara gasped.

Suddenly out of the corner of her eye, she noticed Tom's pasty white face and she jolted at the look in his eyes.

A look of intense horror.

* * * * *

Gushing crimson.

Wet and sticky. Metallic smell.

The familiar pounding began to swell against his temples.

He cursed silently as he watched the crimson liquid continue to pour freely. Blood seeping into the light blue carpet. A man. Around sixty-five, maybe older. A burgeoning pool of blood spreading from where his jaw once was.

Tom shook his head, trying to clear the visions. He didn't want to remember. Not now. Not ever!

The pressure in his head swelled. The pain spread outward from his temples, across his forehead to the back of his head. A tight band formed, squeezing, forcing the thoughts from his brain like a fruit squeezer squeezes fruit.

His heart slammed against his chest. He fought to remain in control. The blood continued to roll freely. He had to stop the blood flow! He raced to the man lying facedown on the floor. But it was too late.

He could tell by the deathly paleness gripping his skin. The man was almost dead. But he had to try anyway.

He reached out and turned the man over. He gasped in horror. Part of his chin and throat had been blown away. Automatically he pressed his fingers against what was left of the man's chin and throat in a desperate attempt to stem the flow of blood.

Thick. Warm. Sticky.

"Tom! C'mon Tom! You're scaring me!"

Sara's voice. He had to snap out of it. Oh, God! Had he killed the old man? He had to find out. He allowed his mind to drift back into the God-awful scene.

His hand felt warm and sticky. He looked down. His hand was covered in blood.

"Tom?" Her voice tugged at him.

He blinked again dashing away the vision until Sara's pretty face loomed in front of him. She reached toward him, grabbing his shoulders with her warm, soft, delicate fingers. Shaking him.

Nausea swarmed in his stomach. His head felt as if it were an exploding watermelon. Just like that old man's.

His hand still felt warm and sticky.

Covered with the old man's blood.

"You shot him." A crisp voice sliced through the air. "You're a damn murderer!"

"Call 911." Tom shouted angrily. "Dammit call 911!"

"I've got witnesses," the harsh voice bellowed, ignoring his plea. "You'll never get away with it."

"Dammit, Tom! Can you see me?" Sara's soft voice cut off the harsh accusations. Her voice became louder. Clearer. Sharper. Insistent.

"Tom! Look at me!"

Cold sweat splashed down his back in rivulets. Pain stretched tight across his head. Why would he kill a feeble old man? And who was the accuser? Don't think about it. Don't remember it! Don't!

His muscles ached like the dickens. His mouth tasted of bile and he felt as if he had the worst hangover of his life.

"You okay?" Her pretty smile wavered into view. It was watery but reassuring. He looked around.

Shards of sunshine splashed against the towering pine trees, and a gentle wind rippled the tall grass in the meadow. The gray-planked veranda floor stood steady beneath his unsteady feet. Then he dared to look down and realized with overwhelming relief his hands were covered with the peppermint tea. Not blood! Best of all, Sara stood beside him.

Desperate, he reached out and took her into his arms. He held onto her for dear life. Prayed to God she wouldn't be taken away from him by his own hand.

* * * * *

Sara's heart thundered against her chest as she stood at the kitchen screen door watching Tom splitting the logs he'd piled in the parking lot earlier in the week. The idea that Justin Jeffries might be in love with her had finally sank in, and she'd begun to analyze the possibility Justin might have been the one who'd murdered her husband.

She'd been so nice to the man. Only because she'd felt so sorry for him. She gripped her fists in anger. Unfortunately, her husband and her children had paid the price. They were dead because of Justin Jeffries.

Somehow, she would have to prove it. But how? She didn't know yet, but the next time she laid eyes on Justin Jeffries he was going to wish he had never met her.

She watched Tom take a moment to wipe the sweat from his brow then he continued chopping.

When the cup had broken, he'd had that vision again. The one about seeing a man lying dead on the ground. Blood pooling beneath his head. And he'd admitted more details.

He'd tried to stem the blood flowing from the man's fatal wound. Why would he do that if he'd shot the man on purpose? And whose voice had he heard telling him he'd murdered the old man?

What had Dr. McKay said? The memories may return spontaneously or be triggered by something. Perhaps something familiar.

The cellar in the abandoned house at Jackfish had triggered Tom's memories of being held captive. And she was pretty sure the mug shattering had triggered the old man's death. But why had he reacted to breaking glass? And what had triggered a violently ill reaction while they'd been sitting in her truck, searching through the paper bag for the headache pain reliever?

Sara shook her head in dismay. How in the world would she sort out this mess before Garry and Jo called?

Hungrily she watched the gorgeous muscles in Tom's arms ripple as he swung the ax downward, splitting another romance log in half. By the fierce way he split the wood, she knew he was hurting.

She had to do something to make him realize she would stand by him no matter what happened.

First though, she needed to do something else. Hurrying out of the kitchen, she went in search for the items she would need.

* * * * *

Chopping wood didn't make him feel a whole hell of a lot better, but it sure made it easier to push away the horrible flashes of memories invading his thoughts. Memories of the old man with part of his face blown away. Memories of panic. Of dread. Fear. And a whole host of other gut-twisting feelings.

Plopping the ax up against the chopping block, he took off his sweat-soaked shirt and used it to wipe away the cool perspiration curling around his neck. His arms ached from chopping for hours. His back was pretty sore and his head ached from the visions.

Taking this rare opportunity to look around, he inhaled at the terrific glow of the orange sunset touching the tops of the towering trees setting them ablaze with fire.

It would be night soon and he could be with Sara.

But was it sensible to make love to her without a future for them?

He clenched his jaw as the pain in his heart threatened to make him cry out. Sensible or not, he just couldn't stay away from her. Couldn't bear the thought of being separated from her for too much longer. His gaze flew to the tiny trail that intertwined through the darkening pine trees. The path led to the tiny cemetery in the field overflowing with pale powder blue forget-me-nots. He'd seen her disappear up it, hours ago. He knew what she was doing. He only hoped it didn't hurt too badly.

Dropping his damp shirt on the parking lot's log railing he picked up the ax and swung with all his might. The metal tip of the ax blade buried itself deep into the flesh of the beech tree log and he could swear it felt as if the ax itself had lodged deep into his own heart.

* * * * *

Hot tears roamed freely down Sara's cheeks as she slowly slid the gold wedding band off her finger and tenderly placed it into the warm grass flowing over the gravesite.

"You died so suddenly, Jack," she whispered to the big gravestone that contained the names of her family. "We left so much unsaid because we thought we had all the time in the world to say them."

Gosh, this was harder than she'd thought. Taking a deep heaving breath, she let it out slowly before continuing. "Every time I see a flashing blue police light, I'll remember you and the first time we met. Your cornflower blue eyes really floored me. I know I never told you that. I guess I should have." Sara swallowed the lump in her throat as she continued. "I'm through mourning you, Jack. I've got to say goodbye. Get on with my life. I know that's what you would have wanted. Keep an eye on our kids, okay? And please don't worry about me."

She picked up the painting she'd been working on when tragedy had struck her life. She'd never finished it. And she never would.

It was a portrait of two young children. Her children. How she'd imagined them to be at about six years old. Her portrait of their twins.

A boy, with gorgeous cornflower blue eyes. She'd made him into a young version of Jack. He was wearing blue jean coveralls over a bare chest and their girl, a young version of herself. Wearing a pretty lavender gardening dress. Her hair, long and flowing with luscious copper curls.

They were walking through the meadow behind the house. The meadow splashed with magnificent wildflowers. They were both smiling up at their father Jack who walked in between them carrying a pitchfork over his shoulder. They'd been on their way to till the vegetable garden.

She'd planned on giving the painting to him the day the twins were born, but it hadn't worked out that way. Instead, she'd give it to him now. Swallowing back the tears bursting in her throat, she laid the portrait beside the gold wedding band.

Turning her thoughts to her unborn babies, her heart twisted painfully as she placed her handmade mobile with the happy faces onto the grass beside the other items.

"I'll never hear your voices or see your faces," she whispered softly. "Or play games with you. Tuck you in at night, or hear your prayers. I wish—" Sara took in another heart-wrenching breath. "I wish things had turned out differently. But I'll rest easier knowing you're with your father and your grandmother. And in God's loving hands."

Reaching out, she lightly touched the wedding ring and the portrait and the happy-face mobile, her shaky fingers committing their touch to memory.

"Remember that I love you all so very much, and I haven't forgotten you just because I'm saying goodbye. Take good care of each other, and keep a watchful eye on your grandma."

Slowly Sara got to her feet and heaved a sigh. It had been extremely difficult to say goodbye, but she felt just a little bit better after unburdening herself of some of her tears. After one long, final glance, she turned her back on the big pink stone and left the tiny cemetery.

* * * * *

The skin on Tom's neck prickled a sensual warning and he halted the swing of his axe in midair.

Lifting his head, he saw her standing there. Her long tousled auburn hair flowed freely around her shoulders and arms in the rising late afternoon wind. His cock tightened with longing and hunger at the sight of her seductively curved rosebud lips. Although her beautiful big brown eyes were swollen and red-rimmed from crying, they hungrily flew over his naked chest, then raked down his abdomen and latched onto the quickly tightening erection he got whenever he looked at her.

His cock throbbed, pulsed and hardened against the prison tightness of his tight jeans. He wanted to reach out. To take her in into his arms. To kiss her until she begged for more. To press into her lusciously tight cunt.

He knew she wanted him. Read the desperate need mixed with wild delicious love shimmering like golden jewels in her eyes. Yet he did not reach for her. He stood stock-still, as if an animal sensing his mate.

He waited. Allowing her to make the next move.

* * * * *

How long she stood there openly admiring the hard contours of his gorgeous body she had no idea, but the erotic waves of lust washing through her made Sara acknowledge she would follow him wherever he went and she'd never leave his side no matter what.

Suddenly he sensed her presence and he looked up, his smoldering green eyes looking directly into hers, capturing her, reading her mind, searching her soul. The fiercely heated look glowing in his eyes made her blood pound hotly. Sweat broke out on her palms. She knew the hunger ravishing throughout his body, felt it gnawing deep inside her.

God! She wanted him so bad it physically hurt.

Without taking her eyes from his face, Sara walked toward him. She read the indecision in his eyes. The pain of wanting to leave in order to protect her. The need to stay and fuck her and love her.

"No strings," she found herself whispering knowing that's the only way he would accept another night with her. Reaching out, she took the axe that dangled from his limp hand and placed it against the woodpile.

"No strings," he replied softly as he slipped his powerful arms around her waist, cupping her ass cheeks in his hot hands pulling her roughly against his hard lean body. His head dipped and his mouth boldly took hers. The impact of his scorching lips upon her eager mouth made Sara groan from the sparks of pleasure.

She lifted her arms and wrapped them tightly around his neck. His tongue lightly grazed against her lower lip, sending electrical shock waves spiraling out of control through her.

Opening her mouth, she allowed his tongue to enter. He probed deep and Sara shuddered from the overwhelming feelings of pleasure exploding in her mouth.

His large hands came up and tangled in her hair as he pulled her closer and kissed her more deeply. Sparks of fire danced fiercely around her mouth and her body responded violently. His mouth became more desperate, insistent. She remembered how hot and hard his mouth had suckled her nipples during their previous lovemaking sessions and her breasts swelled with longing, her nipples tightened into painful peaks.

A desperate groan rattled deep within his chest. Suddenly his mouth left hers and she cried out her anguish. Without a word, he lifted her into his strong arms. Holding her tightly against his damp chest as he carried her across the yard and up the steps onto the wraparound porch.

In one fluid motion, he flung open the front screen door, crossed through the kitchen and living room and carried her down the hallway into her bedroom.

A moment later, she was being lowered onto the bed, the cool comforter pressing against her back. Her entire body trembled with frantic need as his fingers untied her runners and socks, flinging them away. She barely heard her shoes hit the wall as he slid his long fingers beneath the elastic band of her shorts, his heated flesh making her tremble with lust as he skimmed off both her panties and shorts.

"Get your blouse off. I'll be back in a minute," he growled and headed for the bathroom.

Her fingers trembled wildly as she did what he instructed. From the bathroom, she heard a drawer sliding open then a moment later it slammed shut. The harsh sound of a zipper opening split the air and Sara pictured him sliding his jeans over his lean masculine hips, the blue material slowly revealing the fluffy hair that arrowed down and encased his swollen testicles and stiff cock.

She blew out a shaky breath and slid her blouse and bra off, allowing her breasts to be exposed fully.

And then he was there.

Standing beside the bed looking down at her.

His fierce sexual gaze made her whimper. Made her pussy cream. Her nipples harden.

He was naked.

Gorgeously naked.

His stiff cock lifted upward toward his belly. The man was greatly aroused.

Then she saw what he held in his hand.

He'd found her vibrator.

The one she'd purchased via mail order shortly after her sister, bless her heart, had taken out a subscription for her with *Playgirl* magazine insisting Sara start to get back into the swing of things.

The vibrator she'd ordered was thin, with a one-inch wide, six-inch long shaft.

Sara had wondered why she hadn't been able to lose herself in the pulsing vibrations when she'd slid it into her pussy those few times. But she was losing herself in erotic vibrations as they swept through her now.

"I want you Sara. I need you. God! I need you so bad." His eyes were so dark with longing her heart swelled with love.

"You are so damn beautiful," he whispered as he gazed into her eyes.

"Come here," she whispered, holding her arms out to him.

He sank down beside her, and she wrapped her fingers into his newly cut and bleached hair—pulling his head toward her for another searing kiss. She couldn't stop herself from nipping at his luscious bottom lip, from tasting his warm flesh until he emitted a groan from deep in his throat.

The primitive sound rocked her, drove a wild ache deep inside her pussy. He smelled erotically dangerous as he leaned over her and began massaging her breasts. A spreading heat of deep-seated need coursed through her nipples as his fingers plumped her nipples, drawing them out, pinching them, squeezing hard until she shrieked from the raw pleasure-pain.

His mouth broke from her lips.

Slid softly along her neck, his long warm tongue burned an erotic trail over her breasts, all the while his hands slid off her mounds smoothing over her belly, teasing her mons with the tip of the now humming vibrator but not getting quite near enough to her pulsing clit as she would have liked.

Sexual frustration mingled with shooting sparks of desire as he kissed one aching nipple and then the other. He followed up with sensual feather brushes with the bristle of his five o'clock shadowed cheek as his face slid erotically against her ever tightening nipples. When she thought she could stand the scraping tension no longer, his lips fell urgently upon her swollen mouth and she accepted his fiery hot kisses impatiently.

She still wasn't used to these feelings of urgency and passion he brought out in her, and she found herself going freely with the intense sensations.

"I love you," she blurted out against his hot mouth. "God help me, I love you so much."

"I love you, too. I want you. I need you. I never want to leave you," he groaned between kisses.

Her breath caught in her throat at the agonizing truth in his words and she wanted to scream with happiness at what she'd just heard.

Opening her mouth, she welcomed more of his hot kisses. Welcomed the sexual thrusting of his tongue against hers. The intimate plunging.

He sucked fiercely at her lower lip until a hot sexual awareness buzzed through her and the strong need to merge as one with him almost overwhelmed her.

His breath was coming quickly now and the vibrator teased along her inner thighs, prompting her to spread her legs apart. She cried out, jerking wonderfully when the vibrator slammed hotly against her swollen clitoris. He began a fast, hard stimulating rub against her clit that sent her senses roaring.

Sara wanted him.

Now!

Boldly she reached out, grabbing his hard cock. His thick erection pulsed against her palms. The veins bulged against her fingertips. She squeezed and twisted his hot steel rod. His sexual groans ripped through the air—it sounded like erotic music to her ears.

His shaft grew harder, his moans deeper.

Growling fiercely, he grabbed her by her upper arms and threw her onto her back.

She thought he'd penetrate her. Take her quickly and fiercely.

He didn't.

Instead, he moved away from her. Grabbing her ankles, she laughed as he slid her along the bed until her ass touched the edge.

"What are you doing?"

He said nothing as he quickly hoisted her knees so her feet were flat on the bed, then he lifted her ass and propped a couple of pillows under her hips giving him a bird's-eye view of both her holes.

She spread her legs wide and shivered as heat flared in his gaze.

"You're already nice and wet for me, Sara."

"Don't sound so surprised, my love."

"It's still too soon for me to penetrate your ass but…"

She noticed he held a container of her peppermint salve in his hand and she found herself whimpering softly as he edged in between her legs. His gorgeous cock looked so big and hard, his balls swollen and ready to pour his love juices inside her.

He placed the container of peppermint down on the bed and returned her attention to her spread thighs.

She couldn't stop herself from trembling with excitement as he grabbed the flat end of the butt plug that protruded from her and slowly pulled it from her body. She moaned as it slid past the ring of anal muscles and left her. Whimpered as the sweet scent of peppermint sifted beneath her nostrils as she watched him lube all his fingers.

She inhaled softly at the delicious feel of his lubed finger invading the tender opening to her ass. Her inner muscles clenched around the intruder and he began to massage her muscles, spreading her.

"I'm going to try something different, sweetness."

"You are a man of variety." She grinned up at him.

"A man of many talents, I'm sure. Even if I can't remember them."

"You will, with time."

He said nothing, but she noticed the flash of fear zip quickly through his eyes and then it was gone.

He leaned closer, lubed the length of the vibrator and her eyes widened in surprise as he slid the vibrator against her anal opening.

She swallowed tightly as he inserted it.

"Have you ever been double penetrated before, sweetness?"

She shook her head back and forth. He grinned wickedly as he began to insert the vibrator, her anal muscles protesting the intrusion. He pushed harder, then slowly her muscles gave in, quickly opening up to it.

She liked the sensations of the vibrator as he turned it onto a low hum and inserted it deeper into her. The pressure built. The pleasure-pain burned brightly.

His eyes were dark. Dark and intense.

He drew the vibrator back out again then slid it in with long sensual strokes that had her moaning from the pleasure sensations.

"How do you like it?"

"Feels good."

"Play with your tits, sweetness. Pull those nipples. Pinch them for me."

Her vaginal muscles clenched wonderfully at his instructions. She did as he asked, running her fingers over her swollen breasts, touching her nipples until they stabbed into the air like two hard peaks of burning burgundy flesh.

She could feel the vibrator pulse deeper into her ass.

He leaned closer, his gaze catching hers, holding hers.

"Sex is beautiful, Sara. Very beautiful with the right person. What we have is something special. Very special."

He began a slow erotic thrust with the vibrator.

"I know," she breathed as she tried to keep the panic from coming again. Panic that maybe he was saying goodbye?

"Just go with it, sweetness. Relax and go with it."

No, he wasn't saying goodbye. He was giving her a present. She had to remain positive. Everything would work out. She couldn't let her doubts come into their lovemaking now.

He must have sensed her worries, her fright, for his hot fingers cupped her pussy, the erotic heat rushed against her flesh and she calmed down instantly.

Coils of desire gushed through her vagina as he slid the edge of his hand between her pussy lips and sawed lustily against her quivering clit.

Her fingers pulled vigorously at her nipples while he massaged her clit.

The erotic thrusts of the thick vibrator pulsing into her ass scorched her.

Trembling with lust, she watched as he guided his manhood between her legs. His cock was so swollen. So unbelievably huge that she almost came right on the spot.

For a split second, she wanted to remind him of putting on a condom but swiftly changed her mind. They'd already had unprotected sex and she wanted to feel the luscious skin-to-skin contact again. Wanted to have another chance that maybe he'd leave a little of him behind inside her in case, God forbid, something horrible happened to him. She desperately needed a link, any link to keep them together, and if she got pregnant and she lost Tom then she would maybe be able to hold herself together for their child.

Her swollen pussy eagerly opened to him. Erotic pressure built as his massive cockhead speared into her creamy vagina. Biting her bottom lip she moaned at the exotic way his thick shaft stretched her cunt muscles unleashing delicious sensations all around her.

He moved slowly into her, probing deep.

His huge cock pulsed. Desire became unbearable.

Gasping for breath, she lifted her legs and curled them around his waist, her feet digging into his hard ass. Lifting her hips upward, she allowed him a deeper penetration.

Oh, yes! That's it!

Her vaginal muscles eagerly clenched around his hot shaft.

He groaned. Thrust his hips hard. Pumped her cunt.

Long, hard, delightful strokes that blew her mind.

Her pussy contracted wickedly all around his thick flesh and she matched his frantic movements with her own.

Their bodies strained toward the lightning speed of ecstasy.

He whispered her name over and over again. Pumped deeper, faster, harder.

The vibrator filled her ass every time his cock left her pussy. The movements were synchronized so perfectly she couldn't believe the incredible sensations that threatened to tear through her.

Wave after wave of sensual vibrations grew and grew.

Her fingers tweaked and twisted her nipples until the pleasure-pain became unbearable.

His cock sank into her again. The vibrator pumped her ass with wicked thrusts. The pleasure increased. Twirled all around her.

She tightened her legs around his hard hips and then everything exploded.

Her mouth dropped open and a silent erotic gasp escaped her lips. For a moment, she couldn't breathe. Couldn't believe the brilliant sparks of sharp pleasure that ripped her apart.

Such wondrous pleasure.

Then she found her mind again and her sexual instincts took over. Her hips bucked harder against him as she fought to keep the carnal edge of bliss all around her.

Fought to keep her sanity as the painful orgasm rocked her.

Spasms churned through her cunt with lightning speed. Pulsing and burning.

The orgasms continued. One after another.

Sharp-edged. Dazzling.

When she could bear no more, she felt Tom come inside her.

Felt his hot sperm seep deep into her womb and hopefully filling her with life.

* * * * *

The hot spray from the handheld shower nozzle snapped against Tom's face making him shout at Sara who was giggling in the shower stall with him. Her long hair was soaked and tangled and fell all over her bouncing breasts. Her face was sweetly flushed, the aftereffects of him making love to her several times during the evening.

"Just wanted to make sure you're awake to watch this," she cooed as she lowered the shower nozzle and aimed it at his cock.

"Shit! Woman!" he growled as the hot needles of water pulsed against his already painfully hard cock. For a split second he thought he might explode and orgasm on the spot, but she quickly aimed the spray away and against her plump breasts.

The light skin of her curvy mounds quickly grew pink from the pelting hot water. Her nipples, already a burgundy color, darkened and elongated, stabbing into the air begging his mouth to take them.

Her full lips parted a little and her eyelids lowered slightly.

"You know I've had visions of you looking like this," he said softly as he watched her breasts swell beneath the pelting spray.

"Oh?"

"Yeah, of you leaning over me when you thought I was unconscious all those days ago."

Her eyes widened and the tiniest smile tilted her luscious lips.

"By the way you're smiling, I'd have to assume they are memories."

He inhaled a sharp breath as her fingernails scraped delicately along the full length of his shaft. She cupped his scrotum and squeezed gently until he growled and blew out a tense breath.

"Don't try to change the subject, sweetness," he warned.

"Yes, it's true. I confess. I came so close to mounting you while you were unconscious. The sight of your big cock had me all hot and horny." Her eyes dilated with lust. He could barely hear her next words above the sound of the water spraying against her breasts. "You don't know how hot and horny, Tom. I've never felt this way with Jack."

"Never?"

She shook her head and licked a bead of water from the seductive curve of her upper lip. "What Jack and I had was a gentle, tamed kind of love. What you and I have is…" Her voice trailed off as she searched for the right words.

"Something carnal? Lusty? Erotic?"

She grinned seductively and flung a dangling thread of her tangled hair off her face. "All of the above and yet something else, too. Something deep and untamed. Primitive."

"Like, soul mates?"

"I think so."

"You think so? Hmm, maybe I should do something to make you know so?" He yanked the showerhead from her hand and she squealed as he easily grabbed both her wrists. Holding them together, he gently pushed her thin frame against the white ceramic tiled wall.

"Spread your legs for me, sweetness and I'll show you exactly how I can make you know how you feel."

"And if I said no?"

"I'll bite your nipples, if you don't comply. And I bite hard."

She shivered visibly.

"Do it now, sweetness."

A sexy smile tilted her pink lips and her breasts heaved with excitement as she debated whether to test his patience. In the end, she spread her legs wide for him.

"Put your hands on my shoulders and keep them there."

She did as he instructed and he got down on his hands and knees. His cock tightened even harder as he looked up and saw her heavy breasts dangling like ripe melons above him. Her eyes were now dark with desire and she whimpered as his gaze slid to her pussy. Her pussy lips were ripe, pink and swollen. Her clit was plump and purpled with arousal and had dropped past her labia. Cream stained her inner legs.

She was prepared for him. Already wet. Well lubricated. Ready to be penetrated by his weighty and engorged cock.

For a moment he thought of standing, of slamming his shaft into her tight pussy and forgetting about foreplay. Managing to clamp down on the lust threatening to make him lose control, he instead concentrated on grabbing the showerhead where it had fallen on the stall floor and switched it to full pulse.

The warm spray gushed harder. Faster.

Aiming it between her legs, he watched eagerly as the harsh jet of water slammed against her succulent clit. She yelped at the impact, her nails digging sharply and painfully into his shoulders.

Oh, yeah. She was hot and she was enjoying the sharp spray coming at her pussy.

He kept the pulsing showerhead mere inches from her quivering vagina and watched as her nostrils flared. Listened to her erotic moans slip from between her luscious lips.

Her body tightened. Her legs trembled. Her eyelids fluttered.

She arched her hips against the showerhead giving him an awesome view of the bottom curves of her cute quivering ass cheeks, the smooth plastic end of the butt plug he'd placed inside her again. The erotic sight sent blades of lust searing along his shaft.

The muscles in her thighs quivered. She gasped out his name and he cupped her cunt, stopping the spray from arousing her any further. He could feel the sticky heat of her pussy, the plump outline of her clit pressed erotically against his palm. God! She was literally dripping with desire.

The cinnamon smell of her sex slammed into his nostrils and his cock pulsed in answer.

His heartbeat thumped madly in his ears. She cried out as his fingers found her swollen clitoris and he stroked her pleasure nub quickly, efficiently, until her hips gyrated.

When he released the pressure, she staggered. In a flash he stood, his right hand sliding over the sensual curve of her wet hip. With his other hand, he guided his aching cock between her velvety pussy lips and slipped into her tiny cunt in one thrust that had her backing hard against the wall and whimpering her approval.

With the butt plug inside her, she was tight. Unbelievably, beautifully tight. He just couldn't get over it. The eager way her vaginal muscles clamped around his hard flesh had him clenching his teeth against the white-hot blades of lightning that threatened to rip him apart. But he didn't want to come just yet. He wanted to fuck her slowly. Wanted to watch the beautiful pink flush stain her cheeks.

Her nails dug deeper into his shoulders making him wince.

Shit!

He wouldn't be surprised if she was drawing blood. Clasping her hips hard, he started a slow thrust. An agonizing slow withdrawal that had her gasping and her silky, greedy pussy trying to suck him back in.

She shook and trembled as he continued the torturous pace. He could feel the sperm building fast in his testicles. Pulsing and throbbing until the pressure in his balls almost had him dropping to his knees.

Her thighs closed, her vaginal muscles clenched tighter around him as he slammed back into her. It was then that he realized he didn't have a condom nearby.

Cripes! Wearing no condom was getting to be a bad habit.

"Protection," he ground out. He was ready to pull out when her hands curled harder around his shoulders, stopping him.

"Don't," she whimpered. "I want this. I want us. God! I want you, Tom. Just like this. No barriers."

There was a hysterical edge to her voice. It sent a tiny fissure of fear racing through him, but she bucked her hips hard and ground her pelvis into him, chasing away his fear with lusty blades of arousal.

He would think later. Right now, he needed to please her.

He thrust into her tiny slit again.

Hard and fast.

Fierce and mighty.

Her tight cunt spasmed around his length, unleashing something wildly exhilarating. He just about lost his mind in the carnal bliss.

He was so hot now. Consumed with need. With pleasure. Wanting to make love to her. Burning with fire.

Rocking his hips against her, he met her every buck with fierce pounding thrusts. Her slippery cunt clenched harder. He drove his thick rod into her over and over again until the pressure in his balls exploded.

His cock burst like a stick of dynamite spewing hot jets deep into her wildly bucking body.

Both their climaxes seemed never ending. Sweat trickled into his eyes, yet he kept thrusting.

Flesh slapped against flesh.

He ground harder. His balls emptying more of his love juices.

God help him, this climax was awesome.

Her cunt was slick. Well oiled. Demanding.

Oh, so demanding as she milked him dry.

When they came down from their highs, he lifted her weary body into his arms and carried her to bed.

* * * * *

The tantalizing aroma of fresh brewing coffee mingling with sizzling bacon and eggs roused Tom from his satisfying sleep. He opened his eyes and instinctively reached out for Sara. His hand fell on emptiness.

He experienced a momentary panic, but the heavenly memories of last night flooded through him bringing a contented smile to his lips. He didn't have to remember if he'd ever made love to another woman in his life. Something told him that after Sara there would never be another.

No two bodies could fit so perfectly together. All her soft curves matching with his hard angles. As if they'd been molded for each other.

As if they were…soul mates?

The warmth filling his heart froze and a groan of pure anguish ripped through him making him bolt straight up in the bed.

Today could very well be their last day together. When her sister or Garry called again and they discovered he was a fugitive, they'd have no choice but to turn him in.

Unless he did something drastic. Like take matters into his own hands. Like go on the run and take Sara with him.

It wasn't the kind of future he wanted for her but at the moment it was the only way they could stay together. They could use the ten grand they'd found in the bike's saddlebags and hop in her truck and head for Thunder Bay. Once there, they could ditch the truck in a mall parking lot and get on a bus or a train. His heart picked up speed as the idea took root. People disappeared without a trace everyday.

Excitement built as he hopped out of bed and quickly donned his clothing.

They could head way out west. Maybe to British Columbia? He could get a job on the docks. They could have kids.

He smiled as he remembered fucking Sara without a condom more than once. The thought of it made an odd kind of warmth that he'd never experienced before slip through him.

Maybe he'd made her pregnant.

There was no way in hell he'd let a kid of his grow up without a dad. No way he would live without Sara.

What they needed to do was get a real solid plan together, but first he'd put the truck into the barn and get the motorcycle in the back of it.

By the time he was finished with that task, breakfast would be ready and he'd allow Sara one more peaceful meal before breaking the news to her, before telling her he wanted to stay with her forever and they had to go on the run. While they packed, they could plan how to make everyone believe she was on another peppermint product delivery trip. It would keep anyone from looking for them for several days.

If they were lucky, they'd be on the road in a couple of hours.

Yes, this could definitely work.

Grabbing his leather jacket, he put it on and withdrew the truck keys from the pocket before heading for the back door. His heart pounded wickedly in his chest as he trotted across the cool mist-enshrouded yard and opened the barn doors.

Once they got a few miles down the highway, they could dump the bike somewhere on a side road or drag it into the woods so no one would ever find it.

Shit! He really could make this happen. Why the hell had he been so resistant to the idea before? He'd been a fool thinking he could live without her. A dreamer thinking Jo and Garry could help him. There were no guarantees they would even believe him. They might simply turn him over to the authorities. He'd never see her again.

Yes, this idea of going on the run definitely sounded like the way to go. Maybe when he regained his memory, and he'd learn the truth and he was innocent he'd have the ammunition he needed to keep himself out of jail. He and Sara might not even have to be fugitives for long.

Leading the bike to the edge of the open barn doors, he popped the stand and started toward the parking lot where they'd left the truck. He'd taken only several steps out of the barn when he stiffened. A shadow stood in the white fog not more than twenty feet away. For a moment, he thought it was Sara but the gun in the person's hand made him realize he was wrong.

Before he had a chance to react, a woman's determined voice sliced through the misty silence.

"Hold it right there, mister!"

Chapter Fourteen

ഇ

Tom froze dead in his tracks. A cold chill sizzled up his spine.

"Get those arms up in the air or I'll blow sunlight right through your brains," the woman ordered crisply.

He hesitated. If he could make a run for it, he could disappear into the dark bowels of the barn and escape through the back window. Sara might hear the gunshot and have a chance at getting away. On the other hand, she might walk outside and straight into a bullet.

"Do it! Now!" Another voice. A man's voice.

Shit! He was surrounded. No use running. His best bet to save Sara would be to wait for an opportunity to escape. Reluctantly he raised his arms skyward.

"Now move toward us!" the man ordered sharply.

Tom swallowed hard against his nervousness and his gut scrunched up with a sick feeling of dread as he slowly began walking toward the two mist-enshrouded shadows.

As he got closer, the shadows took shape. To his horror, he recognized the man from his earlier hallucinations or visions or whatever the hell they had been, the same man whose blood he'd tried to stop from flowing out of what had once been his throat seemed very much alive.

The only differences between the man in his memory and this man was the white handlebar mustache growing beneath this man's pudgy nose, the gun, which he held in his pudgy hand, and the wheelchair he sat in.

A wave of dizziness swooped over him and he faltered as bright flashes of light produced images.

Shattering glass. This old man yelling at him to run. Then this man's eyes staring unseeing at him. The smell of death hanging heavy in the air.

"My God, I thought you were dead?" The words escaped Tom's lips in a rush.

"Wish I could say the same for you, mister!" the old man growled, his knuckles whitened as they tightened around his gun.

Another figure stepped out of the mist. The woman. "Told you I saw someone lurking in the fog."

The sweet feminine voice instantly captured his attention. A tall and slender brunette with forget-me-not blue eyes. She was very pretty but it was the pistol she trained on him that held most of his attention.

"I'm Tom Smith," he offered to both of them.

A satisfied knowing smile whipped across the woman's lips.

The old man laughed bitterly. "Don't toy with us, pup. We know who you are."

"You know who I am?"

Bittersweet relief swept through every fiber of Tom's being.

*   *   *   *   *

Sara threw a few more strips of bacon into the frying pan. They sizzled crazily and she smiled as the delicious aroma wafted up to her nostrils. This morning she would cook Tom a feast fit for a king. Because that's who he was. A king. And she, his queen.

Last night when he'd made love to her, he'd brought out the woman in her so many times, so easily. And today she looked forward to experiencing the same love.

God, she felt so happy. She'd found another man to share her life with, and this time she'd never let anyone take him away from her. Not even—

The hushed sounds of faraway voices filtered through the slightly open kitchen window. Sara's breath caught in her throat. Was it Justin Jeffries? And the police? Her heart crashed against her chest as she dared a peek out the window. She saw nothing. Had she imagined the voices? Maybe. But just to be on the safe side she'd better go out and take a quick look. She took the frying pan off the stove, setting it safely aside on the counter and tiptoed out onto the front veranda.

"What in the world is going on here!" Sara yelled as she spotted Garry and her sister Jocelyn pointing their guns at Tom.

"Caught this killer lurking out in the barn. Has he harmed you in anyway, Sara?" Jocelyn's cold voice shocked Sara, and she looked at Tom. His eyes pleading for a helping hand out of this mess.

"Dear Lord! Take your guns off him. He's not a murderer."

"Did he touch you?" Garry commanded.

Sara jumped at his rough voice.

"What is the matter with you two?"

"That's the man they say murdered my brother."

Sara's mouth opened in utter shock. "Robin?" Her voice a shocked whisper. She barely heard Tom's strangled gasp. She couldn't think. Her surroundings swam before her eyes.

"Sara, are you okay?" Tom's concerned words barely registered on her ears. She saw him step forward.

"Stay away from her or I'll shoot you dead!" Garry shouted at him. Tom stopped.

This wasn't possible. How could Robin be dead? How could Tom be the murderer of Garry's brother? A sick thought slammed into Sara's gut making her gasp. Tom's memories. The old man in his memories had been Robin. A slow tremble began to jostle her insides.

"C'mon, Sara," her sister urged. "Let's get you inside." Sara felt her sister firmly take hold of her elbow. "Can you handle him, Gar—?" Jo yelled back to Garry.

"With pleasure."

Numbly, Sara felt herself being led back into her house. In the kitchen, she slumped dejectedly into a chair before her legs could give out.

Jocelyn sat down opposite Sara.

"Robin's dead? How? When?"

"A little over two weeks ago."

"This is insane." Sara shook her head with disbelief. "Not Tom. It's not possible."

Jo gently patted Sara's clenched fists. "You've fallen in love with him haven't you?"

"How—?"

"It's written all over your face." Jocelyn sighed deeply.

"Oh, Jo, I was so sure he wasn't a murderer. That what he'd said about Justin Jeffries was true."

"What?" Jo's eyes narrowed curiously. "What has he said about Justin Jeffries?"

"That Justin killed Sam Blake in cold blood and that it's likely Justin killed Jack, too."

"His partner? You mean Sam Blake is dead?"

"Yes, but no one knows about it except Tom, Justin and me."

"Sounds like a lot has been going on around here. I'd like to hear more about this man of yours. But I don't know if we can believe him."

"Why not?"

"They have witnesses against him, Sara. One of them is a high-ranking cop. The other is a detective. Both say he pulled the trigger that killed Garry's brother. They found a stash of cocaine at Robin's house. They said it was a thwarted drug deal."

Sara shook her head. "That's not possible."

Jo smiled weakly.

"That's what's so strange about this case. There's no way Robin would ever be buying or selling drugs. Garry thinks it's a plant. We were checking out all the possibilities. We tried to contact you but the phones were out. Then when I finally got through, I would have left a message, but I wanted to tell you, not speak to a machine."

Sara nodded with understanding.

"Sara, honey, I want you to tell me everything you know about this guy."

She choked back a sob and nodded. She'd tell Jo every single detail if it helped free Tom. Everything.

* * * * *

Out in the barn, Tom sat on a hard wooden stool, his hand was cuffed once again. This time to the wooden leg of a very heavy workbench. A twisted groan escaped his throat as he thought about what Sara was going through. For her to realize he really was a murderer. And to make matters worse he killed someone she loved.

God, he felt sick.

The old man in the wheelchair eyed him stonily. The pale skin of his wrinkled face was well creased like the leather of his old neglected motorcycle saddlebags. Pure hatred brewed in his smoldering blue eyes as they drilled a hole right through him. And the old man's fingers twitched nervously on the trigger as the fingers from his other hand stroked his mustache thoughtfully.

Again, Tom found himself in another life-and-death predicament. And quite frankly he was beginning to get fed up with it.

"If I wasn't involved with the justice system, I'd blow your brains out right here and now."

Tom grimaced at the raw emotion in the man's voice. He wished there was something he could do to ease the man's pain.

"Why did you kill him?" The words shot through Tom like a bullet. How could he respond to the question when he couldn't remember what had happened himself?

"How do you know I killed anyone? You have proof or am I just a convenient scapegoat?" Tom's words seemed to rock the older fellow.

"Witnesses saw you pull the trigger. Plastered my brother's throat and chin all over the walls of his house. You hopped on your bike and tore out of there like the devil himself was after you."

Tom grimaced as a flash of something passed through his mind. He pressed his fingers against his temples, trying to keep it from coming.

Someone yelled at him to run. Yelled at him to save himself. Save the truth. A flittering picture of shattering glass. Then the blood. Trying desperately to stem the flow of blood. Even when he knew it was too late. Images of driving his motorcycle through the coldness of the dead of night.

Tom shook himself from the webs of his memories.

The old man stared at him making him squirm uneasily. He felt as if he was a bug specimen under a microscope and the old man a mad scientist ready to stick a pin into him. The old man's next words shocked him.

"You were a good cop. Why'd you turn?"

Tom's mind reeled. "A cop?" He was a cop?

The idea was both mind-shattering and exciting.

"Garry!" Both jumped at the unexpected interruption. It was the woman. Sara's sister. She stood at the barn door.

"What?"

"Bring him into the house!" she instructed. "Sara has some information you need to hear."

"All right. We'll be right in."

Garry leaned over in his wheelchair slamming the key into the lock of the handcuffs. His eyes narrowed threateningly. "Don't make one wrong move," he warned icily. "I'm keeping my eye on you. So watch your step."

* * * * *

A few minutes later Tom stomped up the back door wheelchair ramp and into the house. His hands were cuffed in front of him. His back prickled under the scrutiny of the gun he knew Garry pointed at him. From behind, he could hear the barely discernible squeak one of the wheels of the wheelchair made, as Garry used his free hand to whip his wheelchair quickly up the ramp.

Tom had to hand it to the old fellow. He was quite efficient in the way he maneuvered the chair with one hand and kept the gun trained on him with the other. He hadn't allowed Tom one second at attempting to escape.

As Tom passed the open doorway to the bedroom, he briefly caught a glimpse of the mussed up covers on the bed he'd shared with Sara last night. Although he hadn't admitted it to her, the first time he'd seen her dashing up the walkway, her wonderful auburn curls billowing around her heart-shaped face in the rising wind, he'd fallen head over heels for the woman.

And now when they carted him off to jail, he'd most likely never hold her again. A great emptiness welled inside of himself and he almost preferred it if Garry would shoot him and put him out of his misery.

Garry instructed Tom to sit down in one of the overstuffed sofas in the living room. All the while, the gun remained trained on him.

A moment later Jocelyn brought in a heaping plate of cinnamon-covered donuts and various croissants, and placed it on top of the coffee table in front of Tom. Tom's stomach heaved at the sight of the food.

"I know it's not a healthy type of breakfast," Jo said as she leaned over and picked up two of the cinnamon-covered donuts. "But once in a while won't hurt. Help yourself."

She seemed genuinely surprised when he didn't take one. "They really are delicious. C'mon," she urged. When he shook his head, she smiled softly at him.

"Don't worry, you'll come around." She walked over to the recliner closest to the fireplace and sat down.

Tom couldn't get over her resemblance to Sara. He didn't understand why he hadn't seen it earlier.

She had the same pretty nose, well-rounded full lips and the same type of heart-shaped face like Sara, but that's where the resemblance ended. She was taller than Sara. Not as thin. Her eyes weren't as wide-set as Sara's, and she had pretty forget-me-not blue eyes.

Her hair seemed darker than Sara's. Chestnuts. That's it. Her hair seemed the color of roasting chestnuts.

"A wonderful woman in town bakes them every Monday." She was still talking to him as if he were an old friend paying a visit instead of a criminal shackled in her sister's living room. She took a huge bite out of the donut. Misty brown sugar caressed her mouth.

He really didn't feel like socializing, so he said nothing. He just wanted everything to be sorted out so he could get on with life. Even if it meant living it behind bars.

Sara entered with a pot of steaming coffee, some mugs and a large paper bag on top of a large tray. He found himself relaxing when she threw him an encouraging smile as she sat down on the couch beside him.

"Don't get too close to him, Sara." Garry warned in an icy tone.

Tom was surprised when Sara whirled on her father-in-law. Her dark chocolate eyes sparkled dangerously with anger. God, she looked so beautiful when she was mad.

"I don't know what's gotten into you, Garry. Or you, Jo, for that matter. I was always under the impression you two believed in innocent until proven guilty."

Jo leaned comfortably back in her chair, seemingly content to watch and observe. A hint of a smile played at the sides of her full lips. Tom got the feeling she seemed happy at Sara's outburst, but Garry's eyes grew dark and fierce with disgust.

"What kind of garbage has this man been feeding you, Sara? There's witnesses. Or hasn't Jo told you."

"Damn your witnesses!" Sara spat at Garry.

Garry looked shocked for a moment but recovered quite quickly. "He's wanted for murdering my brother. Until you give me some information that can change my mind—"

"I have some information."

The donut tray and yet untouched coffeepot and mugs danced crazily on the table as she slammed the bag containing their evidence down with furious determination. If she was looking to get Garry's attention she was doing a good job of it, Tom mused as he watched Garry peer at the bag, obvious curiosity on his weathered face.

"What's this?"

Sara reached in and brought out another bag.

"In this bag is a bomb that Tom found among the ruins of our inn."

Garry's jaw fell open in apparent shock and before he could say anything, Sara produced the familiar note and the handcuffs Tom had arrived in. She handed them to Garry's now eagerly outstretched hand.

"This is a note Tom arrived with. And the cuffs I pried off him."

She proceeded to produce the ashtray containing two bullets. The bullet retrieved from the cabin in Jackfish and the one she'd dug out of his own back. Tom flinched at the memory.

Pointing to one of the two bullets lying so innocently in the ashtray she said rather sharply, "And this is the bullet that attempted to silence your witness."

"Witness?" Garry exclaimed with disbelief.

"That's right. Tom is a witness. To a murder in Jackfish."

The familiar pounding in Tom's temples increased another notch.

Garry's eyes narrowed. "Murder in Jackfish? This is the first I've heard of this. Who got murdered?"

"Sam Blake. As he was attempting to kill Tom. We found Sam's body in the bottom of a well in Jackfish where Justin stashed it after he killed Sam Blake."

"Justin killed Sam?" Garry looked at Sara as if she might be crazy.

"That's right," she replied defiantly and folded her arms across her heaving chest. Garry sighed as he leaned over and picked up the bullet Sara had pointed to from the ashtray. His eyes narrowed as he examined it carefully.

"Police issue. Older model," his gaze flew to Tom. "You're a lucky pup. Newer models cause more damage."

"Hurts just the same," Tom replied sourly.

"I'll bet," he returned the bullet into the ashtray as he continued to peer curiously at Tom. "Where were you shot?"

"In the back."

"I see." Although his expression appeared blank, instinctively Tom could tell Garry was getting quite interested. "And the other bullet?"

"We got it from the cabin where Jeffries and Blake were holding Tom prisoner. When Tom escaped, Justin shot at him. He missed the first time and hit a wall. The second time he got Tom in the back. I can swear to that in court because I'm the one who dug the bullet out of him."

Garry's bushy white eyebrows furrowed as he flashed Tom a quick look of concern. Then his gaze fell onto the note Tom had used to find his way here. As he read it, his blue eyes became dark with anger.

"This is Robin's handwriting."

Sara suddenly burst with excitement. "Tom, where are the keys? The motorcycle keys?"

"I have them. Why?" Garry said.

"Look at them, Garry."

Garry threw her a confused look, shook his head with apparent impatience. With all this evidence coming out of the woodwork, Tom knew Garry was beginning to feel swamped and a bit irritated. Reluctantly the old man dug into his coat pocket to produce the item in question.

"Robin must have given Tom the note and the keys to my place knowing that I go on a lot of delivery trips with my peppermint products," Sara said quickly.

Garry frowned and asked Tom coldly. "Did my brother give them to you? Or did you merely pick the keys up at the scene of the crime?"

Tom shrugged as he felt all eyes fall onto him. A cold sweat popped out across his forehead and scattered across his back. His headache began to gain momentum. He didn't like the tone of Garry's voice.

"I don't know."

"What the hell kind of answer is that!"

"He's got amnesia, Garry," Sara replied quickly.

Garry lifted his hand to press a finger firmly against his temple. Tom noticed the signs. The man was encountering a doozie of a headache. Well, join the club.

Garry chuckled strangely, shaking his head with disbelief. He whipped an amused look at him.

"You couldn't come up with a better one than that? Half the criminals I work with use that line as a defense."

Suddenly he'd had enough.

The dam of anger building through him finally burst.

"Frankly, I don't give a shit about your other criminals. I came here because I found that note in my pocket. It was the only lead I had at the time. I waited for your help and now I'm being treated like a criminal. You might as well just blow a hole the size of a barn door through my head and be done with it, because once the cops get a hold of me, it'll be morgue time."

The room suddenly grew quiet.

After a moment, it was Jo that broke the silence. "Coffee anyone?"

* * * * *

An hour later, Sara and Jo were in the kitchen busily preparing a midday meal. Garry had taken a couple of aspirin for a headache and had escorted Tom to the bedroom so he could lie down and keep an eye on Tom at the same time.

How he could do both was beyond Sara. The least Garry could have done was allow Tom to stay here in the kitchen while Jo and she fixed up a lunch. Thankfully though, Garry had agreed not to contact the authorities. At least not yet.

"I can't believe Garry is being so stubborn," Sara hissed to her sister as she added some more hot water to the brown rice boiling in the pan.

"Sure you can. You were married to his son," Jo chuckled as she reached into the cupboard for some plates to set the table. "Anyway I'm not making any excuses for Gar, but he's only concerned for your safety and so am I."

Sara whirled angrily on her little sister. "I've been around Tom for almost two weeks. If he wanted to hurt me, he would have done it by now."

Jo threw her a puzzled look. "Hey don't get so excited, Sara. We care about you. You can't blame us for being protective, can you? I mean I know you would do the same thing for me if I was in your situation."

She nodded. What Jo was saying was so true.

Taking a deep breath she allowed her anger to ebb away, then decided to ask the question that had been gnawing at her for the past two weeks.

"Do you think Garry will help Tom?"

Her sister visibly stiffened at the question. "Are you sure you want my opinion? You won't like what I have to say."

"Yes, please be honest, Jo. I don't want any false illusions. Tell me what you think."

"With all the evidence we have against this guy so far, I don't think he has any chance, but if he can shed more light on all this and remember what really happened at Robin's house the night he was murdered, then our opinions will change."

Sara stopped stirring the rice and turned to face Jo who was watching her carefully.

"Are you telling me you don't believe the witnesses?"

"I can't say anything, Sara."

"C'mon, I'm your sister."

Sighing heavily, she patted her shoulder affectionately. "I don't want to get your hopes—"

"So there is something," Sara whispered, instinctively knowing her sister was having doubts about Tom being guilty.

"Oh, God, don't get your hopes up, please. It may turn out to be nothing. And don't tell Garry I said anything."

"You have a hunch?"

"Sara...please don't read too much into what I said."

Jo's words of warning couldn't wipe out the excitement running rampant throughout her. Jo knew something and Sara had every bit of confidence Jo and Garry would discover Tom's innocence.

"Not to worry. My lips are sealed." She couldn't stop herself from humming as she returned to stirring the rice.

"Anything else you want me to do after I set the table?"

"That's everything," Sara said, and then suddenly she remembered she'd forgotten something.

"Oh, my gosh. Dessert. I don't have anything for dessert. Garry won't listen to anything I say unless I ply him with sweets."

"Got that covered. Widow McCloud cooked up a batch of her famous fresh blueberry coffee cakes early this morning. She'd taken them out of her oven only minutes before opening the store. There's one on top of the fridge beside where you put Garry's mail. And it's probably still warm."

"That's Garry's favorite! It's perfect." Sara couldn't believe her luck. "Garry will do just about anything for Widow McCloud's blueberry coffee cake."

"Of course he will, and Widow McCloud knows it. She asked me to tell him to pick her up this Friday evening and they would be going to bingo."

"You're kidding."

"Nope. And you know what else? That's where I got my first inkling you had a man about the house."

Oh, God! The condoms she'd bought at the store.

"She didn't mention…"

"The condoms? Yes, she did." Jo laughed. "That's what you get for living in a small town. And even if she hadn't told me, that little box sitting on the bathroom shelf would have clued me in. And by the beet red shade on your face…" Jo's words trailed off for a moment before squealing with excitement and disbelief.

"You didn't!"

Sara nodded, her face flaming.

"Details, girl. Details. Details. Details." Jo laughed. "How? Well, I know how. I mean, so soon? You don't even know him. He's wanted for murder for heaven's sake!"

"I'll tell you all about it…" Sara hesitated before adding "…someday."

Jo crossed her arms and leaned against the kitchen counter throwing Sara a relieved smile. "At least you were sensible enough to use protection."

Sara bit her lower lip and returned to stirring the rice. They hadn't used the condoms every time and she'd already had some time to digest the probability she might be pregnant or maybe something a whole hell of a lot worse.

Maybe it was desperation clouding her sensible side. Maybe she was just plain stupid, but she hoped her instincts about him were right. That he was a very careful man with his bed partners and she wouldn't get anything but pregnant from last night's lovemaking. Nothing else could come from their sexfest. Their lovemaking had been so beautiful, she simply refused to believe anything but beauty would result from having sex with Tom.

* * * * *

Sitting on the edge of Sara's freshly made bed where he'd been handcuffed as Garry snoozed, Tom listened to Sara's cheerful voice drift through the open door. He wondered what Jo was saying to keep Sara's spirits up so high. He wished he could get in on it. He desperately needed some cheering up, too.

"I haven't heard Sara happy like this in quite some time." Tom jerked around at Garry's gruff voice. He could have sworn the man had been sleeping. Garry's eyes however remained closed as he spoke again.

"She used to laugh like that when my son was alive. But then he was murdered. Some say she did it. But I know better. Just wasn't able to prove it."

"Who do you think did it?"

"I'm not at liberty to say," Garry replied. His eyes popped open and he eyed Tom curiously. "So exactly how did Sam Blake die?"

"Blake had a gun pointed at my head. I really wasn't too curious as to watching the bullet escape the gun so I closed my eyes before Blake pulled the trigger. I heard a shot and next thing I know Blake's on the ground. And Jeffries is standing there with a smoking gun. After that, I passed out. When I had a chance to escape, I scrambled out of the basement and then fell over the body. The moon was shining through a window and I noticed the bullet hole between Blake's eyes. I grabbed the gun lying on the floor beside Blake and ran."

Garry's eyebrow arched up. "You have the weapon?"

"I do."

He wiggled excitedly into a sitting position. "Where is it?"

"You take off these cuffs and I'll get it for you."

"Nice try, pup."

"A guy can try, can't he?" Tom chuckled.

"What kind of gun is it?"

"A .32. It's not police issue."

"A .32?"

"He drew it out of his boot."

"A dummy gun. Although it's illegal for cops to carry unregistered guns some do it anyway."

Tom studied his frustrated features. Tightly clenched jaw, shaking hands and bright blue eyes that held loads of pain.

"So why do you want Blake's gun so badly?" he asked Garry.

Garry didn't say anything. He appeared deep in thought.

"I don't know where the gun is," Tom admitted after a moment. Garry's shoulders slumped in defeat.

"Sara knows though," Tom volunteered.

"Good, good," Garry said in a satisfied tone. "So, did you kill my brother?"

The words struck Tom as if he'd been slapped in the face.

"Honestly?" He shook his head slowly as he remembered the sound of crashing glass, and the blood. So much blood.

"Honesty is the best policy, pup."

"I really don't know." *But I'm having some awfully bad flashbacks,* he silently added.

Tom cleared his throat, took a deep breath and finally asked the question. "You said earlier I'm a cop. What's my name?"

"I'll tell you later. Right now I want you to tell me everything you remember," Garry said as he struggled off the bed and into the wheelchair.

Wheeling over to a desk by the window he picked up a notepad. "And I want you to start on what you remember from your first visit to Jackfish."

Chapter Fifteen

ဢ

"Sara, that was a good lunch. As always." Garry patted his swollen belly and leaned back against his wheelchair as they all sat in the living room. "You're a good cook. Isn't she a good cook?"

Everyone turned to look at Tom including Sara who eagerly awaited his response.

"Yes, she is. She's good at anything she does." He smiled at the blush creeping into her cheeks.

Apparently noticing Sara's sudden rosy complexion, Jo came to her rescue. She stood up suddenly. "Well on that note, I'll help Sara with the dishes."

"Forget the dishes. I need to speak with both Sara and—" he studied Tom for a moment then said "—and Tom."

"Then if you'll all excuse me, I've some phone calls to make."

Tom stiffened and Sara jumped from the sofa grabbing Jo's arm in desperation. "You're not going to tell anyone he's here, are you?"

"Don't worry. I won't call the authorities without letting you know first, sis. Just answer all of Garry's questions as best as you can," Jo said then cast Garry a quick glance. "I'll be out on the porch."

Garry waited for Jo to leave before taking a notebook out of his back pocket. He flipped it open and set it upon the coffee table.

Tom cast Sara an encouraging smile that seemed to do little to settle her unraveling nerves. Her fists remained clenched—anxiety tinged her beautiful eyes. Soon Garry and Jo would have little choice but to turn him into the authorities. And they'd most likely never see each other again.

Dammit, why did this have to happen? Why couldn't he have met Sara in some other way? Maybe in town or maybe if he'd come as a tourist to the Peppermint Creek Inn or—

"Sara, I want you to tell me everything. Start with the night Tom arrived. Don't leave out any details."

And so Sara explained when she'd first met Tom, wild-eyed and desperate standing in her doorway. And how he'd saved her life when the beech tree had come crashing down on the front veranda. As her story unfolded, fresh memories of last night washed over him.

He remembered the soft, silky walls of her warm cunt welcoming his cock as he slid into her. Remembered how sweetly she'd cried out every time she'd climaxed. Sometime in the early rays of dawn, they'd stopped making love and he didn't recall when they'd fallen asleep.

He had to force himself to look away from her in order to squash the rising sensations those memories created.

"Money?" Garry's questioning thoughts broke into his thoughts. Garry's expression changed to one of dark fury. "How much money?"

"Ten thousand. U.S.," Tom stated firmly. "What gives?"

"That's the same amount of money deposited from an untraceable source and then withdrawn from Robin's bank account the day of his murder."

He didn't like the tone of Garry's voice. His heart crashed against his ribs with such fury he thought it would leap out. His throat went dry and his headache, which had eased a good bit, toned back in again. For a little while he thought he'd found an ally in Garry.

After he'd spilled his guts to the old man, Garry had removed the handcuffs leading Tom to believe he would be trusted. But now he realized Garry still had his doubts. He cursed himself for being a fool and getting his hopes up.

He shouldn't have trusted this old timer. He should have been figuring out a way to escape instead of allowing his guard down and becoming comfortable in his presence. Garry leaned back in his wheelchair, cradling the steaming cup of black coffee in one hand

and fiddling with a pen in his other. The old man studied Tom quietly for a moment then asked softly, "Do you remember how you came across the ten grand?"

There was something in the softness of Garry's voice that brought flashes to Tom's mind. Flashes of a small, cozy living room.

A beautiful wildlife portrait of a raccoon sitting on a tree stump. A feeling of peace and happiness. In a split second, it died with the shattering of glass and the gut-wrenching blast of a gunshot.

He suddenly grew very uncomfortable in his chair and ran a trembling hand through his hair.

"I-I don't know. I mean… Some things. A living room with a dark blue pull-out sofa, nice wildlife paintings on the wall."

Tom shook his head numbly and shrugged. "I can't remember anything else," he lied.

He cast Sara a nervous glance and in turn, she threw him an encouraging smile, squeezing his hand in reassurance. Then he made the fatal mistake of turning to face Garry again. A mysterious gleam twinkled in his eyes and Tom knew instantly Garry was up to something and he wasn't going to like it. Garry didn't disappoint him.

"Does the name TURDUS mean anything to you?"

The urge to run hit Tom full force. He barely heard Sara gasp as the room began a slow spin. The woodpeckers crashed through his skull and he grabbed at the table to prevent from falling.

"Leave him be, Sara. He'll be all right. Just give him a minute."

He noticed movement beside him but he was unable to stop his mind from leaving the room.

"Oh, God!" The words ripped from his throat as he saw an old man lying facedown on the carpet. A large pool of crimson flowing into the light sky blue carpet.

"What do you see, pup?" Garry's voice sounded gentle and yet it sounded like Robin's voice. He couldn't be sure who was talking. Confusion stunned him.

The voice sounded so far away and yet it was right beside him. Insistent. Urgent.

He looked down at his hands. They were covered in blood. Wet. Sticky. Shaky. Then his gaze swooped over to the old man. He lay in a fetal position.

He reached out and turned the man over. A strangled cry caught in his throat. Robin! His best friend. Half his jaw had been blown away. Oh, God! He was still alive! And he was trying to tell him something.

Tom leaned closer. He didn't miss the tooth lying on the carpet as he tried to concentrate on what Robin was saying.

"Uney. un," Robin gurgled. With trembling fingers, Robin lifted his hand to point at the briefcase lying on the floor in the hallway.

"I understand. I understand," Tom whispered. He grabbed onto Robin's cold hand and held tight. "I understand."

"It's okay, Tom," Sara's voice. Tom grabbed onto her voice as if it were his lifeline and he flew back to reality. Shaken, spent and sweating he shivered as the cold sweat ran down his back in icy rivulets.

"TURDUS is the Latin name for Robin. It was his undercover name." Tom breathed harshly. Anger coursed through his veins. He didn't want to remember what had happened to his good buddy. He just wanted to forget. "The money was for me. To keep me safe for awhile."

Garry chuckled lightly. Tom almost decked him but Sara's gentle voice reined him in.

"It's going to be okay. It'll be all right," she soothed. Her warm arms circled around his neck and he found himself gazing into the deep, hot pools of chocolate brown. He began relaxing against her wonderfully soft frame, but before he could fully settle down, Sara pulled her arms away. Thankfully, she held his hand and remained close.

"Seems you've remembered something. Now I'll give you something else." Tom wished Garry would just shut up and go away but the old man continued. "A week before he died, I received a call from my brother. We were supposed to go down to Florida on our annual fishing trip."

Garry stopped for a moment, took a shaky breath, and plunged ahead all the while Tom's mind kept screaming at him to stop. He didn't want to hear anymore. He couldn't handle it. But he drew from Sara's strength and sat stiff as a board forcing himself to listen to Garry.

"Anyway, he told me he wasn't going to make the trip. Something had come up. Naturally, my lawyer instincts smelled something fishy, so I asked him for some details. He told me he was helping a friend with a case. He told me to keep everything under my hat. Which I did. Until now."

"What case?" Sara asked curiously. Tom wished she hadn't asked.

"He said it was one of the biggest cover-ups involving a New York precinct. Cops involved with frame-ups. Messing with evidence. Evidence mysteriously vanishing."

"Tom's a police officer?" Sara asked in a stunned gasp.

Tom ripped himself free from Sara's warm embrace and abruptly stood up. "Yes it looks like I'm a damned cop," he said coldly. He'd had enough. "I'd be grateful if you didn't say anything else."

Garry nodded then warned, "Your past is catching up with you fast, pup. And you better deal with it now or it's going to run right over you."

Tom turned to Sara and attempted a weak smile.

"I need some fresh air. I could use some company."

* * * * *

An hour later, Sara and Tom stood on the high cliff overlooking the tiny meadow sprinkled with forget-me-nots and the small family graveyard.

"Why don't we just run? Not go back. We can follow the train tracks back to the highway. We can hitchhike. Maybe go to Alaska? We could be free."

"If we run, we'll be running for the rest of our lives. That's no kind of freedom. It's not a life I want for you, Sara. Besides, I can't abandon Garry now. He uncuffed me for a reason. He's put his trust in me to help him. Someone killed his brother. It's up to me to remember if I did it or not. And if I didn't do it, then I was there when it happened and I must know who did."

Sara sighed with defeat, all her strength flowing out of her at the determined look in his eyes. So final. There was no changing his mind. He would go back. And he might even end up in jail.

Hot tears trickled down her cheeks and her hand tightened around his. Her heart wouldn't let him go. Not now. Not ever.

Her eyes flittered over the treetops of the giant jack pines and rested upon the meadow with the forget-me-nots. Whenever she came here, she would remember Tom.

She hated her next words but she knew he needed to hear them. "It's up to you. Whatever you decide, I'll support your decision. Even if I don't agree with it."

He looked at her, smiled that crooked smile of his and Sara melted against him. She wanted to savor this moment, to remember this wonderful view with the man of her dreams.

"Are you okay?" he asked gently.

Sara bit her lip, and then attempted a halfhearted smile. "I'm okay."

He took her into his strong arms and they stood silently watching a couple of loons fly past.

After a few moments, he broke the tranquility. "Are you ready for what's going to happen next?"

Sara frowned. "No. I'll never be ready."

"You're going to have to. Chances are there that we'll spend the rest of our lives separated from each other."

"I don't want to hear this."

"You have to hear this, just like I have to go back and hear the rest of what Garry has to tell me. He knows stuff about my past. I don't want to hear it but I have to…and I want you to promise me something… If things don't work out, I want you to forget about me and go on with your life. I don't want you visiting me in prison and tied to me for the rest of your life."

"God, are you insane? I could never forget you. Don't even tell me to. Besides if Jo's hunches pay off, we won't have to worry too long."

He frowned, his eyes narrowed with puzzlement. "What are you talking about? What does Jo know?"

"She says you're the key. If you remember what happened that night. She can help us."

"Are you sure?"

Sara noticed the tiny glimmer of hope flash in his emerald eyes. The same hope that kept her going. "I don't think she believes the witnesses. From what I understand, neither does Garry."

"Why didn't you tell me this earlier?"

"You never asked."

Tom swore softly, smiled and kissed her. His warm lips slid seductively over hers until she had to grab onto his arms to keep from falling over. It was the most explosive kiss she'd experienced to date and it flew all the way down into her feet to curl her toes.

"Sorry to interrupt you two."

They whirled around to find Jo standing not more than ten feet from them. "But Garry wants to talk to Tom again right away."

* * * * *

Garry sat in his wheelchair on the front veranda, as the three of them climbed the stairs.

"Let's get down to business," Garry said as they crowded around him. "Jo's got an appointment with a judge friend of hers that she trusts. The judge might be able to keep a tight lid on this for awhile."

"She works fast," Tom said as he threw Sara's sister an amused grin.

Jocelyn smiled. "I have friends in high places. What can I say?"

In Tom's excitement, he grabbed Sara's hand and ignoring Garry's frown, pulled her down onto the porch swing beside him.

A moment later Sara asked the question Tom had been reluctant to ask. "Was Tom involved in the cover-ups you mentioned earlier?"

Garry smiled sympathetically. "No, he was the undercover investigator."

"That explains the rat dumped through Sara's window," Tom replied.

Garry's bushy white eyebrows drew together, his frown deepened. "Sounds to me like he knew you were heading here. But you say he didn't recognize you in town because rain was interfering with his vision?"

"I don't know. There was a split second I thought he might have recognized me. I figure if he had, he would have taken me down then."

"Maybe. Or maybe he was just waiting for reinforcements to show."

"The thought occurred to us, too. That's why we were over at Jackfish, laying low and looking for clues," Sara said.

"Go on with this undercover stuff, Garry," Tom urged. Now that things were looking up, he wanted to hear more about his past.

Garry smiled, obviously pleased with his curiosity. "From what our source told Jo, up until six years ago you had a spotless record with the Billings, Montana police force."

Tom leaned forward, fully interested now. "Up until six years? What happened to change my record?"

"One of your brothers committed suicide in jail."

Tom grimaced as the heart-wrenching feelings slithered into him. It had been a double whammy. The horror of seeing his mother wither away day after day under the endless pain of cancer had been brutal, then mere days later the shock of finding out his youngest brother Steve who, being an investigative journalist, had been thrown into jail for possession of drugs.

Steve had denied it vehemently and his other brother Daniel, a prominent criminal defense lawyer had tried every angle to get their brother out of jail. In the end, under suspicious circumstances, their brother had supposedly committed suicide in jail, his body mysteriously cremated before they were able to see him.

Sara gave his hand a reassuring squeeze and he threw her a watery smile.

"And your mother —"

Tom threw up a hand to silence him. "I know. I remember that part."

Garry nodded. "Afterwards you became what they call a 'suicidal cop'. Taking unnecessary chances with your life. Many of your coworkers refused to work with you because they feared for their own lives. So they let you work solo. Then my brother came into the picture and he asked you if you were interested in going undercover in New York City as a crooked cop. Robin had some connections that would enable you to start off in the same precinct where an investigation of the chief of police would take place. Robin told you he suspected the chief as being the one who had your brother Steve framed for drug possession.

"The reason being he had refused to name a source about an investigation he was doing linking that chief of police in some way to a prominent doctor who was allegedly doing illegal organ transplants in various cities in the U.S. You were your brother's source."

Tom blinked totally dumbstruck. "What?"

"You came upon the information through one of your street guys. So you tipped off your brother. Apparently, he had a flair for getting to an impossible story. Somehow they found out he was doing some snooping, planted drugs on him and got rid of him in jail. You were hell-bent on revenge and accepted Robin's offer to go in undercover. You started off by keeping up your suicidal rogue cop routine and slowly the chief took a serious interest in you and began using you. After awhile, you became his right arm man. Using the precinct as a cover, you worked for the chief full time. Does any of this ring any bells?"

Tom shook his head slowly. "I don't know. I can vaguely remember going off the deep end but after that..." Tom shrugged his shoulders. "I can't seem to remember. I've had a lot of dreams though about buying and selling drugs, running plate checks for money, stuff like that. It's all—illegal."

"It was your cover. You had to make it look good," Garry replied soothingly. "You were doing it for a good cause."

Tom knew Garry was only trying to make him feel better. But it wasn't working. The more Garry revealed about his past, the less he liked himself. He wondered if Sara was having the same feeling, too.

Suddenly Jo's cell phone rang and she jumped up with excitement flashing in her eyes. "I'll take it inside. Anyone for more coffee and donuts?" she asked.

There was a round of no's.

Tom waited until Jo went inside before he asked the big question. "You said six years ago I changed into a suicidal cop. And then a year later I went undercover. So I've been investigating one man for five years and have come up with nothing? Either this guy is good or something else was going down. And I take it, it's the latter?"

Garry's eyes lit up and he leaned his arms on the wheelchair's armrests. "It started with investigating the chief but you kept digging up more and more crooked cops.

"Robin and our source figured you should stay under until you'd gathered enough evidence on every single one of the bad apples."

Tom frowned. Robin and the source figured? Had he himself had a say in this crusade? Why did the feelings of dislike for this job suddenly begin to grow?

"Who is this source?"

"This source led you to questionable cases by anonymous tips."

"Anonymous tips?" Sara asked the question before Tom could.

"That's right," Garry answered. He turned to Tom. "That's what is so strange about this case. Robin told me you received anonymous tips from two sources. One a man. The other was a woman. We found the woman. She admitted to being your tipper and she gave Jo the low-down of what you were doing. She also told Jo there was no way you could be responsible for murdering my brother. She'd never met you personally, but Robin thought very highly of you. Apparently you two grew to be best friends. When we got here and saw you heading to the barn we still had to be careful. We had no way of knowing if you'd turned bad. Another reason why you'd better get your memory back."

"You spoke to this woman?" Tom squirmed with excitement.

"Actually Jo spoke to her in person. A pretty brunette. But she wishes to remain anonymous. So she only spoke to Jo. From the looks of it, this woman is important."

Sara broke in. "Why do you say that, Garry?"

"When we went to pay her a visit at a prearranged meeting place, we were surrounded by armed guards. She had one hell of a security system. I tell you, I was impressed."

By the increased pounding of his headache, Tom knew he was venturing into dangerous territory by asking more questions. But he needed to know. "What did she say? Any ideas as to why she wants to remain anonymous? Why the big secrecy?"

"Like I said Jo hasn't revealed the woman's identity. Being a P.I., she takes her job very seriously. If she knows who the woman is and breaks her anonymity, it would hurt Jo's reputation. No one would trust her anymore. You can understand that, right?"

Tom nodded. He could understand it all too well. It didn't mean he had to like it.

Garry continued. "I can only venture a guess as to who the woman is. Like I said, she was surrounded by guards and a hell of a security system. She must have access to some important government stuff. Jo found her by calling in a bunch of favors. She was given a Washington phone number along with the name TURDUS. Both you and Robin it appears were working for her."

"What the hell did we get ourselves into?" Tom wondered aloud.

"Wondering the same thing myself." Garry frowned. "Looks like we may never know. But the woman did mention a couple of cases you were investigating."

Tom's curiosity began to pique again. "Go on."

"One is a five year old case. A raid instigated against a crack house. A very large amount of heroine was confiscated. Worth millions of dollars on the street. The drugs were put into police storage, and tagged to be destroyed.

"Checking the police records, you uncovered something interesting. There was no record of police storage ever receiving that shipment of drugs."

"But how can that be? A big raid like that must have been in the papers. No one can just go in and walk out with drugs?" Sara replied.

Something clicked. "It was an inside job. Someone with authority. There were no witnesses at the crack house. The three dealers had been killed in the raid. Hence no trial. No evidence needed. Clever."

"So you remember?" Garry asked hopefully. His eyes shining with anticipation.

"When you tell me. I can't seem to retrieve it on my own. What's the tie-in to this recent case?"

"I didn't say it was recent."

"Sorry."

"Don't be. You're right. It is a recent case." Garry smiled his encouragement.

Tom nodded solemnly. He didn't know if he should be excited or scared. But by the frown on Sara's face, she was experiencing the latter. Garry continued. "A few weeks back, another raid was instigated against a ship about to leave port in the New York harbor. A sting against a well-known arms dealer. The cops retrieved over a ton of weapons. You name it they had it. Uzis. .38s. Whatever your wish. Again the boat was practically empty of people except for one man. The notorious arms dealer Scout McMaster was supposedly killed in the raid. Hence again, no trial. No records of any weapons. Same scenario as the case five years ago."

"Supposedly killed?" Sara asked.

"I say supposedly because word somehow got leaked on the street it was the arms dealer who tipped off the cops about his own shipment. He'd already sold the guns to the Iranians. Had the money in his pocket."

"Bad move from the Iranians point of view," Sara stated.

Tom smiled knowingly. "Bad deals are made every day. It only needs one weak link to screw things up. Money passing too quickly always leads to trouble."

Garry nodded in agreement then continued. "Story has it, a high-ranking cop in your precinct faked the dealer's death. The crook threw the cop in for an undisclosed amount. Robin said you were working on finding out if there was any truth to this."

Nothing came to Tom's mind. Just an annoying throbbing in his temples. "Sorry, I'm drawing a blank. Give me the name of the top brass."

"Top guy's nickname is Whitey. He's the chief of police you're investigating." Garry's voice grew softer. "And there's something else you should know before I go any farther. His daughter is your wife."

"Wife?" Sara choked.

Tom drew in a sharp breath. It felt like he'd been socked in the stomach. He understood Sara's reaction.

"You married her last month. She's a homicide detective in your precinct. She's the other witness who saw you kill my brother. Robin said the marriage happened quickly and unexpectedly. Says you two flew down to Vegas over a weekend.

"Apparently, you got plastered down there and couldn't remember getting hitched. Needless to say, my brother was quite shocked about it and apparently so were you. I say apparently because we have no way of knowing if you were lying to Robin. Maybe you got hitched with the woman because you truly loved her and wanted to get access to her dad's money. You do understand why we reacted the way we did when we first saw you?" There seemed to be an apology in there somewhere and Tom couldn't help but be a little hopeful again about the situation he was in.

Unfortunately the story about him being married seemed unbelievable. Like some kind of nightmare he couldn't wake up from. And by the devastated look on Sara's face, she was experiencing the same gut-wrenching sorrow for their relationship.

Jo appeared at the door. "Garry? Can I talk to you?"

Garry turned in his chair. "I'll be right in."

He turned to the silent couple. "I'm sorry, but I figured you both should know about the marriage. I'll leave you two alone."

He threw them what Tom figured to be a reassuring smile. But he didn't feel reassured.

Garry said he was married. To a woman he didn't even remember. He felt as if his whole world had just been blown to smithereens.

Chapter Sixteen

ဢ

Sara and Tom sat in silence for quite a long time after Garry wheeled himself inside. Both peered out across the parking lot at the cool forest. Both pondering the horrible bomb Garry had dropped. Finally, Sara gathered enough courage to speak.

"It' s an enormous amount of information for one person to take in all at once."

The dark, shocked look on Tom's face instantly dissolved and he swung his hurt gaze directly on her.

"Especially the part about me being married," he replied softly.

Sara nodded as she fought back the sudden swell of tears. Tom was married. One of her worst nightmares had come true. Even if they somehow got out of this mess, he was married. He would leave her for the other woman.

God, it hurt. Hurt so bad.

She bit her lower lip in frustration preventing the anguished cry to escape her throat.

"I didn't know. I'm so sorry." His shoulders sagged in defeat.

Sara reached out to lightly touch his arm.

"Don't beat yourself over it. We're both adults. We knew what we were doing. No strings. Remember?"

He nodded solemnly.

Love wasn't a chance she had wanted to take again and now she knew why. Dammit. Her heart was breaking all over again.

"Whether I am married or not, Sara, you are someone very special to me. Very special," his whispered cry ripped through her heart.

In a flurry of movement, he pulled her into his strong arms, caressing the tears flooding a hot trail along her cheeks. "I love you. I love you more than my life itself."

A violent shudder shot through her and she buried her face against his warm neck. "I believe you. I truly do. I was happy for a while. I'd almost forgotten what it felt like. For that I'm thankful to you."

His arms tightened around her waist. When she looked into his eyes, she saw tears glistening there. Painful tears of what they had shared and what might have been.

They sat that way for a long time. Wrapped in each other's arms. Hearts beating in unison. Neither wanting to break their embrace.

They were interrupted by the screen door creaking open and Garry clearing his throat. Tom and Sara slowly drew apart.

"Sorry," Garry mumbled uncomfortably. "There's not much time. We have to leave again. Please, Sara, fetch me all the evidence. Everything including the gun he arrived with. I need to speak to Tom."

With great hesitation, Tom let Sara's hand go and casting him a longing look she finally went in search of the evidence.

"How are we going to do this?" Tom asked tightly when Sara was out of earshot. "About me, I mean?"

"I've been thinking on that. Change of plans. I want you to stay here with Sara. Keep a damn good low profile. Stay in one of the cabins out in the woods if you have to. Stay indoors. Stay out of sight. Don't turn on any lights at night. You know the drill."

"Sara has to come with you. I want her safe."

Garry continued as if he hadn't heard him. "I want us to keep this hush for as long as possible. I'd get you to a safe house, but I don't know whom to trust. It would be risky. Can't take the chance that some cop would recognize you. You're face isn't all over the police computers yet and the story hasn't hit the press, but it is just a matter of time. Whitey must have some pretty good connections keeping this suppressed. I guess that's to our advantage. Anyway, I'd like you to stay put. Heck, it's risky asking you to stay here, but I need you by a phone. I may need to get a hold of you at a moment's notice." Tom's mind reeled as he tried to take everything in. Somehow, Garry believed him innocent. The relief was almost too much to bear.

Garry continued quickly, efficiently. If he noticed the shock on Tom's face, he didn't seem to pay attention. "And Jo got us an appointment with Ballistics tonight.

"Bullets have a way of telling the story. I just hope Ballistics will find something. Anyways, I've got to find someone trustworthy to retrieve Blake's body and Jo has to talk to the judge about getting protection for you."

"Are you sure about all this? About me staying here? Aren't you afraid I'll run?"

"You didn't run earlier when I gave you and Sara the chance."

Tom nodded still numb with disbelief at the turn of events.

"And I want you to keep trying to remember everything that happened. I'm putting my faith in you. Don't let me down."

Tom smiled uneasily. A lump clogged his throat.

"I'll try not to, sir."

"Don't try. Do it!" Garry demanded sharply.

Sara returned, and handed Garry the paper bag where all the evidence was located. Tom felt a whole hell of a lot better when she slipped her velvety hand into his trembling palm and clenched it tightly.

He watched as Garry put on a pair of rubber gloves and began placing the evidence into clear plastic evidence bags he produced from a small plastic box sitting on his lap. It seemed the man came well prepared.

Suddenly the note sailed into a bag and something clicked.

"Wait! The note! How the hell did I forget what was on the note!"

Both Sara and Garry looked at him as if he'd completely gone off the deep end.

"The note! Garry, the note!" he sputtered excitedly. "The numbers on the note. There are two numbers on the note."

Garry frowned as he fished the paper back out of the plastic bag. He read it and shook his head slowly. He turned it over.

"No, I'm sorry there are no numbers."

He'd been so delirious and tired that night. Had he imagined the numbers?

Tom plucked the piece of paper from Garry's hands. "Here. Right here. See! This ink spot! It used to have the number twenty-eight, right here. And then the rain came."

"Twenty-eight?" Garry shrugged his shoulders. And then as if a bright light switched on in Garry's eyes he let out a shrieking whoop of joy.

Both Tom and Sara jumped with shock at the sudden earsplitting outburst. In a split second, Jo burst through the screen door. Her gun was drawn, her forget-me-not blue eyes bigger than saucers.

After assessing the situation, she quickly slipped her gun back into her shoulder holster. With a sheepish smile she asked, "What in the world is going on here?"

"Tom may have just handed us the case on a silver platter." Garry laughed.

"I gather the numbers mean something?" Sara asked excitedly.

"When Robin and I were in the police academy we shared a locker. Number twenty-eight. The academy has been abandoned for years. That's where all the evidence must be. But the key? Where's the key?" Garry grabbed at Tom's key chain and sifted through the keys. "Not here. Dammit!"

Then Garry squirmed excitedly in his wheelchair. "I think I might still have mine. In the basement, in my footlocker. Jo, would you go look? It's at the bottom in a small red metal container."

Jo nodded and took off.

Garry turned to Tom and Sara. "Sara, you're coming with us."

"Wait a minute! Go with you? But what about Tom?"

"He's staying here, alone."

She cast Tom a confused look and then a look of sudden understanding crossed Sara's face. It was a fascinating sight.

"I'm staying here with him."

"I'm sorry, Sara. It's too dangerous for you to stay here," Garry replied.

"Then it's too dangerous for him, too!"

Tom frowned as he noticed the defiant, stubborn look fly into her eyes.

"It's okay, Sara. I'll be fine here. I want you safe with Garry and Jo."

Sara whirled on him, determination blazing in her eyes. "You are not staying here by yourself. If anyone comes looking, they'll see me here and think nothing is out of the ordinary. Besides if it comes right down to it I know places I can hide you."

"You have got a point there, Sara," Garry mused. To Tom's irritation, the defense lawyer shrugged his shoulders as if saying to Tom it was useless to even attempt to argue with her. "All right. I'll leave it up to Tom."

"Fine, then I'm staying," Sara said before he could so much as launch a protest.

"You both stay. If Justin had figured out who you were, he would have tried something by now. I'll send Jo back as soon as possible. Maybe late tonight. More likely early in the morning."

"Where are you going?" Sara asked.

"New York. To get the evidence in that locker."

"Found it," Jo interrupted with excitement as she burst up the stairs and held up an old rusty key.

"Excellent. Jo, Sara and Tom will be staying. I'll brief you in the car. Time to go."

A surprised look flittered across Jo's features quickly followed by a somewhat shaky smile. She quickly wrapped her arms around Sara and gave her a warm hug and a big kiss.

"Take care of yourself, Sara. And watch out for this one, will you?" She winked at Tom, then removed her gun from the shoulder holster and handed it to him. It was the greatest compliment he could ever have asked for.

"Take this. You never know when it'll come in handy."

He accepted the gun gratefully and relished the ice-cold silky feel as it slid so smoothly into the palm of his hand. Control surged through him.

"Thanks," he said.

"C'mere, Sara," Garry ordered.

Sara bent down and Garry wrapped his arms around her and gave her a bear hug.

Then Garry extended his hand to Tom and they shook. "Take good care of her."

"Don't worry, sir. I won't let anything happen."

Garry nodded as if he approved of the answer.

"Watch your backs." He warned again as he wheeled his chair down the ramp toward the cherry red Mustang in the parking lot, the evidence bag nestled snugly in his lap.

Jo quickly followed.

* * * * *

Through the binoculars they watched the bright red car steam off down the dirt road. Two figures, a man and a woman stood in the parking lot waving at the quickly disappearing car. The woman turned and went into the house leaving the man to stand by himself.

"That's him," she whispered to her companion.

"I told you it was." He took a deep drag on his cigarette. "Let's get moving on this. All we've been doing is waiting for him to remember. For all we know he's just handed those two the goods and they're heading into town to turn it in."

The blonde woman dropped her binoculars into the open car and stood deep in thought. Her eyes never wavered from the lone figure. Hatred burned in her cobalt eyes. "If he had given them the goods he'd be going along, too. No—" she shook her head slowly "—he hasn't remembered. But he'll lead us to it, soon. In the meantime, I plan on jogging his memory. You stay here."

"But Pauline—"

"Just be quiet! I know what I'm doing. I'll be back for you. And put out that stupid cigarette." Her long blonde hair floated behind her like a bride's veil as she turned abruptly. Leaping into the car they'd hidden behind the nearby bushes, he heard the engine roar to life. In a split second the car disappeared behind a swirl of nearby evergreens.

He did as she said and threw the butt onto the ground and stomped on it, muttering angrily to himself. "I hope that bitch sister of mine knows what she's doing. Cause it's our asses that are going to be kicked when Dad finds out we've just let two potential witnesses drive off."

He drew a pack of cigarettes out of his jacket pocket and lit another one. His frown loosened somewhat as he watched the man standing in the parking lot. "On the other hand, there'll be less competition for me with Sara once that guy is out of the picture."

* * * * *

Tom watched the red tail lights of Jo's apple red Mustang convertible disappear behind the puffy pine trees. Desperation preyed hell on his nerves and he felt as if a vulture was tearing at his midsection. He hoped Garry would find the evidence and Ballistics could ID the bullets and link them to Jeffries. Even then, they would have to prove the gun he'd showed up with actually belonged to Sam. On top of that, he had to worry about the murder rap of Robin. And this marriage to a woman he couldn't even remember.

There didn't seem to be any easy way out of this mess. It was going to be a hell of a long haul.

Suddenly the tiny hairs on the back of his neck prickled in alarm and he got the strangest sensation he was being watched.

Squinting his eyes against the disappearing sun, he surveyed the darkening forest for any signs of movement. He couldn't see anything. Nothing but birds flittering around the branches.

Maybe Garry's warnings had spooked him. Had made his imagination go haywire.

Slowly he stepped onto the porch and heard the rattle of dishes through one of the open kitchen windows as Sara began to wash them before it got too dark. She was trying to act as normal as possible. Pretending nothing out of the ordinary was happening. God bless her for that.

The last remnants of the huge orange sun slipping peacefully behind the tall, dark pine trees caught Tom's attention. This would be their last sunset for quite some time or maybe forever. And he wanted to share it with the woman he loved.

"Sara!" he called out. "C'mere. Check out this sunset."

Quick footsteps clattered against the wooden floor. The screen door swung outward with a creak of rusty hinges. And she was beside him. And he felt whole again.

* * * * *

The dusky air wrapped its chilly arms around Sara and she shivered. Tom came to her rescue by circling his arm around her waist and snuggling up beside her.

Without speaking, they watched the colorful streaks of clouds expand throughout the sky.

It was a beautiful sight Sara had to admit. She wished she could capture it on canvas. The dusty rose billows, thin streaks of turquoise, lavender and powdery sweetheart pink tumbled over one another in the lilac sky.

Ever too quickly though, the fantastic sunset faded allowing tiny sequin stars to burst through the gray satin dusk.

"Pretty wasn't it?" Tom asked.

Sara nodded.

"Want to go inside?"

"No," Sara answered. "Let's stay out a little longer."

He moved behind her. His arms wrapped tighter around her waist and he melted against her. She accepted the warmth his body gave so freely. Accepted the large bulge pressing intimately against her butt.

His arms felt so comfortable and his chest so snug against her back, as if a favorite blanket had been wrapped securely around her. They stood for a long time, watching silently as the sky grew darker and the last pink wisps finally disappeared into the dark velvet sky.

Then suddenly Sara gasped in delight as what she'd been waiting for flew across the inky darkness. Tom pointed excitedly to the spectacle.

"Do you see it? Wow!" His voice echoed with wonder into the crispy night air as if he was a small boy and this his first falling star.

"Quick, make a wish!" Sara shouted.

Closing her eyes, she made her wish.

"I made a wish, Sara," he whispered huskily.

As he spoke, his lips brushed teasingly against the back of her neck. Just a feathery brush. But enough for Sara to ache for more.

She wanted to turn around. Wanted to wrap her arms around his neck and pull him fiercely against her body, to explore his mouth, to make love to him but the sharp lights of a car's headlights blasted through the almost darkness.

"Cops?" she whispered, pulling at him, trying to get him to go inside.

"No, the cops wouldn't come alone. Looks like a woman," he answered stiffly as a dark expensive-looking vehicle drove into the parking lot.

She didn't recognize the car. But a woman sat behind the wheel. When she stopped her car, the door opened slowly and a rather thin, sexy blonde woman emerged from the vehicle.

"Definitely not the cops." Sara sighed in relief. "She probably didn't see the 'closed' sign I had out on the highway."

"Maybe," Tom muttered. She didn't miss his hand sneak around to touch the handle of the gun he'd lodged against the small of his back nor did she miss his worried frown as she bounded down the stairs toward the unfamiliar car. Tom followed close behind. She didn't want to admit it, but his presence gave her that extra welcome sense of security.

"Hello." The newcomer's delicate, airy voice was obviously directed at Tom.

Sara bristled. Instantly she didn't like this tall, honey-haired bombshell. Didn't like the way she was looking at Tom all sweet and innocent. Didn't like her at all.

"Good evening. Can we help you with something?"

He sounded too friendly. She wanted to punch him in the arm.

The young, lithe thing pushed a wisp of stray hair off her forehead. Silvery blue eyes peered curiously at them.

"Yes! Um. I'm lost. Can you direct me to the Johnson ranch?" she whispered seductively. The blonde bimbo's question was unmistakably directed at Tom.

Sara frowned. Her unease toward the woman grew and swarmed over her. There was something about her. Something familiar, but she'd never seen her before.

Suddenly she envisioned pulling the woman's false eyelashes off her face.

"I'd say you're quite lost," Sara replied crisply as she stepped forward. The woman immediately backed away from Tom.

"The Johnson ranch is about a thirty-minute drive to the west. Go back down the road you came from, and once you hit the highway, head west. Oh, I'm sorry," Sara smirked. "Perhaps I should clarify the directions. When you hit the paved road, turn left. Thirty minutes at the maximum speed, you'll see a large sign on the right side of the road. The Johnson's, it says."

The woman cast a scathing glance at Sara.

Sara shot one back.

The lady returned her attention to Tom. Her dark brooding eyes pierced into him. She noticed Tom shift uncomfortably beneath her stare. Danger lurked all around this woman and Sara didn't like the feeling.

Even the blonde's bright, seemingly innocent smile did nothing to dissipate the uneasiness creeping under her skin. Suddenly she wanted this woman out of here.

"You're such a lovely couple," the newcomer mewed at Tom who frowned at the comment. "Have you lived here long?"

"Ages, my dear," Sara said quickly. "Now you better run along before it gets too dark. It's kind of scary out here in the big bad woods. You never know when you'll have car trouble. It's a very long walk at night. Especially since the houses are so far and few between."

The other woman smiled stiffly.

"Why thank you very much for your concern and the info," she replied crisply. "And for your hospitality. I'd better be going."

To Sara's utter amazement, the woman blew Tom a kiss and quickly disappeared into her car. The car squealed as she gassed her vehicle. Wheels spun dirt high into the air narrowly missing both of them.

"The nerve," Sara gasped as she watched the tail lights dim into the night. Hands on her hips, she turned fiercely upon Tom. Why had the woman been openly flirting with him? Did he know her?

Before she could ask him, his troubled gaze stopped her dead. Even in the darkness, she spied the sheen of sweat popping out on his face. When his hand flew up to swipe it away, she noticed his hands were trembling.

What the hell was wrong with him? His face was as white as a sheet. As if he'd seen a ghost.

"Do you know that hussy?" she demanded furiously. Her fists clenched into tight balls at her sides.

"I-I'm not sure," he whispered. His brow furrowed into a deep frown.

"Well I don't see how you could not remember meeting her before."

Her words bit deep into him. She realized it immediately. "I'm sorry. I didn't mean that."

"You're right, Sara. I should remember meeting someone like that."

She spun on him and caught the mischievous glint glowing in his green eyes and a disarming smile tugged at his lips.

"Oh! You are a son of a bitch!" She attempted to take a swipe at him, but his hand gripped her wrist. He pulled her closely against his hot chest and pressed his hips against her, allowing her to feel his hot cock.

"Are you jealous?" he teased softly into her ear.

"I will not dignify that question with an answer," she replied stubbornly.

"You are jealous!" Tom laughed.

"For Pete's sake, wipe that smile off your face."

Pushing him away, she whirled around and tramped angrily up the walkway.

Halfway up the stairs, she felt his hand on her arm and flames of desire erupted within her pussy from his touch.

"Sara, sweetness. Admit it, you're jealous." Tom's voice was low and seductive. Slowly, he turned her around. The knowing smirk on his face pissed her off.

"I wouldn't know jealousy if it came right up and bit me on my nose."

His finger gently touched the tip of her nose and he teased lightly. "There's a big chunk out of it right here."

"Bastard," she whispered and found herself smiling at his teasing glint. "You're right, I am jealous."

"I know."

"It was silly of me to act that way toward her."

"Yes, it was."

Sara frowned. "Do you have to agree with me all the time?"

He answered by bringing his deliciously crushing mouth over hers.

Sara accepted his greedy, sweet tongue as it played against her teeth and opened to him. Fantastic jolts of electricity made her knees go weak. When he raised his head from the kiss, she felt totally breathless.

A moment later, he lifted her effortlessly into his arms.

"What about the dishes?" she whispered huskily.

"Forget the dishes," he murmured in a thick voice and stomped up the stairs.

* * * * *

After they made love, they lay in each other's arms, the blonde woman still on her mind. And so was a whole bunch of other things. Things she needed to get off her chest.

"Tom?" she whispered. "You awake?"

"Mmm?" he replied sleepily.

"When we went to town the other day, I went to visit a friend of mine." It took a good few seconds for her confession to register, and when it did he tensed beside her.

"You didn't say anything about me, did you?"

"No, I didn't tell her about you."

He relaxed and to her surprise, he chuckled. "I guess I'm not so important to brag about to your friends."

"My friends ever see you, they'll snatch you away from me."

He popped one eye open and stated firmly, "Never. I'm yours forever."

She sighed her contentment and snuggled closer to his wonderful naked body.

"My friend. She was my psychiatrist." She let the last word dangle a moment, but Tom didn't respond, so she continued. "I asked her what she knew about amnesia."

His other eye popped open and he smiled at her. "You don't have to worry about me, y'know."

"I know."

"So what did she say?"

"Well, she said amnesia can be caused by different things. A blow to the head or a traumatic experience. She said memory could come back in pieces or right away. Or it could be triggered by something."

Tom moved, turned to face her. The muscles in his biceps bulged wonderfully as he propped his elbow under his head. "Just as I began remembering things when I saw Jackfish. I found the keys and the motorcycle, and remembered what happened in the basement of the cabin. And I know whatever those cops are searching for is somewhere in Jackfish. Just like I know the reason I didn't stay here at Peppermint Creek Inn that first time was because I was afraid I'd bring trouble to you if I got caught here."

"On that map you found in your motorcycle bag, Jackfish was circled. You can't remember who told you about the ghost town?"

Tom shook his head. "I remember cruising around looking for it. But I don't know how I knew Jackfish even existed."

"What if they already found what they were looking for in the cabin? I mean they ripped the house apart pretty good."

Tom shook his head. "It wasn't in the house. It's a strong feeling I have. It's in a safe place." His voice lowered to an endearing whisper. "I just wish you went with your sister and Garry so you'd be in a safe place, too."

"I am in a safe place when I'm in your arms," Sara whispered. "And before I lose my train of thought there's one other thing I need to warn you about."

"What's that?" he said huskily as he reached out to wrap his arms around her, pulling her against him.

"There's a chance you might not remember me when you regain your memory."

"I'll never forget you."

"But Smokey said—"

He placed a gentle finger on her mouth. "Shh. I've already regained some of my memories and I haven't forgotten you, right?"

Sara nodded, suddenly feeling as if a million tons had just been lifted off her shoulders.

Yes he was remembering his past, and yet he still remembered her. She wasn't going to lose him. At least not that way.

"Don't worry, sweetness, okay?"

"As long as I'm in your arms, I won't worry."

Tom nuzzled against her ear, catching her ear lobe gently in his mouth. Sara gasped in pleasure.

"You like?"

"Very much. I didn't know you were an ear man."

He didn't answer as he trailed fiery kisses down the full length of her neck making Sara shiver with delight.

"And a neck man." Sara giggled.

He showered her naked shoulder with light kisses.

"And a shoulder man, too," he said huskily, and Sara watched his magnificent eyes darken with desire.

Her breath quickened as his luscious mouth lowered hotly over her left breast. A low moan escaped from deep inside her throat and he smiled. A few moments later, for the second time in two nights, Sara threw caution to the wind as Tom's mouth worked over her stomach, abdomen and beyond, working miracles on her body. Miracles she never knew existed.

Chapter Seventeen

ဆာ

A stiff, cool autumn breeze blew against Matthew McCullen's face as he sat high in the bright red combine seat, staring in awe at the smooth creamy gold field of ripe grain awaiting him.

The healthy crop extended for acres, fence to fence, as far and wide as his eyes could see. Deep into Montana's foothills. He watched excitedly as the robust wheat, their heads fat and full of hard kernels nodded and waved to him in the wind.

He jumped as Dad shouted at him to get a move on from the edge of the field. Hesitantly he started the engine of the combine and slowly moved forward into the lush, picturesque fields. It was almost a shame to cut all this beauty down. But it was harvest time.

He smiled as the wheat fell before him under the header of the combine and he listened to the satisfying whisper as it rushed out of the auger into the truck box behind. They didn't have to tell him twice this was the bumper crop. It was written all over his parents' faces. This was the harvest of their dreams.

Mom and Dad had been pretty tense all summer waiting for the crop, trying not to get their hopes up. Aside from a couple of close calls, the weather had cooperated. Now he was cutting down his last crop, the crop that would put money on the table, allowing him to head into the big city early next year.

He'd been accepted into the police academy. His parents were both proud of him and sad to see their eldest son go. But he wanted some adventure in his life. He wanted to see the big city. He wanted to help people. What other way to have it all, than by being a cop?

The police academy in Billings was waiting for him. Leaving didn't produce too much guilt. His two younger brothers were still around to help out. Matt gave a happy howl and drove headlong into the swaying fields of gold.

* * * * *

Tears of pain washed out from beneath Sara's lashes as hours later she lay awake in the early gray predawn listening to Tom's uneven breathing. Only two short weeks ago, a bedraggled stranger had entered her dull life. A man covered in black leather and scruffy hair. Little did she know the beautiful feelings of life he would stir inside her.

He'd taught her how to feel alive. He'd given her back her happiness, her joy of painting and most importantly shown her how to love again.

She didn't want to lose him. Couldn't even bear to think it. Maybe she could still persuade him to run. She could wake him up. They could leave right now. Disappear. People disappeared every day without a trace.

She sighed wearily. Deep down she knew no matter how hard she begged him to leave, he wouldn't. He'd made up his mind earlier on the cliff when she'd first suggested leaving. He wanted real freedom. Even if he had to take such a horrible risk in achieving it. Oh, God, why did she have to fall in love with such a stubborn man.

A sob caught in her throat.

She almost didn't hear the strange sound.

A creaking noise that drifted through the slightly open window, mingling with the singing crickets and the croaking frogs. Sara's eyes fluttered open just in time to see the quick blink of lightning flashing in the windows. A momentary shot of panic burst through her body. But almost instantly, she smiled contentedly and snuggled closer to Tom's warm frame.

She wouldn't be frightened, she told herself. Storms couldn't hurt her, only people hurt people.

Another creaking sound spilled into the bedroom. Instantly Sara sat up in bed, fully alert.

Tom rolled onto his back, mumbled something but remained asleep. Sara listened for what seemed a long time but heard no other sound. Could it have been the porch swing out on the veranda? It always made creepy noises when the wind blew. She found herself staring at the curtains, willing them to move. They didn't so much as flutter.

330

Maybe it had been a raccoon or even a porcupine scuttling across the veranda. She wished she could believe it wasn't something bad lurking around out there, but what if it was?

Another flash of lightning lit up the sky. A little closer this time.

Without warning, a shadow flew by the window. So quick, she hoped she'd imagined it. Paralyzed by the sudden fear clutching her throat, Sara froze, and listened.

Above the crashing beat of her heart, she heard the unmistakable moaning protest of dry hinges, as the front screen door was slowly pulled open.

A shiver of familiar fear uncurled inside her body.

Could it be the cops? Her frightened gaze flew to Tom who shifted uneasily in the bed.

Another thought jumped into her head. Garry had said Jo might return early this morning. Sara's eyes flew to the alarm clock sitting on the night table. Exactly six a.m.

It had to be Jo. Perhaps she had good news.

Slowly, so as not to awaken Tom, she eased out of bed, slipped into her track pants and top. Hesitantly she picked up Jo's handgun off the night table, where Tom had placed it.

Just a precaution, she told herself.

Casting another quick glance at Tom, she opted to let him sleep. If Jo had bad news regarding his case, they could wait to tell him.

On her way out of her bedroom, Sara checked to make sure the back door was locked.

It was.

The hallway was semi-dark as she started down the corridor and a feeling of unease swept through her as she passed the slightly open door leading to the upstairs bedrooms.

Her hand tightened around the gun as she remembered seeing a shadow move past her window and the distinct sound of creaking hinges as the screen door had opened.

Maybe she should go back and wake up Tom. If it had been Jo she would have come inside by now.

Just as she turned around, she saw the dark shadow step out of the hallway leading to the upstairs bedrooms, directly into her path. For the briefest instant she prayed it was Jo. But the shock of white hair instantly dashed her hopes.

Sara's scalp prickled with fear and her heart jumped wildly. A warning scream died in her throat as she spied the gleaming gun in the man's hand. And it was pointed directly at her head.

Oh, God!

Her heart sank and she went completely rigid. She could kick herself for not leaving the gun with Tom. She'd left him unarmed and may very well have signed his death warrant.

Drawing in a deep breath, she forced herself to show her anger not her fear. "What do you want?"

The briefest hint of a smile tugged at his lips and the suddenly familiar-looking man cocked his head sideways.

"Where is he?" he spoke in a low crisp voice. A strong confident voice commanding attention and she found it extremely hard to ignore his question.

"I suggest you leave my property before I call the police."

"Now there's really no need for that, little lady," the man drawled. "I'm already here."

Sara jumped to attention as the man's free hand slowly slipped into his open jacket and he produced an official-looking police badge. Her heart crashed against the prison of her chest as she tried to read the badge in the growing dimness of dawn.

Chief Jeffries of the NYPD.

Before Sara could think of a reply, she heard the distinct sound of a footstep behind her coming from the area of the front door.

Her hopes soared. Had Tom heard they had company and woken up? Had he gone out the window and was now sneaking in through the front door to see who she was talking to?

Had the white-haired man also heard the footstep?

Sara didn't think so.

"Why don't you put your gun down, mister, and I'll do the same."

The unmistakable click of a safety catch being released made an icy sensation crawl up Sara's spine. She felt her entire body begin to shake when she smelled the sickeningly sweet perfume of the woman who'd come earlier in her car.

Suddenly she knew why the man looked familiar. He had roughly the same facial features as the woman who'd stopped by last night looking for directions.

Her sister had always told her to pay attention to her gut instincts. Last night when she'd seen this woman, her instincts had screamed bloody murder. Tom had been shaken also.

And he'd made love to her simply because he'd wanted to comfort her.

Shit!

"Drop the gun, girlie!" the woman ordered icily.

Keeping her gaze fixed to the white-haired man, Sara replied sternly to the woman, "If you shoot, I'll take him with me."

"Go ahead," she said icily. "I'll still be alive to finish the job."

Adrenaline squirted through Sara's veins.

Damn! What should she do? If she gave up the gun, then they'd kill Tom anyway. And if she didn't, she'd be dead. But at least she'd give Tom a chance.

Sara's hand tightened on the gun. "Then prepare to die, mister."

"He's in your bedroom, isn't he?" the woman said in a sober, throaty whisper.

A cold snake of fear paralyzed Sara legs. A wave of faintness clutched at her, she fought it away. The small of her back pushed up against the counter for support. The gun in her hand wavered shakily.

Sara could hear the laughter in the woman's voice as she whispered, "I'll go around back and see for myself."

When Sara swung the gun on the woman, she was already gone.

* * * * *

The sharp smell of urine intermingling with the sweet scent of cheap wine assaulted his nostrils as he snuck into the dark alley near the corner of 1st and Maine. The alley was narrow and damp, littered with everything imaginable. Garbage cans, scraps of metal, old lawn chairs, even a dried up Christmas tree.

Matt smiled to himself. It almost looked like the Charlie Brown Christmas tree he'd gotten for himself this past holiday season. It had decorated his apartment quite nicely, adding cheer to his drab surroundings but it hadn't been able to comfort him.

All his family was scattered to the wind. Mom dead. Steve dead. Steve's wife, Emily was now working freelance out of her Prince Edward Island lighthouse. Dad and Daniel were over in Mexico doing some archaeological dig or something. And he was alone in this crazy city feeling sorry for himself.

Well, not exactly alone. He had his so-called wife breathing down his neck all the time. But that problem would be rectified as soon as possible. And he had Robin. Good old reliable Robin. His shrink, confidant and mentor.

Matt squeezed past the piles of sky-high, cast-off tires that lined one wall of the six-story brick building. Gingerly he climbed over a couple of musty, tattered sofas, slipped by the burned out hull of what had once been a Chevy Nova.

Careful not to smash his camcorder against the metal, he quietly kicked aside a few needles left behind by junkies and abruptly halted at the sound of voices. Low and muffled and secretive. A shot of adrenaline surged through his veins and he picked up his trot. They had better not start without him. He'd worked for years getting to the point where Chief Whitey Jeffries and his daughter Pauline trusted him with their lives and the security of tonight's secret meeting.

The fact he was allowed to go around the meeting area freely tonight without being followed or patted down for wires and guns was proof enough that Whitey had vouched for him. Flicking on his camcorder, he quickly and quietly maneuvered past more mounds of debris, stopping only when he reached the end of the alley.

The alley opened up into a tiny court. The moon overhead perfectly illuminated the trio who stood off to the side of the court. A tall woman and two men.

He could see the two burly bodyguards still waiting patiently in the shadows behind the trio while Matt supposedly checked around for anyone suspicious. Thankfully from the looks of it the meeting still hadn't started. Good. If everything went according to plan, tonight would be the last night he'd have to do this lousy job.

Keeping in the shadows out of sight, Matt quickly set up his camcorder on the stand, and snapped the button over to play. When finished he casually walked into the tiny courtyard and headed for the trio.

"Anything?" his boss asked curiously when he saw him approach.

"Checked every little nook and cranny. We're totally alone."

The chief smiled gratefully and rubbed his gloved hands together with apparent excitement.

"Let's get on with it then." He withdrew a thin white business envelope and handed it to Scout McMaster.

Matt still couldn't get over the fact the notorious arms dealer Scout McMaster was alive. He'd almost dropped from shock when the man had appeared at the meet site moments before Matt had taken off to do his so-called security check earlier tonight. Scout had died not too long ago in a raid.

He'd seen him get shot himself. Seen the blood blossom across his chest before he'd tumbled over the ship's railing. The body had never been found but he'd been presumed dead. No one losing all that blood could have lived. And yet, here he stood. He'd have to bring up the conversation of how he'd made it out alive without being too obvious.

Scout chuckled as he peered into the envelope. He whistled happily.

"It's the wire receipt from the bank," Pauline quipped sweetly as she linked her leather-gloved hand through Matt's elbow and pressed her body seductively against him. Matt tried hard not to tense from his wife's affections. He didn't want her to get suspicious. After all they weren't a couple anymore. He just hadn't gotten around to telling her yet. He'd still needed to use her for the case. But it didn't mean he had to like it.

"Your share from the sale of the guns off your boat. The money is in the Caymans like you instructed. Split three ways."

"What are you going to do with your millions, Scout?" Matt asked casually. Scout threw Matt a pleasant smile. The man truly did not have a clue that by morning Matt would be bringing him and everyone else down. Their crooked dealings were finally over.

"Got myself a beautiful island down in the Caymans. Going to retire for a bit of a siesta. You and your wife care to join me?"

"Oh, that is a very enticing invite, Scout," Pauline said and smiling sweetly, leaned over and gave Scout a somewhat innocent peck on the cheek. But instinctively Matthew knew she was doing it for his benefit.

She'd been trying real hard this past month to make him jealous in a desperate effort to get him to consummate their hasty marriage, but he'd remained distant and angry toward her. It was understandable from his point of view. Wasn't everyday you had drugs thrown in your drink and woke up with a gold wedding band on your finger. Personally, he preferred the old-fashioned way of the man asking the woman under romantic circumstances.

Even then, he would never ask Pauline to be his wife. She just wasn't his type. She was too much like her father. Overconfident. Crooked to the core and too vain.

Matt chuckled. "We'll take you up on that offer, Scout. Considering we haven't had a proper honeymoon yet."

Pauline squealed with delight, her body pressing ever closer against Matt.

"You're welcome anytime to come down, Matty. The chief knows where." Scout reached out and shook hands with Matt.

"And by the way, congratulations on your marriage. Pauline's a good catch." Scout threw her a smile and Matt didn't miss her pretty warning pout. He'd heard rumors about Scout and Pauline being an item at one point in the past. But he didn't care. He just wanted this meeting over.

"It's been a real pleasure doing business with you, Scout." Chief Jeffries interjected. "A real pleasure. If you need any more assistance in the future don't hesitate to call on the NYPD. We'll be happy to help."

I'll keep you in mind. But remember, for now I'm dead. Thanks for covering that angle for me, Whitey. If you hadn't had your hand-picked men at the raid then I really would be dead."

Matt fought valiantly to contain the excitement surging through his veins at Scout's unexpected but very welcome confession. An un-coerced confession would stand up in court quite nicely when Matt brought the charges against these three. This was almost too good to be true.

"When I get my new face and identity, I'll be in touch and we can continue our productive partnership. It's been most profitable and — " he turned to Pauline, a secretive smile curving his fat lips " — and a most enjoyable venture."

Pauline nodded, the pout on her pretty face deepening. Matt pretended not to notice.

"Adios, amigos." Scout saluted sharply and disappeared into the shadows with his two bodyguards.

"There goes a very happy man." Chief Jeffries replied as he turned to Matt. "And I'm glad to hear you are going to take my daughter on a honeymoon. It's about time."

"Oh, Dad, isn't this fantastic?" Pauline let go of Matt's arm and hugged her father. Whitey smiled affectionately and said to Matt, "The honeymoon is on me."

"No, sir, we couldn't possibly — "

"I'll hear no objections. You'll head out tonight on my private jet."

Tonight? Dammit! Think fast, Matt.

"Okay." Matt nodded. "How about you drop my wife at the apartment for me, while I pick up something to celebrate on the plane."

Pauline pulled herself from her father's embrace and threw her arms around Matt. He tried not to shudder with revulsion as he was forced to return Pauline's seductive kiss.

When she was finished, she purred, "Can't you take me home?"

"Darling, I'll swing by and pick you up in an hour or so," he lied. "Now, run along. Or you won't have enough time to pack."

Thankfully Pauline scrambled into gear. She grabbed her father's arm and hurried him out of the alley. Matt waited patiently until they'd gone. Then he quickly hustled over to the video camera, grabbed it and the stand, and scrambled through the obstacle course. He flew out of the alley ignoring the stares of curious passersby and hopped onto his bike where he'd left it parked. He removed the stand from the camcorder, stuffed the items safely into a saddlebag behind him and sped off.

The cool wind slapped against his sweat-drenched face and he smiled. It felt good. And for the first time in a long time, he felt alive. It was over. This crap was finally over.

Now, he could quit all this undercover stuff and get on with his life. Maybe even settle down. Maybe he could go up into Canada and visit

Robin's brother's daughter-in-law, the woman who owned the inn. Maybe. His smile widened. Yeah. Maybe.

It had grown quite dark when he pulled his bike in around back of Robin's tiny bungalow. Darker than any night he could even remember. The moon had slipped beneath a black satin blanket and no lights glowed from his windows.

At this late hour, Robin would be asleep. Surely, he'd forgive him for waking him up. Especially when Matt told him the case was finished. Matt banged on the back patio door and waited anxiously for an answer.

Robin would freak when he found out what he'd got on tape. He'd be doing cartwheels down the street. Heck, they'd both be doing them. He knocked again. Still no answer.

Where the hell was he?

He knocked louder. He could feel the glass beneath his knuckles tremble as he pounded harder. He dared a look over his shoulder, his eyes sifting through the shadows checking if anyone was watching. Suddenly the hairs on the back of his neck wiggled in alarm. That always happened when he was being watched by someone.

Nothing moved anywhere. Just a dog barking somewhere nearby.

Despite that fact he couldn't get back into that jovial mood he'd found himself in earlier when he'd thought about heading into Canada and paying a visit to the owner of Peppermint Creek Inn.

Tonight had been easy. Too damn easy. As if they'd presented the evidence to him on a silver platter. But then again, he'd worked pretty hard to gain their trust. Why shouldn't it be easy?

He'd been working undercover for years. Getting into Chief Jeffries' good graces. And now he was Jeffries' right-hand man. It was almost unbelievable that this whole charade was finally over. His only regret was he hadn't been able to nail down the chief as his brother Steve's murderer.

But with all the other evidence he'd collected over the years and handed over to Robin, and then this stuff tonight the chief would end up behind bars anyway.

Matt nearly jumped out of his skin when the patio door slid sideways and an older man stood in underwear and a white T-shirt, scratching his chin.

"Hey, nice of you to drop in Briggsie."

Matt flinched at his nickname. He hated it. It reminded him of the days when he'd gone a little crazy and lived on the edge. Right after his mom and brother had died. His coworkers had promptly nicknamed him Briggsie, after a suicidal cop played by the actor Mel Gibson in a movie called Lethal Weapon.

"Don't call me that," he hissed as he quickly pushed past Robin into the living room.

"Come on in, Little Buddy," Robin chuckled politely.

"I've got to show you something, Robin. And for Christ sake close the door."

Matthew breathed a little sigh of relief when he heard Robin latch the patio door and redraw the drapes.

His partner was smiling at him, his curious gaze raking the camcorder Matt held in his hand. "So? C'mon? What you got there? Why you look like the hounds of hell are at your heels?"

Matt popped the tape out of his camcorder and handed it to Robin.

"Rewind it," he instructed.

"Sit down, kiddo. Before you fall down," Robin chuckled halfheartedly as he dropped the tiny tape into the specialized VCR tape, then slid it into the VCR, turned on the TV and pressed the rewind button.

Matt did as his friend suggested and sat down on the dark blue sofa. Robin's sudden intake of breath captured his attention. They watched the images flicker to life on the television screen. Neither said a word as the scenes unfolded. After about twenty minutes, the tape went blank.

"Wow," Robin whispered quietly. Disbelief etched his voice. Tiny beads of sweat burst out on his forehead. Matthew retrieved his tape and slid it back into the camcorder.

"I can see why you're so hyper, Briggsie. It's not every day one finds out one's wife is a criminal. It's not as if it comes as a big shock. We've been suspecting this for awhile now."

"Any advice as to how we handle this?"

"Just hold on and let me think. Let me think." Robin stood up slowly, and stretched. Then he began pacing the living room floor. The familiar scratching on Robin's chin soothed Matthew's jangled nerves. It was a habit of Robin's and a dead giveaway when he was formulating a plan.

He watched his friend, eagerly awaiting his answer. The silence was never-ending. Finally Robin spoke. His voice sounded quiet. Almost too quiet.

"This evidence will put you into grave danger."

"Thought crossed my mind." He swallowed the tight knot of fear clogging his throat. His stomach literally turned over at his dear friend's next words.

"Didn't know it would be Scout at the meeting."

Alarm bells rang in Matt's head. "You knew about the meeting? How? I never told you."

Robin pressed his lips together. Tightly. As if he'd said something he shouldn't have said. He chuckled nervously.

Shit! What the hell was going on here?

"Remember when you talked that depressive off the ledge?" He didn't wait for Matt to answer as he continued. "That's when you hit the evening news and caught my attention. I watched you crawl out on that ledge. Forty stories up. By golly you had guts, kid. If it was me, I'd have let the guy jump. But you acted as if he was your best friend and you didn't have a care in the world. You got right out there, sat down beside him and offered him a smoke. Afterwards some witnesses told the news anchor lady you'd even offered to jump off the ledge with him. The jumper thought you were nuts."

Matthew frowned. "I was."

"I know, kid. I know," Robin slowly nodded his head. "It was a bad time for you. The way you lost your mom and then your little brother."

"So answer my question, Rob. What gives? What did you know about tonight? Why didn't you warn me? I thought we were in this thing together?"

Robin didn't answer his question. Instead, he plunged down memory lane again. "How about the time you got that anonymous tip about how something illegal was going down in the evidence room right then and there."

"Rob," Matt warned. He didn't like the way Robin was hedging his questions. Robin had never acted this way before.

"You took off with your handy camcorder and recorded those two detectives sprinkling blood on a piece of clothing in evidence. Most cops *might look the other way but you…"* Robin chuckled. *"You reported it to your supervisors. And were promptly blackballed for it."*

Matthew shivered at the memory. *"Those two cops came after me with a vengeance. I almost got my head blown off in the process. It'll be worse this time around, Robin. And you still haven't answered my question."*

Robin smiled unpleasantly. *"You don't want to hear what I have to say, kid."*

"Try me." A shiver of unease crawled up Matthew's spine. Maybe he should tell Robin to forget it. There was something odd about his behavior tonight. Robin never talked about the past. He was always set square in the present.

"Back when we found you, you enjoyed living on the edge, taking chances with your life. We needed someone like you. Someone who wasn't afraid to get his fingernails dirty."

"What do you mean by 'we'? I thought it was just us two in this?"

"That's what I led you to believe."

"So, there's another party involved. No big deal." Matthew shrugged his shoulders as if he didn't care. But he did care. His good friend had lied to him and it didn't sit too good in the pit of his stomach.

"Think about it, Matt." Robin's voice grew gentle. *"I approached you shortly after you were ostracized by your peers for turning in your fellow officers.*

"I told you I suspected Chief Jeffries as having something to do with Steve's death. I wanted to know if you'd help me bring him down by working undercover as a crooked cop. You said you wanted revenge against the man who killed your brother so you accepted my job. You picked up stakes and moved to New York City. We made up an entirely new identity for you. New name. New social security number. The works."

Matthew bowed his head as he remembered those hard days. Robin had been a knight in shining armor. Coming into his life at his lowest point. He would probably be dead by now. Gunned down by some crazy druggie, because a spiteful cop hadn't covered his back.

"I don't understand where this is all going."

"Think about it, kid!" Robin snapped sharply. *"The anonymous tips you've been getting all these years from that woman while working undercover?"* He let the words dangle in front of Matt.

341

"You knew the tippers? Is that what you're saying?"

"Dammit, kid! Do I have to spit it out to you? We're not working on this alone. There's others involved. High government people. F.B.I., C.I.A. People have been feeding you information so you can purposely get the other crooked cops before we brought down Jeffries. They were using you, Matt. And I was the first tipper. I sent you the first tip. The one about the two cops tampering with evidence. I'm the one that got this whole ball rolling."

Matt jolted. His mind reeled with disbelief. "You?"

Suddenly the big picture was staring him straight in his face. And it hurt. Robin had sent Matt into the evidence room. Life had been tough before that day. After that day, life had turned into hell.

"You used me? Set me up?"

Robin said nothing as he bowed his head in apparent shame.

"Coward!" Matt barely noticed Robin flinch at the word. "You hid behind me? You made me risk my life! Risk other people's lives. Why have you betrayed me?"

Robin remained silent.

"Dammit, answer me!" he shouted angrily. "You've knifed me in the back, Rob. I can't believe it. You! The only one I've trusted throughout this whole case. The only reason I hung around so long." Matthew stopped to draw a shattered breath.

"You feel better now, kid?"

"Why are you telling me this? Why now?"

"I promised myself I'd come clean with you when it was over. And with this evidence, it's over."

"To hell with you, Robin! To hell with your goddamn job! I'm outta here!"

Matt's mind reeled as he turned toward the back door. He immediately sobered as a shadow passed by the drapes of the patio window beneath the porch light.

Chapter Eighteen

ဆ

Sara's mind whirled. What should she do? She couldn't go after the woman. This man had a gun on her. But she had one on him, too.

Should she shoot him? Hope her first shot was good enough to bring him down without him shooting her? What about the blonde? Would Tom hear the gunshots and rush headlong into a bullet from the woman's gun?

No, there had to be another way.

It suddenly occurred to her she was being scrutinized by this man. It made her uneasy. He mustn't pick up on her nervousness. She had to remain calm, cool and collected.

But why was he staring at her like that? Smiling at her as if he'd put one over on her. He didn't even look frightened. For all he knew she would put a bullet in his brain any second. So, why wasn't he even the slightest bit intimidated by her gun?

She had to get him scared. When people got scared they made mistakes. And when he made a mistake, she'd be ready.

* * * * *

"Were you seen?" Robin whispered as he watched the shadow move outside the patio doors.

Matt closed his eyes and cursed sharply.

Robin's frown deepened. "Either you were or you weren't, kiddo."

"I didn't see anyone following." He reached for his shoulder holster and withdrew his gun. "Rob, there is definitely someone out there."

"Oh, man, this is great. Just fucking great. They must have followed you. You're losing your touch, Little Buddy."

Robin moved quickly, heading toward a writing desk in one corner of the living room. Matt knew that's where Robin kept his gun.

Along with the gun, he yanked out a notepad and began to scrawl something on it.

"This is no time for an autograph, Robin," Matt joked sarcastically as his fingers tightened around both the camcorder in one hand and his gun in the other hand.

"C'mere," Robin commanded.

Matt edged over to Robin, keeping his eyes on the back patio door. Robin dropped his gun on a nearby table and grabbed a photograph shoving the picture in front of his face.

"Take a good look at this. Memorize these two faces."

Matthew dared a glance at the photograph. Instantly, it gripped his full attention. He'd seen the picture many times.

Five people. An elderly couple and a younger couple about his age, and another woman.

Robin had once told him, the younger woman was the sister to the younger married woman. And he'd even hinted the younger sister wasn't married. But Tom's gaze always flew longingly to the married gal.

Sara. Beautiful woman. Beautiful name. Robin had told him about her husband being murdered a couple years back. How she'd miscarried their children that same day. God, the pain and horror she must have gone through.

Some days he ached to meet her. To talk to her. But the undercover life he'd pursued didn't allow him such frivolous activities as to meet a good woman.

"See these two people," Robin pointed to his twin brother and Sara's sister. "You can trust them."

"I don't understand."

"Take the evidence to this place. Tell Sara I sent you." Robin shoved the sheet of paper at Matthew. Matt juggled the camcorder and the gun in the same hand as he grabbed the sheet.

Quickly he glanced at the address scrawled on the paper and then back at Robin. "Peppermint Creek Inn? Why go there?"

"Just do it!" Robin hissed between gritted teeth. He shoved his hand into the desk drawer again and withdrew some keys.

"Here. The keys to the inn. Sara might not be there. She goes on a lot of trips for her business. Hold up there until she shows. Tell her to contact

my brother Garry and keep it as low-key as possible. Give Garry this note, he'll know what to do with it. Here's the barn key. Take a gander inside. There's an old motorcycle you might want to tinker with. Used to be mine. And take that suitcase." Robin pointed to the small suitcase on the floor beside the sofa.

"You packed an overnight bag? How sweet." Matt smirked.

"Cut the crap, kid! There's money in there for spending. Don't use any credit cards. You'll have to lay low for awhile. When it's safe, I'll contact you."

Apparently Robin had known tonight could be the last night. Why else had he packed a bag full of money? Robin slammed a heavy hand onto Matt's back. "Looks like you'll get to meet Sara after all, eh?"

Suddenly a knock on the glass sliding doors ricocheted through the house.

In a quick flash, Robin picked up the suitcase and flipped it open. Matt's eyes grew wide at the sight of all that money.

"Jesus. How long do you want me to stay under?"

"As long as it takes. I'll get in touch."

Robin grabbed the camcorder, the note and the keys from Matt's hands and dumped them into the case. Then he thrust the case into Matt's hands.

"Get going, kid. Out the bathroom window. I'll distract them."

"I'm not leaving you here," Matt said as he tugged on his friend's arm. "I brought them here. I got you into this. We go together."

Robin smiled sickly. "You didn't get me into this remember? I got you into it."

"It doesn't matter who did what, dammit. Let's get out of here."

"Police! Open up!" A loud booming voice erupted throughout the living room.

Robin jerked away from Matthew's grasp. "I'd slow you down, kid. Don't worry about me. I can handle myself. Keep the goods safe. Go out the bathroom window."

Another round of banging shook the patio glass door. Robin shoved him into the hallway. Before he knew it, Robin had retreated back into the living room.

Toward the door.

Toward danger.

"*Go! Now, you stupid son of a bitch. Do as I say!*" Robin shouted back at him. He saw the fear in his friend's eyes before he turned and headed toward the gun he'd left on the table.

"*God, Robin, what the hell are you doing?*" Matthew hissed urgently as he ran back to get his partner. "*Forget the gun!*"

"*Go! Save yourself,*" Robin commanded again. The crazed look in his eyes made Matthew listen.

He whirled around and started back down the hallway. The sound of shattering glass and Whitey's warning shout stopped him cold. In a split second he was being swarmed by Pauline.

"*Drop the gun, Matt,*" she shouted fiercely.

Matt hesitated. If he gave up the gun, they were both dead.

Whitey stepped forward, his gun trained on Robin. No way out. He had to do what they said.

He dropped the gun and Pauline swooped over to pick it up. She handed it to Whitey.

"*Well, well, well. What have we got here?*" He looked from Robin then to Matthew then to Matt's gun curled in his gloved hand. He inspected it curiously.

"*Strange bedfellows?*"

"*You're under arrest, Whitey. For corruption and a shitload of other things. It's over,*" Robin hissed.

"*For you,*" Whitey replied coldly.

It happened within a blink of an eye.

The gun in Whitey's hand rose in lightning speed. The earsplitting gunshot followed. Blood spattered against the beautiful wildlife painting on the wall beside Robin.

The patio door disintegrated from the bullet that blew part of Robin's throat away.

Matthew's eyes flew wide open. He winced as the sound of breaking glass still echoed viciously in his ears. His heart cracked like a jackhammer against his chest, his body primed for action. He swore beneath his breath and bolted up in bed.

He scratched his bristly chin, looked around the semi-dark room and tried to figure out where the hell he was.

* * * * *

In a desperate attempt to alert Tom, Sara had purposely knocked a pile of mugs off the kitchen counter. The crash reverberated throughout the house so loud it made Whitey cringe. When he recovered from the shock of the noise Whitey took a threatening step toward her.

"He won't get away. Not this time," Whitey growled angrily.

"Stay there! I'm warning you! I will shoot," Sara shouted.

But Whitey still came toward her.

She had to shoot him. She had to protect Tom.

Oh, please, God, forgive me.

Closing her eyes, she pulled the trigger.

Nothing happened.

She pulled it again. Still nothing. When she opened her eyes Whitey was hurtling toward her.

She wanted to run. To scream a warning. But it was too late!

"Next time make sure the safety catch is off," he snickered wickedly as he reached out to grab her.

Sara cringed in horror, as she awaited his wicked touch. But then Whitey froze as a man's fierce shout echoed through her kitchen.

"Hold it right there or I'll blow sunshine right through your brains!"

Sara almost laughed with relief as she spotted Tom standing in the hallway. Clad only in jeans, his hair was all messed from sleep. But his green eyes shone with bright alertness. An old musket clamped firmly in his hands.

Sara stifled a helpless cry. He held the same musket she'd hung over her fireplace as decoration. And it was totally useless. Did Tom know? Would Whitey guess?

Tom glared at the white-haired man. If looks could kill, then Whitey surely would be a dead man.

"You're history, Whitey. Place your gun gently on the table."

The white-haired man chuckled lightly. "I'm history? Have you taken a look at your gun?"

Oh, dear God, he knows. Sara's heart picked up the battering beat.

"Do it! Now!" Tom commanded. The icy authority in his voice jolted her. She peered through the early morning darkness at him.

Something had changed about him.

He seemed different. In the way he held himself. In the cold, no-nonsense authority of his voice. Then realization slammed into her stomach as if she'd just been sucker punched.

That endearing little lost boy look she'd fallen in love with had vanished from his face, the sadness veiling his eyes drawn away to reveal a searing masculine confidence.

She found herself drawn to this new emotional transformation.

"Maybe you don't hear so good, Whitey." Tom leveled the antique musket at Whitey's head. "Consider this a hearing aid."

Whitey's smooth smile slid into a frown. He hesitated a moment. His fierce gaze studied Tom. Sara could hear the wheels turning in the man's head. Was Tom bluffing? Did the musket work?

"As you wish, as you wish. I'm putting down my gun." Slowly, with a great deal of care, Whitey moved toward the kitchen table. Toward her.

"Lady! Get away from him!" It took her a moment before Sara realized Tom was talking to her. A cold shiver of unease slid down her back as she did as he asked. Why had he called her "lady"?

"Keep your hands where I can see them," Tom warned Whitey. And then he swung his cold gaze on her.

"You too, lady." Sara blinked in surprise as he shouted at her. "I said stay clear away from him, lady. I don't want any trouble from either of you. Just follow my instructions and neither of you will get hurt, *comprendez*?"

Why was he acting so strangely? So cold toward her? As if he didn't trust her. Sara's mind immediately supplied the answer. Smokey had said it might happen.

Tom had reassured her only hours ago it wouldn't. But it had. The cold realization made her head swim. Tom had forgotten her.

"You won't get away with this, Matt." Whitey spat as he placed the gun gently upon the table and glared angrily at Tom.

"*Au contrar*, Whitey. I've got the evidence you want. Your fate is sealed. As are the fates of so many of your crooked cops."

"Better think twice what you're saying, Matt. I can merely snap my fingers from prison and everyone you love will be dead including her." Whitey pointed at Sara.

"Her?" Tom's eyes narrowed as he threw a quick glance at Sara. She jolted at the cold hardness in his green eyes and Sara felt the prick of tears blur her eyes as his next words cut a deep gash, straight into her very soul.

"She means nothing to me. What the hell are you talking about? I've never seen this woman in my life."

Sara was too stunned at the cold harshness of his words to fully comprehend the movement she saw in the dark hallway behind Tom until it was too late. Before she could issue a warning, the blonde woman had stepped up behind Tom and jabbed the gun into his back.

"Hi, Loverboy," she drawled.

Tom's face washed to a ghastly white and he winced. If it was due to the gun in his back or the word she'd called him, Sara couldn't be sure. But the icy curve lifting his lips assured Sara he wasn't happy to see the blonde.

"Pauline," Tom sneered. "Should have known you'd crash the party."

"You know the drill, Matt," Whitey said as he grabbed the musket from Tom's hands and threw it onto the kitchen table. With lightning speed, he retrieved his own gun and Sara's.

She watched helplessly as Tom placed his hands against the wall and spread his legs.

"Pauline," Whitey said. "I'll cover them. I'm sure you'd like to do the honors."

"You bet," Pauline drawled seductively as she placed her gun on a nearby chair.

Sara noticed Tom move uncomfortably as Pauline's hands roved slower than necessary over Tom's hips, across his back and belly and then down his legs.

"The only thing he's packing is a nice cock and juicy set of balls," Pauline chuckled as she finished frisking Tom and with the quick swiftness of a scorpion, pulled his arms behind his back and snapped a pair of handcuffs around his wrists.

Pauline swept her gun off the nearby chair and Sara jumped as the blonde swung the weapon on her.

"And you! I should kill you. No one gets away with sleeping with my husband."

"Don't do it, Pauline," Tom warned. "It'll be too messy. I know how you hate to clean up after yourself."

Pauline lunged at Tom. But Whitey's sharp shout stopped her dead.

"He's baiting you. Cuff the girl. Then go outside. Cool off. And keep an eye out for any unwelcome guests."

Sara winced as the blonde cruelly forced her hands forward and snapped the ice-cold cuffs around her wrists. She noticed the satisfied smile on Pauline's face and wished she could punch the woman in the nose.

"I'll deal with you later!" the blonde hissed as she pointed her menacing gun at Sara.

"Looking forward to it," Sara replied coolly as the woman stepped outside.

"Now that I have your full attention," Whitey said to Matt, "you can tell me what I want to know."

"Go to hell!" Sara spat. "He's not telling you a damn thing."

"I guess I can see whose side you're on, lady," Tom drawled coldly. "But I don't need your help. Just shut your pretty little mouth. This conversation is between the big cheese and me."

Sara blinked in surprise as Tom casually returned his attention to Whitey. There had been something in his eyes.

A glint of mischievousness?

"So, let's deal, Whitey. What are you willing to trade to get your hands on the tape I shot?"

"I'll kill both of you quick. How's that?"

Tom lifted his handcuffed hands and scratched his nose thoughtfully before saying, "Someone once told me something. Only the good die young. So, I figure my time isn't up for awhile."

Sara blinked in surprise and tried to clamp down on her soaring hopes. She'd used the same line on him when he was recuperating from the gunshot wound in her bed. He was sending her a message. To let her know he was all right. That he still remembered her.

But why was he pretending not to know her? Was it so Whitey wouldn't use her as leverage against him? Did he want Whitey to believe she meant nothing to him, so he'd let her go? But she wouldn't leave. Not without Tom.

Whitey muttered a foul oath then said angrily, "What makes you think I can even deal with you, Matt? What you did sickens me. Worming your way into my trust, into my business. I allowed you to marry my daughter."

"Your daughter drugged me. It was the only way she could get herself a man. Besides the marriage isn't legal. I haven't used my real name."

"You bastard," the blonde hissed from the other side of the screen door.

"Shut up, Pauline," Tom snarled at the blonde. His cold gaze flew back to Whitey. "I'll hand over the tape, on one condition."

Whitey inhaled slowly. Then let out a deep breath. "All right. Name it."

"You let the lady go."

Sara's wrists tightened against her restraints. Tom was offering his life for hers. She wouldn't allow it.

It was up to her now. She had to figure out how to get out of these handcuffs. She'd done it once with Tom's cuffs on the first night he'd arrived. It should be easier the second time around. When she got free then she'd be able to help him.

Whitey was regarding Tom with genuine interest when she said, "I need to go to the bathroom."

"Where is it?"

"Just down the hall. I can leave the door open if you're so afraid I might escape," Sara taunted. "And I need the cuffs off."

Whitey shook his head. "No. You keep them on. Figure out a way. I'll give you three minutes. You're not back by then I'll shoot Matt in the leg. And I'll enjoy it."

An icy shiver rippled across her shoulders at Whitey's evil grin. Shakily, she headed down the hallway. Leaving the door open, she darted through the adjoining doorway into her bedroom. Breathing a silent thanks, she picked up the item she needed then headed back into the bathroom, flushing the toilet to make it look official.

* * * * *

"C'mon, Matthew. How do you propose I let a witness go?" Whitey smirked.

"She looks to be a smart lady. I'm sure she'd know how to keep her mouth shut. You set her free and I'll hand over everything Robin accumulated over the years."

Whitey looked doubtful. Matt was losing the man and fast. He had to keep him interested.

"How'd you know I was at Robin's house that night?"

"You give me too much credit." Whitey sat down on a nearby chair, the gun trained on Sara as she walked back into the room.

"We didn't know you were a rat. You had us all snowed y'know. Never would have figured you for Internal Affairs."

The chief shook his head slightly. "After the meeting was finished that night and we left you, we came back almost right away. Pauline wanted to tell you to pick her up in two hours instead of one hour. Imagine our surprise when we saw you back in the alley with something in your hand. A camcorder, no doubt. We followed you down the alley, Matt. Saw you hop on your bike with that smug smile on your face. I called my driver on the cell phone. Told him which street you were heading down. He's an expert tracker. Maneuvers like a chameleon in heavy traffic. That's why I hired him. The driver followed you into Robin's neighborhood. Right to Robin's back door." The chief smiled and an icy shiver went up Matt's naked back. "That's the beauty of being a police chief, Matt. I know lots of people. I have something on everyone. I had Robin in my hip pocket, or so I thought."

"So you had something on Robin, did you?" Tom smiled ruefully. "You talking about those bribes he took from you years back?"

Whitey visibly stiffened.

Matt tried hard to contain the raw hurt that still burned inside him from Robin's confession that he was working with a bunch of government people, using him, stringing him along all these years instead of just the two of them working together as he'd been told by his partner.

Now that he looked back on everything that had happened over the past few years, he'd been naïve.

Stupid in blindly trusting Robin just because he'd kept dangling Chief Jeffries over his head as having something to do with his brother Steve's death.

Robin had probably lied to him about that, too.

"Are you talking about Robin accepting a weekly fee of one thousand dollars in return for keeping the heat off Scout McMaster and all his arms dealings? Oh, don't worry, I know all about it. Robin told me everything he did for you. He was your right-hand man. Right up until he got cancer and had to bring in someone new to replace him. Or he would have had you earlier. I worked on you for a long time before you trusted me. You were a tough nut to crack."

Whitey cursed.

"You're a low-life, Whitey," Matt continued. "You've caused too much pain and suffering to people with your crooked dealings. Not to mention the officers you corrupted by waving big bills and flashy cars under their noses. If I had been another type of man, I'd have killed you a long time ago."

"Just like you killed Robin?" Whitey chuckled softly. Matt heard Sara's sharp intake of breath.

"You know the truth, Whitey."

"You were stupid to try and save him, Matt. He was a talking dead man. He stiffed me and you stiffed me. No one crosses me. You see what happens when they do, don't you?"

"So how about it. Let the woman go, and I'll give you the evidence."

"Tom!" Sara pleaded.

"Dammit! Don't call me that!" Matthew snapped back. He hated yelling at her like this, but he needed to make Whitey believe he couldn't use her as leverage against him.

"All right," Whitey soothed. "Take it easy, Matt. I'll let her go after you give me the evidence."

Matt knew he didn't have a choice. Reluctantly he gave in.

"Jackfish. The evidence is in Jackfish. I'll take you there. But you leave the woman here unharmed."

"We'll take Sara with us. Then we'll let her go."

Suddenly Sara interrupted. "I don't know about you guys but I'm awfully thirsty. Do you mind?" She gestured toward her refrigerator, a tight smile on her lips.

Matt frowned. If he didn't know any better he could swear she was up to something.

"Hurry up," Whitey growled impatiently.

Matt caught her quick glance at him as she headed for the refrigerator. It took a long time for her to drain the cup as she stood with the fridge door open, but finally she was finished. And when she rejoined them, Matt had the distinct feeling Sara's demeanor had changed. And changed for the better.

* * * * *

They took two vehicles. Sara drove her truck with Pauline sitting in the passenger seat, a gun trained on her all the time. Tom sat in the passenger seat of the sedan with his hands still cuffed behind him. Whitey drove.

If he didn't have to think about Sara's safety, he would have easily been able to get away by lifting his feet and crushing Whitey against the driver side door. But Whitey had probably anticipated such a move and conveniently taken two vehicles to compensate.

Whitey remained quiet as he drove, allowing Tom to concentrate on a way of getting Sara and himself out of this mess. A moment later, he found himself leaning forward, when up ahead on the highway, off in the not-so-far distance, through the early morning light, he made out a red car zipping along the highway toward them.

His heart began a quick beat.

Could it be Jo returning?

It was at that moment, the two vehicles swung off the main highway onto a gravel road that led them down a steep hill. He glanced out the back window just in time to see the red Mustang whiz past.

His heart sank. Jo sat in the car. And she hadn't seen them. He slumped dejectedly against his seat. They were on their own now.

Chapter Nineteen

ဆာ

After a few minutes, the road narrowed. Branches scraped eerily against the sedan. Towering jack pines shot upward into the heavens blocking their view from the increasingly brightening stormy sky. The road grew bumpy then abruptly grew smooth as they drove over a long carpet of moss. A few minutes later, the two vehicles came to a halt.

Tom's jaw dropped open in shock. Up ahead, a police cruiser blocked the road. And leaning against the car, smoking a cigarette was Justin Jeffries.

"Uh-oh, now we're in trouble," Tom said coolly.

"Shut up, Matt," Whitey growled as he swooped out of the car and came around to the passenger side to let him out.

The air felt heavy with the promise of rain and cool wind played with Tom's face as he got out of the car. His wrists pulled in frustration against his restraints as he watched Justin's lip turn into an evil sneer.

"I thought you looked familiar when I saw you in town," Justin Jeffries drawled. "You were just born to be a chalk outline, Matt. I only wish I could be there to do the honors."

"Hmm. Is that necklace you're wearing a souvenir from one of your other chalk outlines? If I remember correctly it has a bullet hanging from it."

"Shut up you son of a bitch," Justin yelled.

Whitey shook a stern finger at his son. "You keep that temper of yours under control, son."

"What about the necklace?" Sara asked breathlessly. She'd taken the bait and his stomach soured.

"Don't, Sara," Justin pleaded.

"No, I want to know."

He was really beginning to feel sick now. Using the woman he loved to bait these two was unforgivable. But he needed to get Jeffries antsy. Needed to get his old man pissed off at him. He knew Whitey didn't like it when his son and daughter got angry.

Anger in his kids was the one visible weakness he had. It irritated him. He didn't want them around when they were pissed off about something.

He needed to get them apart. Divide them. Divide and conquer.

"Dad, get the dammed evidence from him and let's get this over with," Justin whined.

"Is it... You have the bullet that killed my husband hanging around your neck?"

The disbelief in Sara's voice almost brought Matt to his knees.

Sara grabbed at Justin's shirt, ripping it open. The two top buttons flew into the air.

Gleaming happily against his hairy chest hung the bullet on a chain.

"Good God. You're insane," Sara cried and pushed Justin away from her.

She whirled around to face Matt. He could have died from the hurt look in her eyes. Her lower lip quivered uncontrollably. He wished he could take her into his arms to comfort her, but he couldn't let them know how much he loved her.

"I have a witness who heard them talking," he told Sara softly.

"Who?" Justin interjected. "The only ones down there was Sam, you and me."

"I'm the witness."

"That's not possible. You were unconscious."

"I let you think I was. I heard the whole thing. Sam telling you how much he was interested in Sara. How he should tell her you were Jack's killer. How he'd seen you kill Jack with the final bullet, then took his journal, where he'd written down the whereabouts of the amethyst mine on her property."

"Please stop, Tom," Sara whispered. She was pale and shaky. He ached to take her into his arms. But he couldn't. He had to keep his emotions under control.

"Sounds like you've been real busy, baby brother," Pauline chuckled as she shook her head in disbelief. "You told me you had your eye on some married woman but I never expected you to go this far. Killing her husband in cold blood? And wearing a necklace with the bullet that did him in? That's crude. Even for you."

"If you don't shut up, I'll blow your head off," Justin yelled at his sister. His hand flew to his holster. "Then I'll blow his off. He's lying. That's not the way it happened."

"I've had enough of this bickering," Whitey snapped. "You head back to town, Justin. See if you can't make some inquiries and see what evidence Garry and that Brady woman have on us. Kill them if you have to. Matt will show Pauline and me where he stashed the goods."

"But what about Sara?" Justin whispered desperately.

Whitey's eyes narrowed into mere slits. "I've made a deal with Matt about her. You just get yourself back to town. Get an alibi. This is the end of our conversation."

Justin appeared to want to say something then thought better of it. His shoulders sagged in defeat as he climbed back into the cruiser. Wheels spinning, kicking up dirt, Justin Jeffries took off.

Matt sighed with quiet relief.

One down.

Two to go.

* * * * *

Sara felt as if each step were her last. She had no idea how she kept going but something deep inside her urged her to put one foot in front of the other. To keep plodding along. To be ready. That Tom had a plan. That's the only reason he'd been acting in this horrid way toward her.

Justin had killed her husband and her children. And he wore the missing bullet around his neck. As if it were some sort of trophy.

Tom had been right all along about Justin. And yet she'd still had doubts he'd been involved simply because Justin and Jack had been partners and seemingly such good friends. Now that she'd seen the missing bullet hanging around Justin's neck, she burned with anger.

She hadn't noticed the disappearance of Jack's journal until months after he'd been murdered, not until she'd been able to think clearly enough to remember the strange conversation they'd had on the morning of his death.

They'd been lying in bed, listening to the cheerful chattering of the wild birds outside. Jack's large hand had been cradling her slightly swollen stomach. His cornflower blue eyes had been so sober when he'd said, "If something ever happens to me, Sara, I want you to give my journal to Dad. He'll know what to do with it."

Sara cuddled closer to him trying to dispel the cold shiver his words had caused.

"Nothing's going to happen to you, Jack," she had soothed. "The men at the mill are uttering death threats because they're upset about you helping the government. Things will calm down eventually."

He'd smiled at her in answer. But the smile hadn't quite reached his dark eyes. He'd reached for her and they'd made love for the last time.

Sara jolted as Whitey stumbled on the slippery trail in front of her. Her mouth went dry and her knees suddenly shook. Hopefully Whitey wouldn't turn around and see what she was doing. Twisting her hands at an odd angle, Sara jammed the makeshift key into the hole and began working on the cuffs.

* * * * *

Matt eyed the brooding sky. Thunder crackled somewhere to the north. The plan he'd been formulating depended on the weather. Hopefully if the rain held off and the mist stayed thick, he might be able to get them out of this mess.

When he'd awoken this morning, he'd discovered most of his memories intact. He remembered Whitey lifting the gun, pointing it at Robin's face. Remembered how horribly helpless he'd felt as

359

Whitey pulled the trigger. How Robin's body had jerked wildly when the bullet ripped through his throat.

He remembered his buddy murmur something about the nearby suitcase and other words he hadn't been able to understand. He remembered Whitey, Pauline and Scout hovering around him like vultures, glass crunching wickedly beneath their feet as they'd watched him fervently try to stop the blood from spurting out of Robin. Yelling at them to call 911.

"He's practically dead," Whitey had replied coldly. "And you are a murderer."

Then he'd heard Robin's death rattle. A ghastly sound he'd never forget as long as he lived.

Realizing Robin was beyond help, the full implications of Whitey's words impacted Matt. Whitey was setting him up for Robin's death. He'd grabbed the briefcase with the money and run.

Their gunshots had miraculously missed him as he'd raced into Robin's bathroom locked the door and crashed through the window. Heading over to where he'd stashed his bike, he'd hopped onto his vehicle and raced off.

The trail veered sharply to the right bringing him out of his thoughts. He cast a quick glance at Sara. From the firm set of her lovely jaw and the somewhat shaky smile she cast his way, he allowed himself to hope that she was also working on a plan.

He'd need all the help he could get.

* * * * *

Sara's fingers tightened around the ballpoint pen she was using as a makeshift key to the handcuffs. She almost let out a whoop of joy when the handcuffs snapped open and teetered precariously on her wrists. With some quick fancy maneuvering, she was able to keep the cuffs from falling off.

Keeping her eyes glued to Whitey's back in front of her she had to remain alert. Waited for Tom's sign.

Sara tensed when Tom veered sharply to the right. He turned around and for a split second their gazes locked. She threw him what she hoped was a reassuring smile, to let him know she suddenly understood where they were going.

She allowed the tip of the ballpoint to slip slightly out from between her fingers. Enough to become a miniature weapon and then she prepared herself for all hell to break loose.

As if on cue, Tom came to a dead halt. Whitey cursed loudly as he almost crashed into the back of him.

"Why are you stopping?" he hissed anxiously.

"We're here," Tom said casually.

Sara didn't miss the cruel smile ripple across Whitey's lips. God she hoped the plan worked.

Tom pointed to the other side of the familiar meadow in front of a debilitated cabin.

"It's inside that log over there."

"You go ahead. Show me," Whitey instructed.

Sara's blood ran icy cold. She hadn't anticipated this problem. Her mind raced for an answer. Help came from an unexpected source.

"Oh, for heaven's sake, Dad. Just get it," Pauline urged him.

Whitey threw her a cold look. "Keep them covered."

Matt and Sara watched anxiously as Whitey struggled through the scraggly bushes claiming the meadow. Both poised to move at a split-second notice. But nothing happened. Whitey reached the log without a problem and Sara knew they were in trouble.

Sara's heart pounded frantically against her chest as she watched Whitey lean over and peek inside the hollow.

He looked back at them. A horrible grin sliced his face.

"Are you toying with us, Matt?"

He raised his gun.

Sara flinched as he pointed it at her. "I hope for her sake you aren't."

"It's the wrong log," Sara said quickly, nodding to the other log. "It's that one over there."

All eyes flew to another fallen log a few feet to the right of this one.

Whitey grinned as he scrambled to his feet.

"You've got a lovely lady there, Matthew. She's smart."

He headed toward the other log. Suddenly a cry rang out and the earth swallowed Whitey.

With lightning speed, Sara turned. Holding the pen tight she stabbed Pauline's gun hand. The blonde screamed in pain. An instant later, Tom bowled into Pauline, knocking her and the weapon to the ground.

Sara grabbed for the gun, but froze when dirt flew into the air mere inches from her fingertips.

"My God," she gasped.

Her mind reeled in confusion as a red-haired man with a pockmarked face stepped out of the bushes. A horrible looking semi-automatic was gripped snugly in his hand.

Beside her, Matt and Pauline stopped struggling.

"What took you so long?" Pauline quipped as she scrambled away from Tom, stooped over and grabbed her gun.

"I'm here," the man retorted smoothly. "And not a moment too soon, Pauline. You can't keep your own husband under control?"

He turned to Tom, a fierce hatred in his eyes and a truly high-spirited smile on his ultra-thin lips.

"Greetings, Matty."

"Scout," Tom acknowledged stiffly.

This sorry-looking character was Scout McMaster? The supposedly dead arms dealer?

"I should put a bullet in you for deceiving all of us."

"Go ahead," taunted Tom. "Right between the eyes. It seems to be in the air around here."

"If you shoot Tom, then you're up a creek without a paddle so to speak, aren't you?" Sara said in the sugariest voice she could gather. She needed to keep this horrible man's attention off Tom.

Scout swung his gaze on her and she shivered involuntarily at the crazy glint in his stormy blue eyes. He studied her for a long time before replying with obvious interest, "And who are you?"

"She's nobody," Matt interjected quickly.

"She looks like a somebody to me. Somebody I'd like to get to know," Scout drawled.

"Scout would you take a look see if Dad's okay?" Pauline pointed to the gaping hole of the well Tom had fallen into the other evening. It was barely visible in the gray misty light.

As he quickly headed toward the well Scout threw Sara a look, a heated look that made her shiver with revulsion.

"Hey, Whitey? You okay down there?" he called down the hole.

No answer.

Sara's frantic gaze flew to search the tall grass. She'd lost the pen somewhere on the ground nearby when she'd stabbed Pauline. And now she couldn't find it.

"You looking for this?"

All the fight rushed out of her body as Pauline held the pen up.

Her only weapon, her last hope was gone.

"No answer," Scout replied as he continued to peer down the hole. "I can't even see him. It's too dark. He's probably knocked himself out."

"Leave him for now. We'll get him later," Pauline said sternly. She turned to Matthew but the gun in her hand never left Sara.

"Please, no more games, Matt. Where is it?" she said wearily.

"You'll have to undo my cuffs," he stated calmly. He sounded a hell of a lot more calm than he felt.

"I don't think so," Pauline spat.

"I can't swim without my hands."

"Swim?" both Pauline and Sara asked in unison.

Tom nodded. He nodded down the hill toward the fog-enshrouded Jackfish Bay.

"It's out there. On the island."

* * * * *

A few minutes later, they stood on the sandy beach.

Pauline had unlocked the handcuffs and Matt had stripped down to his underwear. He stood in the cool morning mist, shivering uncontrollably awaiting a decision as to who would accompany him.

"You go with him, Scout," Pauline instructed.

"Can't."

"Sure you can. Follow him out to the island. Make sure he doesn't do anything stupid, like take off."

"Can't swim. You go with him. I'll stay here with the lady. I'm sure we can amuse ourselves."

Matt stiffened at the remark. He wanted to belt the scum, but he had to keep his cool. If Scout only knew how much he loved her. Matt shuddered to think what would happen to her. And Scout would make sure Matt watched the whole thing.

Pauline rolled her eyes heavenward in disgust.

"Forgot my bathing suit," she said. "Just get the evidence, Matt. All of it. You don't come back, she's a goner. Is that clear?"

"Crystal."

He took a step toward the giant black waves rolling onto the sandy beach.

"No! Please." Sara's cry tore at his heart. "He can't go in there! There's a storm coming. The waves are too big. He'll freeze to death. Maybe there's a boat around here somewhere he can use."

Matthew tensed and anxiously waited as Pauline cast her gaze across the fog-shielded inlet and the white-capped waves rolling onto the beach as if pondering Sara's plea then she replied icily, "Don't worry. He'll think warm thoughts of you. Go ahead, Matt."

Before Sara could protest again, Tom took a deep breath and with one fluid motion, he dove into the brooding black water.

* * * * *

Chilly rain pellets stung Sara's face as she watched the swirling dark waves get higher with the oncoming wind. Thunder crunched overhead, making her jump involuntarily. Ice cold fear for Tom's safety slithered through her like a cobra.

He'd disappeared beneath the frothy waves quite a while ago. She'd searched the misty waters for one more sign of him. One more glance for her memory. But he'd never resurfaced, most likely opting to come up for air under cover of the veily mist.

She hoped and prayed he wouldn't come back. Any important information he'd accumulated and left on the island belonged to the authorities. Even if her life needed to be sacrificed. Knowing Tom would be safe gave her all the reassurance she required to endure just about anything.

"What's taking him so long?" Scout McMaster said.

Sara spun around to face him as he stepped closer to her. His gun was pointed at her stomach. An ugly sneer gripped his pockmarked face and his grubby eyes raked over her body. Sara swallowed the horrible chunk of dryness threatening to clog her throat.

"The island is a fair bit to swim to," she replied trying to appear calm.

"If it's really there at all," he whispered softly.

He reached up with his free hand and Sara tried not to flinch as he ran his slimy fingers through her hair. His lips parted. Sara cringed inwardly at the sight of his yellow teeth. She smelled his nauseating breath grate over her face, yet she resisted the overwhelming urge to lift her knee and sock it to him where the sun doesn't shine.

Stall him, Sara. Stall. Tom needs more time.

Her heart pounded fiercely against her rib cage at what she was about to do. She felt faint as the air tried to squeeze into her constricting lungs. The gun poked painfully into her rib cage and Sara forced a seductive smile to her lips.

* * * * *

It didn't take long before Matthew's arms and legs grew numb, but the fear of what would happen to Sara if he didn't return propelled him into blanking out the numbness.

Breaststroke. Kick. Sidestroke. Kick harder. Keep moving. The icy fingers of the water slithered along his cold body. God, he needed to get warm.

Sara.

He needed to think of Sara. An agonizing ache erupted deep inside his heart as he thought of last night. She'd moved in perfect rhythm beneath him. Her velvety body luscious and smooth. So beautiful.

The woman of his dreams. A great mother for their children. A passionate, talented woman. Desirable, strong and independent.

Fire breathed into lungs and he found himself gasping for air. His arms and legs began to slow, to grow heavy. Panic notched up a few degrees. Something hard cracked against his knees and arrows of pain shot way up into his hips. He cursed loudly. His hands grazed against rock. A large jagged rock. Then another.

He lifted his weary head. Through the white mist, a wall of sheer gunmetal gray loomed like a giant in front of him. He'd hit the damn island. By golly, he'd made it. He would have let out a shout of success but he was too pooped to even gasp.

Climbing out of the black waves, Matt shivered as the cool raindrops nailed into his naked skin. He sat down on one of the boulders catching his breath and looked around. Mist swirled everywhere, through each crack and crevice, across every boulder. His gut clenched. Nothing seemed familiar.

Maybe he was wrong about this island. Maybe he'd put the evidence somewhere else? Maybe he'd only dreamed it was here?

Swallowing hard, he fought the overwhelming panic threatening his sense of confidence and forced himself to stand and to start walking. He had to stay strong. He had to think. *Think, man, think.* Where could he have stashed the evidence?

He was so deep in thought when a few moments later he realized walking had become easier. He'd stumbled off the stony beach onto sand. That's when he saw the overturned kayak and that's when he finally remembered where he'd put the evidence and how he could get back off the island and rescue Sara.

* * * * *

"Who killed Robin?" Sara asked the question the moment it popped into her head.

Thankfully, Scout's dry lips stopped mere inches from hers. His eyes narrowed and he shook his head slowly. "You sure know how to ruin a party, gal."

The gun left her ribs and he savagely pushed her away from him.

"He got in the way of a bullet," he replied angrily. "What do you think? Whitey had to clean out the pest. Can't work proper with varmints double-crossing you."

"Then Tom didn't do it?"

"Why the hell do you call him Tom anyway? His name's Matthew Brown. Least ways that's the name the rat went by in New York." He stroked the barrel of his gun with apparent affection. "And I can't wait to kill him."

Lifting his head, his piercing dark blue gaze fastened onto Sara, his eyes roving over her breasts and settling between her legs.

"But first I'll let him watch while I take pleasure in fucking you. I'll enjoy your screams as I come inside that sweet little pussy of yours. Alas in the end we'll have to part so to speak and you'll join your boyfriend in the truck where you'll both meet an unfortunate accident as your truck stalls on the train tracks."

Sara shivered at Scout's horrible words. She'd been wondering how they'd do it without causing too much attention. What better way than to make it look like a train accident.

Scout continued to pet his pistol and his eyes glazed wide with wonder. "Don't you see how easy it was to frame Matty? All the chief had to do was say the man was guilty and everyone believed it. Brownie's just another chump, a sucker, who thinks he can sweep the streets clean. He can't do it himself. There's too many of us out there."

McMaster laughed harshly. "Now c'mere, I want to party with you."

She shrieked with disgust as he grabbed for her again, his slimy hands circling around her waist with an iron steel grip. He pulled her close. Too close.

She could feel the hard bulge of his small cock rub against her thigh, and squelched the need to scream her head off. His face lowered again and he nuzzled his clammy lips against the base of her neck.

God help her, she was going to start fighting him any moment. She almost did a double take when she spotted movement in the misty waves. Before she could pinpoint the location or attest to what had captured her attention, it was gone.

Quickly she turned away from the gray waters and forced herself to stare directly into the nearby bushes.

"What's the matter?" Pauline called from where she sat on a gnarled tree stump several feet down the beach.

She forced herself to stiffen, to look nervous, to act as if she were trying to cover something up. Which she was.

"N-nothing. I just thought I heard something."

Scout, sensing possible trouble, followed Sara's gaze to stare at the thick bushes she'd been looking at.

Trying to appear as casual as possible, Sara glanced back out over the waters where she'd spotted movement a moment earlier. Her eyes widened.

Shit!

Tom sat in a tiny wooden kayak, the oar laid horizontally across the boat, the choppy waters throwing him wildly about as if he were a mere plastic toy. Yet miraculously he remained afloat.

In one hand, he held up a plastic wrapped package. In the other hand, he held a gun. He waved at her to move away from Scout. But before she could follow Tom's instructions, Scout McMaster, having detected Matt, grabbed Sara and pulled her roughly to his side.

"Drop the damn gun, Matty!" he shouted down to Tom.

Pauline whirled around, a sinister smile plastered across her thin lips. "Look who the current dragged in."

"Drop the gun! Drop it now, Matty! I'm warning you!" Scout was shouting now. Anger laced his voice. Anger and a tinge of panic.

Sara winced as the open tip of Scout's gun kissed her temple.

"No way in hell, Scout," Matthew shouted back. "Here's the evidence. Let her go. Do it now! Or I kill you!"

"Toss it up," Pauline demanded. "You keep the gun and she goes."

Matthew nodded and threw the package. It landed on the wet sand-packed shoreline. Pauline didn't waste a moment. Running to the water's edge, she retrieved it. Ripping away the plastic exterior, and the brown wrapping paper, she let out a small cry of glee. Reaching inside the snack-sized milk carton box, she withdrew a small camcorder tape.

"This is it!" She held up the tiny tape.

Scout McMaster loosened his grip on Sara and strained to see.

"I trust it is the original?" Scout hollered down to Matthew.

"You can trust me all you want. Let Sara go! Now!" he ordered. "You have what you want. It's over."

"Throw the tape in the lake," Scout McMaster ordered Pauline. She did as he instructed and hurled it far. Sara's stomach sunk as the tiny tape was instantly swallowed up by the massive waves.

"Walk toward me, Sara." Matthew ordered.

Scout nodded his head and let her go.

Not believing her immense luck, Sara didn't hesitate. She walked quickly toward the beach.

Toward Tom.

His eyes widened in sudden fear and she turned her head just in time to see Scout lift the gun and aim it at Tom.

"Now! It's over!" Scout shouted.

With a wild helpless fascination, Sara watched Scout McMaster pull the trigger. Gunshots rang out.

She gasped as she heard a horrible grunt from Scout McMaster. Pauline screamed as the notorious gun dealer clutched his head and pitched forward.

Sara whirled back around. Thankfully, Tom still sat safely in the kayak. But he was quickly disappearing in the thick mist. That's when Sara noticed Pauline lifting her arm and the gun rising slowly, aiming at Tom.

Instantly Sara ran toward Pauline.

More shots rang out.

Tom flew backward into the water.

Sweet God! He disappeared beneath the waves.

Sara whirled on Pauline to see an evil, satisfied smile cross the blonde woman's red painted lips.

Her gun hand began to swing around toward Sara.

A sinking feeling slammed into her guts. She wasn't going to make it out of this alive. But she kept running. As long as she had breath in her lungs, there was still a chance.

She heart shouts from behind her.

She kept running.

She heard more gunshots.

Something tugged wildly at her hip followed by a sharp, searing pain. Sara gasped at the intensity of it. Stumbled. Quickly caught her balance, and started running again.

Then came to an abrupt halt as she noticed the bullet hole in Pauline's forehead. Pauline was dead before she hit the beach.

A scream lodged deep inside her throat. She stopped herself from losing it. Now was not the time to freak out. Someone had accidentally shot Pauline instead of her. She needed to get to Tom. Needed for them to get out of here.

She turned toward the waters and barely heard a familiar woman's voice cry out to her. A moment later, she crashed into the cold black waves where she'd seen Tom go under.

"Tom! Dammit! Answer me. You son of a bitch!" Sara screamed as she dove in and started swimming out.

"That's not a way for a lady to talk," a disembodied amused voice answered from somewhere close.

"Tom?" Sara gasped as she tried to stare through the thick white mist.

She heard him answer with a cough and quickly swam toward the sound.

And then she heaved a terrific sigh of relief when she spotted him, his face stark white in contrast to the dark waves as he swam toward her.

"You okay?" he sputtered as he grabbed a weak hold of her cold waist.

Tears of joy sprinkled down her cheeks and she didn't miss the blood oozing from a bullet wound in his shoulder.

"You're alive. That's all that matters," she cried.

"What the hell happened?" His teeth were chattering. He looked frail.

"I don't know. Scout's dead. Pauline's dead. I don't know who shot them."

A frantic voice cut through the fog.

It was Jo.

"Your sister," Tom mumbled. His teeth were chattering louder now. Or maybe it was hers?

She nodded and her heart thundered to the beat of the storm lashing down on them as they both swam through the giant frothy waves. When their feet touched the sandy bottom, she felt his warm embrace and his hot searing mouth covering hers.

How she'd waited for this. To feel Tom's warmth surround her body once again. To suddenly feel whole.

The pain in her hip intensified.

Sara stumbled.

Concern flashed in Tom's eyes.

She began to feel sick to her stomach.

"Sara? What's wrong?" She saw his lips move but he sounded so far away.

"She's hit." Jo's frantic voice echoed in her ears.

"She must have found my message?"

"What message?" Tom's voice was beginning to sound as if he was talking in slow motion. A prickle of fear sputtered along Sara's spine. Blackness hovered at the edges of her vision.

Oh, shit! She was going to pass out.

"She put one of those old tin pots she collects out here into the fridge," Jo replied just as slowly. "She knows my stomach so well."

"We've got to get her to a hospital, Jo." She heard Tom's desperate wail.

"I called the hospital on the cell phone. They're sending a chopper. It should be here in a few minutes."

"Is someone sick?" Sara heard herself asking.

"Yeah, you, sweetness," Tom replied softly. She felt herself being lifted into strong, warm, safe arms.

"It's all my fault. All my fault," Tom whispered into her ear as he held her close. "I should have walked that first night I saw you. The first night I fell in love with you."

"Ahh, love at first sight. You don't strike me as the type," Sara murmured.

The prickle of fear vanished as she cuddled closer to Tom. She felt so loved. So safe. So warm.

Closing her eyes, she allowed the safety net of unconsciousness to capture her.

Chapter Twenty

ஒ

The unmistakable odor of medicine slammed into Sara's nostrils urging her to open her eyes. She felt dopey. Out of it.

Pale moss green drapes greeted her and she heard hushed whispers from somewhere far off.

Her gaze fell upon Tom who sat slumped in a small uncomfortable-looking metal chair. A couple of day's growth shadowed his sexy face. The steady rise and fall of his chest proved he was asleep. He had one arm in a sling. The other arm stretched over her bed, his warm fingers intertwined with her own.

Sara smiled.

Matthew. His name was Matthew, not Tom. It tumbled over and over in her head. He looked like a Matthew more that he looked like a Tom.

Sweet. Honorable.

Tough. Dangerous. Sexy.

A warm sereneness washed all around her and she closed her eyes drifting off to a dream where rain dropped in silvery torrents and a magnificent emerald-eyed stranger made exquisite love to her on tangled sleeping bags in an old boathouse nestled on a sandy beach with a lone candle flickering in the window.

Sara didn't know how long she slept, but the next time she awoke she felt a bit more aware and quite thrilled to find Tom—Matthew—she'd have to get used to his name—to find Matthew sitting in the same chair and his fingers still intertwined with hers.

This time he was awake, but staring off into space like some sort of zombie. She found herself frowning at the dark circles under his eyes, the haggard, haunted look about his face.

As if sensing she was watching him, he blinked then leaned forward in his chair, his fingers tightening around hers.

"You awake?" he whispered anxiously.

"Mmm. You okay?" Sara asked softly. Her gaze raked over the sling.

"Me?" He shook his head in amazement.

Sara nodded. "Yes. You. You don't look so good. Are you okay?"

He lifted her hand in answer and gently kissed each finger. The light touch of his lips made Sara tingle with excitement.

"And you're a finger man, too. Nice. Very nice."

He smiled, but concern clouded his eyes. "Your hip hurt real bad?"

"A wee bit."

He reached for the nurse's button. "I'll call a nurse. She can give you something for the pain."

"No, It's okay. I'm fine. Really." She watched him relax. "So, did we get the bad guys?"

"Yeah, we got them."

"We make a good team, huh?"

His fingers tightened desperately and she almost cried out at the way he was squishing her fingers. It was a direct contrast to the delicate way he brushed his bristly cheek against her knuckles.

"Yes, we do." His voice had softened to barely a whisper.

"So? What happened? I remember Jo being there and then nothing."

"She saved your life."

Sara tried to smile but she was beginning to drift off again. She had to keep him talking. Keep herself awake. She didn't know why but there was something in Matthew's sad eyes that frightened her. He appeared somewhat distant and yet he so obviously cared for her. What was wrong?

"Tell me everything."

"You sure?"

Sara nodded.

"It's a long story."

"I've got time." She stifled a yawn.

"Okay. Well...after getting your ingenious message in the refrigerator, Jo shot over to Jackfish. I saw her from the kayak. Through hand motions, I signaled she cover Pauline and I'd take care of Scout. Turned out she couldn't get a clear shot at Pauline from where she was. Before she could let me know, all hell had broken loose. My mistake."

Matthew shook his head slowly, the tiny lines around his gentle mouth deepened into a grimace. "I should have known, but I wanted Scout. He was too close to you. I was — afraid."

He chuckled or at least she thought it was a chuckle until she spotted the sprig of tears brightening his emerald eyes.

"Oh, God, Sara." His voice broke making Sara even more frightened at the torment and apparent guilt he harbored. "I'm so sorry all this happened. I figured you'd be okay. But you weren't."

"I'm okay," Sara soothed. "You're okay. Everything's okay. It's over now."

Her eyelids felt so damn heavy.

"You're tired. You should sleep."

"No," she managed to mumble. "Stay. I want to hear your voice. Keep talking to me. What else happened?"

She heard him take a deep breath. "Pauline's dead. She wasn't my wife. She'd drugged me, forged my signature on the marriage certificate. The undercover name I used isn't legit and the marriage was never consummated."

The idea Matthew was a free man seemed almost too good to be true. She dared to hope that they would someday be together.

"Scout's not dead. He's gonna live. He'll be a vegetable. Won't stand trial for his criminal dealings."

"At least he can't hurt anyone by selling guns."

"I guess." He hesitated a moment then said, "Garry's back. He found the evidence in a locker in that abandoned police academy he was talking about. The same academy Whitey, Robin and Garry attended. Apparently they'd been friends up until a point where Garry took a bullet for Whitey Jeffries."

"What?"

"Garry and Jeffries were partners at one point in their career. One night a man high on drugs jumped them when they were on foot patrol. Whitey Jeffries used Garry as a shield. Garry took the bullet."

"Oh, God. I didn't know it was Whitey. I thought it was the druggie."

"Garry never told anyone except his brother…and that was years after the fact."

"But why keep something like that quiet? I just don't understand why Garry would cover up something like that."

"Because Garry didn't want to go through the blue wall of silence that cops live by. If he'd turned in Whitey, there would have been an investigation. According to Robin, there was no physical proof what Whitey had done. It was his word against Garry's. If Garry had talked then his life and his family's life could have been in danger. Some cops don't like the idea of other cops ratting each other out, no matter what. Garry could have been killed. Or worse, a member of his family could have been killed. He decided that keeping quiet was the only way he could protect his family."

"How could Garry live with that knowledge? How could he stand to watch Whitey rise through the ranks to chief of police knowing he was such a coward?"

"According to Robin, it ate at Garry for years until he finally told Robin. Robin wasn't one to sit idly by and let this go. That's why he finally went after Whitey on his own. Went undercover as a bad cop for a while, but then he got cancer. Had to stop his crusade against Whitey and then he recruited me."

Matthew continued. "Justin Jeffries didn't kill Jack. I remembered a vicious fight between Blake and Jeffries when Jeffries spotted the necklace with the bullet around Blake's neck. It was the same caliber as the one that…they removed from your husband. The missing bullet that someone had dug out of the wall."

"But Justin was wearing the necklace. You said he…"

"I know. I remembered that I'd seen Jeffries take the necklace from Sam's body that night right after he'd shot him in the back. I'm so, so sorry I said what I did about Justin being your husband's killer. At the time I was desperate and trying to find a way to get

Justin upset. Whitey gets quite irritated when one of his kids is upset. It worked though. Whitey got rid of Justin. I just wished I didn't have to put you through that hell."

She should be upset with him for tearing her heart out that way. But she wasn't. He knew Whitey's weaknesses and had worked quickly to try and get them out of danger the only way he could under the circumstances.

"He says he saw the bullet necklace around Blake's neck asked him about it and Blake laughed and bragged at how he got away with murder. That was the argument I'd heard while I was semiconscious in the basement of the cabin. After their argument Blake had left for awhile and Jeffries had kept an eye on me but when Blake returned and wanted to kill me, Jeffries killed Blake instead and —"

"And tried to pin the murder on handy you."

"A frame-up. Like father, like son," he admitted.

"But why would Sam kill my husband? You said something about Jack's journal?"

"Here's the theory the provincial police came up with after interviewing the folks in town. Shortly before Jack died, the local surveyor confirmed an amethyst mine find on your property. The local land surveyor and Blake are brothers. Brothers talk. Blake started to get ideas. Knew Jack and his partner Jeffries were good buddies. Justin says shortly before Jack was killed, Blake started pumping Justin for information. Asking all kinds of questions about Jack and your property. Started making friends with your husband. Started coming around a lot with Justin."

"My God, they were around quite a bit toward the end."

"But why kill Jack for the mine? They couldn't do anything with the minerals. The government would get the claim anyway. They have all mineral rights here in Canada."

"Blake and his brother, the land surveyor, made all the records of the claim disappear."

Sara sighed her confusion. "I don't understand. How would anyone know about the mine if they got rid of all the records?" Her mind was groggy but she wasn't so out of it that she couldn't see there were a lot of unanswered questions.

"That's the beauty of this whole scheme. They've been illegally mining out on your north quarter for more than a year. Cran Simcoe just told one of the investigating officers that a drinking buddy who was hired to work at the mine and was getting paid big bucks to keep his mouth shut, spilled his guts about the mine only a few nights ago when he was drunk. Cran was scared to go to Jeffries. So he drove down to Thunder Bay and told the police down there. That's how everything started rolling. They flew a police helicopter over your property and discovered the mine and the rest is history."

It was too much to take in all at once. Tom hadn't been kidding when he'd said this was a long story.

"Then why vandalize my place?"

"Maybe Blake wanted you off the property. You'd sell to him and he could control what happened on the land. Keep out trespassers and pocket the proceeds from all the illegal sales."

"But he doesn't smoke," she said when she remembered the smell of cigarette shortly after she'd entered the cabin the night Jack had been shot.

"Oh, yes, he does. Closet smoker like Jeffries. Not a good image for a cop to be a smoker these days."

My God, this was a horrible tangle of information.

"How did they know you were at Jackfish in the first place?"

"Jeffries and Blake overheard Mrs. McCloud and some other woman who works at the store having a conversation about a scruffy-looking character on a brand new Harley who came into the store asking for directions to Peppermint Creek Inn. And how later that day I came back to ask if there was a cheap place to hold up until you returned. She suggested a couple of hotels but I figured since my bike had stolen license plates, I'd better keep a low profile. I casually hinted I was low on cash and if there was anywhere I could camp and she mentioned the ghost town. So that's where I headed."

"Her name's Sue. She works at the store Friday nights."

"That's right—Sue. I gave her a fifty to copy a tape for me. I addressed the original to Garry care of Peppermint Creek Inn. I still have to tell Garry to go and pick it up."

Sara remembered Widow McCloud's conversation about a handsome guy on a motorcycle who'd come into the store then she'd given Sara the mail including the package for Garry.

"I've got it."

"You do?"

"Yes. Don't you remember? When we were returning from town? You had a headache. You looked in the bag for medicine? You must have seen the package then, and it triggered some flashbacks and you got violently ill. I thought you'd seen the condoms."

"Condoms were in the bag?"

"They were in the bottom. I thought you didn't want to have sex with me... I know it was silly, but at the time that's all I could come up with."

Suddenly he laughed. A good laugh. Hearty and from deep inside his chest.

Sara giggled, his laugh contagious.

"I bought some, too! I hid them in the barn." He immediately sobered. "But we didn't use condoms every time."

She noticed the flash of pain or maybe it was regret in his gorgeous green eyes.

"No strings, remember?" she said quickly, trying to relax him.

He frowned and leaned back in his chair, his fingers finally breaking their lock on hers.

A bad feeling, a sorrowful feeling, dug deep into her heart. Maybe he didn't want a child with her? Maybe he thought it was all a big mistake? Well, too bad. It was over and done with now. If she was pregnant, then she would raise their child alone.

"I don't have any STDs. I've always used protection...until us."

She'd known he was a careful man but now that he'd said it out loud, a wave of relief splashed over her.

"Where is Whitey?" she asked, trying to change the subject. Now was not the time to talk about all this. She needed to get Garry and Jo to help him, but first she needed to know how bad things stood for Matt.

"In jail with a broken leg and a concussion. He won't be getting out for a long time. If ever. At least if that tape holds up in court."

"So, it's really over. And you're free. Free to do what you want. Be with whoever you want."

She closed her eyes. She was tired. Drifting. Drifting away from Matthew.

"I want you, Sara." His low whisper permeated the thick layers of sleep clogging up her brain, and Sara loved what she was hearing. "I love you, Sara. Do you hear me? I love you more than my own life, more than my own happiness. Remember that always. No matter what happens."

I love you too, Tom. Matthew. I love you, too.

* * * * *

The next time Sara awoke, she found Jo sitting in the chair beside her with a huge smile plastered on her face, but the smile didn't reach her concerned eyes.

Instantly Sara sensed trouble.

"Morning, sis. How you feeling?" Jo asked brightly. A little too brightly.

"Better."

"You look better. A whole lot better. You had us all worried."

Sara licked her suddenly dry lips. "What's happened?"

"The bullet lodged itself right against your hip bone. They had to operate to remove it. No serious damage. You'll be up and walking in no time flat."

"No. I mean what's happened to Matt. Where's Matt? His shoulder?"

Jo frowned.

Sara felt an awful sinking feeling in the pit of her stomach as her sister leaned over and patted Sara's shoulder reassuringly.

"He's fine. Um, here, he left this for you," Jo lifted a lavender envelope out of her purse and handed it to her. "He asked me to give you this the instant you woke.

"You want me to stay?"

"No, I'll be fine," she lied fighting against the sharp sting of tears that were blurring her eyes.

"I'll be right outside, if you need me."

She nodded numbly and waited until Jo had stepped outside before she tore open the envelope and withdrew the single lavender sheet.

My Love,

I wish I could tell you in person again, how much I love you. But the longer I stayed, the greater the risk of you being hurt. I don't want anything to ever happen to you, I wouldn't be able to live knowing I've caused you any more pain.

You deserve a chance at happiness. To be a mother, a wife to some lucky fellow. I know I'll hate the guy's guts but you're a good judge of character. I'll trust your judgment. As long as you're happy, Sara.

The best way for me to show you how much I love you is to keep you safe. Away from me. I know I'm a coward in doing it this way, but if I'd told you in person, I wouldn't have been able to walk away. It's better this way. I'll always love you.

Matthew. "Tom."

Bastard.

Her head spun.

Coward.

How could he do this?

Her mind reeled.

Her heart felt as if it had been pierced by a bullet as she remembered the way his crooked smile curled her toes, the way his gentle touch made her melt in his arms, the sad way he'd looked at her the last time she'd seen him.

He'd been saying goodbye. And she'd been too doped up to know.

"Sara, I love you. Don't ever forget that. I love you more than my own life, more than my own happiness."

Anger broiled and she clenched her fists.

Ripping the letter to shreds, she threw the tiny pieces onto the floor. She wouldn't let him get away with it this easy. She'd find that son of a bitch. She would confront him.

If it took her the rest of her life to find him.

She'd do it.

* * * * *

Garry and Matthew watched the TV screen go blank.

"You did a good job, Matthew. Robin picked a good man to help him," Garry's compliment did nothing to dissipate the sadness clutching Matt's heart.

He wondered if Sara had woken and read the letter. It was the only way he could think of to keep her safe.

He would have to stand trial for Robin's murder, even if he hadn't done it. Whitey wasn't talking and Pauline and Scout certainly weren't.

Jo and Garry hadn't been able to come up with anything to disprove that he hadn't killed Robin. The fact that Whitey was now a criminal would certainly discredit his testimony against Matthew, but it was still Matthew's gun that had been used and his bullet that had killed Robin. Not to mention only his fingerprints all over the weapon.

Garry had said he might be able to get the charge reduced to manslaughter and Matthew would get out in a few years, but he couldn't ask Sara to wait for him. He wouldn't do that to her.

Standing, he crossed the room to rewind the tape. Reaching out he was about to push the stop button when the screen on the TV suddenly flashed to black and a familiar voice sliced through the room.

"Get going, kid. Out the bathroom window. I'll distract them." It was Robin's voice. A bit muffled but it was his voice. And he sounded scared.

"My God, what is happening?" Garry's voice cracked from behind Matthew.

"I'm not leaving you here." It was Matt's voice and the sudden realization of what they were hearing slammed into his gut like a torpedo. "I brought them here. I got you into this. We go together."

Matthew's jaw dropped open in shock.

"You didn't get me into this remember? I got you into it."

"Police! Open up!" A loud booming voice erupted from the TV set.

"That's Whitey's voice," Garry said as he wheeled up beside Matthew.

Matthew shook his head in disbelief. "I didn't know it was taping. Robin must have accidentally pressed the button on the camcorder before stuffing it into the briefcase." Matthew pressed the stop button—full realization as to what Garry was listening to sunk in.

"Oh, God, Garry, you don't want to hear this."

"The hell I don't."

"No you don't. It's—"

"I think I know what it is. And if it is what I think, then you're in the clear. Turn it on."

Matthew shook his head. "I can't listen to this."

"Do it or I will."

"I can't…." Matt choked. If that tape had been recording everything he wanted nothing to do with reliving it.

"I'll listen to it, Matt," Garry's voice softened. "You go on now. Like we planned. I'll listen to the tape and take care of everything."

Matthew nodded numbly and headed toward the door.

The instant he cleared the room he winced as the unmistakable roar of a gunshot echoed from the TV.

* * * * *

That Friday night, true to Jo's word, Garry took the Widow McCloud to bingo. Enjoying her company so much, Garry continued to take the widow out to bingo every Friday evening and dinner at her place every Sunday.

As for Tom? Or maybe she should start thinking of him by his real name, Matt.

She didn't hear a peep from him.

If Jo and Garry knew where he was staying, they weren't saying.

But just the thought that Matt wouldn't have to stand trial for any murders and that he was alive and safe somewhere, gave Sara the courage to remain cheerful and determined she would get her wish to see him again.

One afternoon in mid-June, while returning from a trip to town, Sara discovered a new hand-carved sign had been hung out on the road replacing the old weather-beaten sign people had complained about.

Racing up the laneway, she'd discovered a newly planted beech tree in the same area as the old romance tree had once stood. Heart cracking against her ribs with excitement she rushed to the barn, and found the old sign.

Curls of wood and sawdust littered the floor where the carving had taken place. Sara's breath quickened at the sight.

Matt had been here. He'd finally come close.

Now it was her turn.

* * * * *

Matthew bolted upright in his sleeping bag. Cold sweat drenched his back, dampened his face. His breath escaped in ragged gasps. His heart beat frantically against his chest.

He'd had the dream again. The same dream he'd had every night, replaying the events of the day he'd been so helpless in the foggy waters off Jackfish Bay when he'd seen Scout McMaster grabbing Sara and pointing the gun to her head.

Matt's own gun forced from his fingers as Pauline's bullet had slammed into his shoulder, then he'd watched in stunned terror as Pauline aimed the gun at Sara on the beach.

The mist had enshrouded him blocking his view of what was happening to her. At that point, gut-wrenching sounds of gunshots had ripped through him. He'd almost slipped under the water and just allowed himself to drown at the thought that Sara was dead.

But then he'd heard Sara call his name.

She'd found him in the water and they'd gotten back to shore. She'd fainted in his arms, and his heart had stopped at the sight of the blood flowing out of her.

All that blood.

The same question still burned inside him. Why hadn't he shot Pauline instead of Scout McMaster? He'd made eye contact with Jo mere seconds before all hell broke loose. He'd indicated to Jo to cover Pauline and he would take out Scout. He'd thought Sara had been safe.

But she hadn't. Sara had still gotten shot.

He'd made a wrong calculation and it had almost killed her.

He heaved a shuddering sigh. He'd let Sara down. And he'd let Garry and Jo down. He'd promised to keep Sara safe.

And he'd failed all of them. Big time.

Unzipping the sleeping bag, he crawled out and stood on the cold wooden boards of the boathouse he'd shared with Sara.

Christ! He missed her like crazy.

Grabbing for the matches, he lit the tiny Coleman lantern that Garry had given him.

His let his hand run over the smooth plastic exterior of the camcorder. The police officials had found it inside the suitcase Robin had given him. Apparently Justin had found it in the cabin Matt had been staying in when they'd jumped him and thrown it into the well with Blake.

He'd been able to clean the grunge and water from it and it now worked perfectly. But he didn't know if he could ever use it again. It always brought back memories of the night he'd seen Robin killed.

Maybe someday he'd use it again. For pleasure. Not work. But he needed time to heal. Lots of time.

Garry wanted Matthew to tell Sara he was back from his debriefing with the FBI and the CIA, and even National Security had been in on it, but Matt couldn't be near her.

He was too damn dangerous for her.

Chief Jeffries didn't know his true identity, but the chance existed Jeffries may find out. Matt had contacted his younger brother Daniel and his father who was helping Daniel on an archeological dig in Mexico, and had warned them about possible retaliation from the chief.

He'd also contacted his sister-in-law Emily who lived on Prince Edward Island, and Sara's parents and her brother Jessie, warning them of potential danger regarding the case.

Then he'd returned to Canada.

He'd opted to stay at Jackfish. At least he was near to Sara. For one more night anyway.

Matthew padded barefoot to the rusty basin he'd found in one of the houses in the abandoned town. Cupping his hands, he splashed the mild water against his face, relishing in its freshness. After tonight, he'd be whisked off to a safe house somewhere in the world. He'd return to New York when the trial ensued. And then who knew what would happen.

He might have to stay underground forever. Or perhaps Chief Jeffries, after having cooled off, might follow the police code of honor and call off any hits on Matthew after realizing Matthew had just been doing his job in uncovering crooked cops.

Not bothering to wipe the water from his face, he headed outdoors.

Bullfrogs greeted him as they croaked loudly from the shoreline. Fireflies blinked with enthusiasm throughout the thicket and the moon, full and bright, shone down onto Jackfish Bay illuminating it like a mirror.

He stopped on the sandy beach in the area of the shooting.

Dammit!

He missed her. Missed her with every inch of his body, every fiber of his soul. More now that he'd visited Peppermint Creek Inn and hung the new sign out on the main highway for her. He'd planted the tree while she'd been in town today. Last night he'd snuck into her bedroom and watched her sleep. He'd touched her hair, her eyebrows, her pouting lips. Had memorized every inch of her.

It had taken every ounce of willpower not to wake her, to ask her to come with him.

But too much danger surrounded him. Hadn't he proved it when she'd been shot?

He let his hot feet sink into the coolness of the still water.

Four weeks. Exactly four weeks ago today, he'd stood here on the beach, clad only in his underwear, much the same way as he did tonight.

Back then Sara had tried to stop him from going into the frigid waters. He only wished she could be here now with him, talking him out of going into hiding.

He looked out over the bay at the island where he'd stashed that copy of the tape. The island stood dark and giant, popping out of the moonstruck bay like a huge whale, taking a midnight swim.

Matthew shook his head at the silly thoughts creeping into his head. Lack of sleep did that to him. Kept him off balance.

Lightning flashed somewhere to the north and a welcome cool wind picked up, brushing softly against his naked skin.

It felt good. Soothing almost.

He should be with Sara. They should both be lying here on the beach, intertwined in each other's arms, watching the storm come in.

Closing his eyes, he took a deep breath.

Shit! He missed her so much he could even smell her sweet minty aroma waft over him. Tugging at him. Luring him into her arms. Her hushed whispers comforting him, telling him everything would be all right.

At his thoughts about Sara, his cock hardened, thickened, pressed fiercely against his prison-tight underwear.

A sting needled at his elbow and he cursed wildly, quickly swatting a pesky mosquito. Then he cursed again when another one bit behind his left knee.

A soft giggle split the air from somewhere behind him. His heart leapt with joy.

"Sweetness?" he whispered beneath his breath. He was too stunned to do anything but to stand there.

"Got something here for you," she said softly.

Slowly he turned around, his breath catching in his throat.

She looked so beautiful. So damned beautiful clad in a sweet body-hugging Spring floral dress, her hair tumbling down over her shoulders, covering her breasts. He barely noticed the white box she held in her hand as a strong desire erupted within him.

The urge to reach out and run his fingers through her silky strands was powerful. He wanted to push aside the thin fabric covering her breasts, to touch her naked skin, suckle her nipples. To press her naked body onto the sand and sink his throbbing cock into her warm, welcome pussy and feel her bucking beneath him as he thrust into her over and over again just to show her how much he loved her.

It took every ounce in his being not to do it.

"Baked you that peppermint cheesecake you hinted at during our picnic."

The wonderful picnic. He could still imagine the sweet taste of her velvety cream gushing against his lips, as he'd tongue-fucked her on that quilt. It seemed so long ago.

Her cheeks were flushed in the moon glow as her gaze riveted to his engorged erection. Oh God! He wanted to take her into his arms so bad, the hurt twisted through him like a sharp knife.

"How'd you find me? Did Garry tell you?"

"You left this behind." She held up an old rusty tin pot he'd found in one of the Jackfish buildings. He'd been sure she would enjoy fixing it up and entering it into one of those contests. He'd left it in her painting loft, sure she wouldn't be going up there for at least awhile now that she was too busy with the new log building of Peppermint Creek Inn being erected.

He kicked himself for not being more careful. It had been a stupid gesture now that he thought about it. And it could very well have signed her death warrant.

"Were you followed?"

"No. I took every precaution. You know it's still a bit cold for camping out in a boathouse all by yourself. Don't you think you should come home? Have some of this yummy cake?"

She held the box up.

Matthew swallowed the tightness suddenly clogging his throat.

Home. Home-baked food. Sara.

It sounded so good. So safe. But with him around, her home would only turn into a death trap. He'd almost gotten her killed once. He wouldn't take the chance again.

He willed himself to stiffen against the love that shone like jewels in her eyes. He had to tell her why it had to be this way. Why they couldn't see each other ever again.

Why he could never go home with her.

"Before I went undercover to work for Robin, I dreamed of a life with a woman like you. I dated. Came close to getting married. Once. But she couldn't handle my being a cop. And I wouldn't give up my work. She settled on a plumber instead."

Sara stood still. Barefoot and picture pretty as she smiled at him. A sensual smile.

"So what are you trying to tell me?"

"I was an undercover cop. A lot of the time I had to wear a wire. A hidden microphone hooked onto a recording device. I slept with my eyes open. I carried two guns besides my police issue one. Both were 'throwaway' guns, in case I needed to kill someone in self-defense. We couldn't afford any questions that could break my cover. One I hid in my boot, the other small enough so I could hide it with the wire. Both the wire and gun were taped to my groin."

"I guess you can't go to the bathroom while you're working," Sara whispered softly.

Dammit, the woman wasn't getting the point.

"I went by a different name while I was undercover. If they find out my real identity, everyone in my family, anyone around me, could get killed. I'm known now as a rat, a cop who broke the code of silence. I crashed through the blue wall the police hide behind and now I've got many enemies who would love to see me squirm as they slit your throat."

"I'm not scared."

"You should be." Matthew sighed. "What it comes right down to is, I'm not husband material. Not even good father material."

"Are you finished?"

"No." Matthew took a deep breath and forced his voice to grow cold, emotionless.

"You were just a distraction for me, Sara. A one night stand. Heck, a two night stand. I don't love you," he lied. "There's nothing between us. Please, just leave me alone."

He couldn't bear to go on. The words had impacted her strongly. He could tell by the way her face turned milky white. He'd done his job, and it made him sick to his stomach.

Quickly, so he wouldn't change his mind, he brushed past her stock-still form.

* * * * *

Sara found him inside their boathouse. The same one they'd made love in during their stay at Jackfish.

He was packing.

"Why are you lying to me?"

"I'm not." He didn't look up.

She watched him roll the sleeping bag up. With madly shaking hands, he attempted to tie it up with its attached strings. After a couple of attempts he succeeded, then quickly shoved it into its carrying case.

"You're scared, aren't you?" Sara asked.

Matt stopped cold. He straightened and faced her.

Pain, and hurt and fear shone bright in his emerald eyes.

"Yes. Scared shitless," he admitted. He didn't reach out to her. But he wanted to. She could read it in his eyes. He wanted to and it was killing him not to.

"Matthew—"

"What if it happens again, Sara? What if some guy who's got it in for me comes gunning for me and gets you instead?" His eyes grew wide with panic. He shoved a shaky hand through his hair. "What if it happens and—"

"Listen to me. You're living with 'what ifs'. What if this happens? What if that happens? What if it doesn't happen, Matt? What if it doesn't?"

"What if it did?" his voice caught. He sat down on top of his rolled sleeping bag, looking up at her. His mouth clenched tight.

He was shaking. Shaking so hard.

"Stop it! Just stop it! Don't listen to those 'what ifs'. Because if you do, they'll drive you to grab your gun and put it to your head. You don't want that to happen do you?"

Matthew let out a long breath. "Maybe it's better that way."

At his answer, she felt the anger inside her unleash itself.

"No! It's not! Damn you! It's my life, too! No one has the right to say how I live it. No one. Just me. Do you understand?" She ignored his shocked look. "My God! You don't own me. I had a life before I met you, and I'll have a life if you don't want me. But I want you in my life. Danger. Risks and all. I love you for who you are. Not what you do.

"So why don't we just sit back, enjoy each other's company and see what happens? But if you don't want me, if you truly don't love me, at least look me square in the eye and tell me! At least have the guts to do that!"

For a long time, he didn't speak. He sat stiff as a board upon the rolled sleeping bag, his jaw clenched so tightly, Sara noticed the muscles in his cheeks twitch abnormally.

Behind him, a flash of lightning lit up the glassless window, but she wasn't afraid of the storm brewing outside.

She was afraid of the storm inside him.

His answer terrified her. What if he did look her in the eye and tell her to get lost?

She'd come here with full intentions of fighting fiercely for him. Could she let him go so easily as she'd said? Could she simply turn around and walk away?

Rain began to pitter against the moss-covered shingles on the roof. She barely heard it. She scarcely felt the cool, misty drizzle sprinkle against her bare arms as it blew into the boathouse through the open window.

The cool wind did little to soothe her hot tears.

He wasn't going to say anything. He was going to let her walk away.

Her body began to tremble. Not because she was cold, but because she had been wrong about Matthew. She'd let him into her soul. Inside her heart. And now he was ripping her heart apart. Not by his words but by his silence.

How can she fight silence?

Feeling as if she might collapse, Sara turned to leave.

"Life without you is impossible. I do love you, with all my heart and soul." His hoarse whisper made her turn around.

He was standing now. Tears glimmered in his eyes.

With one shaky hand he reached out, his trembling fingers were cold as he gently brushed away the tears gushing over her cheeks. Then, without warning he swept her into the safety of his loving arms.

"I'm sorry I left you," he whispered softly against her ear. "Seems like I've wasted a lot of time."

"You needed the time, Matthew. Just don't ever leave me again. Promise me?"

"Okay. Okay. I promise," he chuckled then his voice grew serious again. "We can probably never go home. I hope you know that. I'll be living like this. Out of tents. In safe houses all over the world. Moving all the time. I have to testify because of all the evidence I've collected over the years. It could take years. I'll be taking a lot of people down."

"I'll go anywhere with you. For as long as it takes. For better or worse."

"But what about Peppermint Creek? Your peppermint product business?"

"I've already recruited Garry and Hilda. They're moving into the house as we speak. And I've rehired a couple of last year's peppermint helpers to assist them with the ins and outs of the business end of things."

"You think of everything." He softly brushed his lips against hers. A scorching brush that left her aching for more.

"I don't want to be apart from you anymore. I want you to make love to me," she whispered, desperate to feel him inside her again. Anxious to feel his love.

Without hesitation, his trembling fingers were at the front dress buttons. In seconds, his warm hands were sliding inside the opening, cupping her quickly swelling breasts.

Immediately her nipples grew harder, desire pulsed in her pussy.

Oh, God! It felt so good to have him touching her again.

"I've quit this undercover stuff. When the trial is over, if it's safe, we might be able to move back to the inn and raise our kids there, but the chances are really slim."

"As long as we're together we can live anywhere."

He grinned his gorgeous crooked grin that left her breathless. His gaze dropped to the box containing the cake she held in her hand.

"The cake can wait," Sara whispered huskily. Her fingers let go of the string and the box dropped at her feet. Hopefully the fall wouldn't totally ruin it, but at the moment she didn't care. She had more important things to do, like make love with the man of her heart.

She found herself eyeing the ropes dangling at the moorings. One of her fantasies zipped into her thoughts. A fantasy of him tying her down, of being his sexual hostage. Of him taking her in the ass from behind as he'd once said he'd do the last time they'd been in this boathouse.

She heard his breath quicken as he followed her gaze, his eyes flared with arousal and understanding.

"I've missed you so much," he whispered, his fingers tweaking her hard, aching nipples to this side of pain. His firm mouth felt like an aphrodisiac as his warm lips slanted over hers. She trembled against him when the hard head of his huge cock prodded against her quickly drenching pussy lips.

Oh, yes! She'd missed this.

She'd lain awake in bed, alone every night, the erotic scent of him on her pillowcases, her vibrator never enough to satisfy the sexual cravings he'd unleashed during their brief time together.

Now she had him back and she wanted him to fuck her senseless.

"I've been wearing one of those inflatable butt plugs off and on over the past month, preparing myself for you. I took it out just before I came here," she said softly as he broke the intoxicating kiss and unbuttoned her dress allowing her to step out of it.

He cursed softly at her words, or maybe he swore at the fact she wore no panties and now stood totally naked in front of him. Erotic heat mounted inside her, and she trembled with a desire so fierce and wanton she just about climaxed at the lusty way his gaze caressed her every curve. He let go of her, and bent over to release the sleeping bag from its restraints. Rolling it open on the nearby single air mattress, he helped her onto her hands and knees instructing her to do a cat stretch by placing her head down, her arms lifting out over her head, her legs apart and her ass up in the air.

She shivered from the carnal position, the wild sensations ripping through her as he tied the ropes around her wrists. Yanking at them, he made sure they were secure then he crawled behind her.

"I dreamed of tying you down the last time we were here when I inserted the plug."

She turned her head and caught him grinning wickedly at her, his gorgeous eyes twinkling with arousal.

"Why didn't you?"

"I didn't want to scare you away."

"You could never scare me. I trust you. And I want you to play out your sexual fantasies with me just as I want to play out mine with you."

She frowned as she caught him untying the strings around the cake box.

Suddenly anxious to have his attention back on her, she wiggled her ass at him.

He ignored her. "Do you by any chance have some whipped cream on this cake?"

"Oh, my God! Matt! Don't make me wait."

"You look so cute when you're desperate to get fucked."

She inhaled sharply as his hot fingers ran a feather-light trail of fire over her right ass cheek. With his other hand, he lifted the cake out of the box.

"Ah perfect, whipping cream and peppermint sauce."

Was he nuts? Was she nuts for putting up with this delay? If she didn't have her wrists tied she'd be straddling him right now.

"Why are you hungry now?" she blurted out, impatience making her hornier. She watched as his fingers dipped a long swath over the peppermint syrup as he effectively destroyed the pretty decoration swirls of whipping cream she'd placed on top.

She should be upset that he was ruining her cake so casually. Strangely enough, she wasn't. Her gaze riveted to his engorged cock. It was flushing an angry red, the thick veins pulsing wickedly. His cockhead looked absolutely delicious with the dot of pre-come at the slit. Whatever he was thinking of doing was turning him on big time. She didn't have too long to find out what he was up to.

"This isn't for me, sweetness. It's for you. Lubrication."

Oh, my gosh! If she wasn't so hot for him right now she'd be laughing at the thought of using her peppermint cheesecake for *that* purpose.

He brought his fingers to his mouth, his long pink tongue licking off the cream as he watched her.

"Tastes damn good."

His tongue scooped another swath off his fingers. This time he didn't eat it. Her pulse quickened as his head lowered to her ass. His breath caressed her flesh and his fingers and tongue massaged cool whipping cream and gooey syrup over her hot ass cheeks. He scraped more of the thick cream and she groaned as a slippery finger, hot as a flame, slid over her throbbing clitoris with smooth firm strokes.

Pleasure enveloped her at his touch. It came so quickly, so wantonly, it made her tummy clench. Made erotic heat flush inside her vagina. Lusty sensations consumed her, made her tremble.

"They say the way to a man's heart is through his stomach. But I always say a way to a man's heart is through his stomach and his cock. And you and your cake, sweetness, are extremely good for my cock."

A moan escaped her lips as his flaming finger left her swelling clitoris. She turned her head in protest and watched in awe as he began spreading the whipped cream up and down the massive length of his solid erection, covering the web of veins weaving through his cock from her view. She found herself tugging at the restraints, wanting to do the smearing herself. Wanting to touch his thick flesh, aching to lick the cream from his shaft. But devouring her lubrication wouldn't be such a good thing. A big, thick cock like his going up her ass was going to need all the lube it could get.

"So, what you are effectively saying is if I wasn't a good cook, I'd be in trouble?" she teased, deciding to talk her way through her mounting pleasure.

"That's what I'm saying, sweetness."

"Do all men feel that way?"

"I won't answer for them," he chuckled.

"Why not?"

"It's just like me asking you if all women cook damn good peppermint cheesecakes like you do."

She laughed and found herself thinking about her sister Jo—about how she didn't like to cook and how she should have a man like Matthew in her life. A man who made her feel special, and wanted and safe. And brought such exquisite pleasure to her like Matt did to her.

"Does your brother want a woman who cooks?" The words popped out of her mouth before she'd even realized what she was saying.

That erotic blazing finger of his once again slid across her throbbing clit with another healthy dose of cream, the coolness of it doing nothing to vanquish the heated sensations he'd already created.

"He'd be a perfect match for your sister Jo," he admitted.

"We'd have to think of a way to get them together. Does he have the same requirements as you do about wanting a good cook and good sex?"

She trembled when she felt a peppermint-syruped finger pierce her anal opening.

"I don't know. You'd have to ask him that yourself."

His long finger stretched her muscles as he explored, and she welcomed the erotic sensations of his intimate touches. He withdrew, then a moment later inserted two syrup-laced fingers. He slid in easily—his heat-seeking probes sparking off a lustful heat.

"Would it bother him if she didn't cook at all?"

"I think it's safe to say if she cooks in the bedroom as good as she cooks with her temper when she's angry, they'll connect in ways we've probably never dreamed of."

"Sounds promising."

"So does your ass. Sweetness, you are so beautifully tight. Absolutely perfect."

She felt the first bite of pleasure-pain as a moment later he sunk three syrupy fingers into her ass. He prepared her slower now. His fingers pressing into her, caressing her muscles, building erotic pressure against her rapidly dazed senses.

An untamed eagerness zipped along her nerves. A carnal need she'd never imagined began to take hold of her. An intense need to have him burying his cock inside her ass. To feel him plunging into her.

She could literally feel her vagina dripping with her desire as he continued to stroke her plump clit. An odd emptiness gripped her pussy. There was a need to be filled there, too. But it wasn't as powerful as what was happening inside her ass.

A moment later, he pulled his fingers out and she felt the head of his cock poised at her back entrance.

Her skin flushed hot. Her body hummed. She could smell her arousal.

"Ready, sweet stuff?"

Her fingers gripped the sleeping bag, fear of the unknown mingled with the excitement of having him making love to her needy ass.

She nodded.

He didn't waste any time powering into her.

He was big. Unbelievably big.

Muscles stretched wickedly as the hot, hard intrusion quickly and confidently penetrated her, burned her.

Oh, my gosh, that felt quite different. Quite good.

Silently she thanked the inflated butt plug for preparing her so nicely for him.

Matt groaned, a strangled cry of arousal that sent sharp shockwaves of desire rippling through her pussy drawing her closer to the edge of bliss. She found herself wondering how in the world a sound could bring her so close to the edge of a climax?

As if sensing her impending pleasure, his finger backed off the pressure on her whipped cream soaked clit, making her cry out her frustration.

Thankfully his finger remained, stroking, massaging, seducing.

"Not yet," he ground out. "I want us coming together."

He stuffed his gorgeous cock deeper. The thickness burned.

She closed her eyes melting into the eroticism, her muscles eagerly opening to his length.

Sweat popped over her flesh. Her breasts felt swollen as they dangled—her nipples ached as she continued to rasp them against the sleeping bag.

His breath grew just as labored as hers and he began a tender thrust. He stroked into her tight ass with deep, confident plunges, each impalement lessening the pleasure-pain and increasing the pleasure.

She found herself widening her legs, steadying herself, as his thrusts grew deeper, harder, fiercer.

The flaming finger at her clit became desperate, his touch more insistent. She found herself pulling at her restraints, bucking her hips backwards, eagerly accepting his flesh—allowing a deeper penetration.

Pleasure flared, burst, tore into her with wickedly delicious spirals. Gritting her teeth, she tried not to cry out, tried hard to wait for him to come with her.

His plunges grew harder, faster. Her cunt muscles spasmed, gripped an imaginary cock. The slippery finger at her engorged clit quickened. Her anal muscles tightened.

He groaned. His cock surged harder. In and out. Long powerful thrusts.

He came hard, his cries of arousal ripping through her every fiber, unleashing her, throwing her into her own orgasm.

She jerked as spasms splintered around her, roared through her with fevered lightning. Tore her apart. Made her cry out shamelessly.

So beautiful!

"Oh, yes!" he shouted. She could feel his release gushing deep inside her, seeping out of her, dripping along her inner thighs.

Instinctively she knew these would be moments they would cherish. Moments they would use to lose themselves in a world of immense pleasure.

A world that would help them forget all the troubles they were sure to encounter in their dangerous future together.